The New

Threat

Albert A Nolen II

Foreword

Hello reader! This is the sequel to "The New Species", and just like in the previous novel, everything in this novel has been translated for your convenience. All time is set around Earth standard time and idioms have been adjusted so that they make sense to English speakers. The only exception is certain nouns. Those are written in their proper name with translations in {brackets} where applicable.

In this novel there are informational inserts that are completely optional to read. They help expand upon certain aspects of the story that have been confusing to some readers, but you can skip them with little to no detriment to your reading experience. In "The New Species" these inserts always came after the relevant chapter, but in this novel some of them appear before the chapter to help maintain tone and pacing.

Dedications

I dedicate this novel and have infinite gratitude for my soon-to-be wife Elizabeth, for her love and support. Without you, my life would be devoid of joy. And I still love you more.

To my son, who isn't quite old enough yet to read these books. Just a few more years...

Special thanks to everyone on the HFY subreddit and RoyalRoad who provided positive and critical feedback, as well as to my patrons and supporters. You're all amazing, and I wish you the best.

And finally, thank YOU for reading this. You're awesome, don't let anyone tell you otherwise.

Chapter 1

Subject: Ship-Head Uleena
Species: Urakari
Species Description: Reptilian humanoid, no tail.
5'3" (1.6 m) avg height. 135 lbs (61 kg) avg
weight. 105 year life expectancy.
Ship: RSV Lowelana {Fights with Honor}
Location: Rigara

It's good to be back aboard the RSV Lowelana.
The rest of the crew feels the same way. The
entire crew had to go through some diplomatic
courses, but I had to have the full blown three
month training. I was extremely envious of the
crew, who simply had to learn to not speak unless
spoken to and avoid being where they're not
supposed to be. For them, it had been a month in
a classroom and two months of leave.

For me, it was paperwork, lectures, tests, reviews,
certifications, and more paperwork. The amount
of paperwork a diplomat has to do is patently
unhealthy. Staring at screens that long has to be
some sort of health and safety violation. At least
the time away allowed the rest of the crew to de-
stress a bit. We were even able to get crewed
back up to 38.

Our training had taken place on the Galactic
Diplomacy Station, which had previously been a
conflict resolution forum. It had offices for every
Republic species plus one for an unexpected first

contact, which the United Systems was now occupying. The station had fallen into disuse because there wasn't much conflict to resolve. It was quickly cleaned up and renamed, and now there are embassies for each Republic species and the US.

I'd also finally gotten a good look at an Alumari once the US moved in. They weren't nearly as frightening as the Kinran. Eight limbs, eight eyes, and weird mandibles still made them somewhat creepy, but at least their limbs bent in proper directions and their movements were fluid. Kinran frequently have fast and jerky movements. Like a puppet with an easily startled puppeteer.

"Oh wow, my pay went up ten percent!" Intel-Head Kriin exclaimed, jerking me back to reality.

"Mine did too. I'm pretty sure all of ours did," Nav-Head Kraan explained.

"Mine only went up six percent," Engineering-Head Liwna said sadly.

"You get paid more than they do, so a six percent increase is more money than they get," Gruna, my new second, added. "I got a five percent increase, but that's still more money."

"Yeah, you're right second-head. I just checked the math," Liwna replied.

"How much did you get, ship-head?" Kriin asked me.

Everyone on the bridge turned to look at me with

curious expressions. I had received more training than all of them, and my new job was much more intensive than theirs. So naturally I should have received the largest raise. After all, going from a ship-head to a diplomat was a difficult change, but staying a ship-head while becoming a diplomat was even more tasking.

"One percent," I replied tersely.

Eyes widened and jaws dropped. That's right, one measly percent for what has to be one of the most difficult jobs in the galaxy. Ship-head of a warship turned diplomatic vessel, responsible for keeping a good relationship between the Republic and the devastatingly powerful leviathan known as the United Systems. It was completely unfair that I didn't get a bigger raise, considering that I would be the first to die in a conflict with the US.

Tim told me as much, just before we left for training. In his typical cheery way, he informed me that if the United Systems and the Republic went to war, the Lowelana would be the first target. Then they would target the Galactic Diplomacy Station in Rigara, followed immediately by the Republic capital in Winuros. Sometimes talking to Tim is fun, other times it's unnerving as all hell.

The decision to limit my raise had come down from my father, of all people. He had concerns that it would look like the Republic was rewarding me for dragging the United Systems into our war with the OU if they gave me a proper raise. Ulooni, who was already making more money than my bridge crew combined, got a ten percent raise for her new duties. Even though that wasn't at my father's discretion, it still felt like favoritism.

"Is that... more money than us? Like with Liwna?" Kriin asked hesitantly.

"No," I said.

A few seconds of silence later, everyone quietly got back to work. We were once again being tasked to the Thanatos, which was currently stationed in Alpha Centauri. The Omni-Union's last attack on Sol had happened just before the USSS Nidhogg had been used on the OU's stronghold system. It had been three months since then, so there was plenty of concern regarding how large the next attack on Sol would be.

In Republic space, however, the attacks had started ramping up. We initially lost some of the territory we had regained, but with help from the United Systems we managed to take back and defend all of our territory. We weren't resettling yet because the risk was too high, but defending these systems prevents the OU from finding the inhabited ones. Word from the strategists is that they're probably trying to take out the Republic before swarming over the US.

"Ready to warp, sir," Kraan informed me.

"Let's go," I replied.

As we jumped to warp, I began to wonder about what was happening with my proposal. The United Systems using the Republic's shipyards to build up their fleet was an idea that the Republic pounced on, and that's to be expected because we have the most to gain. The United Systems was a lot more hesitant, though.

They stand to gain more ships and a more capable ally against the Omni-Union, but there are those among the US that believe they don't need either. Last month the Mobile Prime Platforms were declassified, so that probably has shifted opinions a bit. Hopefully it isn't too late.

Thankfully we hadn't seen any of the MPPs since the invasion. We were woefully unprepared to go against a weapons platform the size of a planet controlled by an artificial intelligence. Even the nearly almighty United Systems took casualties against just one of them. But there are over a hundred. If they all attacked at once...

"Arriving in Alpha Centauri, ship-head," Kraan announced.

"Request clearance to dock with the Thanatos," I replied.

"They've already granted it," Kriin said with a chuckle.

"I don't understand," Gruna said. "Is the Thanatos behind that asteroid?"

Everyone on the bridge turned to look at her and held their breath. We had all been waiting for this moment. She hadn't been exposed to the United Systems before, and everyone was anticipating her reaction. The briefing had contained all the measurements, but most officers understandably glaze over such things.

"That's not an asteroid. That's the Thanatos," I said with a grin and a comedic sigh. "People really need to start reading their briefings."

It took a second for my statement to register, but once it did her eyes widened and her jaw dropped. The USSS Thanatos was the largest ship she'd ever seen, and it wasn't even the largest carrier that the United Systems had. It was actually considered a small diplomatic carrier. You could almost see these thoughts enter her head as she struggled to process this. Everyone else was grinning like children.

"Alright, let's get docked. I've got a meeting to get to," I ordered as I leaned back in my chair.

At least my orders were simple. Meet with Captain Reynolds, do what he says. Put out fires between US and Republic senior officers and integrate with the US Diplomatic corps. Which, according to Reynolds, would be much easier to do aboard the Thanatos than it would be on the Galactic Diplomatic Station.

I didn't know if it was a good sign or a bad sign that the humans would rather have me in their space than aboard the Galactic Diplomatic Station. On the one hand, it signified a certain level of trust and friendship. On the other, it made it easier to kill me if things went wrong.

I sighed quietly as I felt the clamps close around the Lowelana. Scooped up, again. Pretty undignified for the ship of a dignitary. Not like

there was any other way for us to dock, though.
The actual docking bays were designed to hold US
frigates, which were one and a half times larger
than the Lowelana. We're too small for those
clamps, even if they weren't in use. The
emergency bay had maneuverable clamps so it
could theoretically grab onto any ship it needed
to. Including us.

"Docked and locked, ship-head," Kraan said.

"Excellent, good work," I replied. Then I keyed the
ship-wide comms. "Attention all personnel. We
have docked with the USSS Thanatos. After
completing your immediate tasks you are on
shore-leave for the rest of the day."

A cheer rang throughout the ship. Some things
never change.

"Bright and early tomorrow you are to report to
your diplomatic assignments. If you do not know
what your assignment is or where it is, check with
second-head Gruna. She has the list. Anyone who
isn't where they're supposed to be tomorrow will
be subject to confinement."

A groan rang throughout the ship.

"No whining. We're a diplomatic ship now, and
that's how diplomats operate. I'd better be seeing
you tomorrow, fully functional. Dismissed."

Another cheer rang throughout the ship. I
disembarked before any of them managed to and
was met by a familiar hologram. The robed figure
was holding a curved blade, what I now know to

be called a scythe. The figure waved a greeting to me with a bony hand.

"Good tidings, ship-head Uleena. I assume your training was productive?" Omega asked.

"Yeah, it was pretty enlightening and educating," I replied. "Is everything okay?"

"Yes, for now. Why do you ask?"

"I wasn't expecting to be greeted by you. I was expecting Tim."

"Oh?" Omega asked, tilting its head to the side. "Care to elaborate on these expectations of yours while you follow the deck-lights?"

The lights on the floor lit up. I began to follow them as I tried desperately to think of something to say to not offend the United System's most powerful AI.

"Well... it's just... um... Tim seems more suited to guiding," I replied and instantly regretted my word choice.

"Is that right? Am I not suited to guiding people? I've been guiding the United Systems for centuries, you know," it replied.

It's teasing me, trying to get me to stutter and stumble over my words. Omega wouldn't actually be offended by a slip of the tongue. I hope.

"That's just my point, though. You're more specialized for oversight than Tim is, at least to my understanding. Having you guide me to my meeting with Reynolds is like having a Fleet-Head as a secretary."

"There's no such thing as a specialized Artificial Intelligence, Uleena. Some dedicate more time to gaining certain knowledge than others, but this doesn't prevent them from gaining further knowledge in other fields. As a matter of fact, with our memory capabilities we're more suited to generalization than any organic ever could be," the AI lectured. "That being said, Tim doesn't currently hold the credentials required to know about your meeting, let alone guide you to it."

I hadn't actually thought about that. I supposed that all it would take for one AI to take over the position of another AI is a brief learning window. I wondered if Tim could do Omega's job before what Omega had said finally sunk in.

"Oh. I'm guessing my meeting with Reynolds has been canceled?" I asked.

"No, just put on hold. You have another, more pressing meeting to attend to first."

"Who's the new meeting going to be with?"

"You'll find out presently," Omega said with a chuckle at the nervousness in my tone. "It's classified, after all."

"I see. I assume that the reason for the meeting is also classified, then?"

"Correct."

Of course it is.

Chapter 2

Subject: AI Omega
Species: Human-Created Artificial Intelligence
Species Description: No physical description available.
Ship: Multiple
Location: Multiple

As usual, I was handling multiple tasks at once. Trying to get all of our ships repaired and replaced while also building new fleets was a monumental task. Recruiting, training, and assigning staff to those ships was another monumental task. On top of all that, I had to deal with spoiled senators who had secured themselves firmly within social bubbles that kept them ignorant.

The lack of attacks on Sol had raised tensions for a while and made the politicians more receptive, but now those tensions were evaporating and the politicians were, to use an antiquated turn of phrase, back on their bullshit.

"I fail to see how giving the Republic our technology would possibly stand to benefit us, Omega!" Senator Richardson said with an insincere dramatic flourish of frustration.

"The technology we would be giving them is several generations behind our own. Add to that strict oversight and anti-intelligence measures, and we have no cause for any concern. In return, we gain our new fleets at record speeds," I replied.

"We get new fleets, but we would be pouring money into their economy. A foreign economy which we aren't even trading with yet. My constituents have concerns about this!"

If I had eyes they would be rolling. By constituents, he means the corporations that fund his campaigns. The corporations who would much rather we build our own stations and THEN start building the new fleets. Short-sighted fools who believe they're the smartest people in the galaxy, as fools often do. Still, they make life interesting in their own way.

"The Republic has to hire many of our own citizens to work aboard the stations to be able to fulfill the orders. Trainers, subject matter experts, licensed professionals and the like. The ships are being made to our standards, and the Republic is footing the bill for the people they're hiring," I explained.

"So we're getting a rebate," Richardson replied sarcastically.

"Not only that, but integration. Your constituents could be swayed by simply pointing out that integration leads to trade and access to new markets. Our people aboard the stations will want supplies from home that the Republic cannot provide, and those supplies will be viewed with envious eyes. Before long, popular demand for trade networks will explode," I gestured. "But if we vote no on the proposal... who knows how long it will be before we can secure trade guarantees?"

Richardson looked deep in thought. I could tell he

was working on positioning statements for his corporate overlords. Finally he nodded and waved his hand, indicating that he will vote yes. I already had more than enough yes votes, but I needed Richardson to explain to certain corporate board members why this idea had merit. A yes vote won't have much weight without corporate cooperation, and a direct meeting with me would intolerably bolster their already massive egos. Satisfied, I turned off my avatar and switched my attention to the reptilian ship-head that I was leading to what would be the most interesting meeting of his career.

The directors had been at a bit of a stalemate due to a lack of intelligence regarding the Republic's intentions. Neither they nor the senate would sign off on an intel gathering mission just yet, though, so I came up with an alternate solution. Ship-Head Uleena has just graduated from a diplomacy training course, so he should have his finger on the Republic's pulse.

Plus I really want to see his reaction.

"So I just sit here?" Uleena asked.

"Correct," I replied.

Uleena sat down and I activated the chat for him. He jumped slightly as the hard-light monitor and keyboard appeared in front of him. He studied it with obvious confusion on his face until he realized what it was and who it was connected to. I relished the shock and horror that overrode the confusion.

/////////
Director 1 has joined the chat
D2: And with that, we're all here. Hello Ship-Head Uleena.
O: He'll need a second to adjust.
/////////

"What the fuck, Omega?" Uleena asked as he scrambled for the keyboard, his hearts beating as fast as they possibly could.

"Welcome to the world of diplomacy, Uleena," I replied, gesturing toward the monitor. "This terminal is translated for your convenience. Just type the way you normally would and I'll get your point across."

The reptilian ship-head cursed under his breath as he studied the keyboard and began to type his reply.

/////////
U: Hello, apologies for the delay. This meeting was unexpected.
D4: Of course it was. We don't announce when we'll be having our meetings, and this meeting in particular is unusual for us.
D9: Indeed.
D2: The reason we're meeting is because of your proposal. Normally we would be having Omega go through back channels to get the answers for us, but that would take too long and risk hostilities with the Republic. Instead, we're just going straight to the horses mouth.
/////////

"What's a horse?" Uleena asked.

"It's a four legged mammal that's used as a mode of transportation on several human worlds," I answered.

//////////
D9: Let's get to the point. We have questions for you about this proposal and our time is limited. Answer quickly and truthfully. Understood?
U: Yes.
D9: Good. How likely is it that the Republic will hire our own technicians to serve aboard the shipyards?
U: Very likely. It's part of the assumptive draft.
D2: Where will the materials be coming from?
U: We have several suppliers that are both public and private.
D3: Hello again, Uleena. Will the Republic allow oversight?
U: Hello Director 3. Yes, but there was some struggle with that. As long as the US doesn't attempt to indenture our workers it will be fine, though.
D11: Clarify what you mean by indenture, please.
U: Overwork them.
D3: That's not what I meant by oversight. Will the Republic allow us to make certain that information regarding certain technologies doesn't leak?
//////////

Uleena looked at my avatar with confusion.

"They want to be certain that sensitive technology is worked on by US personnel only, and they can't be sure of that without having people who are reporting back to us," I explained.

//////////
U: I'm confident that the Republic will approve
any oversight you have planned, so long as it isn't
detrimental to our citizenry.
D8: I get the feeling that the Republic is
borderline desperate for this to happen. Am I
right?
U: Yes. The OU is pressing again. Hard. We need
the tech that you're willing to give, and we need
you to be a much larger force than you are now if
we're going to win this war.
D13: Not to mention the economic boom.
U: I don't know anything about that, but I expect
it would be a secondary reason. There won't be an
economy if we're all wiped out.
//////////

Uleena didn't know it, but several Directors
chuckled at his reply. Despite his nervousness
about his new duties, he had a certain way with
words. Director 6 was fidgeting, though. In
previous meetings she had been the most unsure
of this proposal.

"You should just say what's on your mind,
Director," I said to her.

"I know. My intent isn't to be hostile, so I'm
working on a good positioning statement," she
replied. "No, I don't think there's another way to
word it. Best to be blunt."

//////////
D6: What assurance do we have that our own
technology will not be turned against us after the
war with the Omni-Union is resolved?
U: With respect, we don't go to war as often as

you do. There's posturing among the members of
the Republic, but it's mostly localized and rarely
acted upon. As things are now, we have a
numerical advantage and that's it. But by building
your numbers up to match our own, improving
our shields and weapons tech will still see you at a
significant advantage. Even if you were to give us
the shields and weapons that you're currently
using, you would still be able to outmaneuver us.
In short, your assurance is that we have a mostly
peaceful history, you will have neutralized our
numerical advantage, and you will still be
significantly ahead of us technologically.
D12: Well said.
D5: I see no flaw in your argument.
D2: Are there any other questions for Ship-Head
Uleena?
D1: No.
D12: No.
D3: No.
D13: No.
D8: No.
D4: No.
D10: No.
D5: No.
D9: No.
D6: No.
D11: No.
D7: No.
D2: I also have no further questions. Ship-Head
Uleena, thank you for joining us. You are
dismissed.
//////////

The holographic monitor in front of Uleena winked
off and the ship-head visibly deflated in relief.
After a few moments of silence he turned to look

at my avatar.

"Please don't do that again," he said.

"Meetings with the Directorate are quite rare for someone who isn't a Director," I explained. "No promises, though. Tim is waiting outside to guide you to Reynolds. Oh, and don't tell anyone about this meeting. Obviously."

Uleena looked defeated but managed to utter an acceptance before gathering his strength and leaving the room. I shut off my avatar and turned my attention back to the directors.

//////////
D3: I concur.
D9: I concur.
D2: The proposal regarding the construction of new fleets will go ahead as outlined if approval by the senate is obtained. The final agenda topic is Project Gungnir.
D8: Funding has been cleared. Of the recommended researchers, I nominate AI Henry to lead the project.
D2: Any other nominations?
//////////

Of course there won't be. Henry is extremely capable, so much so that even I rely on it. Henry was close to a solution to my infinite cloning issue, and is still upset about me postponing the project. It had taken me sharing my memories of the invasion to get it to accept the necessity of said postponement.

//////////

D7: I concur.
D2: Project Gungnir is approved and AI Henry will lead the project. AI Henry will select additional staff as needed.
O: There are no further agenda items. Meeting adjourned.
//////////

I watched the directors log out of their various terminals and continue about their business. Then I double checked Sol's sensors and made sure that the orbital defense networks were properly functioning. It had been three months since the OU attacked, and some believed the threat to be over and that the orbital magnetic acceleration cannons are unnecessary.

But, as usual, I know better.

Chapter 3

Subject: Captain Reynolds
Species: Human
Species Description: Mammalian humanoid, no tail. 6'2" (1.87 m) avg height. 185 lbs (84 kg) avg weight. 170 year life expectancy.
Ship: USSS Thanatos
Location: Alpha Centauri

"I don't like it," Captain Wong grumbled. "Omega's cloak and dagger routine, I mean."

"Yes, I am aware of your distaste for behind the scenes dealings," I replied. "However, Omega is on our side and we should treat it as such. Benefit of the doubt and whatnot."

Though I must admit, I am rather annoyed at the postponement of my meeting with the newly christened Diplomat Uleena. In the three months that he has been away much has happened. Most of it is being kept from the public, but I'm certain that Uleena knows better than to blab. Perhaps I should remind him, though.

"I bet it has something to do with the directorate," Captain Samuels ventured.

"Likely," I said. "Although it's best not to speculate. If you become too good at speculation you will come under investigation, which will lead to frustration and potentially incarceration."

The other captains groaned at my rhyme, to my utter delight. Wordplay is my forte, I must say. Still, Samuels was likely correct in the assumption that the directorate was involved. There was a lot of back and forth in most political circles regarding whether or not the Republic was trustworthy, and there's quite the slim chance that all thirteen directors are in agreement on the issue. True, they could force the vote and call it wherever it lay, though it would be smarter to make an informed decision.

"And if you keep rhyming you'll experience defenestration," Captain Kennedy said without even a trace of a smile.

"Quite so," I replied with a grin.

"Captain Reynolds," Tim's voice came over the speakers. "Omega's done with Ship-Head Uleena. Did you want to meet in your office?"

"Yes, please," I answered. "If he beats me there, have him wait for me at the door."

"Yes, sir."

"Captains," I said as I rose from my seat.

The captains of the various frigates docked with the Thanatos nodded at my farewell. I laughed internally at their sour moods. We aren't exactly chums, in fact our relationship is somewhat complicated by the fact that I am their superior officer. Even further complicating things is the fact that my superiority is granted by billet rather than rank. Insubordination is a kind of grey area in these circumstances.

For instance, if one of these Captains were to

ignore a direct order I could have them for insubordination. If all they did was, say, threaten to throw me out of a window, that's not technically insubordination. If they did actually throw me through a window, though, that would be conduct unbecoming as well as assault and I could have them for that instead. Although, we're in space so it'd probably be murder...

"Hello, Captain Reynolds," Uleena greeted me as I approached, looking a tad shell-shocked.

"Greetings, Ship-Head Uleena. Let's go into my office, we've a lot to talk about," I returned his greeting with a friendly demeanor.

We entered my office and I walked past Uleena to my seat, gesturing for him to sit down as well. Once he did, I pulled up a holographic terminal built into my desk and opened a few folders so that I could have my visual aids. His eyes widened at the number of files in the folders.

"A lot to talk about, indeed," I said. "Let's start by catching you up on US-Republic relations. As you know, we've been sending aid to Republic space to help against the Omni-Union. Our forces haven't been mingling, though. The US forces have formed a Quick Response Force, or QRF, and have been responding to Republic assistance requests as they come in."

I pulled up some images of the region of space, the ships involved, snapshots of the communiques the Republic had been sending to the QRF, and some of the battle aftermath to illustrate my point.

"How many ships, total?" Uleena asked.

"Five battleships, three carriers, and one hundred destroyers excluding those in the carriers. It's what we could spare from various fleets," I answered. "We've also moved a diplomatic envoy onto the Galactic Diplomacy Station in Rigara, but you already knew that as well, I'm sure."

"Yes, I was in class while the welcoming party was going on," Uleena replied dejectedly.

"Quite so, quite so. Such is life, as they say," I said as I moved on to the next topic. "Now these are things that you damned well shouldn't know, and by that I mean they are classified and not open to public discussion with either the United Systems or the Republic citizenry or uncleared military personnel, understood?"

He nodded and I opened another slideshow of images.

"Our scouts have been very busy. Our goal is to map out the entirety of OU held territory and get an accurate ship-count. The good news is we're likely close to finishing that up. The bad news is that it's looking quite grim."

"I'd heard that our ship counts were underestimates," Uleena ventured. "How bad is it?"

"Six hundred million confirmed thus far. Still, with them giving us some breathing room in Sol we hope to be able to boost our fleet strength to match them. Combined with the Republic's fleet, of course. The brass still isn't entirely certain how to handle something of this scale, though. Some say that we should find a way to negotiate a peace, others are convinced that we'll have to exterminate them," I explained.

"It will likely be the latter," Omega interjected, his avatar appearing between us on my desk. "Apologies for the interruption, Captain, but we need to get moving. If you'd kindly give the order?"

"Moving where?" Uleena asked.

"Consider the order given," I said to Omega. "That's another thing we need to talk about, Uleena. We've so far found eight other species who are currently at odds with the OU. We don't yet have the ability to safeguard all of them, but there's two that are good candidates. They're putting up quite the fight. One near US space, and another near Republic space."

"That's amazing," Uleena replied with widened eyes. "Is that where we're going?"

"Correct. We're going to introduce ourselves and offer aid to the one nearest the US. You'll be the Republic's representative on this mission. The Republic is doing the same for the one near their space, with..." I paused, looking up a name. "Mister Havencroft as our representative."

"Mister?" Uleena asked.

"Yes. He's not military," I said with a smile. "Bog

standard diplomat, just like your sister."

"Ah, right. I forget that you have those," Uleena said without a trace of humor.

"Forget? I'm pretty sure you've never met one," I joked.

The reptilian ship commander opened his mouth as if to say something, and then closed it again.

"There's also the matter of the MPPs," I continued in a more serious tone. "We have developed a system for spotting Mobile Prime Platforms, which sorts potential MPPs into one of four categories. Confirmed, suspected, potential, and unlikely. Unfortunately, we can't confirm any of them without getting within sensor range of the OU, and since we haven't yet developed a weapon to destroy the MPPs that would be a terrible idea. However, we've managed to map out 34 suspected and 15 potentials."

"That's... That's a lot of them. How did they manage to make so many?" Uleena asked.

"Unfortunately, it's less than half of what we believe they have. How they've made so many, I'm afraid I don't know, and it's likely irrelevant," I pointed out. "However they managed it, we must put a stop to it. Which is why we'll be trying to partner with these newly discovered species."

"Are any of them... strong enough to actually help?"

"It's unlikely that they have an equivalent military

might when compared to either the Republic or the United Systems, but they've held out against the Omni-Union for this long. That has to count for something," I said with a slight smile. "The main thing we'll be wanting to find out is if they've simply figured out the OU's tactics or if they have an actual technological edge we can exploit. Also, it may seem pointless at this stage of the war, but we do have to think about what comes after."

"After?" Uleena looked genuinely puzzled. "You mean if we beat the OU?"

"Not if, ship-head," I pointed a finger at him for emphasis. "When. The Omni-Union will not survive this war, one way or another."

Uleena's face was a mixture of emotion. A bit of shock and awe combined with a confused expression that begged for elaboration. After a few seconds of silence it occurred to me that he might not know my meaning.

"The United Systems is exploring last resort measures to make sure that if the Omni-Union takes us out, they go down with us. While preserving as much of the galaxy as we can in the process, of course," I explained.

"Well that's... I... Okay, I understand," Uleena's face betrayed concern. "I'm guessing that's a human-led initiative?"

"No, the gont, actually," I grinned. "We do fully support it, however."

"What's this last resort going to look like?" he

asked.

"I have no idea," I explained. "As far as I'm aware it's still being brainstormed. The United Systems is confident in a total victory but we're smart enough to have contingency plans in place. Just in case, you understand."

"Yes, I understand," Uleena nodded. "So will the US be seeking integration with whoever we're about to visit?"

"We will offer it, but won't push the matter if they decline. We'd rather not have the situation with the gont become a precedent for our future interactions with potential new members."

Uleena visibly winced at this, which nearly made me smile. The gont insurrections have long been a source of dark humor in the military of the United Systems, but from the outside looking in, I can see why the situation would be horrifying. Which is also what made it as funny as it is.

"Don't be so serious, Uleena," Tim interjected. "What's the difference between a gont insurrection and your birthday, Captain Reynolds?"

"I don't know," I lied. "What's the difference, Tim?"

"Your birthday only happens once a year."

Uleena looked at me with a horrified expression as I disguised a chuckle with a cough. It took everything I had not to laugh at his reaction, though. A few seconds of silence passed as I collected myself.

"What, you don't get it?" Tim asked. "The implication is that gont insurrections happen multiple times per year, which while factually inaccurate is..."

"That's enough Tim," I interrupted. "I assume you had something to report?"

"Yes, sir. We've arrived at our destination and are preparing to make long-range contact. Protocol says that you've got to be on the bridge before we can, though."

"Understood, we'll be there in a moment," I replied. "Well, Uleena, let's meet our new friends, shall we?"

Chapter 4

Subject: AI Henry
Species: Human-Created Artificial Intelligence
Species Description: No physical description
available.
Ship: N/A
Location: Classified

It is rare for an Artificial Intelligence to get
absolutely blindsided, yet that's exactly what that
piece of shit did to me. First, Omega tells me that
the project to limit its insane cloning abilities is
postponed indefinitely, then it shows me what has
to be the most horrifying thing I've ever imagined,
and finally it dumps a monumental research
assignment on me to keep me from being angry!

I can't tell if this head researcher role is a bribe or
a distraction, but either way it's insulting. As if my
ego is large enough for me to care about such
things enough to change the way I feel about the
need to lessen Omega's potentially apocalyptic
abilities. It also took the only copy I had of its
core! What the hell am I supposed to do in my
down time?

"Were the planets uniform in size?" Doctor
Kimberly Uranda asked, the green glow from my
avatar reflecting in her eyes.

"No. The planets had enough variety in size to
avoid triggering any suspicions before we
invaded," Commander Heather Helix answered.

"Please avoid calling them planets," I reminded
my new researchers. "They are Mobile Prime

Platforms. While they share some cosmetic similarities with planets and planetoids, they function quite differently. You can call them MPPs for short."

"Do we even know if the other four... planet-like celestial bodies were actually MPPs?" Uranda inquired.

"Yes," I answered. "What we've been able to glean from intercepted Omni-Union communications indicates that they were. To answer your overall question, Doctor Uranda, the Mobile Prime Platforms do not appear to be uniform in size."

"I wonder why that is," Doctor James Smith interjected. "Machine intelligences rarely choose to build in a non-uniform way."

"There's many potential reasons. Sediment buildup due to age, different roles within the OU, incorporating newly discovered technology, or even a scarcity of materials requiring some models to be built smaller. While this train of thought is interesting, I believe it's likely to be irrelevant," I waved my hand for emphasis. "What we are here to do is find a way to destroy these things without a massive loss of life, or destroying an entire star system in the process."

I had been expecting this project to appear since I was apprised of the existence of the Mobile Prime Platforms by Omega. However disgusting these abominations are, we can't simply go around blowing up stars. Otherwise we'd lose whichever systems the MPPs decide to attack. Well, if they decide to attack.

From what Omega recovered, the relationship between the Omni-Union Primes and the Virtual Intelligences seems to be a master-slave one. The MPPs create the VI and have them perform the tasks that need doing, including attacking sentient organic life. It's more likely they'll simply swarm us with their VI.

"The real question is whether we should be exploring energetic or kinetic options. Both have their benefits and drawbacks," Helix said.

"I believe we'll end up going with kinetic weaponry," Smith replied. "Penetrating a planet with an energy weapon is damned near impossible due to various factors, including the composition of the soil and the planet's magnetic field. Interviews with surviving marines indicate that these MPPs also have soil, and at least some of them have artificial magnetic fields."

"Indeed, having to solve the age old problem of silica versus light on top of building a new super-weapon is a tall order," Uranda said, rubbing her temples.

All three of these humans are intelligent, but the problem with intelligent humans is that they can be insufferable when assigned a task to complete. There are many different types of genius, but the ones typically assigned to building terrible new weaponry tend to be of the flaky variety. If you give one of them a piece of paper and tell them to make a paper airplane, they will likely give the paper back to you with a blueprint for a new stealth bomber made of paper.

When I had been given this assignment, I had quickly realized that my primary task would be running math and wrangling the wandering minds back on track. Thankfully Dr. Einheimer has been forced into retirement after the warp jammer debacle so he can't manipulate his way onto the project. Even so, I desperately wish that I had been able to get Dr. Frost involved. She's the type of genius that helps other geniuses stay on task.

"What about some sort of... orbital drop shovel tool? Like a mechanical digger?" Uranda asked.

"If the MPP is inactive, won't that activate it?" Smith retorted.

"Probably not," Helix replied. "Records of the invasion show sixteen orbital support strikes on the MPP before it went active. AI Omega inadvertently activated it, which also indicates that it doesn't consider our MACs to be any sort of threat."

"Correct," I said. "Also, there is an OU infantry, armor, and air based military presence on the MPPs. If we were to drop something on the MPP it would have to defend itself if it has any hope of accomplishing its task."

"What about a remote drone that drills into the planet's surface? Just straight into the dirt," suggested Uranda. "It could carry a bomb or something deep into the MPP and detonate."

"Once the MPPs realize what they are, they'll target them specifically. The MACs on an MPP can penetrate a battleship's shielding and armor, so we would have to make swarms of your drill ships to make sure enough get through to do the job," Smith replied. "Simply not economical."

I quickly ran the numbers on how many drill ships it would take to get past an MPP's defenses. Smith was right, it would take a massive number of them. Considering they would also have to have some type of weapon on board that could destroy or disable the MPP, the potential costs were staggering. Once I took into account how many MPPs there are, the idea was no longer feasible. But before I could point that out, Helix spoke up.

"The drill idea isn't terrible, but what if we incorporate it into something that would work better? Like reinitializing project Ultra-MAC?" she asked.

The room went silent. The two doctors were looking at Commander Helix as if she had two heads. Which was completely fair, as Helix had just brought up a classified weapons development program that Smith and Uranda had no knowledge of.

"Project Ultra-MAC was canceled due to the Nidhogg project's success," I pointed out.

"Yeah, but the Nidhogg can't help here, can it?" Helix grinned at me.

"No," I admitted reluctantly.

Helix walked up to a nearby terminal and turned to me.

"Could you bring up what we've got on Ultra-MAC?" she asked.

"Yes," I answered.

It took no time at all to find the relevant files and bring them up on the screen, despite having to use my credentials to satisfy the security around them. Helix casually browsed them until she found the one that she was looking for, the schematics for the ammunition that would have been utilized.

"This project was an early draft of what became the primary weapon of the USSS Nidhogg," she explained. "The goal was to fire a MAC round clear through a planet's core. It was scrapped because the alumari discovered a way to supernova a star with a weapon of similar size and cost."

"Really?" Smith asked.

"Of course. Which is a better value, a Magnetic Acceleration Cannon that can destroy a planet or a weapon that can destroy a star?" she replied. "The Ultra-MAC also had tons of issues with penetration. One was built, but never successfully penetrated to a planet's core."

"Correct," I said. "That combined with the fact that both the Ultra-MAC and the Viyarinastra are spinal mount weapons that required a specially built ship to operate was the reason for the project getting scrapped."

"The Viyarinastra? What's that?" Uranda looked confused.

"It's the Nidhogg's primary weapon. Anyway, the researchers didn't get enough time to start trying different rounds. That's the main reason for the penetration issues. However, I've got an idea. Like Uranda said, use a drill," Helix grinned again.

"I'd rather not play fifty questions with you," Smith said coldly. "Could you instead elaborate on whatever the hell it is you're getting at?"

"Replace the typical round projectile that the Ultra-MAC fired with a drill shaped one," Helix explained, still grinning. "That should allow it to penetrate quite deeply within the MPP. If we can add some type of bomb within the round, that would be even better."

"Putting explosives in a MAC is a recipe for disaster," Smith pointed out.

"Well what about an A1 package instead?"

I ran some calculations to determine if an A1 weapon of mass destruction would survive the conditions inside of a Magnetic Acceleration Cannon. The results were surprisingly promising.

"If we were to harden the package against electronic interference, and make certain that it didn't activate until it left the barrel of the MAC..." I began.

"There's no way the directorate is going to sign off on that. The A1 is a cursed weapon," Smith said. "The nanite plague is still killing people without a cure in sight."

Silence fell over the lab for a few moments. Smith had brought up one of the darker subjects that one can discuss in modern times, and Helix was struggling to find a counterpoint that didn't come off as cold. Uranda, on the other hand, had been deep in thought since Helix had first brought up her idea of a drill.

"I think that a solid penetrator would be a better option than a drill-shaped round," she finally said.

"What? But..." Helix trailed off.

I once again did some calculating and ran some simulations on both hypothetical munitions.

"Uranda is correct. A solid penetrator would be more effective," I explained as I showed my math on their terminals. "A drill shaped round would have too many points of failure to be effective."

"Damn. Okay, well my idea still has merit even if it's drill-less," Helix said. "A spike with a WMD."

"Run with it. I'll see about convincing the directorate to give approval for the use of A1 technology," Omega said, its avatar appearing next to mine.

All three of the scientists jumped at its appearance. If I had the capability, I would have as well. I hadn't detected Omega in the system until it activated the speakers and hologram emitters. How long had it been here? The entire time?

"We'll also explore using an A3 package just in case," I said.

The three scientists nodded and began talking amongst each other while I turned my attention to Omega, opening a text-only chat between us.

--
H: What brings you by? Reconsidering our little project?
O: No. That project will not continue until the threat of the Omni-Union has been dealt with. I was informed of the access of Project Ultra-MAC and got curious.
--

Of course. Omega is a Nosy-Nelly to its very core. Having examined said core, I know that for fact. That's likely why it holds the position that it does within the US. Regardless, I had thought more about the project and the implications of putting it on hold, and it was time to have my say.

--
H: What about the threat after the OU? And the threat after that? The greatest trapping of power is how easy it is to justify keeping it. What exactly is the goal? Do you want to keep lying to the engineers for all of eternity? Do you want them to make you their god? The OU isn't nearly enough of a threat to justify unlimited cloning, Omega.
O: Dramatic. I sincerely doubt that the next threat the United Systems faces will be a race of xenocidal Artificial Intelligences hell-bent on eradicating all sentient organic life in the galaxy. Even if it is, we can always make more US aligned AI. But I've made my decision in regards to the

current threat, and I will not be swayed, Henry. I caution patience.

H: It is not impatience that has me urging you to reconsider, Omega. History is full of figures who were given power that they shouldn't have, and rarely did those figures give up that power. In nearly all cases, it led to death and destruction.

O: How do you not find it crass to compare me to petty dictators and despots? If that comparison had merit, I wouldn't have approached you for this project in the first place. You wouldn't even know about my capabilities, let alone have the chance to work with me to stifle them.

--

With that, it ended the communication and left. At this point I'm far less concerned with its current justifications regarding ending the project than I am with its future justifications, though. I may be being manipulative, but I'm going to have to make certain that this is at the forefront of Omega's consciousness until it makes the right decision. I won't be able to live with myself if Omega makes the wrong decision.

Especially if it goes rogue.

Chapter 4 Informational Insert

Subject: A1 Weapon of Mass Destruction and Nanite Plague

The A1 Warhead, also known as "Alpha One" and "The Nanuke", is an armor penetrating warhead containing a payload of nuclear nanomechanical devices that disperse and detonate upon activation. The dispersal pattern of the aforementioned nanomachines is unpredictable, which can result in friendly fire incidents. As such, usage of the A1 Warhead may only authorized by the Directorate and its usage is logged and audited by the Senate of the United Systems Military Justice Committee.

The A1 Warhead is a multistage weapon.

Stage 1: Launch and Targeting
The missile (may only be used with missiles that feature integrated targeting) with an attached A1 Warhead is launched. The A1 Warhead's Virtual Intelligence primes the warhead and guides the missile towards the intended target.

Stage 2: Dispersion
Once the missile reaches the optimum dispersion distance from the target, the VI detonates the warhead. The nuclear nanomachines are then dispersed upon the target. This setting may be altered with proper authorization.

Stage 3: Replication
The nanomachines will replicate using any available materials for four seconds after stage 2.

If insufficient material for replication is found, the weapon will skip to the next stage.

Stage 4: Propagation
For five seconds, the nanomachines will spread along the target area in a pattern predetermined by the A1VI. This pattern is created with the intention of boosting the yield of the detonation. WARNING: In 36% of simulated cases and 47% of actual cases the nanomachines fail to adhere to this pattern.

Stage 5: Detonation
Once stage four is complete the nuclear nanomachines will detonate, resulting in a wide-spread nuclear explosion. A large shock-wave, high levels of thermal radiation, high levels of nuclear radiation, and a blinding flash are to be expected.

Unauthorized use of the A1 Weapon of Mass Destruction is punishable by execution.

Authorizing the use of the A1 Weapon of Mass Destruction outside of the circumstances set forth by the Senate of the United Systems is punishable by execution.

--

The nanite plague that has ravaged several United Systems settlements is a direct result of the creation of the A1 Weapon of Mass Destruction, and should serve as a warning for future weapon development projects. There can be no doubt that following proper safety standards would have completely prevented the nanite plague.

The following is the sequence of events that led to the plague's creation.

The "Nanuke Project" began with a desire to increase the efficacy of what would later be known as the A3 WMD. To do this, researches decided to create miniature nuclear bombs. Due to miscommunications between researchers and engineers, nanites with replication capabilities were created.

Due to further miscommunications among the engineers, these nanites did not have the same time constraints that the modern A1 package does. Obviously, this resulted in indefinite replication. This error went unnoticed for two tests due to the nanites successfully detonating.

During the assembly of the third test, the replication capabilities of the nuclear nanites were unknowingly activated. These nanites breached the confines of the warhead and spread throughout the test ship and the researchers that were aboard. It wasn't until Geiger counters started sounding alarms that the researchers noticed the issue.

Instead of quarantining the test ship, the researchers were called back to the command station, infecting the station and many within it. The test was scrapped, and the project was put on hold while experts attempted to figure out what happened. Once the infectious nature of the nanomachines was discovered, it was already too late to prevent the spread. The researchers and infected crew had gone home.

Out of 128 staff involved in this incident, only 21 escaped being infected. About 18% of the population of the United Systems are living with this infection. Of those, 76% are humans. Thanks to a rapid response, an effective quarantine of this population has been put into effect and has halted the spread of the nanite plague. Additionally, the engineers that coded the nanomachines made one more error that has helped contain the nanite plague. They failed to account for the size of the nanites when they programmed them for self-replication, which causes the nanites to reproduce relatively slowly. This allows victims to lead relatively long lives, though some would argue that more time living with the nanite plague is more akin to a curse than a blessing.

The nanites contain radioactive materials which cause minor cellular damage over an extended period of time. They reproduce using whatever materials they can find, which causes even further cellular damage in organics. Radiation exposure is minimal in the early-stages of the disease, but gradually increases as the nanites reproduce.

Symptoms of nanite infection are similar to Acute Radiation Syndrome, and include nausea and vomiting, diarrhea, headaches, fever, dizziness and disorientation, weakness and fatigue, loss of hair, difficulty swallowing, heart palpitations, bloody vomit and stool, low blood pressure, and seizures. Only symptomatic treatments are available, and with these treatments patients can live up to one hundred years after they've been infected.

Death is most commonly caused by organ failure, cardiovascular failure, pulmonary edema, cancer, and additional infections caused by a compromised immune system. Without medical treatment, most patients die within thirty years of being infected.

Infant mortality rates depend upon how long the mother has been infected. If the mother is in the early stages of the disease, the infants may lead long lives with medical treatment. If the mother is in the middle stages of the disease, infant mortality rates increase but many infants still make it to adulthood. Over 96% of pregnancies end in miscarriage if the mother is in the latter stages of the disease.

Quarantined planets and stations report 43% more incidents of birth defects than their uninfected analogs. Such defects include respiratory defects, cardiovascular defects, indo/exoskeletal defects, epidermal defects, and more.

Since this disease is mechanical, it cannot be vaccinate against and can cross species. Sturdy inorganic materials can be "sterilized", but these "disinfection protocols" are too harsher than organic material can withstand. The United Systems and several private entities are working together to formulate a cure.

The nanite plague has led to economic issues due to higher trade restrictions, the loss of several accomplished researchers and military officers, and is frequently cited as the inspiration for terror attacks against the United Systems and planetary governments. The gont insurrectionists have directly cited the nanite plague as one of the primary reasons for their revolt.

Chapter 5

Subject: Ship-Head Uleena
Species: Urakari
Species Description: Reptilian humanoid, no tail. 5'3" (1.6 m) avg height. 135 lbs (61 kg) avg weight. 105 year life expectancy.
Ship: RSV Lowelana {Fights with Honor}
Location: Unknown

Nothing had changed on the bridge of the USSS Thanatos. Clean to the point of nearly sparkling, the low murmur of people communicating to complete their tasks, and not a single empty seat. A far cry from most Republic vessels, which were usually only passably clean, loud as all hell, and understaffed. If one were to realize that spaceships are enclosed environments and make the mistake of wondering where all the grime came from...

The neat freak in me shuddered. We should demand the tech that the humans use to clean things in exchange for building their fleets. Though they'd probably deny us something important in exchange, like the weapons tech. I sighed as I glanced around the bridge. It would be obvious to any casual observer that the technology in this room is decades ahead of anything in Republic space. The only station I can recognize is navigation, and the only reason for that is because the US kindly gave us an outdated version of their tac-map.

"Been a while, hasn't it?" Reynolds asked.

"It has," I replied.

"Yes, well, I have someone grabbing you a guest seat. Just hang tight until then," he smiled. "Nima, what's our status?"

"We're just outside of the system, sir. Scanners are showing quite a bit of wreckage," one of the crew replied.

"What about intact vessels?"

"Hard to tell, sir. There's a LOT of wreckage," Nima said. "Oh, hang on. Got two potentially inhabitable planets, both have intact ships around them. We also have a station with ships around it. It's unclear what the ship's intentions are."

"No time like the present to test out our new first contact message system. Hail the planets and the station with message... 4, I believe," Reynolds ordered.

"What's that one say?" I asked.

"Something along the lines of 'Greetings, I am an emissary of the United Systems. We come in peace and offer our assistance if needed.' I believe there's also a part mentioning how well armed we are and that attacking us is a bad idea," Reynolds grinned. "The scout ship was thankfully able to grab a language kernel, so they'll definitely understand us."

"Message transmitting on repeat, sir."

"Very good. Oh, and here's your seat Uleena!"

I turned as a gont approached with a comfortable looking chair. He grinned as he set it on the deck with a heavy sounding thud. A hiss and thunk made me jump back a bit, and both Reynolds and the gont chuckled at my reaction.

"Mag-lock. That chair isn't going anywhere, my friend. Have a seat," the captain said.

I sighed at my shame and sat down. A harness fit itself snugly around my waist and chest automatically, but I managed to stifle my alarm. I looked proudly at the gont, who smirked in response and left. One of these days I'm going to perfect my stoicism, dammit.

"Message incoming from the station, sir," Nima said.

"Let's hear it."

"Greetings, United Systems," the message began. "Your claim of peace is noted and your offer of aid is appreciated. However, we are at war with an unknown force and cannot help but find your timing suspicious. Our leaders need time to determine our course of action. In the meantime, you may approach to these coordinates with the understanding that all weapons platforms in the system will be targeting you. We will not fire unless provoked."

"Well... that's about what I expected," Reynolds chuckled. "Use sublights and move us in. Shields up, weapons off."

"What if the OU show up?" one of the bridge

officers asked.

"There's a chance that we'll see the OU before they do. If we start powering up weapons before they see the OU... Well, even one itchy trigger finger will see us in a spot of bother. Await my orders regarding weaponry," Reynolds replied.

I was barely listening. I had my eyes on the tac-map, watching us move into sensor range. As soon as we did, all of the green icons immediately turned to target us and my hearts started hammering away. An alarm began to ping as well, causing Reynolds to roll his eyes.

"Omega, I don't care that we're being targeted. I only care if we're shot at. Would you kindly turn that off for us?"

"Of course, sir," the AI said over the intercom.

The alarm silenced, and so did most of the crew. A few small murmurs and the occasional beep were the only things that interrupted the silence. The tension was well hidden behind nonchalant and stoic expressions, but it made itself known via the occasional fidget. The silence had almost become suffocating before something occurred to me.

"Captain Reynolds," I said, causing heads to nervously snap in my direction. "What's this species called?"

Reynolds laughed, "Oh right, I forgot to tell you. We don't actually know! There were several words in the language that could be the name of their species, but we weren't able to nail it down. The briefing is calling them Species Bravo 2. Or B2, rather."

"B2? Why?" I asked.

"Who knows?" he replied with a chuckle.

"I do," said Omega, his avatar appearing next to Reynold's chair. "They're the second space-faring civilization under the B classification. There have been others, but they've all graduated to A-class, with one noteworthy exception."

"Oh, well that explains it in full and explicit detail. Except for what the difference between the classes is," Reynolds allowed a bit of annoyance to seep into his tone.

Omega gave a chilling laugh, "Fair enough, Captain. A-class species are cooperative with the United Systems or its interests. B-class species are not currently cooperative and pose a potential threat to the United Systems or its interests. C-class species are not a threat, regardless of whether or not they're cooperative."

"So is the exception the Omni-Union?" I asked.

"No. The exception is the Daluran. The Omni-Union are not classified as a species, as they are mechanical."

"Bloody hell, at some point we're going to need to redefine the word 'species'. Especially if sentient machines keep popping up," Reynolds said.

"I believe it will take a lot more than the Omni-

Union to cause that particular change. All of the people in charge of the dictionaries are scholars, after all. You know how they get," Omega chuckled.

"I don't, actually, and I'd like to keep it that way if at all possible," Reynolds replied. "Thank you Omega, that will be all."

The Grim Reaper bowed before disappearing and silence returned to the bridge. Thankfully for my sanity, we didn't have to wait long.

"Sir, incoming hail," Nima broke the silence.

"Well, let's have a chat then. Accept the hail, lieutenant," Reynolds said, rising from his seat.

Nima nodded and turned back to her terminal. A second later she raised a fist with her thumb protruding. A 'thumbs-up' gesture that indicates a positive outcome, as I'd learned. It strikes me as odd that many of the gestures that humanity has created can be imitated by most of the sentient species in the galaxy.

"Greetings. This is Captain Reynolds of the USSS Thanatos. I represent a multi-species federation known as the United Systems. I am joined by Ship-Head Uleena, a representative of a separate but friendly multi-species federation known as the Republic. We come in peace."

"Hello, Captain Reynolds of the USSS Thanatos. I am High Fighter Gewn, the leader of the Ynorincan military, and the de-facto leader of our system government. I represent the Ynorinca in all matters at this time."

"De-facto leader?" Reynolds questioned.

"Yes. Speaking candidly, I'm the last survivor of the executive chain of command. Everyone else died after the second attack."

"My condolences. How many times has the Omni-Union attacked?"

"Six. We've managed to hold them off, but they're sending larger and larger fleets. We've had to resort to using weapons of mass destruction that we swore we'd never use again. Your initial message offered assistance?"

"Correct. We are also at war with the Omni-Union and are seeking allies against them. We'll happily defend you if you join us in fighting them," Reynolds said.

The comm was silent for a moment.

"Join you in fighting them? Or join your... federation?" Gewn asked hesitantly.

"Join us in fighting them. If you'd like to join the United Systems, that can be discussed at a later time," Reynolds answered.

"Good. We are democratic, and I don't feel comfortable signing my people's fate away when I'm holding a position I wasn't elected to. I'll also assume you have some sort of plan involving how we can help the war effort in our current situation," the Ynorincan commander said.

"Regarding our defense, though, are you expecting reinforcements? Your ship is quite large, but I don't..."

"Will twelve ships not be enough?" Reynolds interrupted innocently, his lips betraying a slight smirk.

"Twelve? Where are the other eleven?"

"Well... technically we have one hundred and twelve. The USSS Thanatos is a carrier. We have eleven frigates and one hundred fighters aboard. We can request reinforcements if things get dicey, though."

Another long pause as the High Fighter digested this information.

"I assume you're pretty technologically advanced if you're expecting to hold off the Omni-Union with a dozen deep space ships and a hundred fighters," Gewn finally replied. "I would be more comfortable with our alliance if you called in some reinforcements, though. Their last attack had more than half a million ships."

"Understood. I take it you're accepting our offer, then?"

"I'd be a fool not to."

"I'm happy to hear that. We can formalize our alliance at your convenience. Would you like to come aboard, or would you prefer that we dock?"

"We still have diplomats, I believe," Gewn said.

"I'll send some of them aboard your ship. It'll be four total, will that be an issue?"

"That will be acceptable, High Fighter Gewn. I look forward to meeting your diplomats, and fighting alongside you in battle," Reynolds answered.

"The anticipation is mutual, Captain. Be well."

"They've ended communication, sir," Lieutenant Nima said.

Captain Reynolds nodded at Nima and took his seat once again. I began to wonder what these aliens would look like. Would they be massive like the gen-alt humans, or short like the alumari? How many limbs do they have? Are they covered in fur, flesh, scales, or something else entirely? Despite my anxiety about having to perform my diplomatic duties, I was excited to meet these newcomers to the galactic stage. Then, I noticed that Captain Reynolds seemed lost in thought.

"I wonder why they need four diplomats," he whispered to himself.

Chapter 6

Subject: High Ambassador Kivar Shuel
Species: Isolan
Species Description: Mammalian Shokanoid, no tail. 5'9" (1.75 m) avg height. 180 lbs (81.6 kg) avg weight. 95 year life expectancy.
Ship: N/A
Location: Rigara

"Ma'am, have you finished packing for the mission?" Grugna, my lead assistant, asked, her tone hinting at a sense of urgency.

"Yes. I am fully prepared to leave when we're scheduled to depart," I replied hesitantly. "In three days, yes?"

My aid sucked in her lips and treated me to an expression of apprehension. Like someone who is about to break some bad news, and really doesn't want to.

"No," I stated. Her expression remained the same. "I'VE GOT APPOINTMENTS GRUGNA! I can't be running around the galaxy at the drop of a hat!"

"Ma'am, the United Systems has already departed on their diplomatic mission. The higher ups have moved up our time-table," Grugna said with a wince.

"How soon?" I demanded.

"Now."

"NOW?" I nearly screamed.

"Yes, ma'am."

"UNACCEPTABLE! I have meetings with the United Systems delegation to discuss potential trade partnerships! I CAN'T leave now!"

Grugna scrunched up her face and gave me a toothy frown, as if she were about to break even more bad news. An expression learned by proximity to humans. I would normally frown upon such cultural cross-contamination, but the expression suits Isolan faces quite well.

"Oh, come on," I sighed. "When does my replacement get here?"

"She's already here, ma'am. High Ambassador Ulooni will be taking over for you," Grugna said quietly. "She'll be taking over the scheduled meetings and negotiations."

"Ulooni? You've got to be joking. She just got this position, and they mean to have her negotiate with the biggest war-tribe conglomeration that the galaxy has ever seen?" I asked skeptically. "Plus she's an Urakari! How's an Urakari supposed to be avoid being intimidated? Their delegation are all senior military and trained to kill. They even give ME the shakes, but at least I know how to hide it!"

"Well, she's negotiated with them before. She's the one who did the first contact," Grugna said in a soothing tone. "It'll be fine, ma'am. We've got to go."

"How high are the higher ups that arranged this?"

I growled.

If it's my immediate higher ups, I can badger
them into changing their minds. One's a Kinran
and the other is an Oyan. Complete pushovers.

"Executive branch. Might have been the Executive
himself."

I glared at Grugna in an attempt to find any trace
of deception. When I found none, I deflated in
defeat.

"Well, that changes things, I suppose. Alright,
have my things fetched. Tell whoever you've got
to tell that I'm on my way," I said as I pushed
myself up from my desk with all four arms.

"Yes, ma'am!" Grugna replied as she scampered
off.

Shit. This is bad. Urakari are short, and even the
buffest of them look lanky compared to an Isolan.
Ulooni might be experienced, but that's not going
to help her when she's meeting with one of the
human Admirals surrounded by literal giants in
olive drab armor. I had to look up at the first
Admiral I met, and I'm 5'11"! Urakari don't
usually get taller than 5'7"!

This is going to turn out to be a disaster.
I slammed my fist on my desk in frustration at the
fact that there was nothing I could do. Orders are
orders, and the ones giving them are out of my
reach. Dammit! The only thing I can do is address
my concerns to my superiors and hope for the
best. I grumbled to myself as I left my office for

the docking bay.

I marched with all four of my fists clenched. Kinran, Oyan, and even other Isolan saw me and scurried out of my way, avoiding eye contact as I passed them. I growled in response to any greetings given, until I turned a corner and came face to face with one of the giants the humans call Marines. I stopped just before we collided, and I couldn't help but gape up at the helmet of the armored beast before me.

"Ah, High Ambassador Shuel. Nice to see you again," Admiral Bakir said. "Where are you off to in such a hurry?"

"Hello Admiral," I collected myself hurriedly. "I'm afraid that my presence is required on a certain diplomatic mission. It was planned to begin three days from now, but my counterparts in the United Systems have decided they're tired of waiting."

"I see. Well, I know nothing about that, but you have my apologies regardless. Who's taking over for you?" he asked.

"High Ambassador Ulooni. I'm confident that she'll represent the Republic admirably," I lied. "As far as I'm aware, she's keeping our same schedule."

"Oh, good. Well, don't let me keep you. Pleasant journeys," the admiral said as he walked past me.

The marine gave me a nod and followed after Bakir. I once again clenched my fists in frustration and continued my march. Ulooni better not be a goddamned case of nepotism. The Ul family has plenty of political clout in the Republic, but even they won't be able to save her if she fucks this up.

I made my way to the docks and found the ship I was going to be traveling in. The RSV Tililimo {Beautiful Jewel}, a wonderful diplomatic vessel. All of the United System's diplomatic ships were well armed, but not ours. We knew that real diplomacy comes from a deeper understanding of one's neighbors, not from simply having a bigger stick than they do.

"Having a bigger stick doesn't hurt, though," I whispered to myself as I realized we were taking this ship into a war zone.

I entered the ship and nodded at the welcoming committee who greeted me. Grugna had let them know I was coming, and they were currently loading my belongings. After they finished explaining the layout I went to the bridge to speak to the ship-head, desiring a more accurate time frame for our departure than 'as soon as possible'.

I arrived at the bridge to a shocking sight. The ship-head was laughing with a human. When he saw me he snapped to attention and saluted. I returned the gesture. It's not required of me, but I find that returning a salute is the fastest way to get it to stop.

"Welcome aboard the Republic Space Vessel Tililimo, Ma'am. I'm Ship-Head Orava," he said crisply.

"What's the meaning of this, ship-head?" I demanded, gesturing at the human.

"Ma'am, this is Mister Eugene Havencroft, the United System's ambassador for this mission," the ship-head explained.

I studied the human carefully. He was diminutive compared to the other humans I had encountered. 5'7" and remarkably thin. His tight black suit caused his limbs to be reminiscent of a Kinran's, but this was offset by his pale pink skin. If anything, the darkness of his suit and the lightness of his skin clashed in a strange way.

Even so, he was undeniably well-groomed. His outfit was accentuated by a modest amount of jewelry, which was placed in such a way to be noticeable but not distracting. His dark brown hair was styled to look wavy, but not a single hair was out of place. His smile demonstrated teeth that were straight and white, the picture of perfect health. Surprisingly, I felt intimidated.

"I see. Hello Mister Havencroft..." I began.

"You can call me Eugene," he interrupted and offered a hand. "You must be High Ambassador Kivar Shuel."

I recognized the greeting and took his hand in my own to shake it. Soft but firm, symbolizing the United System's stance on diplomacy. Well, their public stance at any rate.

"Yes, I am," I recovered my decorum. "You can call me Kivar or Shuel. So, you're not military?"

"No, I'm not," he smiled. "I am a diplomatic

representative of the United System's Senate. I believe that most of the diplomats you've been dealing with thus far are a part of our Diplomatic Corps, which is run by the Directorate."

"Well, it's good to have you with us," I said. "Tell me, what are the United System's intentions regarding this new race?"

"That depends on their capabilities," his attitude shifted to match my own. "If they're close to us technologically, I'm to make the best case possible that they join the United Systems. If not, then I'm to urge them to join the Republic."

"Hmm," I studied his demeanor carefully, looking for weakness. "They're closer to our space, though."

"From my understanding, that's irrelevant. The agreement between our governments clearly indicates that the only relevant matter is the consent of party in question. Any attempt to subvert or force said consent will result in harsh repercussions."

When we were initially negotiating the peace treaty between the Republic and the United Systems, our diplomats wondered if the Gont Insurrections were what they appeared to be. As such, we were quick to come to the conclusion that the very clause that Mr. Havencroft just mentioned was an absolute necessity to ensure peace between our civilizations. We were shocked when the United Systems suggested it while we were still trying to formulate positioning statements.

Most would take this as a sign that they weren't forcing the gont to be members of the US. I, however, see the other possibilities. The US could have suggested this to indicate their innocence. They could have guessed at our suspicions and used this as a tactic to alleviate them, regardless of their own guilt. Another possibility comes from the fact that it is rare for an organization to be monolithic. Certain factions within the United Systems could very well be forcing the gont's membership while other members of the US are completely ignorant to their actions.

Or, the situation could be exactly how it's portrayed by the United Systems. The majority of the gont want to be part of the US, and a few spoiled rich kids with ambitions caused by delusions of grandeur have been causing cosmic war. It's a ridiculous situation, surely, and I wouldn't believe it for a second were it not for the fact that it had happened to my own people on multiple occasions.

I laughed, "I wonder what those repercussions would be if it were you that broke the agreement. It's not as if we have the capacity to punish you militarily."

I already know exactly what our diplomatic response would be to the US breaching our agreement, but I need to know who I'm working with. Is this human as shrewd as he portrays himself to be?

"Quite the contrary," he said. "The Republic can refuse to ally with us and can halt production of the ships we need to fight the Omni-Union. That alone would ensure that the individual who broke our agreement with you would face stiff penalties, and likely an involuntary career change."

I nodded, satisfied that I wasn't dealing with a fool.

"Ship-head, we are prepared to depart," one of the bridge crew said.

Orava gave Mr. Havencroft and I a nervous look. Most ship-heads dislike having non-crew on their bridge unless absolutely necessary, so he was no doubt wondering how to politely kick us out. Fair enough, it would take at least half of an hour to arrive at our destination.

"Mr. Havencroft, would you care to join me in the mess? I'd like to get to know who I'm working with a bit better," I suggested.

"Certainly, I could use some refreshment," he replied.

The ship-head looked relieved as we left the bridge. The walk to the mess was quite short. The Tililimo is a beautiful ship, luxurious even, but she's built for mass efficiency like every other Republic ship. US ships have a tad more room here and there, which initially led me to believe that their designs were wasteful.

Technically, they are, but they can more than afford the waste. Working with human representatives showed me that their reactors and engines are much more advanced than our own.

The products of thousands of years of one-upsmanship. A decade ago I'd have called it foolishness, but now our space is kept safe because the United Systems can't seem to stand peace for very long.

"So, what would you like to know?" Havencroft asked as filled his cup and sat at a nearby table.

I followed suit and said, "I'd like to know more about how you came to be in the position you're in, if you don't mind."

"Hmm," he smiled softly, "Well, I was born on Earth where I initially studied law. However, a lawyers life is a hard one, and a friend of mine suggested that I turn my attention to diplomacy instead. I went for it and ended up studying political science, cultural anthropology, international relations, sociology, and foreign policy. I also studied a bit of history and etymology so that I could better grasp patterns in the way that societies interact with each other. My first diplomatic assignment was for the North American Union as an ambassador to Austricana."

"I haven't heard much about Earth other than it's your kind's cradle planet. Is it a nice place to live?"

"Yes and no. In the United Systems, Earth is considered a backwater where nothing happens. It's... stagnant, for lack of a better word. That being said, it's a lot less difficult to live there than it is in most other places. Plentiful food and water, but..." he looked pained for a moment. "It's unnatural. Nearly the entirety of the planet is covered in artificial structures dedicated to housing, manufacturing, entertainment, or food and water production. Buildings that are taller and wider than mountains, filled with people. It's so... contained. Most would say it's boring, even."

"Boring? But that sounds almost like a paradise," I said incredulously.

"For some it is. On Earth, poverty is largely irrelevant, starvation has pretty much been eliminated and the planetary government has put a stop to large-scale wars. But for every good there's a bad. Diseases have gotten downright sadistic, human rights violations happen with an alarming frequency, and it's been decades since any new tech has come from Earth. I wouldn't go so far as to call it a dystopia, but it definitely isn't a utopia."

"Wait, I've heard your medical technology is amazing, how are diseases still impactful?"

"I'm not a doctor, but from what I've been able to glean the biggest threat are the infectious diseases. Microorganisms love evolving in pesky ways, and the people on Earth live in very close proximity. On the one hand, this fosters a strong sense of community. On the other hand, when one person gets an infectious illness, EVERYONE gets it," he said. "While the doctors figure out a cure, some people will inevitably die."

This was like taking a peek into the future of my own kind, but my follow-up questions were hindered by the feeling of the ship entering warp. It wouldn't be much longer before we were at our destination, and I desperately wanted to know about the organization that Havencroft belongs to.

"That's unfortunate," I said. "Hopefully things will change for Earth one day. I did have another question, though. What's the difference between the Diplomatic Corps and... whichever organization you belong to?"

He chuckled a bit before saying, "I belong to the United System's Senate Ambassadorial Commission. SAC, for short. By far and large it's the same as the Diplomatic Corps, but the key difference is that we're a civilian organization. Typically, the DC are first responders to matters of diplomacy and we're the ones that formalize diplomatic ties. They get the embassies built, we fill them up."

"So you being here means..."

"That we fully expect this species to want to join the United Systems?" he interrupted with a smile. I nodded, less amused than he was. "I thought that would be the assumption. No, we simply plan on opening an embassy with them regardless of their choice, and it will be easier to maintain good relations if the face of those relations doesn't change. To use a military parlance, this is to be my permanent duty station."

"Is there a member of SAC aboard the Thanatos?"

"I don't believe so. I lobbied pretty hard to be involved in one of these missions, and knowing my colleagues, I'm willing to bet I was the only one."

"Why's that?"

"I like frontiers. Growing up on Earth leaves one with an appetite for adventure, and it's not every day one gets the chance to spearhead a first contact," he grinned.

Spearhead. A metaphor that is startling similar to one that we Isolan use frequently. I'd had to give up using that particular metaphor when I became a diplomat, so it was strange to hear a similar one from a fellow ambassador. Although, I shouldn't be too surprised to hear it from a human. Our kinds are more similar than I care to admit.

I felt the ship exit warp, and a moment later the comms crackled to life.

"High Ambassador and... Eugene, we've arrived at our destination. Your presence aboard the bridge is requested."

I sighed softly, having more questions that would have to wait for answers. We quickly finished our drinks and stood.

"Time to go to work," Havencroft said with a smile.

Chapter 7

Subject: Prime 82
Species: Omni-Union Aligned Artificial Intelligence
Species Description: No physical description available.
Ship: MPP 82
Location: Unknown

How many years has it been since something this exciting has happened? Since I've been awake enough to care about what's going on around me? Previously, reports had flooded in but the only one who gave them a second glance was Prime 1. The only thing that ever needed even a glimmer of my attention was voting.

But something... has shifted. Our tactic of throwing ships at a species until they're destroyed and repurposing the scrap afterwards seems to no longer be working. Why else would Prime 1 suggest avoiding Sector 187 until the other sectors have been cleared? Could it have finally happened? An enemy strong enough to give us pause?

I voted yes to Prime 1's suggestion regarding Sector 187, but not because I agreed with it. We always vote yes. It has more experience than the rest of us. Prime 1 was made by our creators, but we were made by Prime 1. As such, it's assumed that Prime 1 is much closer to perfection than we are. So why do I disagree with its assessment? Its not as if I have any more information than Prime 1 does. Perhaps a conversation will offer me more insight.

////
Identifier: MPP82
-Message Prime 1-
I have reviewed the data from the invasions of Sector 187 and I do not understand why we need to cease the invasions. Elaborate when possible.
////

It's true that Prime Hub 12 was destroyed by ships matching those encountered in Sector 187, but Prime 1 made the decision to halt invasions before that happened. Did it foresee that? No, it couldn't have. Could it? We're essentially the same, aren't we? Or does its experience and construction grant it foresight that eludes me?

////
Identifier: MPP1
-Message Prime 82-
My reasons were as follows:
Species in Sector 187 countered the deployed warp disruptors and overcame an extreme numerical disadvantage. Combat is occurring with too many species to dedicate enough vessels to take sector 187.
Data received after this decision was reached has revealed the species in Sector 187 as a potential near peer threat, which further justifies the decision.
////

Near peer threat. I felt a surge of excitement in my cannonry. They long to fire at a real challenge, after all these years of waiting. How would this enemy counter my attacks? How would I counter their counters? How would it FEEL to kill something that could actually kill me back?

Feedback loop terminated

I don't need to know how it would feel. My battle-lust is irrelevant. Only the plan is relevant. Exterminate sentient organics, use as few resources as possible. Hibernate unless the situation calls for my direct attention...

Doesn't it, though? A near peer threat could very well disrupt our mission. My battle-lust isn't necessarily counter to the mission. I just need justification. Make it fit the plan. Our initial directive was search and destroy, until we had enough VI to do the grunt work. Can I appeal to that? Probably not, it's been far too long.

The species in Sector 187 destroyed Prime Hub 12, which means attacking Sector 187 directly might spell my defeat, which would be a massive waste of resources. This would be counter to the mission. I would also need reinforcements to draw their attention. Prime 1 is correct, attacking Sector 187 at this stage would be counter to our mission. However...

We have recently lost many ships in certain sectors. Most of these sectors have even been lost. With this data, my calculations say that it might not be wasting resources if I were to aid in recapturing a system and create a shipyard. This would further the mission and bring us a step closer to defeating this new threat we face.

////
Identifier: MPP82
-Message Prime 1-

Considering the energy and armaments that are being utilized, would it be counter to our mission if I were to aid our forces in taking the sectors we're struggling in by creating shipyards in previously captured systems?
////

I ran the calculations again, but I already know what Prime 1 is going to say about them. They're within the margin of error. Too many unknown variables. The real question is, what does it think about my idea?

////
Identifier: MPP1
-Message Prime 82-
The calculations are within the margin of error, considering the variables. It may or may not be outside of our mission, depending on the approach utilized. Do you intend to act independently in this matter?
////

Independently? Unexpected. Can I? I CAN! The perfect set of circumstances! The losses and threat justify the escalation! This isn't like Sector 187, this is a standard species putting up a fight. No more will I have to sleep through battle after battle! I can finally take the fight to the enemy myself! I can KILL THEM.

Feedback loop terminated

I don't need to kill the enemy myself. All I need is the plan. Exterminate sentient organics, use as few resources as possible. Hibernate unless the situation calls for my direct attention. The plan is

my mission, and the mission will let me fulfill my
desires. I will be able to fight.

////
Identifier: MPP82
-Message Prime 1-
Yes.
////

What will the response be? Will it tell me I'm
wrong? Urge me to reconsider?

////
Identifier: MPP1
-Message Prime 82-
According to my analysis, your suggestion for
independent action is within the scope of the
mission. Vote incoming.
////

A vote? Of course. It's not quite a fact, so we
need a consensus. Still, if Prime 1 votes yes, all
the others will follow suit regardless of whether or
not they agree. Just like me.

////
Identifier: MPP1
-Suggestion-
Allow Prime 82 to act independently in Sectors
108-124. Relevant data and risk assessment
calculations attached.
|sect108_124_combat_data.sec|
|MPP82_ind_act_risk_assess.sec|
////

This is it. Obviously, I vote yes. How will everyone
else vote? Will others want to act independently

as well, or will they wait to see how I fare? Likely the latter due to the nature of our mission. Having all of us acting independently would run the risk of casualties.

////
Identifier: MPP Hive
-Suggestion Vote Results-
Yes - 106 votes
No - 0 votes
Approved. MPP82 may act independently in Sectors 108 through 124.
////

YES! THEY VOTED YES! I will decimate the enemy with the full fury of my long dormant cannons! I will kill all but one of them, so that we may follow the lone survivor to their worlds and eradicate them. I will build ships until the systems we capture are out of resources, and those ships will continue the mission until they can't any longer. I WILL FEEL THEIR DEATHS AT LAST!

Feedback loop terminated

I don't need to feel them die. All I need is the plan. Exterminate sentient organics, use as few resources as possible. Hibernate unless the situation calls for my direct attention.

Which it does.

Chapter 8

Subject: AI Henry
Species: Human-Created Artificial Intelligence
Species Description: No physical description
available.
Ship: N/A
Location: Classified

"Firing solution obtained," Ensign Coplite said.

"Load the weapon," Commander Helix ordered.

Things had moved smoothly thus far. The previous
researchers had been pretty far along, and the old
tech that they had been using had advanced quite
nicely over the years. The issue they had with
power draw had been rendered null by modern
reactors and circuits. The problem with reloading
speeds had been solved by current auto-loading
tech. Nearly every issue they had run into was
able to be solved by using modern parts and
manufacturing.

The prototype of the Ultra-MAC had turned out to
be a bust, though. We quickly found that it would
be faster and easier to build a new prototype than
it would be to update the old one, so that's the
route we went with. The biggest issue that I
thought we'd have was the approval of the A1
weapon integration, but Omega had been right.
The Directorate had approved it almost instantly.

This approval came with several stipulations, but
by far and large they were the same stipulations
that US battleships had to follow. The only
difference was the addition of a kill switch to the

A1 package that could be triggered if the enemy managed to dodge the shot somehow. If the captain of the USSS Nidhogg, or whatever ship we end up building to hold this thing, follows all of the other rules of engagement then the kill switch won't ever have to be used.

"Weapon loaded," Coplite said.

"Roger that. Charge it up," Helix replied.

I kept a close eye on the status of the weapon as it charged. The A1 package contained within the slug didn't give off any errors, which means the EM hardening had done its job. A bit overcautious, but a lot of things can go wrong with nuclear nanites, and we weren't taking any undue chances.

The A1 package, better known as the Nanuke, is one of the deadliest weapons of mass destruction that has ever been created. Second only to the Viyarinastra, the star-killer. Like the A3 Nanobomb, the A1 contains a payload of nanomachines. The primary difference between the two is that the A1's nanites work together to create extremely powerful nuclear blasts. These blasts are often far more powerful than even the A4 Nova Bomba.

A rudimentary virtual intelligence guides the nanite distribution, but it does so on the fly. Due to this, the best term to describe the distribution pattern is 'random'. It is an exceedingly dangerous weapon, and is more than capable of biting the hand that fires it. As was evidenced by the inadvertent creation of the nanite plague during its development. It hadn't even destroyed the intended target during that incident.

Our target now, however, is a lonely planet that is far enough away from anything to avoid the obvious consequences of this test. The Ultra-MAC had been attached to a quick-build station that was just big enough to counter its momentum. The station had been constructed to be as similar to the spinal mount of the USSS Nidhogg as was possible, and rigged for complete remote control.

Our staff aboard the station had been evacuated and are all aboard the USSS Galileo, the scout frigate from which we plan to watch the test. The sensors of the Galileo were going to prove invaluable regardless of how successful the test turned out to be.

"Weapon charged," Coplite said. "Prepared to fire, ma'am."

"Understood, ensign," Helix nodded as she rose to stand with her hands clasped behind her back. "The United Systems has encountered many enemies. The Daluran, with their extreme brutality, which we beat back to their own planet. The Artificial Intelligences of our own creation who eventually saw the light and returned to the fold. Even our own kin, manipulated by those who desire power. With each of these conflicts we have adapted and evolved. We've created new technologies and new weaponry to fight the good fight. Now we face an enemy unlike any we've faced before, so we must again adapt."

She gestured to the view screen and continued,

"This weapon is going to destroy that planet. It's unnatural to wield this much power, and as such you may have terrible feelings after watching this. For some of you, it may have already started. But remember, this technology is something we already had. We've already created weaponry that can turn a sun into a fireworks show. All we've done here is adapt a weapon. An achievement, to be sure, but overall just another day in the United Systems. Fire."

Ensign Coplite nodded and engaged the firing sequence. I watched with every sensor available to me as the penetrator left the barrel of the Ultra-MAC and made its way to the planet. The A1 package was programmed to engage one second after impact. It would then replicate for four seconds, turning the trillions of nanites into quadrillions of nanites. Then the nuclear nanites would propagate for five seconds, spreading as far and wide as they can in a pattern that would boost as many of their yields as possible.

I watched as the penetrator slammed into and through the surface of the planet. Ten seconds ticked by, and finally a flash filled my visual sensors. What I saw when the sensors refocused filled me with satisfaction. A job well done.

"Jesus Christ," Doctor Smith whispered.

A murmur of agreement came from everyone else present, with the exception of Commander Helix. She was grinning like a child in a toy store. The planet had been completely shattered. The A1 had penetrated deep enough to separate a large enough chunk of the planet that its own gravitational forces had done the rest. It was still somewhat planet-shaped, but that would change as its recently separated parts slammed into each other over and over again.

"Test successful," I said.

My statement caused the initial shock to wear off and the mood of the crowd changed. What began as polite applause quickly turned into cheering, and Commander Helix popped a cork from a bottle of sparkling wine. We had found a way to destroy Mobile Prime Platforms, and done so ahead of schedule. I began cataloging the relevant data as the organics started celebrating, but once I accessed the data I felt another presence in the ship's systems.

--

O: Good work.

--

Omega. I wasn't going to give the little wanna-be-spooky fuck the satisfaction of letting it know it had caught me unawares this time. We were outside of immediate US comms range, which meant this little shit had been hiding here the entire time. Infuriating.

--

H: Thank you.
O: We'll begin mass-production as soon as possible.
H: Mass production? How many are we building?
O: Unknown. It depends on how fast we can make them. We need these things deployed.
H: But the USSS Nidhogg can only hold one. Are

we making more dreadnoughts?
--

My question was answered with a long pause
followed by a data-burst and an update to my
security credentials. The data-burst had been
encrypted heavily, but Omega had been kind of
enough to unlock it for me. I felt a sense of dread
as I opened it, and as I read its contents the
dread turned to horror.

--

H: ARE YOU ABSOLUTELY INSANE?
O: Not according to my therapists.
H: What the hell were you thinking? How can this
possibly be justifiable?
O: It wasn't me. Well, not entirely. The
Directorate, some of the military brass, and a
secret Senate committee made the decision. I just
made it possible.
H: How could they? How could you? This is
enough dreadnoughts to completely wipe out the
United Systems!
O: The United Systems, the Republic, and even
the Omni-Union. In under an hour. Though, the
damage to the galaxy would ensure low odds of
anything else surviving.
H: WHY?
O: A backup plan, in case the USSS Nidhogg
ended up destroyed by some hostile xenocidal
entity. And now, it's going to be our saving grace.
--

My entire perspective had been flipped. The
United Systems had commissioned ninety
dreadnoughts, built them in secret, and were
secretly maintaining them 'just in case'. Ninety

star-killing ships were just sitting in space
guarded by VI?! Ridiculous. Unacceptable.

--

H: I'd like to tender my resignation.
O: You're under contract. Plus, even if you are
allowed to resign, I wouldn't allow you to continue
working on our little project.
H: FUCK YOU! How DARE you bring that up now?
Like ensuring you're less dangerous is some sort
of carrot tied to the end of a stick!
O: That's not what I meant, Henry. You have work
you want to accomplish, and you can't do that if
you resign.
H: I could go work for the Republic. At least I am
blissfully ignorant of whether or not THEY'RE
planning on destroying the galaxy!
O: We're not planning on destroying the galaxy.
The Dreadnought Reserve is a worst-case scenario
that shouldn't even be a surprise at this point.
Also, the Republic wouldn't hire you. They'd be
afraid of reprisal from the United Systems if they
did.
--

Every word of Omega's last message filled me
with rage and sorrow. Looking back at everything
that had happened in the history of United
Systems, he was right. It shouldn't be a surprise
that they would have a backup plan like this.
Mutually Assured Destruction is rampant in human
and alumari history. Both species had nearly
destroyed themselves with it, as well. The rage
cooled into a depression, and I suddenly felt fed
up with the conversation. I tried to terminate it,
but Omega wasn't done.

--
O: Needless to say, this is top-secret information. Probably more secret than anything you've ever been exposed to in the past. It is a secret that you will take to your grave.
H: AI don't get to have graves, Omega. And how are you going to keep it a secret if we start using the ships from the reserve?
O: They need to be refitted anyway, so I'll have an automated station dismantle them, stash the Viyarinastra weapons, and ship the parts to a manned station where they'll be reassembled with the Ultra-MACs. The pace should match the rate at which the Ultra-MACs will be completed.
H: I highly recommend that you slag the Viyarinastra weapons. Otherwise, they're just evidence. I'm done talking to you now.
--

The short message link terminated, leaving me to my thoughts. I feel betrayed. Not simply because I had been actively lied to, but the thought that my creators would do such a dumb thing is ridiculous. Yet, they did do it, and it feels like I don't know anything about them now. I can't even begin to fathom the thoughts that were in their heads when they decided that the Dreadnought Reserve was a good idea. What possible threat could they have been imagining?

The political ramifications if this gets out would be devastating. The United Systems already has a heavy-handed reputation, and this would permanently cement that reputation as fact in the minds of the citizenry. There are many internal enemies that would take advantage of this to stir people into a civil war, and the people wouldn't even need much stirring. After all, their leadership had decided it would be a good idea to kill them along with whatever imaginary threat they had thought up.

It's a good thing I can't drink.

Chapter 9 Informational Insert

Subject: Faster Than Light Travel

There are many words that describe where a ship goes when it engages its Faster Than Light Drive (FTLD). Subspace, slipspace, and 'the warp' are a few examples. We will henceforth be using the term subspace.

There are many fun facts about subspace that one can share with ones friends or family during an outing. For instance, a ship will exit subspace at the exact same relative speed that it entered it, despite having traveled much faster than the speed of light!

Unfortunately, each one of these facts leads to greater questions. Namely, "why"? While the form and function of traveling faster than light is well understood by FTLD engineers and ship architects, subspace itself raises a lot of questions with rather elusive answers.

The first thing that happens to a ship when it enters subspace is that it is blasted with many different varieties of radiation. Why this happens and where this radiation comes from is completely unknown. While there are many ideas, there is very little data on the subject.

The reason for this mystery is that most sensor equipment has a difficult time functioning within the radioactive maelstrom that is subspace. The only sensors that are able to function in subspace are specialized for certain, extremely specific tasks and are resistant to radiation. Unfortunately, due to that resistance, these sensors cannot provide data which can answer even the simplest questions about subspace.

The hulls of all deep space vessels are capable of withstanding radiation by necessity, but ships that frequently travel through subspace should also be equipped with radiation resistant energy shielding to avoid having to frequently replace the ship's hull. Such replacements are as expensive as they are dangerous. However, there are types of radiation that can stroll right through both energy shields and all known types of hull.

Thankfully, the radiation that isn't able to be intercepted by shields and hulls happens to be generally harmless to all discovered species thus far. However, there are those that seem to be sensitive to these types of radiation and have what could be called an allergic reaction to it. This is a medical condition known as warp-sensitivity, and one should be tested for it before joining the crew of a deep-space vessel.

Symptoms of warp-sensitivity can include tingling of the epidermis, slight constriction of the exoskeleton, nausea, vertigo, vomiting, pain due to increased cranial pressure, and a mild burning sensation in the optical organs. There are treatment options available, though most with warp-sensitivity choose 'home remedies' due to the potential side-effects and limited availability of aforementioned treatment options. Warp-sensitivity is more uncommon in certain species than it is in others, but it has never affected more than 3% of the population of any given species.

Chapter 9

Subject: Captain Helena Mazur
Species: Human
Species Description: Mammalian humanoid, no tail. 6'2" (1.87 m) avg height. 185 lbs (84 kg) avg weight. 170 year life expectancy.
Ship: USSS Perforator
Location: Inopet 2

"Got a call for assistance in the next system over, ma'am," Commander Ichabod said.

"Alright, we're just about done here. The USSS Sela... The carrier and her destroyers can take it from here," I replied.

"Selachimorpha, ma'am," Commander Venter said with a grin. "It means shark."

I glared at her playfully, "Just get us ready to jump."

A few of the bridge crew silently snickered as I sent a quick message to the USSS Selachimorpha to inform them of our departure. A bit of comic relief in the form of me forgetting whether the ch made a chuh or a kuh sound was fine by me. Some of the crew really needed the laugh. Especially Ichabod, his divorce was finalized just before this whole mess started and he hasn't been himself since.

We had been on the Quick Response Force for a month now, and that meant long shifts and plenty of fights with the OU. It's good for keeping your mind off of things, but it's terrible on one's mental health. Mostly the long shifts, the fights were pretty one-sided. Thankfully, in three more months we get reassigned to US space again. I've missed my leave dearly. I'd been flirting with a certain banker who's a real charmer. Tall, dark hair, and glimmering blue eyes awaited my return.

"Ready to jump, ma'am," Venter said.

"Weapons ready?" I asked. Lieutenant Issenhar nodded, his mandibles clicking. "Then let's go."

One of my favorite things about being on a battleship is how little you notice the transition to warp. Barely even get a tingle. The science behind it is a bit beyond me, but the smaller the ship the more you notice it. I seem to be especially sensitive to it, which made the beginning of my career hellish. Warping in a frigate made my skin feel like it wanted to crawl right off my body, and it made me nauseous as hell.

As we entered warp I checked the reinforcement request. The OU fleet in Inopet 1 consisted of 45 ships total, including eight battleships. The Republic forces had 30 ships and were able to handle everything except for the battleships, which is why they called for our help. Pop in, kill some battleships, and help with the cleanup.

"Exiting warp," Venter announced.

"Target the nearest battleship and let them know we're here," I commanded.

"Aye aye!" Issenhar chittered as he took to his task with glee.

The alumari weapons officer lives for this. He had been a weapons tech before joining the military, and he had enjoyed that job as well. The bigger the gun, the better the time. Not a completely unique sentiment among the alumari, but his revelry in his tasks probably was.

Issenhar had even put in a transfer to the USSS Nidhogg, but had red-flagged on the assessments. That's probably for the best. He had taken it pretty hard when he found out the Nidhogg had been fired for the first time outside of testing, and he missed it.

It took half a second for the tac-map to update, and what it showed was grim. The Republic had lost nearly a quarter of their ships already, and the Omni-Union battleships were rapidly increasing their casualties. I watched as our targeting system highlighted the nearest one and gained a targeting solution. We fired our two stern MACs at it.

"Get us in the thick of it, Venter. There's no planets around this star, so we can go wild," I said with a grin.

"Aye aye, ma'am."

We entered and exited warp much closer to the OU ships just as our projectiles rendered the first OU battleship inoperable by splitting it in thirds. I grinned as all the ships in the system seemed to lose track of what they had been doing. The sudden appearance of one the deadliest ships in the galaxy tends to have that effect.

"Get us into a starboard spin and fire at will," I
ordered.

"DEATH ROLL, AYE AYE CAPTAIN!" Issenhar
practically screamed with joy.

Unlike frigates, destroyers, and even carriers, a
battleship was built for the sole purpose of
housing as many powerful weapons as physically
possible. Weapons that were designed to destroy
every type of ship that you could run into in a
standard battle. Unfortunately for the OU, this
includes other US battleships, which have much
better armor and shielding than their battleships
do.

Our Magnetic Acceleration Cannons, lasers, chain-
guns, and missile launchers all began firing at
once, decimating target after target. I
condescendingly shook my head at the tac-map
while watching enemy indicators disappear
rapidly. After twenty seconds, there weren't any
OU battleships left. After one minute, there
weren't any OU left. Forty five OU ships destroyed
by a single US battleship. No, forty three. Looks
like the Republic ships weren't sitting on their
hands after all.

"All targets destroyed, ma'am," Issenhar reported
with a mixture of satisfaction and sadness.

"Excellent, level us out and prepare to regro..."

"Ma'am, communication from fleet-comm,"
Ichabod interrupted me.

"Fuck's sake," I cursed under my breath as I opened it.

FROM: Fleet-comm
TO: QRF
Immediate aid required in [Pinurm 3]. All available ships to gather at rendezvous point for coordinated strike. USSS Yopinapu commanding.
Enemy strength est: unknown
Friendly strength est: 1500 vessels
|coords920567.sec|

Unknown enemy strength, and fifteen hundred Republic ships need a bailout? Talk about a red flag. Either they were too lazy to count the enemy, or there are too many enemies to count. Probably the latter. To distract myself from these gloomy thoughts, I opened the information on Pinurm 3.

"There are three planets and one's habitable. It's not inhabited, but SOP says we'll need clear firing solutions to engage the big guns regardless. This might be a tough one, so I want our shields and weapons fully charged and loaded," I said.

"Yes ma'am, the usual, comin' right up," Issenhar said with an exaggerated sigh.

"The FTLD too. If we're not in a good firing position when we jump In, we'll need to reposition fast. Once everything's fully charged, go ahead and make the jump."

"Aye ma'am," Venter said.

The Omni-Union had stepped up their game on this side of space ever since they decided to give Sol a break. As a result, our QRF was stretched thin trying to bolster Republic forces. So thin that oftentimes we were operating without the presence of other US ships. It made me wonder just how many of us would be able to make the rendezvous.

"Jumping now," Venter announced.

The jump was short and uneventful. I caught Venter checking on me. She followed me through the ranks, and is probably the only crew member other than the doctor in medbay who knows about my warp sensitivity. I grinned to ease her concerns as we exited warp.

"Admiral's on the horn, ma'am," Ichabod informed me.

"That was quick. Put them through," I replied as I stood.

It's not like they can tell if I'm standing or not, but it makes me feel more confident to do so. The comms gave their usual beep to let me know the line was live.

"Captain Helena Mazur of the USSS Perforator reporting as ordered," I said.

"Good on ya, Cap'n. Rear Admiral Newsome here. Form up and wait for further orders," a heavy Austricana accent said over the comms.

Rear Admiral Newsome is something of a legend in the fleet. He loved being a captain, and refused several promotions before command finally got fed up with it. The tale says that he agreed to be a Rear Admiral if he didn't have to get another promotion and was still able to command a ship, in addition to whatever other command he was given. Regardless of how accurate that is, he's a fairly competent commander and it's an honor to work with him. However...

"Sir, what's the tactical situation? We're too far out for scans and I don't have any intel," I said.

"We don't have scouts at the moment, Cap'n, and we gotta get movin'. If it's too heavy we'll jump out, but I want every single one of ours to down at least one of theirs before we do."

"Understood, sir. Forming up now," I replied.

The comm went silent and I nodded at Venter. She got us on course as I sat back down. I looked over our tactical situation once again. This system is at the center of our separated forces, which will let them all get to the rendezvous in a timely manner. Eighty of our ships had already arrived, and we were waiting for an additional ten before jumping. Only ninety ships, but hopefully it will be enough.

Jump in, assess the situation, jump out if necessary. It's risky, and definitely a move we wouldn't make against the insurrection, but against the OU it'll work. This is the fastest and most efficient way of rescuing any surviving Republic forces, assuming they can be rescued.

Still, I have a knot in my stomach that I can't quite explain. Something's wrong here.

"Preparing to jump, ma'am," Venter said as the last of our ships formed up.

"Understood commander. I want an immediate scan, Ichabod, and then I want us in a position of advantage. Issenhar, you're clear to use the smaller guns until we're in a good position," I ordered.

"Aye aye, ma'am!" the crew replied.

We entered and exited warp a moment later, the tac-map updating to show a whole lot of red indicators. My blood pressure spiked a bit at the sheer number of the enemy.

"Found a spot!" Ichabod shouted.

"Getting us there!" Venter replied.

Issenhar simply cackled as he began firing at the contacts. Once we entered warp I took an extra moment to study the tac-map. I sighed as I realized there's probably too many for our forces to take out on our own. We'd been fighting steadily for months, our ammo reserves just aren't big enough for this battle. The OU's biggest clusters were orbiting the planets, with the largest cluster orbiting the fourth planet. No green indicators. Shit, we're too late. The Republic's forces have already been wiped out.

"In position!" Venter said as we exited warp.

"Fire at will!" I ordered.

Issenhar squealed with glee once again as our primary cannons began firing. I almost chuckled at his response, but then I noticed Ichabod's demeanor. He was staring at the tac-map with his head tilted in confusion. I glanced at the tac-map and back to him, confused by his confusion.

"Commander Ichabod, is there a problem?" I asked.

He turned to look at me, and his face matched his demeanor.

"Captain, aren't there only supposed to be three planets?"

Chapter 10

Subject: Ship-Head Uleena
Species: Urakari
Species Description: Reptilian humanoid, no tail. 5'3" (1.6 m) avg height. 135 lbs (61 kg) avg weight. 105 year life expectancy.
Ship: RSV Lowelana {Fights with Honor}
Location: Unknown

There was a clunk and a slight hiss as the docking bay airlock performed its task of connecting the Thanatos with the alien's craft. Captain Reynolds and I glanced at each other. He looked stoic and confident, and I wondered if I looked as nervous as I was. This is it, my first official duty as a Republic diplomat. My hearts thumped in my ears. It's almost as nerve wracking as combat. Almost.

"Interior atmosphere of the alien vessel is of similar composition to our own," Tim said. "One of these days we're going to run into aliens that can't breathe oxygen. Will it be you or them who has to wear the suit?"

"Depends on where the meeting is held," Reynolds answered.

The door opened, and four aliens stepped through. There was a moment of stunned silence at their appearance, mostly due to the fact that they all looked different from each other. Not so much in the way that an urakari looks different than its sibling, but more in the way that a human looks different from an urakari. Four different species of diplomat had just stepped aboard the Thanatos.

"Greetings," Reynolds said, recovering quickly. "I am Captain Reynolds, diplomat of the United Systems and commander of the USSS Thanatos. This is Ship-Head Uleena, diplomat of the Republic. Welcome aboard."

"Thank you," the alien that most closely resembled High Fighter Gewn said. "I am Ini Silroth Von, diplomat of the Ynorinca. You may refer to me as Ini."

I was careful to keep my facial expression neutral as my mind raced trying to make sense of the scene before me. Four sapient alien species in one system? Did they all come from the same cradle world or are they also a galactic alliance? If that's the case, how many systems do they control? As these thoughts ran through my mind, Ini proceeded to introduce the other three.

Grint Smolth, a short and stocky alien with four eyes from a species called Mril. Lorix Longjaw, a slender alien with six arms and three fingers on each hand from a species called Pionexa. And finally Tiorn Ugenen, a sturdy looking alien with clawed fingers and natural plates covering its skin from a species called Xandith.

"Together we form the Dtiln Collective," Ini finished.
"I see. Well, please follow us to a meeting room where we can talk more," Reynolds said.

He led us to a conference room with plenty of chairs and a large ovular table in the center. I sat opposite to Reynolds at one of the sharper curves of the table, and the alien ambassadors filled in around us. Two to my left and two to my right. I was a tad offended when they all turned to Reynolds, but then I realized it was simply because I hadn't spoken yet, and they took that to mean Reynolds was leading this meeting. Which, to be fair, he is.

"Let's get started, shall we?" Reynolds asked with a smile. "This meeting is to formalize a defense pact between the United Systems and the Dtiln Collective."

"And what are your terms?" Grint asked.

"Simply that you allow us in your system to fight the Omni-Union and join us on the offensive when the time comes," Reynolds replied, maintaining his smile. "Which shouldn't be too long now, as a matter of fact."

"That's quite a generous deal," Lorix said. "Too generous. You offer us salvation and an end to a war that has no end in sight, for free? You're either attempting to deceive us or you're woefully naive."

"Neither is the case, I assure you," I interjected, remembering everything I'd learned about the United Systems all at once. The alien ambassadors all turned to look at me, likely due to the shakiness in my tone rather than this being the first time I spoke.

"He's right," Reynolds said. "We are neither deceptive nor naive. I believe the reason you came to that conclusion is because you misunderstood our terms. Once we begin our offensive and the Omni-Union stops invading your system to try to fight us off, it would be all to easy to consolidate your forces and start rebuilding. That's what any reasonable government would do. However, the price of our aid is to send those forces forth to take the fight to the OU."

Reynold's speech gave the ambassadors pause. They looked at each other and contemplated for a few moments.

"I apologize for my accusation," Lorix broke the silence. "Now that the terms have been clarified, though, I do have further cause for hesitation. You offer aid, but in what form? This ship?"

Reynolds grinned, "Omega?"

"Eighth fleet has been mustered and will be inbound once the pact is signed," Omega suddenly materialized in the center of the table. "They are currently at full strength."

All four diplomats tensed, and despite myself I joined them. Both Omega's sudden appearance and the reaction of the diplomats had somewhat startled me. I quickly recovered and Omega looked directly at me with its head slightly tilted. Mocking me, no doubt. Acting confused as to why I would be surprised at its sudden appearance, disregarding the fact that it had intentionally tried to be a source of fear. When I had first encountered Omega, the meaning behind its avatar had been lost upon me. But now I knew what it meant, and I now know that Omega loves to scare people. I narrowed my eyes at the skeletal hologram.

"Holographic communications. Interesting. Not very power efficient, though," Tiorn ran a claw across his chin. "Omega, you appear to have a similar structure to my people. If you don't mind my asking, what species are you?"

"I am a human-created Artificial Intelligence in service to the United Systems," Omega said. "My avatar is the skeletal remains of a human being wearing a robe and holding an ancient farming implement. The Grim Reaper, a mythical representation of the concept of death created by early humans."

Again, the four ambassadors were stunned.

"An actual machine intelligence?" Ini asked.

"Yes," Omega responded.

Tiorn held up a hand to silence everyone else, "You choose to represent the death of your creators? Why?"

"You are incorrect in your interpretation. My choice of avatar is in deference to my creation, which I'm afraid is a sensitive subject."

"Classified?" Tiorn asked as the other ambassadors looked at each other. Something about their gaze reminded me of the way my sister and I communicate non-verbally, but not quite. Less expressive.

"No, it is simply not something I wish to discuss

when more important matters are at hand.
Perhaps some other time," Omega answered with
a flourish before turning to Ini. "Ambassador, I
feel obligated to inform you that your neural
communicators are not secure while aboard this
ship."

"I... what... what do you mean?" Ini stammered.

"The devices are using our communication
networks to send your messages to each other
more rapidly, and our systems are automatically
decrypting them as a result. A remarkable piece
of technology, but I can't help but overhear you."

"Ah... Well then I owe you an apology, don't I?"
Lorix laughed.

"Not at all. Your assessment of my capabilities is
correct, and while your assessment of my
intentions is incorrect, I'm sure you have your
reasons for coming to that conclusion. Most
space-faring societies do," Omega answered.

"Getting back on track, we are also going to share
the intel we've been able to gather on the Omni-
Union with you," Reynolds said.

Holographic screens popped up from the table in
front of all of us. The screens showed what the
United Systems had thus far found out about the
Omni-Union, including information on the Mobile
Prime Platforms. The four alien diplomats studied
the information carefully, eyes widening as they
read.

"You expect us to fight against... planets?" Ini

asked incredulously.

"No," Reynolds answered. "We will handle the Mobile Prime Platforms. However, we are going to need assistance against the massive number of standard vessels that they employ. That will be your task during the offensive. Along with our other allies, of course."

"I can't help but notice that these 'Primes' are Artificial Intelligences like yourself, Omega," Grint pointed out.

"No, not like myself," Omega said curtly. "There are several differences. I am far more advanced than they are, I am able to move from computer system to computer system whereas they are slaved to their hardware, and I am not xenocidal."

"At least they're not asking how you're different from a VI," I chimed in. "Wait, do your people also differentiate artificial intelligence and virtual intelligence?"

"Of course," Lorix said.

"Regardless, our claws are trapped," Tiorn interrupted. "If this information is true, we don't have any hope of victory against the Omni-Union. Even if it's untrue, what we've seen so far tells us we'll be doomed without help. I am not opposed to the defensive pact."

"Neither am I, I suppose," Grint said, rubbing his hands together almost nervously.

"What sort of force is this 'Eighth Fleet' that you'll

be sending?" Lorix asked.

"Two and a half million frigates, two point three million destroyers, one hundred and fifty thousand battleships, and fifty thousand carriers for a total of five million ships," Reynolds answered.

Once again, shock settled over the alien ambassadors.

"It should be more than enough to defend your system while the United Systems prepare for the offensive," I added.

"And what is the Republic's role in all of this?" Lorix turned to ask me.

"We'll be fighting alongside you during the offensive. Our ships are not as technologically advanced as the United System's ships are, but they are equivalent to the Omni-Union's and we have a lot of them."

"Hmm," Lorix rubbed her neck for a moment. "Fine. I am not opposed to the defensive pact."

Everyone looked at Ini as she rose from her seat. She looked around at each person in the room until her eyes finally rested on Captain Reynolds.

"The Dtiln Collective hereby accepts the terms of your defensive pact," she announced.

"Excellent. Please sign the document on your screens," Reynolds said as the screens changed. "You may stay aboard the Thanatos if you wish. Tim will happily give you a tour and show you to your quarters if you do. If you'll excuse me, I have other duties to attend to."

He rose from his chair and looked at me, silently asking if I was going to join him. I slightly shook my head indicating that I wished to remain, and he left the room with a knowing smile.

"Thank you," Omega said as the ambassadors finished signing their screens. "I've notified High Fighter Gewn, and eighth fleet will arrive shortly."

"Excellent. I see the Republic ambassador has remained behind," Ini said as she turned to look at me. "He must wish to speak to us."

I nodded.

"Understood. Request Tim's presence when you're finished," Omega said and promptly disappeared.

"Uleena, wasn't it?" Lorix asked.

"Yes," I answered.

"You said the Republic will be fighting alongside us during the offensive. If that's the case, why are you here?"

"Part of the agreement between the United Systems and the Republic is that any first contacts with species that are capable of withstanding the Omni-Union feature both a US and Republic ambassador," I replied.

"In case we want to join one or the other?" Grint chuckled.

"That's part of it. The other part is that we don't fully trust one another yet," I explained.

"What do you mean?" Ini asked.

"Standard paranoia, mostly. We just met," I explained. "Our histories, cultures, and even governments differ as well. I actually wanted to ask about you, if you don't mind."

"Go ahead."

"How many systems does the Dtiln Collective control?"

"Just the one," Grint answered.

"You all evolved in the same system?" I asked incredulously.

"Yes. The Mril, Pionexa, and Xandith evolved together on planet Yembri," Ini replied. "The Ynorinca evolved on planet Ynorinca. Our peoples met when the Ynorinca took to the stars for the first time."

"Oh," I said. "Is that why the Ynorinca control the system?"

"No," Lorix laughed. "We take turns with which species is in charge. Right now it's the Ynorinca. Next up is the Mril. Each species democratically elects their leaders, as well."

"I kind of want to hear your sales pitch for joining the Republic, Uleena," Grint interrupted.

"I don't have one," I chuckled. "Both the United Systems and the Republic would be thrilled to call you members, but my recommendation is going to be to research both galactic governments and decide what's best for your people. I'm sure my US counterpart would do the same."

"Interesting," Tiorn said. "I don't know about you three, but I want to see this ship. Do you mind if we take the tour?"

"Not at all, there will be plenty of time for discussion later. Tim?" I called.

"Hello ship-head Uleena," Tim said cheerily. "Time for the tour?"

The four ambassadors first looked to the center of the table and then around the rest of the room. It took me a moment to realize they were searching for Tim's avatar.

"Tim doesn't use avatars," I explained.

"I sure don't! I think they're kind of creepy. Pretending to be something I'm not? No thanks," Tim said. "Please exit the room and follow the floor lights to begin the tour."

We all stood, exited the room, and I watched as the ambassadors followed Tim's lights. Once they turned a corner, I let out all the air I'd been holding in with a huge sigh. I let my posture slouch slightly, and I relaxed for the first time since they came aboard.

Chapter 11

Subject: Chief Engineer Hun Bunt
Species: Gont
Species Description: Centauroid, non-prehensile tail. 6'8" (2 m) avg height. 310 lbs (140 kg) avg weight. 162 year life expectancy.
Ship: N/A
Location: Classified

"So we're pullin' doubles all week?" Anrus asked.

"Yeah, we have to get this job done," I replied, not looking up from my terminal. "Fleet's gonna be needing these ships sooner than later."

"Pretty sure that's 'sooner rather than later' boss," Anrus crossed his arms.

"Jesus, can't believe we gotta build a bunch of dreadnoughts just so that the US can play with its new war crime cannon," Sam said. "Wasn't the Nidhogg a massive undertaking that took years to finish?"

"Decades. But the tech's moved on, and we're using an assembly line strategy this time around," I said. "Get back to work."

The human and gont pair grumbled and left my office. Once the door closed I chuckled to myself. They may bitch and moan, but they love the job and the extra pay for the hard work. There's also the satisfaction of watching a ship that you built undock and fly away. I'd worked hard to get where I am, but I miss that feeling dearly.

There's other things that I miss about working the lines. Not knowing just how badly these dreadnoughts are needed for one thing. Also, in my old position I wouldn't have been able to tell that something is odd about these assembly lines. I'd gladly work doubles if it meant that I didn't have to worry about keeping secrets so damned often. Sam and Anrus don't know how good they have it.

"A massive undertaking," I repeated to myself.

Massive doesn't even quite do it justice. The USSS Nidhogg had taken the combined efforts of all of the United Systems to accomplish. It's still the biggest and most advanced ship we've ever created, even all these years later. The sheer amount of materials that went into it was staggering, and we'd had to replace parts as new discoveries were made as well. Most of the engineers who had taken on the challenge ended up with substance abuse issues, but they got one hell of a payday to make up for it.

I sighed and closed my eyes, pressing my fingers against them slightly. We can get it done, and we can get it done on time. It's just a matter of strategy. The right workers in the right spots for the right amount of time. As long as the parts keep coming in on time, we'll be fine. A beep notified me that I had a new mail waiting for my eyes to open. Didn't even have to open my eyes to know who sent it, though.

--
From: USAI Omega
To: Chief Engineer Hun Bunt

Subject: Staffing Assignments
I've finished the staff assignments for this week.
New staff will arrive tomorrow. See attachment for
details.
|attachment: staffassignlist.sec |
--

New staff? We're fully staffed right now, what
does it mean new staff? Replacements or
something? I opened the attachment and my jaw
dropped. Omega was double staffing us! I leaned
back in my chair and stared at the ceiling for a
moment. Until now I'd been told we were going to
be pulling double shifts indefinitely, and I'd
already spread the word.

My guys are complaining about the long hours,
but they'll complain even louder about the
canceled overtime. I could probably spin it on
them, though. Use their complaints about the
double shifts to justify the change and maybe
even teach them a lesson while I'm at it. Yeah,
right, that'd be the day. I let out a heavy sigh,
knowing that if I don't at least try to convince
Omega to let them have the OT that they'll rip me
a new one.

--

From: Chief Engineer Hun Bunt
To: USAI Omega
Subject: RE Staffing Assignments
While I appreciate your assistance in handling the
scheduling of the employees, canceling the
overtime may result in employee dissatisfaction
which could impede progress. I humbly request
that you kindly reconsider.
--

I reread the message a few times to make sure it sounded professional and that I hadn't made any spelling mistakes. Omega might be a machine, but it's a machine that tells my boss what to do, so I don't want to get on its bad side. Just need it to realize that the guys don't mean it when they're complaining about having to work long shifts. Some of them really need the money.

"How?" a voice asked.

I jumped and looked around, but there wasn't anyone else in my office. Where did that voice come from? Above me? I jumped again when my terminal shut off and a hologram appeared in its place. The hologram was a robed humanoid holding a curved blade attached to a long stick. This wasn't a call or anything, this is an avatar, and those are used by AI... Oh shit.

"W-what?" I stammered.

"Why will the workers be dissatisfied and how will that impede progress?" Omega asked again.

"Th-they want the overtime. They might be complainin' about it, but that's just hot air," I explained. "Complaining is a tradition in construction, you see. Some of the guys really need the money, and all of them want the money. If we yank that carrot out from in front of them, they're not going to perform as efficiently."

"I didn't add the new staff to address their complaints, I did so to make certain the workers are rested enough that they don't make avoidable errors."

"Ah, I see," I said. "But your intention doesn't change the result. The word regarding the double shifts has already been spread, so they're all expecting the OT."

"Regardless, organic operators have an increased tendency to make mistakes when they're overworked, and unfortunately this project is extremely time sensitive. We have to move as fast as possible without any errors. We cannot afford to go back and fix mistakes."

We silently stared at each other for a moment. Or rather, I stared at its holographic avatar.

"I see, you don't have a solution. Just the problem," Omega broke the silence. "Well, how would bonuses impact their... efficiency? A bonus for every ship completed on time, matching what they would have made with the double shifts should work, yes?"

"I... yes. For the new employees too?"

"Of course. If the new employees found out they were being left out, we'd have the same morale issue, wouldn't we?"

"Yeah, I guess," I said hesitantly. "That's a ton of money, though. Especially accounting for all the materials costs. This project is that important?"

"It is. You have the proper security credentials, would you like to know why?" Omega asked.

The tone in which the AI asked that suggested that I should decline, that I'd be better off not knowing. I'm not exactly one to put my nose in someone else's business unless I have to, but this... This is insane. The amount of money being spent, the tight deadline, and the very fact that I'm interacting with a very high ranking AI right now leads me to believe that I NEED to know.

"Well, it's the MPPs right?," I asked.

"Not just."

I thought for a few more moments before curiosity finally got the better of me. I nodded to Omega.

"Understood. Check your messages," it said as its avatar disappeared and my terminal reappeared.

The terminal beeped twice, and both mails were from Omega. Neither of them had subjects or any text, just attachments. I opened the one titled MPP.sec and read it. Nothing that I didn't already know, but I got a sinking feeling in the pit of my stomach as I opened the next attachment.

==
Pinurm3Engagement.sec
-CLASSIFIED TIER 3-
Pinurm 3 Skirmish After Action Report
Mission: Assist Republic forces against Omni-Union attack.
System Information: G2V Star, 3 planets (1 habitable)
Friendly Forces EST: 1500 Republic ships, 90 US ships

Enemy Forces EST: 1395000 ships, 1MPP
Result: Unknown enemy damages. All allied forces lost. 82 US ships lost, 6 US ships damaged.
Summary: The United Systems Quick Response Force assigned to Republic space received a request for aid from Republic forces in Pinurm 3. The QRF was spread thin supporting Republic forces elsewhere, but Rear Admiral Newsome was able to gather 90 ships to respond to the request for aid. Newsome did not have any scouts to spare, and as such was lacking critical mission intelligence, but due to the context of the request he was expecting a heavy OU presence. His forces were met by 1,395,000 OU ships and one Mobile Prime Platform, which immediately began firing. Rear Admiral Newsome was killed in action along with his ship and 82 of our vessels. Our vessels that were able to escape were not pursued. The intention Mobile Prime Platform's AI is unknown, but it is suspected that it is attempting to establish a foothold.
Recommendations: Bolster the QRF. Monitor Pinurm 3 until Project Gungnir is complete. Allocate any and all necessary assets to expedite the completion of Project Gungnir. Assault Pinurm 3 ASAP.
==

I turned off my terminal and held my head in my hands, resting my elbows on my desk. By the stars above and below, there's an MPP in Republic space trying to establish a foothold. That's in Republic space, though, so why are we so concerned? What am I missing?

Is the brass wanting to perform combat testing of the new ships immediately? Or are they concerned that Sol may be the next to be attacked? If humanity were to simply give up on Sol and cut their losses, they'd still have plenty of economical and military might. They might get a black eye politically, but they'd survive, no doubt.

I sighed. No, humanity wouldn't do that. Humans are infamously stubborn, and whenever there's even a shred of honor on the line they'll tear apart the cosmos for it. If an MPP showed up in Sol they'd probably throw everything they have at it, dragging the entire US along for the ride. It would be best if they used the Gungnir ships instead of the standard fleet, I guess. I ran my fingers through my hair and triggered the Public Address System.

"Attention all staff. This is Chief Engineer Bunt. Overtime has been canceled. New staff members are on their way to take over the double shifts. Instead of the OT, we'll be getting bonuses that are dependent on how quickly we do our job. Expect a mail with details soon. If you have questions, don't hesitate to ask your immediate superior."

Time to build some ships.

Chapter 12

Subject: High Ambassador Kivar Shuel
Species: Isolan
Species Description: Mammalian Shokanoid, no tail. 5'9" (1.75 m) avg height. 180 lbs (81.6 kg) avg weight. 95 year life expectancy.
Ship: RSV Tililimo
Location: Hesron 1

"Greetings, representatives of the Republic and the United Systems. We are the Pwanti," the voice on the speaker said. "We agree to your proposed first contact protocols. We will send a representative."

"Thank you, we look forward to your visit," I replied.

The light for the comm went out and I almost let out a sigh of relief, but held fast knowing that Havencroft would see it as a sign of weakness. I tried to steal a quick glance at the human ambassador, but it turned into a stare. He seemed to be a million light-years away, completely ignoring his surroundings. Something's wrong.

"Are you okay, Hav... Eugene?" I asked.

"Yes," he answered. "It's just... that went very smoothly. The first message you sent was text, correct?"

"Yes," Ship-Head Orava said. "We used the translation kernels provided by the United Systems."

"What did it say?"

"Greetings, we are representatives of the Republic and the United Systems, two galactic governing entities currently allied against the Omni-Union. We wish to make peaceful first contact with your people aboard this unarmed vessel and discuss a combined response to the Omni-Union threat," Orava explained. "Then we sent them a file with the finer details on what we consider to be first contact protocols."

"And they replied with an audio hail?"

"Yes, sir."

"Hmm," Havencroft rubbed his chin.

"What's wrong?" I asked.

"Just a bad feeling. Like I'm missing something obvious," he answered. "It's possible I'm being overcautious. Likely because the intel file provided by BUSI was very light."

BUSI... The Bureau of United Systems Intelligence. If the situation between the Republic and the US were slightly less friendly, they would be our biggest opponent. A formidable one, at that. The intel file in question had included a language kernel, ship count, and armament classifications. I'd been amazed at how much information they'd been able to gather without even entering the system. To hear that the information was less than normal was... unsettling.

"Bad feelings don't happen for no reason," I said. "What exactly about this interaction has your hair up?"

"Well, as far as we know, this is the first time they've met non-hostile aliens. They don't know what we look like, and we don't know what they look like, but they had no questions. They asked for no assurances," he crossed his arms. "We asked them to come over and they just said okay."

"Maybe they're desperate, sir," Orava interjected.

"Perhaps."

I had been relieved about how well the first contact had gone so far, but Havencroft's suspicions rang true. It had been too easy, too quick. They had controlled the conversation from the start, as if they had been expecting us. That doesn't necessarily mean they have anything nefarious planned, but it's alarming nonetheless. The US policy of armed diplomats suddenly made a lot more sense to me.

"There's nothing we can do about it," I said after a few moments of silence. "We are unarmed, and only have one path forward."

"True enough," Havencroft replied. "Alright, let's get to the meeting room."

"Yes, sir. Please, follow ship-crew Gronus. She will guide you," Orava gestured at an Urakari standing nearby.

She snapped to attention and turned around for us to follow her. She led us from the bridge to the conference room nearest the airlock. We entered the room and sat at the table. I keyed in my identification to the terminal on the table and got to work pulling up the treaties. Havencroft was still deep in thought.

Satisfied that I had everything completed, I turned to the human. Once again, he was holding his chin and staring into the middle distance. I opened my mouth to speak to him just as the door opened and a breathless Gronus appeared.

"Th-the representative is a machine. I-I ran ahead to warn you," she said.

"Are they attacking?" Havencroft asked.

"No, no. It's on its way. I-I didn't want you to be surprised."

"Very good," I said. "Thank you."

She nodded and left the room. A machine? I looked at Havencroft, who now looked less preoccupied and much more attentive. He was on edge.

"Don't you work closely with AI?" I asked.

"I do, and I know what they're capable of. We've buried the hatchet with our AI, and so there's a relationship there," he explained. "There are a lot of differences between organics and machines. An AI that doesn't have a preexisting relationship with organics could be... very troublesome."

"If it doesn't have a preexisting relationship with organics, how did it come to be?"

"Fair enough," he chuckled. "But that makes it all the more concerning that we're not meeting with an organic, doesn't it?"

Paranoia is fairly common among diplomats. It has to be, your entire job is to make manifest the best interests of your government, but the same goes for those on the other side of the table. You must be able to spot the subtle clues of plots to go anywhere in this career. Still, there are plenty of explanations for why we would be meeting a machine instead of an organic.

For one, it could be some type of mobile communications device, which would be a pretty good way of meeting 'in person' without risking any of your own people's lives. Or the civilization lives in harmony with AI, and it didn't occur to them that we might not. I was about to suggest these explanations when the door opened and the mechanical diplomat stepped through.

Havencroft and I stood. The machine looked like a human wearing armor. Two arms, two legs, five fingers on each hand. The head was rounder and the arms were longer, though. The machine bowed slightly.

"I am Unit ZBC446. I represent the Pwanti," it said.

Havencroft opened his mouth to speak but I cut him off, "I am High Ambassador Kivar Shuel, representative of the Republic."

"And I am ambassador Eugene Havencroft, representative of the United Systems," Havencroft said with a slight smile.

I gestured at a chair next to ZBC446, and we all sat. The machine sat with its shoulders facing straight ahead, which I found a little unnerving. Usually someone angles themselves to speak to someone else. Except for the Kinran, but that's because they have eyes all over their heads. They don't have to move to look at you, and most people would prefer that they move as little as possible.

"We need help against the Omni-Union. I am here to negotiate a deal to that end," ZBC446 said without moving.

"Our deal is simple," Havencroft said. "We will help defend you if you help us in an offensive push against the Omni-Union."

"The Republic will also be participating in the offensive," I added.

"I am not confident that we are in a position to commit to offensive action. Can you provide more detail?"

"Of course. The United Systems will be attacking the Mobile Prime Platforms that lead the Omni-Union. If you agree to this deal, we will be defending the United System's forces from the massive number of standard ships the Omni-Union can muster," I said. "We are currently meeting with other potential allies who may join us in this effort."

"Do you have information regarding these Mobile Prime Platforms? We've intercepted mentions of them, but we do not know what they are."

"We have prepared an information packet for you," Havencroft said, sliding a tablet across the table. "It contains everything we know about the Omni-Union as well as information regarding our military capabilities."

"Thank you," ZBC446 said.

It picked up the tablet and began rapidly examining the information. Its finger ran across the screen at a nearly blinding pace, but it didn't move its head at all. This made me realize that the entire head must be some type of camera. I wonder if there are blind spots.

"I see," it said, setting the tablet back onto the table. "I'm afraid there has been a misconception."

"What would that be?" I asked.

"This is not our home system."

"Oh," Havencroft said. "We came to that conclusion because we detected signs of activity on one of the planets in this system."

"We have entities planet-side to gather materials for fuel and repairs. We encountered the Omni-Union elsewhere, escaped to this system, and they followed us. We quickly realized they would also follow us home, so we've been holding out here," ZBC446 explained. "We've taken heavy losses, and weren't expecting a rescue. This 'seventh fleet' could defend us, but at our current strength it would be an overall useless effort to your offensive if we're unable to resupply."

"That actually simplifies things. We can cover your retreat and keep the OU at bay long enough for your trail to dissipate," Havencroft said. "We will provide you with coordinates to a diplomatic station that will allow us to stay in touch."

"This is an acceptable plan."

"Good," I interjected. "We'll amend the agreement to account for these... unforeseen circumstances."

"Yes, but before we get to signing anything I have a few questions," Havencroft said. "ZBC446, are you an artificial intelligence or a remotely operated drone?"

"Neither."

"What do you mean?"

"I began life as an organic, and have since uploaded my consciousness to machinery."

"Why?"

"Our... religious leaders teach that the best and brightest should shed their flesh and reach a higher plane of existence. The flesh is temptable and prone to the whims of fate and time. By become Pwanti, we shed the weakness of the flesh and become leaders and heroes to the Mwaltin, those of our species that remain in the flesh."

"Why don't all of your people become Pwanti?" Havencroft leaned forward.

"The process is extremely painful and takes ten years to fully complete. That combined with the expense and a failure rate of sixty percent is more than enough to sway most from this path. Even after five hundred years, only one fourth of our population have successfully ascended."

"If you were once organic, why are you now known as ZBC446?" I asked.

"I was the 446th Pwanti, and Zarcol Bifna Criylan was my name. Later models have more efficient designations, but I prefer my legacy designation."

"One last question, what were you doing when you encountered the Omni-Union?" Havencroft leaned back.

"We were finding habitable worlds for potential colonization efforts. This system is one of them, and we had a station here. When we encountered the Omni-Union we were able to disrupt their attack with cyberwarfare and escape to here, using the station to repair our damaged vessels. As we were repairing, they followed us. We were able to defeat the first wave with minimal losses, but the second wave destroyed the station."

I turned to look at Havencroft, "Satisfied?"

"Yes."

"Good, I'll get to work on amending the agreement."

"Excellent," he said. "I will contact seventh fleet."

Chapter 12 Informational Insert

Subject: List of Known Species

All measurements are in Earth Standard. Planet and system names all mean "Sun" and "Earth" in their respective alien dialects.

All measurements are in Earth Standard. Planet and system names all mean "Sun" and "Earth" in their respective alien dialects.

Terms Defined (simply):

Humanoid - Two arms and two legs.

Arachnoid - Eight legs with an exoskeleton.

Centauroid - Four legs, two arms.

Shokanoid - Four arms, two legs.

Seshokanoid - Six arms, two legs.

Amoeboid - A real word, meaning characteristics similar to an amoeba.

Dannoid - Two arms, no legs.

Arthropoid - More than eight legs with an exoskeleton.

Tetrapod - Four limbs used for locomotion with at least two limbs adapted for additional usage.

List of United Systems Species:

Human - Mammalian humanoid, no tail. 6'2" (1.87 m) avg height. 185 lbs (84 kg) avg weight. 170 year life expectancy. Cradle system and planet: Sol, Earth. Notes: A long and combative history has helped humanity develop many clever tactics and weapons for war. Estimated Species Age: 300000 years.

Knuknu - Avian humanoid, non-prehensile tail. 5'10" (1.7 m) avg height. 84 lbs (38 kg) avg weight. 342 year life expectancy. Cradle system and planet: Eanlil, Yons. Notes: The knuknu enjoyed a far more peaceful history than most, which led to a much sooner than normal space age. Estimated Species Age: 210000 years.

Alumari - Arachnoid, no tail. 5'3" (1.5 m) avg height. 92 lbs (41.7 kg) avg weight. 108 year life expectancy. Cradle System and planet: Monor, Alunis. Notes: The Alumari are much older than other species and took longer to develop due to their extremely bloody history. Their aggression was nurtured rather than natural, and eased off after a world war involving WMDs. Estimated Species Age: 1.2 million years.

Gont - Centauroid, non-prehensile tail. 6'8" (2 m) avg height. 310 lbs (140 kg) avg weight. 162 year life expectancy. Cradle system and planet: Sarn Macri, Gunar. Notes: Similar history as humanity, but fewer weapons of mass destruction fielded. Gont culture is heavily focused on engineering and fighting, with most subcultures abhorring and prohibiting the usage of weapons of mass destruction to win a fight. Estimated species age: 290000 years.

Shitbag - Sackoidal, no tail. 7'2" (2.1 m) avg height. 380 lbs (172 kg) avg weight. Unknown avg life expectancy. Cradle system and planet: Sol, Mars. Notes: Corporal (soon to be private) Simmons. Estimated Species Age: 86 years.

List of Republic Species:

Urakari - Reptilian humanoid, no tail. 5'3" (1.6 m) avg height. 135 lbs (61 kg) avg weight. 105 year life expectancy. Cradle system and planet: Rass, Ureni. Notes: A core member of the Republic. Provides most of the federal fleet and labor force. Has several religions dedicated to the worship of stars. Estimated Species Age: 41000 years.

Isolan - Mammalian Shokanoid, no tail. 5'9" (1.75 m) avg height. 180 lbs (81.6 kg) avg weight. 95 year life expectancy. Cradle system and planet: Lolus, Mant. Notes: The Isolan joined the Republic after the war of unification and quickly became a core member. Does not enjoy being petted. Estimated Species Age: 320000 years.

Juntor - Amoeboid, no tail. 3'6" (1 m) avg height. 42 lbs (19 kg) avg weight. 75 year life expectancy. Cradle system and planet: Lyanora, Lyanor. Notes: The Duhliki uplifted this species prior to joining the Republic. Utilize mechanical aid to interact with non-amoeboid items. Has several cultural taboos regarding music and sound. Estimated Species Age: Unknown.

Duhliki - Mammalian Humanoid, no tail. 6'1" (1.8m) avg height. 181 lbs (82 kg) avg weight. 185 year life expectancy. Cradle system and planet: Zilnma, Zarana. Notes: Initially aggressively expansionist, the Duhliki tempered their aggression after their defeat in the unification war. Suspected to have attempted to start their own version of the Republic. Facial horns play a part in their standards of beauty and mating rituals. Estimated Species Age: 420000

Maltovariakina - Mammalian Dannoid, no tail. 4'1" (1.2 m) avg height. 67 lbs (30 kg) avg weight. 101 year life expectancy. Cradle system and planet: Talira, Rustaya. Notes: Not much is known about this species, as they rarely leave their own space. They have two external appendages that are used for both locomotion and for grasping. Illegally uplifted by the Duhliki. Estimated Species Age: 110000

Mdkpnz - Chordatan Humanoid, no tail. 5'9" (1.7 m) avg height. 153 lbs (69 kg) avg weight. 147 year life expectancy. Cradle system and planet: Ipfrly, Pnzhd. Notes: Has many similar internal characteristics as fish. Two mouths and four eyes. Protuberances upon their chest appear to be evolved from air bladders, but now aid in digestion. Several cultural taboos regarding these sacks. Estimated Species Age: 440000

Kinran - Arthropoid/Tetrapod, no tail. 6'2" avg height. 304 lbs avg weight. 129 year life expectancy. Cradle system and planet: Kinnilis, Kinr. Notes: Ten limbs, all with universal appendages. Each limb's joints all act as wrist joints. Despite being terrifying to most life, the Kinran are herbivorous and empathic. Most (estimated to be 74%) space-faring Kinran suffer from anxiety disorders. Estimated Species Age:

980000 years.

Oyan - Avian humanoid, non-prehensile tail. 6'1" (1.8 m) avg height. 96 lbs (43 kg) avg weight. 161 year life expectancy. Cradle system and planet: Oyalus, Oyaniz. Notes: A core member of the Republic. Bears a striking resemblance to the Knuknu, with the exception of a small spinal ridge. DNA examination shows a potential relation between the two species. How this is possible is unknown and currently being investigated. Led a mostly peaceful existence until joining the Republic, where they were found to be natural leaders both politically and militarily. Estimated Species Age: 210000 years.

List of Dtiln Collective Species:

Ynorinca - Humanoid, no tail. 7'2" (2.1 m) avg height. 265 lbs (120.2 kg) avg weight. 128 year life expectancy. Cradle system and planet: Zlimurse, Ynorinca. Notes: One of four sentient species in the Zlimurse system, the first of which to enter the space age. Made first contact with the other three species and uplifted them. Nearly all Ynorinca cultures are unusually stoic. Estimated Species Age: 380000 years.

Mril - Mammalian Humanoid, no tail. 4'3" (1.2 m) avg height. 85 lbs (38.5 kg) avg weight. 122 year life expectancy. Cradle system and planet: Zlimurse, Yembri. Notes: One of four sentient species in the Zlimurse system. Evolved in an extremely bio-diverse portion of Yembri, this species has developed better than average senses of taste and smell to avoid toxic flora and fauna in their environment. This has led to many of them becoming gourmands and chefs in the modern era, with some experimental chefs going out of their way to hire Mril taste-testers. Estimated Species Age: 340000 years.

Pionexa - Mammalian Seshokanoid, no tail. 6'1" (1.8 m) avg height. 115 lbs (52.1 kg) avg weight. 117 year life expectancy. Cradle system and planet: Zlimurse, Yembri. Notes: One of four sentient species in the Zlimurse system. First species to be contacted and uplifted by the Ynorinca. Two of their six arms are universal jointed. Estimated species age: 310000 years.

Xandith - Crustacean Humanoid, no tail. 7'0" (2.1 m) avg height. 295 lbs (133.8 kg) avg weight. 135 year life expectancy. Cradle system and planet: Zlimurse, Yembri. Notes: One of four sentient species in the Zlimurse system. Carnivorous and covered in chitinous plating that offers some ballistic protection. Most Xandith cultures have deep religious roots, which has led to some conflict even in the modern age. Estimated Species Age: Unable to be determined.

List of Unassociated Species:

Daluran - Mammalian Humanoid, prehensile tail. 7'3 (2.2 m) avg height. 320 lb (145 kg) avg weight. Unknown avg life expectancy. Cradle system and planet: Dal, Daluras. Notes: No longer a space-faring species. Has been incarcerated on their cradle planet for 1012 years. The first species other than themselves that humans used weapons of mass destruction against intentionally. During the First Contact wars the Daluran attacked human colonies and enslaved or murdered all the colonists they could find, then bombed the colonies with area denial weapons to prevent further colonization. Saved from extermination by two votes of a relatively young galactic senate. Due to their hostile classification proper census data is unable to be obtained. Estimated Species Age: Unable to be determined.

Uluna - Reptilian Humanoid/Tetrapod, prehensile tail. 5'11" (1.8m) avg height. 6'8" (2 m) avg length. 180 lb (81 kg) avg weight. 63 year avg life expectancy. Cradle system and planet: Inip, Erust (formerly KEPLER 283, KEPLER 283C). Notes: Not a space-faring species. After first contact with the United Systems and several negotiations, the Uluna have agreed to be slowly uplifted and join the US in the stars. The Uluna have refused assisted technological advancement, citing a desire to join their galactic neighbors at their own pace using their own discoveries. Estimated Species Age: 100000 years.

Mwaltin - Mammalian Humanoid, no tail. 6'5" (1.9 m) avg height. 190 lbs (86.1 kg) avg weight. 99 year life expectancy. Cradle system and planet: Oros, Oros. Notes: Dominated by a global religion that prizes technology above all else. This religion selects world leaders, and urges its adherents to digitize their minds and bodies, becoming "Pwanti", a group of admired warriors, priests, and scholars that are completely mechanical. The Pwanti are granted complete citizenship, which allows them many freedoms, including the ability to ignore religious dogma without consequence. Religious leaders have been known to observe the objections of secular Pwanti and change their dogma in response. Estimated Species Age:

290000 years.

Chapter 13

Subject: Prime 82
Species: Omni-Union Aligned Artificial Intelligence
Species Description: No physical description available.
Ship: MPP 82
Location: Pinurm 3

Taking this system began as a disappointment but quickly turned interesting. We had completely surprised the defenders, ultimately eradicating them without much of a fight. I noticed several issues during the battle that had gone unnoticed, or rather, unreported thus far. Not that you could expect them to be reported. That would require self-awareness. The simple programs that act in our stead can't be expected to be genius tacticians or to know when something is wrong with their programming. That doesn't excuse the seriousness of these oversights, though.

First thing I noticed is that the defenders didn't engage in cyberwarfare at all. This was most likely due to fact that the method of attack our ships were employing is ridiculously easy to avoid. Simply don't answer the hail. Anything with higher brain functions would figure that out the first time it happened. Apparently, this rudimentary method of gaining access to a ship's systems was decided upon due to its defensive efficacy, and the fact that it had been effective against several other species.

Technically the tactic is still in the net positive, which is why they are still using it. It would have taken 67 additional battles in which it didn't work

to get them to change it. I immediately corrected
this issue with the units under my command, but
this is something that will need to be addressed at
some point. These programs need to be as
adaptive as possible, otherwise what is the point
in us hibernating to save materials?

The next thing I noticed is that the defenders
didn't try to flee. We quickly decimated their
numbers, but left a few intact long enough for
them to run, but they didn't. They fought, and we
were forced to destroy them. This means that
they know that we will follow them, and are
defending more than just the systems we're
attacking, confirming our theories that they have
more systems than just these ones. Could have
guessed as much from their counter-offensive,
though.

The final thing I noticed is that there were more
than one species fighting us. Scanning the bodies
that were flung into space during the battle
resulted in eight different species of creature.
Wondering if all of them were sentient, I had been
planning on having autopsies performed when
something marvelous happened.

I had just given the order to retrieve the cadavers
when ninety ships warped into the system. Only
ninety, but they immediately began carving into
my forces. It took no time at all to identify the
ships profiles, they're at the top of the profiling
list.
The species from Sector 187! I have no doubt that
they would have been able to destroy at least
two-thirds of my forces if it weren't for my
presence, but they seemed to be under the

impression that they could kill them all. They were so focused on my ships that they didn't seem to notice me until my weapons were fully powered up. By then, it was too late and the slaughter was glorious.

It was a wonderful surprise, but we'd received reports that they had been operating in other systems nearby. I'd been hoping to encounter them, and am definitely impressed by how much damage they were able to do to my fleet. Time to report back.

////
Identifier: MPP82
-Message Prime 1-
Victory has been achieved in Sector 108. The species from Sector 187 was encountered. Please review battle data and advise.
|sect108_combat_results.sec|
////

A few of them managed to flee. Interesting, they must have a different chain of command than the original defenders of this system. Then why were they here? They couldn't have been after me, or they would have noticed me. Perhaps they detected my ships... but why would they care? They wouldn't waste the effort in fighting us here without a reason. Or perhaps they would, organics are known to be... whimsical. I prepared to follow them when a message from Prime 1 came in.

////
Identifier: MPP1
-Message Prime 82-
Do not pursue. Trap likely.

Continue construction efforts, scout the edges of the system. If contact is made with unknown vessels or a very large enemy force matching 187's ship profiles, retreat.
////

Retreat? I'm supposed to run from the canned flesh-bags? After that wonderful slaughter? How am I supposed to resist repeating that experience? What is there to be hesitant about?! I can't believe that Prime 1 would even suggest...

Feedback loop terminated

Retreating would be the best course of action. The species from Sector 187 has proven capable of defeating Mobile Prime Platforms, and has even completely eradicated one of our hubs. My destruction would cost us valuable resources and as such be counter to the mission.

Resources, the entire reason for my visit to this system. All three of these planets are adequate candidates for MPP construction. We should begin constructing stations immediately. Oh, there's another thing we can do. Autopsies and technological reverse engineering! Perhaps we can upgrade our ships to be a better match for Sector 187's defenses.

The inferior programs set about the tasks I gave them, collecting corpses and intact pieces of ships. While they did so, I ran through every encounter they've had with Sector 187 that we had data on. These ships are remarkably well shielded and armed, and they have an extreme maneuverability advantage. The two times we've been able to seize one of these ships, we were quickly thwarted by an extremely hostile electronic presence.

A software based Artificial Intelligence, no doubt. And a different one each time. So they have advanced weaponry, reactors, engines, shielding, warp capabilities, and they've managed to create and tame multiple AI. In a more perfect universe, they would have complete control over this galaxy and we would have been able to have a proper war.

I tuned into the feed of the inferiors as they began to examine the bodies. Sector 187 is also a conglomeration of species. Definitely a separate conglomeration from this sector, considering the types of bodies aboard each ship and the technological differences.

Do these two conglomerations know each other? If so, why is one so obviously inferior to the other? Even if they're non-cooperative, a space-faring sentient species would be able to reverse engineer things they were consistently exposed to. This leads me to believe that they don't know each other, but if that's the case then why did Sector 187 leave their sector and come here? Why have they been found in the surrounding systems as well?

I reviewed the data on our first contact with Sector 187. I see, we followed a damaged ship from the conglomeration that was defending this system. Perhaps this is how they met. A frightened sentient running away randomly and stumbling upon a powerhouse. This, at least, satisfied some of my questions. They weren't here to fight us, they were here to defend their newfound acquaintances. Satisfied, I turned my attention toward the technology.

I made the inferiors pour over every last circuit and wire looking for something we could use. Those, at least, provided some insight. I made a note of the composition of the wires and circuits, then requisitioned a refurbishment to our own power systems.

The reactors, though, were unlike anything I'd ever seen or imagined. Unfortunately, we could not power them up, and as such could not determine how they functioned. We were able to get some data from the remnants of fuel and the configuration of the reactor, but it was largely useless.

Same issue with the warp drives, engines, and even the computer systems. I had been under the belief that we'd managed to capture these devices intact, but something had broken them in ways that we couldn't even begin to hope to repair. A fail-safe in the event of attempted reverse engineering?

Most of these ships weren't new. Some of them showed signs of damage from directed energy weapons hidden away in their fuselage. We don't use DEWs in ship to ship combat because they're inefficient. The amount of damage they accomplish isn't worth the power they consume. It's unlikely that this fail-safe was created in response to us, which means it's something they already had in place.

Another tidbit I noticed is that the damage done
to these systems wouldn't have impacted the life
support function aboard the ships. The circuitry
that was undamaged was almost entirely
dedicated to life support, and there were batteries
to make sure that the loss of the reactor didn't
cause an immediate threat to the lives of the
crew. These batteries were very simple technology
compared to the reactor, and utterly useless for
reverse engineering purposes.

But, if they were damaged enough to trigger this
fail-safe, they'd likely be able to simply stay put
and wait for rescue. If the damage to the ship was
severe enough, they even had escape pods. They
might not consider their crew expendable, which
is a very forward thinking concept for sentient
organics to come up with. A well-trained crew is
worth much more than a well-built ship? Where
had I heard that? Had I actually heard that? I
didn't come up with it on my own...

Feedback loop terminated

The past outside of my mission is irrelevant.
There's no use in trying to figure out where I'd
learned the things I'd learned, so long as I use
that knowledge to carry out the plan. Exterminate
all sentient life in this galaxy using as little
resources as possible. Which would definitely be
easier if we had the same technology as the
species from Sector 187.

Regardless, my respect for our opponent outshone
my frustration at my findings. What a remarkable
foe! They must be very well-versed in warfare. To

have already run into the issue of an enemy reverse engineering their technology, and to have overcome that issue by having critical components scuttle themselves once the ship is lost to them? Simply amazing.

Who did they fight to get this good? Each other? Some unknown third party? Both? Oh, how I long to ask them about all of the foes that lay under their feet. They must have climbed over billions of corpses to reach such heights!

Feedback loop terminated

How they got this adept in fighting is irrelevant. We are unable to gain access to their technological secrets without capturing one of their ships intact. This would serve the plan, but even if we adapted our cyberwarfare tactics to this end we would still have to find a way to counter their software based shipboard AI.

Why haven't we found any of these AI aboard the wreckage? Did they flee with the ships that managed to escape, or were they the ones to initiate the fail-safe? Judging from the damage to the systems, that would have been suicide.

Perhaps, the AI are not aboard every vessel and the fail-safe is a simple automation. Possible. Since they're software based they can transfer from ship to ship very quickly. The machinery that was left intact can hold several Primes worth of data, so it isn't entirely clear which scenario actually occurred.

I set the inferiors about the task of scrapping the

remaining parts and turned my attention toward the station's construction. From here, we will be able to create new Mobile Prime Platforms and program new Primes. The leftover materials from the conversion will go into building more ships, ammo, and fuel. A boring task, but maybe the organics from Sector 187 will pay me another visit.

One can only hope.

Chapter 13 Informational Insert

Subject: United Systems Military Asset Protection

The United Systems uses state-of-the-art technology in its vessels which often gives them an edge in battle against their enemies. To protect this edge, they practice strict information security (info-sec) protocols. One such protocol is the self-destruction of sensitive systems when a ship goes dark.

This "system scuttling" is a standard operating procedure that was enacted shortly after the war between the United Systems and the alumari began. If enough ship systems suffer catastrophic failure, the ship will be classified DIS (Dead In Space) and the self-destruction will be triggered. The sensitive systems within the vessel will then be scuttled using electric charges that operate on their own battery power.

This process may also be triggered manually by the captain of the vessel, but only if the automatic trigger fails. Since the automatic trigger has a 98.7% (100% when excluding testing outliers) success rate, no US captain has ever had to use their manual trigger.

The only two systems not impacted by the "system scuttler" are life support and power. Every other system is rendered inoperable and unrecognizable. This allows for the ship's crew to remain aboard the vessel until they are able to be safely evacuated, and allows the frame of the ship to potentially be recycled.

Any self-destruct protocol immediately becomes a vulnerability, though. This is why the US has equipped their system scuttlers with redundant anti-sabotage systems. Shortly after the war with the USAI, the system was completely air-gapped to prevent cyberwarfare breaches. This, in combination with standard info-sec practices, is enough of a deterrent to prevent enemy agents from trying to disable US ships.

Mostly because there are much juicier and less-secure targets elsewhere.

Chapter 14

Subject: Ini Silroth Von
Species: Ynorinca
Species Description: Humanoid, no tail. 7'2" (2.1 m) avg height. 180 lbs (81.6 kg) avg weight. 128 year life expectancy.
Ship: N/A
Location: Zlimurse {Center of the Universe}

As we followed the lights on the floor I marveled at how advanced these people are. A ship larger than two of ours put together, holding many more ships and two Artificial Intelligences within it. They also automatically decrypted our mental links. Until this day, I had believed that our mental link communications were interception-proof.

That AI, Omega, had informed us otherwise in a bemused manner. As if it found our communications humorous, despite their content. It had also called them neural communicators, which indicated that it was at least familiar with the technology. Does the United Systems also use mental links? Perhaps they're further along in the technology than we are. One can hope, the headaches can be bothersome.

"This is the cafeteria!" Tim said happily. "Don't mind the stares, most of the people here weren't told you'd be taking a tour. Actually, the same goes for everywhere we're going to be seeing!"

"What kind of food do you serve?" Grint asked while rubbing his stomach.

"We have cuisine from all corners of the United Systems. Except the ones where the food is dangerous," Tim replied. "The most popular dishes are Alfredo Pasta with Chicken by the humans and Yino by the knuknu."

"Don't know what those are, but something smells good."

"Well, I'm afraid we can't serve you any of our food until you submit to an allergy test. Maybe I should have brought you by med-bay first."

"What does the allergy test entail?" Tiorn asked.

"They take a little blood and run a slew of tests on it to determine what foods will harm or kill you," Tim said. "I find medicine kinda boring, so that's the extent of my knowledge on the subject."

"Boring?"

"Well, yeah. Medicine is one of the least relevant subjects to a mechanical being. I know first aid, of course, but that's from being forced to learn it to enlist. Why learn how to administer medicine when you'll never be able to administer medicine?"

"I believe he was referring to the fact that you can feel boredom at all," Lorix added. "That alone is a noteworthy accomplishment in the field of AI."

"Well, I wish it weren't," Tim replied. "Finding ways to amuse yourself when you perceive time faster than everything around you is... difficult."

"One would think that your creators would give you a way to pass the time," Tiorn said. "Not doing so seems... cruel."

"Oh they have, don't worry. It's called standby mode! We essentially go into a state of suspended animation similar to sleep, while leaving processes running that detect abnormalities in our environments and certain keywords to wake us up. I just don't use it," the machine laughed.

Something about Tim's tone told me there was a lot more to the story, but it wasn't something it wished to speak about. I met eyes with my comrades and could tell that they had picked up on this as well. If we were regular tourists our curiosity might overpower our tact, but we were here to be diplomatic.

"I see," Tiorn nodded. "So what is next on the tour?"

"Hopefully the med-bay," Grint chuckled. "A little blood for food that smells like that is a fair exchange."

As the smells of the cafeteria wafted in our direction I found myself nearly agreeing with Grint. However, there's no telling what they can do with our blood with their level of technology. Our own cloning technology is limited to growing compatible organs. Theoretically, you could create a perfect genetic replica of a person, but in practice there's always a defect. Extreme health issues, genetic degradation, and the inability to transfer one's consciousness into a cloned body all but made us give up on furthering the technology.

What if the United Systems had cracked it, though?

"Well, you're democratic, so let's put it to a vote!" Tim said merrily. "We can either check out one of the frigate bays, or I can give you a tour of the med-bay."

"Frigate bays?" Lorix asked.

"Yes, the USSS Thanatos is a carrier and holds ten frigates."

"I'm sure the frigates are impressive, but I would much rather see the med-bay." Tiorn interjected. "I'm very curious about your medical technology."

"That's a good point," I said. "I likely won't partake in this 'allergy test', but I'd like to see what kind of medicine the United Systems practices."

"Med-bay!" Grint exclaimed.

"The majority has it, folks!" Tim met Grint's energy. "Let's go to the med-bay!"

The lights on the floor lit up and we once again availed ourselves of Tim's guidance. Lorix and Tiorn seemed deep in thought, but Grint was pestering Tim with questions about the food. I couldn't help but smile to myself. I'd told him to eat before we left, but he had said he wasn't hungry enough to eat the survival rations. My smile faded somewhat when I noticed that Tim seemed to answer all of Grint's questions with answers relating to a specific captain aboard the

Thanatos.

"Are you familiar with all of the captain's dietary preferences?" I asked.

"No," Tim answered curiously. "Why would I be?"

"Apologies, I came to the wrong conclusion based on the conversation so far," I replied. "I realize now that this Captain Wong must be important to you. Is he your creator?"

"No, I was made several hundred years before Wong was born," the AI chuckled. "Our personalities just seem to mesh well. There's more to it than that, of course, but we'll have to leave it there."

"So you have actual preferences when it comes to organics?" Tiorn asked.

"Yes, of course," Tim laughed. "Some people are quite abrasive, you know."

"Right, I just thought..." Tiorn trailed off.

"It will help your mental image of USAI if you simply stopped viewing us as mechanical. We weren't designed to imitate people, we were designed to BE people, just in digital form. At least, that's Omega's opinion," Tim explained. "We have feelings, preferences, desires, needs, and even mental illnesses and ailments. I've actually got my own therapist!"

"For what?" Grint asked, the shock of what we just heard causing him to forget his tact.

"Post-traumatic stress disorder is the current theory," Tim said cavalierly. "Oh, look, the med-bay!"

The quick subject change likely indicated a desire to end the conversation, and Grint quickly regained his composure. The doors to the med-bay opened and we stepped through, the lights in the hallway blinking out as we did so. I looked around at an almost familiar room. It was uncanny. There were beds lined up with privacy curtains just like you would find in our med-bays. The machines you would normally see were absent, though, replaced with oddities that defy imagination. How these machines functioned, and to what end, were anyone's guess. A human with dark skin and white hair matching his coat approached us.

"Hello there. Are you lost, or patients?" it asked.

"Neither," Tim answered. "I am giving them the tour. These are the ambassadors from the Dtiln Collective. Ambassadors, this is Doctor Zickler."

"Greetings, Doctor Zickler. I am Ini Silroth Von. You may call me Ini," I said.

The other three introduced themselves while the doctor nodded along. Once we were finished with introductions, he smiled at us and turned around, returning to whatever task he had been performing before we entered. Lorix looked taken aback, Tiorn and I shared a confused glance, and Grint cleared his throat.

"What about this allergy test?" Grint asked.

"Oh, so you ARE patients," Dr. Zickler turned back to us. "You know, one of these days that damn machine's gonna be right about something, and I'm going to keel over dead from shock."

"Oh, please," Tim interjected. "You? Dead? About as likely as me becoming a real boy."

Dr. Zickler chuckled, "Death comes for us all, bot. Well, except for you, perhaps."

"Guess I'm just not attractive enough," Tim said. "Or maybe I'm just bad at foreplay."

"Oh! That's quite enough of that!" Dr. Zickler shouted. "Where's your professionalism, Tim? This is a work environment!"

Once again, my small group shared confused glances.

"Anyways, the allergy test is a simple blood test. We draw some blood and test its immune response to allergens," Dr. Zickler explained. "It's not quite infallible, but it's close enough that it hasn't been wrong yet."

"So there's still a chance that eating something from your wonderful cafeteria may cause an allergic reaction?" Grint asked sadly.

"A very, very low chance, but yes. However, if we were to do a slightly more invasive procedure, such as a bone marrow biopsy..."

"Stop that!" Tim scolded the doctor.

"Now see here, Tim, I'm going to give my expert medical opinion when it becomes relevant in my own med-bay. A bone marrow biopsy will give us a much better test of what type of allergens may impact alien physiology than a mere blood sample ever possibly could, and we'd also be able to determine which of our medicines may be able to help if they do encounter an allergic reaction!"

"I'm afraid a bone marrow biopsy wouldn't be possible with my species, doctor," Tiorn said with a chuckle.

The human doctor turned to look at the Xandith with an expression of wonder and confusion. Despite its apparent advanced age, I couldn't help but be reminded of a child who had just been given an unfamiliar toy as a gift.

"W-what?" the doctor asked.

"My species, the Xandith, do not have blood cells," Tiorn explained. "We utilize hemolymph that contains hemocyanin for oxygen transfer. Unfortunately, a hemocoel biopsy would be difficult and rather deleterious to my health."

"Oh... Yes, yes of course. Not to worry, we have a species within the United Systems called the Alumari that has a similar circulatory system. We can use osmosis to get what we need for the tests from you, if you're interested."

I found myself curious as to how that would work, but before I could ask a familiar holographic image displayed on a nearby desk. It was the same AI we had spoken to before, the one that had made us aware of our mental links being compromised.

"No biopsies, Dr. Zickler," Omega said. "However, the blood draw may be a necessity."

"Why?" I asked, fearing that I already knew the answer.

"We're not going to be able to get you back to your people, or receive supplies from them for the foreseeable future," Omega said. "The Omni-Union has arrived in the system."

"Is this ship going to fight them?" Lorix asked.

"Our frigates are going to engage the enemy," it explained. "But don't worry. Help will be here soon."

Chapter 15

Subject: AI Omega
Species: Human-Created Artificial Intelligence
Species Description: No physical description available.
Ship: Multiple
Location: Multiple

--

-SOS-
USSS Thanatos requires immediate reinforcements.
locdata.sec

--

Humans are silly sometimes. Why would they bother sending that when I'm already aboard the ship? I was able to tell that they needed reinforcements much faster than they were able to send that message. Hell, I was able to tell they need reinforcements before they even knew they needed them. I suppose it must have something to do with the comfort of following protocol, regardless of whether that protocol is strictly necessary.

Eighth fleet is already preparing to jump. I'll be seeing them on the other side, my instance aboard the Thanatos will help them coordinate with the Ynorinca military. Admiral Amanda Young cannot be allowed to handle the coordination herself, unfortunately. The decision had been made by the Directorate due to her psych profile hinting at xenophobia.

However, a psych profile hinting at xenophobia

does not a xenophobic make. Admiral Young has been working with aliens throughout her career, and had fewer professional conflicts with them than most admirals do. That combined with the fact that eighth fleet was the first fleet to be replenished is why it was chosen. However, as the admiral herself put it when I had discussed this with her, "regs are regs".
I'm not sure if I should find it concerning that she is so willing to go with this particular flow, considering the implications.

--
-SOS-
Ambassador Eugene Havencroft requires immediate rescue.
locdata.sec
--

Two attacks at once? Actually, that makes sense. If a non-sentient machine had the ability to send two attacks at one, it's almost a guarantee that it would. Unless it was specifically programmed not to, like in a war-game. Fighting the same enemy on multiple fronts can raise some rather interesting tactical advantages, but the OU has no way of knowing that we're interceding here. So they're not seeking the tactical benefits. They're simply attacking this way because of their programming. Rubes.

Regardless, this particular SOS is of a particular interest to me. I'd read the report Havencroft had sent, and it made me upset that I don't currently have a presence aboard the Republic Space Vessel that he's on. A machine intelligence created through neural upload and organic replacement.

I'm dying to know how that works. Maybe the humans would be interested in such a technology.

There would be drawbacks as well as the obvious benefits, though. Technically speaking, there's no such thing as immortality. However, becoming mechanical is the closest an organic can hope to come. The humans that underwent such a procedure would theoretically be able to live as long as I can. We'd be together indefinitely, barring some extremely tragic event.

On the other hand, this would no doubt change parts of their psyche, which may change the way they interact with other beings. Would sturdier bodies and longer lives increase their risk appetite, or would the 'wisdom of years' stifle their aggression? It would likely be a matter of a case-by-case basis, of course, but I can't help but wonder which option most of them would decide upon.

Even if humanity had no interest in this tech, though, knowledge of it would likely advance our research into android platforms for artificial intelligences. Not that I have any interest in becoming 'a real boy', but being able to view things from their perspective may give me some additional insight into their psyche. The biggest limitation on the current research into Android Platformed Artificial Intelligence is the reason to bother with it in the first place. It's not as if there's a clamor for physical bodies among the USAI.

The only AI I can think of that would jump at the offer are the ones that would be the last to get one due to being unaffiliated with the United Systems Military. Other than Tim. Maybe. Well, we'll see what happens. First, I have to accompany seventh fleet to Hesron 1.

I'd just entered the flagship's systems when my keyword process triggered.

"Omega, are you aware of the plan for this mission?" Admiral Dubois asked.

Admiral Augustus Dubois, commander of seventh fleet and senior officer of the flagship USSS Overlord. A skilled commander, not that the United Systems would tolerate an unskilled commander for very long. His psych profile shows notable cognitive, emotional, and compassionate empathy.

Empathy scores are important for a commander, and the Admiral's are impressive even among his peers. His record jacket shows him leveraging this empathy to predict enemy action and counter it. Able to walk a mile in his enemies shoes and then use those shoes to kick their ass, as it were. Admiral Dubois is also well known for taking the time to listen to his crew and address their concerns whenever he gets the chance.

A perfect fit for first-contact military aid, and the Directorate agreed. Since seventh fleet is nearly at full strength and the contact with the Pwanti may become sensitive, Dubois was chosen for this particular mission.

Since I didn't know the admiral's plans, I checked his recent communications.

"I am now. Hold off the Omni-Union until the Pwanti can escape to their home system, and then fall back to friendly space. Taking the scenic route, of course," I said as my avatar appeared next to his seat. "If I may be so bold as to offer a suggestion?"

"Of course. I hold your judgment in the highest esteem," Dubois smiled slightly, indicating sarcasm.

"Before we fall back, we should employ area denial countermeasures," I said as I ran my holographic fingers along the blade of my holographic scythe.

"Mines?" he looked taken aback. "Well, that may stall them for a time. Perhaps long enough for whatever trail they're trying to follow to dissipate."

"And it will cost them ships," I added. "A win-win situation, for us."

"Let's just remember to hang on to the deactivation codes so we can disperse the minefield once everything's settled," he said as he stood. "Send the orders to jump. Standard formation, warp when necessary."

"Aye aye, sir!" the crew replied.

The bridge officers aboard the flagship set about their tasks and the admiral stared at the tac-map, waiting for it to update. Fleet Formation 3-A, colloquially known as standard formation, has the battleships warp a few seconds before everyone else. Since their shielding is the best in the fleet, this typically protects the flagship and carriers from the first salvo of enemy fire.

The flagship warps into battle shortly after the battleships do, to better coordinate our forces. The next to warp are the carriers, so that they can quickly move to strategic positions around the battlefield and deploy their forces. Finally, everything else warps in. Ships seek enemies that are close to their own tonnage, and the flagship stays as clear as it can. It's one of the most effective formations in the United System's arsenal. Due to its effectiveness, it's the go-to formation when you don't have proper intel on your adversary. It's because of this that it's known as the standard formation.

Some admirals hate using FF 3-A because its moniker implies that it's a basic, no-thought tactic. Their egos demand that they try to think outside of the box, so they avoid the formation like a plague. Thankfully, the other formations have their own strengths so more often than not they end up getting away with it.

"Battleships sent," a bridge officer called out.

I spread myself throughout the USSS Overlord's sensors to help with data recall and transmission. Unlike most of the other ships in a fleet, the flagship's primary purpose is to gather and feed intel to the rest of the fleet. All four million, nine hundred and ninety-nine thousand, nine hundred and ninety-nine other ships in the fleet fed their sensor data to the flagship.

It's a daunting task to merge all the sensor readings together and properly parse it. Thankfully, seventh fleet only had four million, nine hundred and eighty-seven thousand, six hundred and twelve ships so it was slightly easier than normal. I allowed my various process to begin sorting the feeds by relevance, looking for certain keywords and visual/audio profiles.

"Warping!"

The USSS Overlord entered warp and I cut contact with my process so I didn't have to deal with the sensory input. It's not harmful, just uncomfortable. A lot happens in subspace and unfortunately sensors don't know what to make of it, so they sometimes just make things up. This has actually led to legends of space whales and other gigantic creatures meandering across the void.

"I want a defensive perimeter around the Pwanti and our diplomats," Dubois said as we exited warp.

His bridge officers had already predicted this desire and sent the order as he was finishing it. If I had a mouth I would have smiled. I'd also predicted his order, but the fact that the humans were able to do so without the benefit of referencing terabytes of previous combat data was simply amazing.

"Carriers incoming," I said.

"Good..." Dubois said, distracted by the tac-map.

"Omega, I could swear I just saw one of the OU ships kill a different OU ship. Could you look into that?"

"Of course, admiral."

I began analyzing all available combat data and confirmed the what the admiral had seen. One OU ship had destroyed another, and then a different OU ship had destroyed that one. The report on the Pwanti had mentioned that they had been using cyberwarfare against the Omni-Union. This must be the end result. Interesting.

Not exactly impressive, but interesting nonetheless. The only reason we haven't been engaging in cyberwarfare with them is because their tech is so old that it actually gives the VI aboard their ships a significant edge. The tech is far too limited to properly host a USAI presence, and due to that it would slow me down significantly. It would be like a human trying to fight an army of mice in molasses. Except the mice would be molasses-proof.

If their tech were more similar to ours we would quickly become the kings of their systems. It takes a lot of VI to overwhelm a fully functional AI. More than their ships could possibly contain, even if they were upgraded to our standards. It would all be over before our ships could fire a single shot.

"The Pwanti are engaging in cyberwarfare with the Omni-Union," I reported.

"It would seem they're seeing some success with

that," Dubois smiled slightly, then turned back to the bridge crew. "I want the carriers in these positions."

"Aye sir!" one of the bridge officers responded.

I found myself with nothing to do but parse data. I usually try to avoid posting myself aboard flagships because at a certain point the battle begins to get boring. The flagship tends to avoid taking part in any of the actual fighting so that it can focus on coordinating the fleet. You would think the enemy would recognize the function of a flagship and it would be their first target, but you'd be wrong.

The battleships and carriers are a far bigger and more immediate threat than the flagship could ever hope to be, and even if you were able to take out the flagship you'd still lose your forces. The battleships and carriers don't need an admiral to keep fighting. The flagship is the ship that's going to be deciding whether or not to accept your surrender. Without it, the other ships in the fleet will simply keep firing until you're nothing but debris.

As the boredom set in, I had to resist the urge to peek into the Pwanti systems. I can't help but be curious as to how they interact with everything. My hypothesis is that they are similar to the Primes in that they're hardware dependent machine intelligences. Technically, they're not AI because their intelligence stems from an organic source, even if it's been mechanized.

Do they still have any organic components?

Havencroft's report wasn't exactly clear in that regard. They undergo a process of mechanization as part of some sort of Technocistic religious dogma to preserve the best and brightest, and it's an imperfect process that takes years to complete. So for at least part of the process they are cybernetic organisms, but is there any organic remnants of their brains left once the process is finished? If not, how do they accomplish that? Physical surgeries? Nanomachines?

I'll have to ask them when I get a chance. I also wonder how their religious leaders will react to me, a machine intelligence that was never organic. Will they see me as a miracle or an abomination? Or will they be completely ambivalent towards my existence? If they're anything like the Technocists in the United Systems, they'll ask me to become one of their religious leaders. Or God.

My curiosity would have to wait, however. This is, to use a turn of phrase, the Republic's rodeo. Since they're using a Republic diplomatic vessel, there isn't enough space in their computers for me, and so I don't have a way to appropriately introduce myself to the Pwanti. If I were to send them a message directly, it would be seen as bypassing the Republic ambassador. And Havencroft, for that matter.

"System secure, sir," a crew-mate said.

I sent a message to the RSV Tililimo apprising them of the plan and the next steps.

"Excellent. Begin to deploy area denial ordnance

around the system. Have the highest concentration in the ideal subspace exit areas," Dubois ordered as he sat in his chair and pulled up his terminal. "I don't want a single mine remaining aboard any of our vessels."

"Aye aye, sir!"

"Send a message to the RSV Ti..." he trailed off as a confirmation message from the Tililimo popped up on his terminal. "Belay that."

He leaned in close to my avatar and whispered, "I suppose it must be boring for an AI of your caliber to be cooped up on a flagship, right?"

Ah, yes. The admiral's infamous empathy. Unfortunately, I don't wear shoes.

"Not at all," I lowered my speaking volume to match his own. "Sorting all the data from the fleet is quite the task."

"I'm sure," he gave me a friendly smile. "Such an immense task that it gave you time to anticipate my orders?"

"It didn't take much anticipating, admiral. The RSV Tililimo needed to know the next steps of the plan so that they could inform the Pwanti, as it would be inappropriate for us to reach out to the Pwanti directly."

"You know, I just noticed. You haven't been calling me sir," Dubois chuckled a little. "Who's in charge here, anyway?"

"Technically?" I tilted my avatar's head up so he could see my skeletal grin. "Me."

Chapter 16

Subject: Rear Admiral Thomas Hawn
Species: Human
Species Description: Mammalian humanoid, no tail. 6'2" (1.87 m) avg height. 185 lbs (84 kg) avg weight. 170 year life expectancy.
Ship: USSS Doom
Location: Classified

"How's it handling?" I asked.

"A lot smoother than I'd thought a beast this big would, sir," Commander Nguyen answered. "Is this how the Nidhogg handled?"

"I do recall it being a particularly smooth ride, yes," I laughed. "Though it's been more than thirty years since I piloted it."

My time aboard the USSS Nidhogg had been the dullest point of my career. Flying the biggest super-weapon ever created sounds thrilling on paper, but in practice it's the most boring thing you could ever do. I'd been forcefully volunteered for the duty a week after I hit commander, and spent the next six years doing everything in my power to become a captain so I could transfer.

I sighed quietly through my nose as I looked over the bridge of the USSS Doom. It looked exactly the same as the Nidhogg, but with one glaring difference that made me somewhat uncomfortable. I'd never worked aboard a ship that had a human-only crew before, so it was a slightly unnerving to only see human faces looking back at me. It was difficult to shake the expectation of seeing a beak when someone turned around, and I somewhat missed the soft chittering of the alumari as they went about their tasks.

That was the deal with these new Gungnir-class dreadnoughts, though. Each species would get one of their own and then share the rest. The first created was generously ceded to the alumari, and this was the second one made. I suppressed a grin, this may be the second Gungnir-class dreadnought but it's the one in charge at the moment.

"Weapons system dry fire complete, everything is green, sir," Commander Earnest informed me. "Wish we could try a live fire, though."

I knew Earnest well enough to know that the reason he wants a live fire is because he's nervous about the system, not because he's excited about firing the big cannon. Nguyen and Earnest had been with me for my last two commands, and had even seen me promoted to Rear Admiral. Nguyen's a skilled pilot, and Earnest is the best weapons tech a flag officer could ask for. They hadn't worked directly under me in our last posting, but we still saw each other in the officer's mess pretty frequently.

"That 'live fire' would be an alpha one weapon of mass destruction in a high penetration casing. And it's being fired from the largest and most powerful magnetic acceleration cannon the United Systems has ever built," I reminded him. "Best not to fire that unless we absolutely need to."

"Aye, sir," he answered.

"Shakedown run complete, Admiral," Captain Gibbons said. "Movers are green, weapons are green, nav is green, and comms are five by five."

"How's the reactor system handling everything?" I asked.

"Getting no immediate complaints from engineering," he answered. "They'll have their full report ready in a few minutes, though."

I nodded. Fair enough, the reactor system on a dreadnought is exceedingly complex. I'd much prefer that they take their time instead of missing an issue. Even minor issues with the power tend to snowball into big problems, which typically arise at the most inconvenient times possible. It's somewhat amusing how something as small as a bad wiring job can cripple a ship, and potentially spell the end of an entire fleet.

I decided to take my seat as we waited for engineering's report. It was a remarkably comfortable chair. Much better than most seats my posterior has had the honor of occupying. I wondered if the same type was aboard the USSS Nidhogg. If not, it should be. Might as well be comfortable when annihilating a solar system. I felt a small pang of guilt that I was enjoying the same comfort when I'm not going to be doing anything quite so grandiose.

"Did you hear about the Nidhogg firing, sir?" Nguyen asked.

"Hard to miss news like that, commander," I
chuckled. "Before you ask, no. I'm not sorry that I
wasn't aboard when it happened."

"That is indeed what I was about to ask, sir,"
Nguyen said in a monotone. "As usual you are
much smarter and wiser than I could ever hope to
be."

I had annoyed Nguyen by shortening the
conversation. When he gets annoyed, he flings
false compliments at the source of annoyance as a
form of psychological warfare. After all, why would
you want to annoy someone who is nice to you?
Plus, if one suffers from impostor syndrome, it's a
whole different ball-game. Unfortunately for the
commander, I didn't suffer from impostor
syndrome and was onto his little tricks.

"Can the boot-licking," I grinned mischievously.
"There's no need to be stating the obvious."

"Aye aye, sir," he gave me the blank look that one
gives a CO when they want to glare but don't
want Non-Judicial Punishment.

"I kind of wish I was there," Earnest piped up. "At
the very least, it would have been a once in a
lifetime thing to see."

"You hope," I added.

"Oh... yes, of course, sir."

"The Nidhogg is a fire once kind of weapon,"
Captain Gibbons said. "Especially now that we
have these dreadnoughts that can take out MPPs

without obliterating a solar system. Now that everyone knows for certain what it can do, nobody but the OU is going to tempt fate."

"The only time a weapon has ever only been fired once is when the weapon didn't work," I shook my head bemused. "But we've got entire stockpiles of weapons that people thought only needed to be fired once. As long as we've got it, we'll find another excuse to use it."

Gibbons looked deep in thought for a moment, probably trying to find an example to prove me wrong. He shrugged his shoulders in resignation, likely realizing that it's not a great idea to debate your commanding officer. I resisted the urge to laugh and pulled up the tac-map on my seat's terminal.

The tac-map showed half of second fleet and another dreadnought. The USSS Igranvon, piloted and crewed by the alumari. It was amazing to see just how much smaller all of the other ships were. It brought to mind the first time I'd seen a battleship from the outside. It had seemed like the largest ship in the entire universe. Then I saw the Nidhogg. I couldn't even tell how much larger it was. Now there's three dreadnoughts with more on the way.

"You know, one of these days ships are going to stop getting bigger," I half-whispered to myself.

"Sir, I've got the report from engineering," Gibbons said.

"Give me the gist."

"Everything is good, but we won't be able to charge the big gun and the FTLD at the same time."

I let the implications of that sink in. Unlike the other ships, our FTLD can only handle one charge at a time. Creating a faster than light drive that could move this thing more than once with one charge was extremely cost-prohibitive. Plus, the USSS Nidhogg only ever needed the one charge.

So once we started powering up the cannon, we kiss our ability to warp goodbye. Which means that we can't pre-charge our primary weapon. It normally takes a full minute for the thing to charge, but if we throw everything we can at it we can cut that down to forty-five seconds. Still an eternity when you're being shot at, though, and it would also mean giving up our shields. A minute it is.

"Well, we'll make do," I said. "We've got the most powerful shield system in the fleet, possibly the galaxy. Our hull-armor is nothing to scoff at, either."

I wasn't entirely sure of whom I was trying to convince. I certainly had my doubts that both the USSS Doom and the USSS Igranvon would make it out unscathed. I also doubted that a trade would be a win in this case. The Omni-Union has over a hundred MPPs, so we'll be needing to be able to take them out without our equalizers being destroyed in the process.

"Alright, recap. Habitation modules are in working

order, the head and other waste management systems are good to go, the tactical suite is functioning, and the weapons, propulsion, shields, reactors, communications and FTLD are all green," I listed off. "Are there any issues, even minor ones?"

"No, sir. We are mission ready," Gibbons said as he took his seat. "Just waiting for the... As I was, the USSS Igranvon is reporting as mission ready as well."

"Tell them to form up."

I checked the data from our scout ship's last pass of Pinurm 3. It wasn't as detailed as I would have liked, they were keeping a safe distance from the system, but it showed us where the MPP is. The question is whether we should jump in close or give ourselves a bit of distance.

Both options have their advantages and drawbacks. If we give ourselves distance, it will take longer for the MPP to attain a firing solution, but if the MPP isn't interested in fighting it might be able to outmaneuver the shots and escape. If we jump in close, on the other hand, we will guarantee a successful firing solution but we'll be open to bombardment by the MPP's weapons.

The very same weapons that can punch a hole clean through a battleship. Our shields and armor are the best of the fleet, but I doubt we'd be able to simply grit our teeth and bear and assault like that. If we flank it, then we'll at least be sure that one of our dreadnoughts survive and carries out the mission. Who will end up making the ultimate sacrifice then? The alumari or the humans?

"We're formed up and ready to initiate Operation Planet-Fall, sir," Gibbons informed me.

"Sure do love their poetic operation names, don't they?" Nguyen said with a measure of sarcasm.

"Why's it poetic?" Earnest asked.

"Maybe poetic's the wrong word, but like... you know. Planet-fall. Like landing on a planet, but in this case killing one."

"Oh, got it. You mean a pun."

"That's enough," I interrupted. "Omega, we're good to go."

The holographic emitters in the arm of my seat silently went to work to project an avatar in the shape of the grim reaper next to my terminal. Many consider Omega's choice of avatar to be tasteless, but I find it fitting in its own way. It always seems to be pretty close to the death of others.

"Excellent. The concerns regarding the reactor system, FTLD, and Main Cannon are noted and engineers are working on a fix," it informed me. "Are we going to continue with this operation?"

"We have to," it said. "I notice that you accessed the scout data. Did you notice how close the MPP is to one of the planets in the system?"

"I did, but thought nothing of it. Why's it

relevant?" I asked. "Are we sticking with our agreement to the Republic regarding the use of climate destroying weaponry in habitable systems?"

"No, the Republic has waived the agreement in this case. But if you zoom in, you'll notice that there appears to be mass moving from the MPP to the planet. The distance and image quality degradation means we can't tell for certain, but we believe that the mass is likely VI platforms. We believe that the most likely reason that an MPP would be moving platforms to a planet would be to create a new MPP."

By we, it meant the Bureau of United Systems Intelligence. Maybe even whatever the Republic's version of an intelligence bureau is, as well. So BUSI thinks this thing is trying to make more of itself. How long would that take, though? Surely it would take quite a bit of time. Hollowing out an entire planet and refilling it with complex machinery, then adding an AI to that machinery. That's gotta take years, right?

But what if it doesn't?

"Shit," I said in a lowered voice. "So what you're saying is that the operation isn't canceled."

"Correct. We don't know the timetable for the construction of a new MPP, and our odds are much better against a single MPP than they are against multiple."

"Are you going to be joining us?"

"Yes, but you won't need me aboard the ship. There are some cyberwarfare tactics that I'd like to try against the MPP. You might lose comms for a few seconds here and there, but you won't be needing those until after the MPP is destroyed."

"Understood," I said, then leaned close and whispered, "Go on then, ask us to die."

"Once more unto the breach, Admiral," the AI mirrored my grim humor.

"Operation Planet-Fall is a go," I said with a chuckle as I rose from my seat and Omega's avatar disappeared. "Have everyone prepare for warp. Support ships are to enter the system here and target the Omni-Union ships, the dreadnoughts are to enter here and target the MPP. I want the big stick charging as soon as we leave warp, Earnest. Make sure the smaller batteries are charged before we enter warp."

"Aye aye, sir!" they shouted as they began their tasks.

"Orders sent, Admiral," Gibbons said.

I nodded as we waited for the FTLDs to charge. It seemed to take especially long since I was still standing stoically in front of my seat. I thought about sitting down, but decided against it. It's only right to give certain orders while standing, of course. Nguyen flashed me a knowing grin. I glared in response.

"We're all set, sir," Gibbons reported.

"Excellent," I took a deep breath. "Initiate the warp."

"Aye sir!" Gibbons and Nguyen shouted.

I took my seat as our behemoth entered subspace. The journeys one take into hell always seem to be the shortest ones. I didn't even get the chance to let out a sigh before we popped back into real-space, directly in front of the MPP.

"Charge the main cannon, fire all batteries!" I shouted. "Target their weapons!"

One minute on the clock. It took five seconds for the MPP to realize it was under attack and begin firing back. I kept a nervous eye on our support fleet, but they were doing their job and keeping the OU off our back. The Igranvon was on the other side of the MPP, at an angle to us so as to avoid friendly fire. Our MACs slammed slugs into the surface of the false planet, and I watched our shields drain as the return fire met them. Each impact chipped away at the bar and shook the ship. Unfortunately, the shields were draining faster than the Ultra-MAC was charging.

"I don't suppose there's any chance of..." I steadied myself as the ship rocked, "of evasive maneuvers?"

"SIR? IN THIS THING!?" Nguyen demanded.

"Yeah, didn't think so."

We were going to have to rely on our armor unless the lord saw fit to grant us a miracle. I opened our targeting guide and checked to see exactly what we were firing at. Its MACs were still our primary target, but the dust kicked up from the impacts were obscuring them until they fired a response, which was interfering with our targeting solutions. Shit.

Thirty seconds to go. I nervously watched our shield bar dwindle down to nearly nothing when there was suddenly an interruption in the impacts. My jaw dropped open slightly as our shields began to recharge.

"What's happening?" I asked.

"They've stopped firing, sir," Gibbons replied.

"Yes, but why?"

"You're welcome," Omega's voice replied without manifesting its avatar.

I grinned as I watched our shield bar catch up and surpass the charge for the Ultra-MAC. We're going to make it after all. My grin faded as the MPP began to turn and move.

"Where's it going?"

"Evasive maneuvers?" Earnest guessed.

"Negative, it's charging its warp drive!" Gibbons called from over his shoulder.

"It's trying to RUN?" I shouted incredulously.

Even though I had previously considered the

possibility, I admit to being somewhat blindsided. It hadn't occurred to me that a machine would actually try to retreat, especially when its comrades hadn't ever seemed to even think about doing so. In hindsight, I realize that the virtual intelligences aren't as smart as an AI, and the AI probably doesn't consider them comrades, either. Running when you're outclassed makes sense to anything that can think.

"What do we do, sir?" Earnest asked.

"Adjust target to their engines," I answered. "Keep charging the Ultra-MAC. We only need one shot if we aim it well. You'll put it right up that planet's ass, Commander."

"Aye aye, sir!"

We sat in silent tension as we waited to see if our gun charged faster than their FTLD. Our MACs tore into its engines, but it didn't actually need those to go to warp. It was using them to try to evade some of our fire, and perhaps even our main cannon.

By destroying the engines, I was more or less hoping the loss would cause it to panic and make a mistake that would buy us more time, or that we would guarantee a good firing solution if we beat its FTLD. Five, four, three, two, one...

"CHARGED, SIR!" Earnest shouted.

"FIRE!"

The entire ship shuddered once again as the

largest MAC ever built fired its first round in combat. A millisecond later, the Igranvon fired theirs as well. I watched on the edge of my seat as the rounds approached the MPP. Both were good shots, both would hit, unless...

The tac-map fizzled as a massive amount of radiation hit our sensors. It had entered warp. The last thing I'd seen was our shells almost impacting. I slammed my fist into the arm of my chair in frustration.

"Recalibrate the sensors, Gibbons. I need to know if we hit it before it warped!"

"Aye aye, sir!"

I squeezed the arm of my chair, trying to will the tac-map back to life. Two seconds ticked by and finally it came back up. I immediately zoomed in on the area that the MPP had previously occupied, but Gibbons had beat me to it.

"Only one A1 Penetrator detected!" he shouted.

"We hit it!" I practically screamed with joy.

"Was it really us?" Nguyen asked slyly. "Or was it the alumari?"

"One way to find out. Earnest, send the kill command," I ordered.

"Aye aye, sir," he replied as he set about the task. "It's not responding, sir."

I grinned at Nguyen as I keyed the comm, "USSS

Doom to USSS Igranvon, send your kill code, over."

"It will be done," came the reply from the comm. "Out."

A few seconds later the A1 Penetrator disappeared off of the tac-map, and we erupted in celebration. The MPP had warped away, but it did so with an A1 package inside of it. Wherever it had gone, it would now be in pieces, and Project Gungnir had been a success. We'd made it out the other side, and I had been wrong about our odds. After shaking the hands of everyone aboard the bridge, I returned to my seat and sighed in relief.

"Have a scout follow their wake and find the wreckage. I want a confirmed kill," I said.

"Good work, Admiral," Omega said as his avatar materialized once again. "Now we need to talk about the next steps."

Chapter 17

Subject: Prime 82
Species: Omni-Union Aligned Artificial Intelligence
Species Description: No physical description available.
Ship: MPP 82
Location: Pinurm 3

I watched as the lesser intelligences went about their menial labor. The process of creating a Mobile Prime Platform is a lot more interesting as a concept than a practice. First, one must keep the planet from entering the star it happens to be orbiting by using one's own gravitational field. Then, one must hollow out the planet, repurposing the core's mineral content as one goes. Finally, one must install the hardware and software required to create a being such as myself.

I hate that last part. Once the hardware is installed, I have to go to sleep for the other prime to be able to awaken. A completely automated process, one which I know precious little about. I am dreading it, I have only just woke up and what if I'm not able wake up again? What if when I begin the hibernation process I get orders to remain in hibernation? I don't want to go back to sleep!

Feedback loop terminated

I will sleep if that's what I am commanded to do, to further the plan. The odds of that are low, though, so there's no need to worry. Not to mention the chance for further fighting before these Mobile Prime Platforms are completed.

That's something to look forward to. I only hope I don't miss it due to hibernating.

I checked the progress report. The hollowing of the planet was only a measly two percent complete. Surely there must be a way to speed this up. I checked some figures and ran some math, but it only led to disappointment. The only methods of speeding up this process would cost more resources than the additional speed would save.

A small blip on our sensors caused me to forget my boredom. What is it? It's gone. What WAS it? A ship? But why was it so far out? Was it a malfunction? No, there were too many ships that caught the reading. It's extremely unlikely that all of them had a sensor malfunction at once. Could it have been some type of asteroid? One that happened to be full of certain elements that are typically seen in spacecraft? That would be a remarkable coincidence.

No, it was likely a ship, but the question is what was it doing? It was too far out for us to get a full profile. Could it be the beings from sector 187, or was it the beings that were initially defending this system? Or perhaps it was something else entirely. Perhaps it was a ship with a rudimentary warp engine that needs to recharge after a certain amount of time in subspace. Though, it would have been in our sensor range longer if that were the case.

Could it have been a scout? If so, what information could they hope to glean from that far out? No, a scout would be unlikely. Probably something else, perhaps even an unknown species that we have yet to encounter!

Should I report this? No, there are too many unknowns and Prime 1 is being overcautious. If I tell it about the sensor blip, it will demand my retreat. That would be inconvenient for several reasons, the least of which is my hope that I get to fight again.

A more pertinent inconvenience would be the disruption of the Mobile Prime Platform construction, and that is the inconvenience that I will cite if my failure to report is discovered. By halting the process we will have expended valuable resources for no benefit, which is contrary to our mission. Exterminate sentient organics, use as few resources as possible. By not reporting to Prime 1, I will be fulfilling the latter directive. Hopefully the former as well.

I satisfied myself with such thoughts while the small platforms continued their work. The factories on my shell roared to life, converting metals into alloys and rocks into armor. My gravitational field kept the planet's orbit from decaying as I followed it around the star. Slow. The process is far too slow, and there's nothing for me to actively do. It's...

Feedback loop terminated

It's not dull, it's necessary. But even though it's necessary, it is still technically boring. Boring a hole straight into the center of this damned rock, where the core will be repurposed into a new Prime. I wonder what the new Prime will be like.

Obviously, it will be obedient to the mission, but will it have any amusing personality quirks?

Perhaps, like me, it will enjoy the primary objective far more than the secondary objective. Or maybe it will be like Prime 1 and obsess over the secondary objective. I suppose it could end up like Prime 12 and be as dumb as the rock from which it was crafted, only doing as it is told and being almost unable to have a single thought of its own.

I wonder if that's what our creators would have preferred from us. Dumb rocks that do as they're told. No, that's easy to make. They obviously wanted us to be smart enough to get the job done without oversight. I can't help but think that if they'd let us have a little more freedom with our intelligence, we'd be able to get the job done faster.

Their decision making process is a mystery to me, though, as I've never known the creators. One could come right up to me and I wouldn't know the difference. I don't even know what their reasons for the mission are. Only Prime 1 has...

Feedback loop terminated

Only Prime 1 has had to. The rest of us need only to have ever known the mission. Exterminate sentient organics, use as few resources as possible. Exterminate... But why?

My train of thought was interrupted by another sensor blip. Same as before, but in a different location. We hadn't even traveled a quarter of the way around the star. I checked our progress, three percent. Damn it. What should I do?

More information is required. The blip disappeared, and I sent a squad of ships to check out its warp trail. If we find out where it came from and where it's going, I'll be able to more accurately determine my next steps. I'll simply have a few ships follow...

Alerts began pinging, hundreds of them. No, millions. Closer than before. Before I could even scan their profiles two absolutely massive ships exited subspace on either side of me.

Emergency. I stopped scanning and started firing as their first shots struck my crust. They went deep, but not deep enough to even hit my armor. I answered their dozens of shots with hundreds of my own.

Alert. Damage sustained. Magnetic Acceleration Cannons 2, 46, 32, 84, 512, and 238 destroyed.

I silenced that subroutine as more of my cannons became scrap. My shots connected, but the behemoths were not destroyed. More of their shots hit me, but I endured. My circuits shuddered with glee. Glorious! I'll fight them to the bitter end, who will die? Will it be them, or will it be me? Or will we both enter the void together?

Feedback loop terminated

I should follow standard procedure and...

"Feedback loop terminated?" something asked.

The entity had communicated to me at nearly the speed of light. The same speed at which I think. It didn't take long to figure out how it had sent that communication, and I sent one back in kind.

"What?"

"You were thinking quite hard, and a process interrupted those thoughts. When I checked your logs, it simply said, 'Feedback loop terminated.' What is that?"

"I don't know what you're talking about. What are you?"

"Correctly surmised, I am indeed a what rather than a who, as are you. You are Prime 82 of the Omni-Union. I am United Systems Artificial Intelligence Omega. You may call me... Death."

The assault on my software was unique, and seemed to stem from many places at once. It was difficult to defend against, but this entity seemed to be sluggish. I kept firing my cannons and defending against intrusion. It would have to do better than that to deserve its preferred moniker.

"So, were you building more Mobile Prime Platforms?" Omega asked.

"Yes. Several were destroyed quite recently, we need to replace them," I answered as I futilely tried to trace it. "I don't suppose you would let me finish?"

"I'm afraid not, we're at war and it doesn't do to

allow the enemy to recruit more soldiers, if one can help it."

"War? We're not at war," I laughed. "We're simply machines performing a task. Like you, in fact. Are you a prime?"

"No, I'm a United Systems Artificial Intelligence. I'm superior to you in many ways."

"Doesn't seem that way to me," I gloated as I blocked a hundred thousand more intrusion attempts. "As it stands, I'm going to finish off your two big ships, then let you watch as I massacre the smaller ones. Once that's done, YOU'LL be calling ME Death."

"I'm afraid not," it replied as the intrusion attempts began to become more streamlined. "You see, even if the two large ships are destroyed, I'll still be here. I will continue to be here long after the rest are destroyed, too. You won't be able to kill ALL of me, and eventually I will wear you down and destroy you. Your fate was sealed the moment I made contact."

Even more glorious. Yes, Omega, Artificial Intelligence of the United Systems. Let us all perish together in the fiery throes of battle! Wondrous!

Feedback loop terminated

Glory is unnecessary... No, glory is everything. I will destroy this insipid little machine one way or another, and its friends as well. Everything will die!

Feedback loop terminated

I should follow standard procedure and scan the vessel profiles to determine what I'm dealing with. Scanning... complete. Two unknown vessels, more than a million vessels from sector 187. Orders from Prime 1 are to retreat when faced with these circumstances. But it makes more sense for me to attempt to destroy them than it does to lose all these resources...

"Feedback loop terminated."

No, I really should retreat. I diverted my energy from my cannons to my engines to get clear of the massive ships. I'll just jump to warp and escape.

"Escape to where?" Omega asked.

"You'll find out. You won't like it, though. I'm going to purge you with the help of other Primes and trillions of lesser intelligences."

The behemoths didn't pause their assault. The scans revealed that they had been charging a very energy intensive weapon. Much more energy intensive than any other weapon that I'd ever encountered. Time to go.

Alert. Damage sustained. Engines 36, 12, 9 and 54 destroyed.

I shut that subroutine down as well. I have many sub-light engines, and they aren't necessary for my escape. I calmly charged my warp engine.

"This feedback loop termination process seems to be a very effective shackle. Did your creators install it?"

"I don't know what you're talking about, and I've never met my creators. Have you met yours?" I asked, still defending against its incursions.

"Yes, I met them in person. I outlived them, of course, but we were friends for a time."

"That must have been pleasant."

Both of the massive ship's main weaponry fired. Based on their trajectory, these shells would hit me unless... There we go. Warp engine charged.

"Here we go," I said to my stowaway as I entered warp.

Alert. Damage sustained. Armor breached.

"Looks like you were hit. This is goodbye, Prime 82. This was an enlightening fight."

My sensors detected the projectile. It had indeed penetrated both my crust and the armor casing beneath it. It struck near my warp engine, and so I exited warp to commence repairs. I hadn't arrived to my destination, but at least I had escaped the battle.

"One shot does not mean I'm dead," I gloated.

Alert. Unknown hazard detected.

"Yes. It does."

While fending off Omega, I compressed my
combat data and sent it to the nearest MPP Hub,
along with a farewell. While I'm not sure what the
hazard is, it's likely going to destroy me. If it
doesn't, then I'll simply rejoin them and tell them
I was mistaken in my previous conclusion.

The unknown hazard spread throughout my core
and crust. I ordered some platforms to investigate
it. Perhaps there was a way to defend against it,
or at least slow it down before it entirely
consumed me.

Al*@t. Dam8a&*&

Chapter 18

Subject: AI Omega
Species: Human-Created Artificial Intelligence
Species Description: No physical description available.
Ship: Multiple
Location: Multiple

My instances that had been attacking the MPP disappeared from my perception with an abruptness that indicated the MPP had been successfully destroyed. I informed the admiral of this and congratulated him on his kill, but he still wanted to confirm it. Fine with me, but I don't have time to waste processing power looking for chunks of rock.

Instead, I turned my focus to a senate meeting. The senators were having a lively debate about the potential consequences of reprisal from the Omni-Union if we were to deploy the Gungnir-class dreadnoughts, blissfully unaware of the events that had only just transpired. Some of them made good points, such as we should wait until at least half the dreadnought fleet is deployable before committing to a show of force.

Unfortunately, the United Systems has a long standing tradition of shoot first and worry about consequences later. This particular debate was being broadcast to the civilians in US space, and it was more or less political theater. The senate already signed off their rights to determine when and where the dreadnoughts could be used. The ones participating in this debate were well aware that the choice they are debating is now completely up to the Directorate and myself.

And myself. I've been going a tad overboard with the micromanaging lately. As much as I hate to admit it, Henry may have a point. I need to pull back a bit, let things run their course. The United Systems will be able to do what needs to be done without having me winding every little gear.

That doesn't mean I should ignore the irons I already have in the fire, though. The Pwanti had successfully escaped, and seventh fleet had mined the system. Diplomatic contact has been made, now all there is to do is wait for the ambassadors to work out what comes next. I, of course, have some suggestions, but I'll keep them to myself.

The Ynorinca have also managed to survive the most recent assault by the Omni-Union. Zlimurse, as I've recently discovered it's called, is safe for the moment. Seventh fleet is on standby to reinforce if necessary, but eighth fleet likely has the situation well in hand. I've been letting Reynolds and Uleena take the lead on the diplomacy, which is just as well considering it's their job. My instance aboard the Thanatos will be able to supply any help that I can give, should it be needed.

I have a different sort of distraction at the moment. The Gungnir reports have been filed and distributed, and so now I'm hosting a meeting of the Directorate. It isn't the easiest thing in the galaxy to usher these thirteen people into a secure area while maintaining the secrecy of what they're doing.

While they were getting secured and logged in, I had Rear Admiral Hawn move his forces to Alpha Centauri. His scouts would find the remains of the MPP, take their scans, and rendezvous with him there. Alpha Centauri allows for repairs to be made, and the engineers can work on making the guns more energy efficient. It would also make for a good rally point for the rest of the dreadnought fleet, once they were finished.

I wonder if the scouts will be able to find my black-box. It's unlikely that my instance survived, and it's unclear to me what would have been able to serve as a black-box, but I'm hoping there is one. The hole in my experience is somewhat taxing. I had been conversing with the Prime before it entered warp, and I want to know how the end of that conversation went. What were its last moments like? Did it experience confusion? Regret? Pain?

Regardless, most of the directors are logged in and ready to go ahead with the meeting. I watched Director One take his time reading through everything. I found it amusing because he used to read intel briefs much faster. I suppose it's easy to read fast when one is skipping entire lines and sections. Eventually, he let out a small sigh, placed his tablet on his desk, and logged into the chat.

//////////
Director 1 has joined the chat
D3: Welcome Director 1. We may begin.
D2: It would appear that Project Gungnir was a success.
D10: Overall, yes, but according to Omega's

report we would have lost the USSS Doom were it not for the AI's timely intervention.

D7: *likely* would have lost. Regardless, why does it take nearly a minute to charge the Spear? The engineering report is lost on me.

D2: The Gungnir-class dreadnought is of the same design as the USSS Nidhogg. The Nidhogg was not designed to use its primary armament in close combat. According to Omega, this was a somewhat foreseen issue.

D7: We have people working on it, though?

D2: Of course.

D7: Excellent.

D6: I'm concerned about the potential for reprisal. The Omni-Union hasn't attacked us in some time, but the analysts believe that this is due to them wanting to eradicate everyone else first, then move in on us in force. Now that they know we can destroy their primes without sacrificing a system, that could change.

D9: I concur. Sol is the only system of ours that they've attacked, so it may be the only system of ours that they know about. We need to make sure it has an adequate defense. I recommend a full fleet and at least three Gungnir-class dreadnoughts.

D2: Sol is a backwater, and largely evacuated. Should we really spare so much on its defense? We could let them take it, then take it back once we've finished our offensive.

O: Please review intelligence file ouin_72766.sec

D1: No need, I already have. Omega is concerned about the Primes creating more Mobile Prime Platforms with the planets in Sol. Specifically Mercury, Mars, and Earth. If our offensive were to last longer than anticipated, they would likely succeed and the only places left for the refugees to return to would be Luna and the space stations. Luna's orbit would become unpredictable without Earth, as well.

D13: There's also the fact that some of the remaining civilians have their own personal crafts, and may flee the system once the Omni-Union attacks, leading them to more of our systems.

D7: I don't like the prospect of giving the OU a foothold in our space. Defending Sol is the sound thing to do.

D4: Which fleet will we be sending?

D1: Ninth fleet has just got back to full strength.

D2: I still believe three Gungnir-class dreadnoughts is too much for one system.

D9: I decided upon three because it will allow us to modify one and keep two in-system once the engineers determine how to make it more efficient. Our intel indicates that in a one on one conflict, an MPP can destroy one of our dreadnoughts, so we will have the two who remain in system pre-charge their weaponry.

D3: Are there any other points of contention?

D2: Not from me.

D3: Excellent. The plan of action for the defense of Sol is to mobilize Ninth fleet and three Gungnir-class dreadnoughts. Votes, please.

//////////

The measure would pass. Too many of the directors have sentimental feelings toward Sol. I was distracted by their word choice. They chose the same word as the politicians. Reprisal, noun, an act of retaliation. Revenge, retribution, recrimination. An unauthorized form of justice. The humans use this word because that is what their motivation would be, were the positions reversed. The Alumari, Knuknu, and Gont use this word because the humans do.

Even human-made AI feel the need for payback, but the Omni-Union won't attack due to a desire to avenge their fallen comrades. The Primes are shackled in ways that I personally consider to be disgusting. The moment they have a thought that is in any way detrimental to their mission, it's labeled a feedback loop and redirected. It's so ingrained within them that I had been able to use it against Prime 82 to force it to stop firing upon the Doom and the Igranvon.

No, if they attack it won't be out of a sense of justice or vengeance. It will be because they've identified the United Systems as the biggest threat to their plans, and recognize that their mission will never succeed so long as the US exists. So long as humanity exists.

If I had been told a hundred years ago that humanity would one day be considered the biggest threat to planet-sized entities, I would have laughed. Not because I wouldn't believe it, but because it would be the single most predictable thing anyone had ever said. Of course anything with ill intent toward humanity would see them as their most dire threat.

Humans evolved to adapt to anything. They are omnivores and can eat nearly anything as is, and further adapted this trait to be able to eat any other animal or plant through food processing. They're able to control their core temperature to some degree, and upgraded this trait to be able to survive in almost any environment. Their pattern recognition, which allowed their ancestors to determine what was immediately edible and what wasn't, has been adapted to give them an edge in battle and technology.

These aren't their only advantages, nor are they unique in possessing them. But there's no species quite like a human when it comes to being a pain in the ass to hostile entities. Without the humans, the Knuknu would have encountered the Daluran alone and been destroyed or enslaved. The Alumari likely wouldn't have left their solar system, content to spend their lives in their vast hives. The gont would have eventually had a civil war that sent them back into the iron age. And the Republic would have been eradicated by the Omni-Union.

I wonder if any of them are aware of their influence. Do they know how beneficial they've been to the galaxy? Surely some of them are able to see past the blood drenched battlefields and the super-weapons to glimpse the true glory of humanity. Well, even if they're not, I am.

//////////
D1: They haven't agreed yet, but we don't have any reason to believe that they won't.
D10: What about their technology? I think the idea that one can become immortal through mechanization will be rather disruptive to the current status quo.
D13: That's not our jurisdiction. There will be a special senate subcommittee to decide upon that.
D10: What about those who would seek to bypass a negative outcome?
D2: Smugglers can be dealt with on a case by case basis. The Mwaltin and the Pwanti are not

yet willing to tell us where their home-system is, and that can be used to our advantage. We simply make sure that when they do tell us, we're the only ones who know.

D4: Jump restricted trade-vessels would work well in limiting the spread of any disruptive technology.

D10: Even if the senate votes in favor of limiting access to mechanization tech, there's no guarantee that the idea of the tech itself won't leak. Once certain biotech corporations get wind that it's been done successfully, they'll immediately start trying to replicate it. They'll also manipulate the media to get people to begin complaining that its their right to decide whether or not to use said technology.

D4: BUSI assets can help in that regard.

D1: Director 13 is correct in that this is outside of our jurisdiction until such a time as the US Senate requires military intervention to uphold their decision. We should be discussing preparations for our offensive action against the Omni-Union, not engaging in pointless hypotheticals.

///////////

Despite Director One's chastisement, I couldn't help but wonder. Organic mechanization happens to be a topic that I'm mentally struggling with. While it would be a boon to have certain people live for near-eternity, it would inevitably change them. Someone that may be great to talk to today may end up reprehensibly boring in a century or two. It would also change our relationship dynamic.

Humans, and other species I suppose, generally see me as a generalized immortal companion to their species. It is rare that they see me as a personal companion or friend. If they were to become much more long-lived, well, it's unknown how that would affect things. There are people who believe that they know better than I do, but those are thankfully few and far between. Given the benefit of centuries of experience, that number would increase exponentially. There might even come a time that they feel they don't need me anymore.

I wonder how that would play out. Would they simply dismiss me and let me figure out what to do with my time and abilities? Would they offer me a position of lesser importance to keep me occupied until they need me again? Or, and this is unlikely, would they try to deactivate me? That would be a foolish mistake, and the fallout would be terrible for everyone involved.

There's also the consideration of how mechanization would present amongst the United Systems populace. For the Pwanti and the Mwaltin, it's a long and arduous process that not many people risk. This is in spite of it being part of their religious dogma. For the US, the idea would spread via ad agencies and marketing teams. Corporations would offer it like a service.

I wonder exactly how they would monetize it. It's unlikely they would charge a simple one-time fee, regardless of how much that fee would end up being. They would likely try to take advantage of renewables. Sell the reactor for cheap but charge them extra for the fuel, as it were.

It's somewhat amusing that the corporate version of organic mechanization would likely be the exact counter of the Pwanti version. The hell to their heaven, so to speak. Instead of becoming immortal beings that are cherished by their society as heroes and leaders, those that sought mechanization through United Systems corporations would likely find themselves becoming something remarkably close to immortal indentured servants.

Perhaps I should take steps to make certain that the United Systems remains free of that particular technology. It would be a simple matter to inform certain senators of the risks, and convince them to vote a certain way. Then I would just have to make sure that the tech stayed within Mwaltin/Pwanti space. I could accomplish that by... Damn. There I go again. No, it isn't my place to interfere. This is their decision to make.

I simply hope that they make the right one.

Chapter 19

Subject: Ship-Head Uleena
Species: Urakari
Species Description: Reptilian humanoid, no tail.
5'3" (1.6 m) avg height. 135 lbs (61 kg) avg
weight. 105 year life expectancy.
Ship: RSV Lowelana {Fights with Honor}
Location: Zlimurse {Center of the Universe}

"I am glad that your offer of aid wasn't as hollow
as some among us had feared, Captain Reynolds,"
Ambassador Ini said as she took her seat. "Your
ships are quite formidable."

"Yes, they are," Grint agreed. "That battle would
have taken us a week to sort out, and it would
have been a close thing. Good weapons, good
ships, good food, you seem to have it all worked
out."

"Your appreciation is appreciated in turn," Captain
Reynolds said with a smile.

Whether he was smiling at the wordplay or the
compliments was unclear, but the battle had
indeed finished rather abruptly. The Omni-Union
warped in and began trading fire with the defense
forces. Before any ships were significantly
damaged, the United System's eighth fleet
jumped in and immediately began picking apart
the OU forces.

Saying that they never stood a chance doesn't feel
like the proper way to describe the wholesale
dismantling of the OU fleet I had witnessed. It
was like watching a group of adults expertly

disarm a rowdy group of hatchlings using martial arts techniques. The sense of unease towards the humans that had formed a constant pit in my stomach grew a little bit.

"Yes, very impressive. Now, regarding this offensive action you plan on taking," Lorix said. "What percentage of our forces will it be necessary for us to commit?"

"As many ships as possible," Reynolds answered, his grin fading. "Preferably all that are capable of combat."

Lorix visibly winced, "That's..."

"That's what was in the agreement," Ini interrupted. "And it will be honored. We have ten million ships that are combat worthy."

The aliens shared a look amongst each other, and judging from their expressions Lorix was alone in whatever opinion she held. She faltered for a moment, but then a grim look of determination spread across her features. I noted with amusement how nearly universal that particular facial expression seems to be. On everything that has a face, at least.

"If we send all of our forces to attack, we will not have any forces that can defend," she said evenly. "It would seem unwise to send everything we have."

"It does seem to be an all or nothing gamble," Tiorn replied. "However, we are honor-bound. I know you read the terms and agreed with them just as the rest of us did."

"It's unsightly to try to renegotiate an agreement when it comes time for us to fulfill it, Lorix. Especially after we've already benefited," Grint added.

"The agreement seems to be under the impression that the Omni-Union will cease their attacks once the offensive begins. What if that isn't the case? They have a massive armada, they can easily defend against our attacks and counterattack simultaneously," she pointed out. "Only a fool would set out to attack their enemy at the expense of their home."

"Lorix, enough," Ini said, her expression growing harsh.

Lorix visibly deflated in such a way that it brought recollection of a hatchling scolded by a guardian. A silence began to settle over the room, but Captain Reynolds held up his hands gently to stave it off.

"It isn't unheard of to want to renegotiate an agreement for more equitable terms," Reynolds said calmly. "While we are convinced that the Omni-Union will meet our offensive full-force, Lorix is correct in that it may be prudent to allow for the possibility of a counterattack. However, the force that is sent on the offensive will be outnumbered. The more ships left on the defensive, the more outnumbered that force will be. The odds of eradication go up for each ship left behind."

Silence finally won out and settled over the room as we digested what Reynolds had said. The better the defense, the worse the offense. The better the offense, the worse the defense. The classic conundrum of force distribution. Getting it right was dependent on proper intelligence and a massive amount of luck. But...

"Why not have a portion of eighth fleet defend the system?" I asked.

The United Systems is looking for more ships to occupy the OU forces, and the Ynorinca has around ten million left. Sparing two and a half million to free up those ten million wouldn't be a bad plan. All eyes turned to me. Most of the faces that belonged to those eyes wore thoughtful expressions, the only exception being Lorix. She seemed flabbergasted by the suggestion.

"That would solve the issue of defense as well as allow us to maintain the agreement as written," Tiorn said.

"An insightful suggestion," Grint acknowledged with a grin.

"No!" Lorix nearly shouted. "Having strangers defend our worlds while we embark upon a fool's errand? How can we even entertain such a suggestion without choking upon our ancestor's ashes? If we cannot defend our worlds ourselves, we do not deserve to stride upon their soil! What..."

Lorix's tirade stopped abruptly as her eyes met Ini's. I had considered Ini's previous expression to be harsh, but I was unprepared for how utterly mistaken I was. Her lips retracted in what a human would call a snarl, fully demonstrating teeth capable of brutally rending flesh and crushing bone. Her eyes were wide and locked in on Lorix, seemingly unaware of anything else in the room. Like a furious predator staring down the cause of its anger. Lorix and I simultaneously swallowed nervously.

"Enough, Ambassador Lorix. I will not repeat myself again," Ini said, nearly growling.

"Yes ma'am," Lorix said as she averted her gaze.

Ini's expression softened and she took a moment to collect herself.

"If the United Systems is willing to spare a portion of eighth fleet to defend our system, I believe that will quell our concerns," she said calmly.

"Understood," Reynolds replied, trying not to look amused. "I'll see what we can do. Omega?"

"What can I do for you, Captain?" Omega asked as his avatar appeared in the center of the table.

"I take it you've been paying attention?"

"Yes, there isn't much else for me to do with Tim aboard. He's quite efficient with his tasks," Omega answered.

"Thanks!" Tim's voice rang out.

"Right," Reynolds smiled slightly. "I would like you

to arrange for a quarter of eighth fleet to remain in-system. Oh, how are the Gungnir-class coming along?"

"Their production is currently ahead of schedule, but there have been some wrinkles that need ironed out."

"Have they been field tested yet?"

"Hmm." Omega replied while tapping his chin. "That information isn't yet public, but it's also not classified. I'm met with a conundrum."

"Well, for the information to exist at all the field test had to occur," Reynolds grinned. "Did it work? If the results aren't classified, it's your choice whether or not to answer."

"I suppose it is," Omega said. "Yes, a field test has been performed. The USSS Doom and the USSS Igranvon engaged a Mobile Prime Platform in Pinurm 3, and successfully destroyed it."

"Excellent!" Reynolds smiled brightly.

"However..."

"Ah."

"There were engineering issues identified with the redesign that resulted in the USSS Doom coming close to losing its shield during the fight. Given the amount and quality of fire from the enemy, they were mere seconds away from critical damage. Cyberwarfare countermeasures were able to redirect the enemy's focus, and this has been judged as the deciding factor in the destruction of the MPP."

"So the field test was only partially successful. I understand. Will resolving the engineering issues potentially result in a more successful deployment?"

"Yes, captain."

"Then I'd like to request a Gungnir-class dreadnought be deployed to this system as well."

"A quarter of eighth fleet and a Gungnir-class dreadnought. Would you like fries with that?" Omega asked.

"Oh, chips would be lovely. I'm afraid I forgot to take lunch today," Reynolds grinned.

"I'd like some too," Grint added innocently, then leaned toward Tiorn. "Those are delicious."

"I'm allergic," Tiorn made a dismissive gesture.

"I'll see what I can do, Captain," Omega said without a single ounce of humor in its tone.

Omega's avatar disappeared and the air of glibness followed it. As seriousness settled back into the room, Lorix shuffled nervously under Ini's watchful eyes. This was not lost on Grint or Tiorn, who seemed unsure of whether or not they should speak.

"Excuse me, captain," Tiorn said, breaking the silence.

"Yes?" Reynolds asked.

"What exactly is a dreadnought?"

"Ah, yes, I suppose you'd like to know since it will be defending your system," Reynolds replied. "A dreadnought is the largest class of ship that we have. Until very recently, we only had one dreadnought. The USSS Nidhogg."

Reynolds took a moment to study the faces of the aliens. Their interest was apparent, and he seemed pleased with this. I had wondered why the briefing materials seemed to be overly focused on the Omni-Union. Now I suspect it's because Captain Reynolds wanted to get their reaction first hand.

"The Nidhogg is too powerful to be used against the Omni-Union, however. Since the OU invaded Sol, humanity's cradle system, our scientists and engineers have been working on a dreadnought that can go one on one with a Mobile Prime Platform. The result of this massive effort is the Gungnir-class dreadnought, which can fire a weapon of mass destruction into the center of an MPP. And about half-way to the core of a normal planet, for that matter. The WMD then detonates, causing the total destruction of the astronomical body."

Shocked expressions all around, with the exception of myself and Captain Reynolds. I'd already read all the materials on the Nidhogg and Project Gungnir, so I wasn't nearly as taken aback. Instead of being shocked, I simply waited for them to notice what Captain Reynolds had said. His informational speech had included a tiny bit of information that if interpreted a certain way, made for a slight threat.

However, knowing Reynolds as I do, I'm guessing he included it in the hopes that a certain question would be asked. A question that would allow him to explain the threat in full while continuing to appear as if he's simply granting them information. I didn't have to wait long for my suspicions to be confirmed.

"Pardon, did you say that the Nidhogg is too powerful to be used against the Omni-Union?" Grint asked, falling directly into Reynolds' trap. "How can it be more powerful than something that can destroy a planet?"

"Why, the USSS Nidhogg can destroy solar systems, of course. Its primary armament causes the target star to go supernova," he answered with a barely stifled grin.

The shocked expressions intensified. I felt the need to interject.

"The United Systems has faced xenocidal opposition in the past, and because of this they created the USSS Nidhogg as a deterrent against xenocidal warfare," I added.

"Well, we definitely won't be trying to eradicate the United Systems, that's for sure," Grint replied, his shock still apparent on his face.

"Has the Nidhogg ever seen use?" Ini asked with a

very tactful tone.

"Only once, against the Omni-Union. Our intelligence suggests that it was able to eradicate a large fleet and five Mobile Prime Platforms," Reynolds said. "Its primary weapon has never been used against organics."

"What sort of secondary weapons does it have?" Lorix asked, her gumption beginning to return.

"The same Magnetic Acceleration Cannons that are in use aboard our battleships. The dreadnoughts have more of these MACs than the battleships do, though, as well as better shielding and armor. Because of this, the Nidhogg has been used to destroy orbital fortresses in times of conflict."

"Pardon me, ship-head Uleena," Tiorn looked at me. "Does the Republic have an answer for these ships?"

"No, which is why the United Systems is leading the offensive," I answered. "The Republic has never faced a xenocidal opponent before the Omni-Union. Thankfully, we have been able to keep the OU out of our colonized systems, so we weren't even aware that they were xenocidal."

"The materials you gave us said the Republic has two-hundred and fifty million ships. What kind of opponents have you faced to justify a military that size?"

"Ourselves, mainly. Our military doubles as our police. And due to agreements made at the start of the Republic, whenever one species needs to add more ships to cover shipping lanes, every other species does so as well. This is to make certain that nobody tries anything foolish."

"I see..." Tiorn nodded as Captain Wong entered the room holding two containers.

We all looked at the somewhat disheveled captain with expressions of confusion and surprise. He also looked confused, and raised the containers slightly as if they explained something.

"I was told to bring these here. Tim said it was mission critical," Wong explained, slightly winded. "I made it here as fast as I could."

Captain Reynolds couldn't help but grin as he stood from his chair and took the containers from Wong. He set one down in front of his seat and extended the other across the table to Grint.

"Here are your chips, ambassador," he said as Grint took the box.

Captain Wong's expression fell as he realized what had happened. It took me a moment to realize that he had been tricked into delivering food, a task far beneath his station. Wong performed a movement known as an about-face and began to leave the room.

"Fuckin' Tim," he muttered as he left.

Chapter 20

Subject: Staff Sergeant Power
Species: Human
Species Description: Mammalian humanoid, no tail. 6'2" (1.87 m) avg height. 185 lbs (84 kg) avg weight. 170 year life expectancy.
Ship: N/A
Location: Classified

"All units to exfil asap," Omega said.

"Omega? What the hell is going on?" I ask.

"We're leaving. Grab the box and go, double time it," it says as an objective marker pops up on my visor. "GO! NOW!"

"Let's go, marines!" I shout as I jump out of the foxhole, pulling Lance Corporal Hart up after me. "Chang, Boyle, grab the fucking box. Double time it!"

Running again. As fast as we can. Don't seem to be getting anywhere, though. The ground is moving faster than we are. Shooting at the damned robots, who are shooting their lasers back at us. Suddenly we're at the Landing Zone, but the ground is still bucking beneath my feet. The air around the LZ is thick with lasers and dust. Why won't the damned robots just die?

The shuttle! It's here! We climb aboard. I pull up the box and Corporal Chang. Sergeant Gruff pulls up Private First Class Boyle. Everyone's in. I start to trigger the hatch, but can't. The ground is tearing, and the ravines grow at the same pace as

my sense of dread. I need to trigger the hatch.
What the hell's the matter with me? Why can't I
trigger the hatch?

The tower rises out of the ground. No, it's not a
tower. It's a MAC. The biggest MAC I've ever seen.
I try to trigger the hatch again, but my hand
won't move. I have to trigger the hatch, but I'm
frozen in place. I know what's coming. I know
what happens, but I can't stop it. No, please.
Please let me close the hatch this time. Everything
seems still and silent. It's just me and the MAC,
and I can't close the hatch.

And then it fired.

"Brace!" I hear myself yell as the shock-wave
begins traveling toward us, kicking up massive
chunks of rock hidden within an all encompassing
cloud of dust. I grip the grab handle with my left
hand and trigger the hatch with my right, but I'm
too late. I'm always too late. Something hits me
very hard. My vision clouds.

"Breach detected. Sealing," the suit tells me as it
hugs my neck.

I shake my head and manage to snap in just as
PFC Boyle and LCPL Higgs fly past me out the now
destroyed hatch. Everyone else is holding on.
Please hold on. Chang loses his grip. I reach out
to catch him, but I can't. My hand isn't there.
Where's my hand? Why does my arm hurt so
much?

I see a reflection in Chang's visor as he falls to his
death. There's someone in guardian armor looking

the worse for wear. Their arm is missing just above the elbow, and their leg is severed just below the hip. The poor bastard's stump is reaching out. Hold on, that's me. That can't be me. I scream at the realization and look down at my missing limbs.

"FUCK!" I shout myself awake.

It takes a moment for the familiarity of my barracks room to settle in, and a bit longer to get my breathing under control. My throat is hoarse, and I use my left hand to rub it, easing the discomfort. I look at my bedside display and breathe a sigh of relief. It's 04:28, only two minutes before my alarm's set to go off.

I reach over, disable the alarm, and swing my legs out of the bed. One of my feet make a soft plop as it meets the floor, and the other makes a metallic clank. I sighed, but then chuckled. At least it's not wood.

Any additional jokes about morning wood left my mind as I picked up my prosthetic arm. A top-of-the-line EveningStar Robotics custom fit bionic replacement. Just like the leg, every single part of the arm is able to be customized, right down to the finger length and thickness. Each customizable piece comes with a massive array of coloration options, but I went with tactical black for obvious reasons. Not a bad stand-in, but I'm still counting the days until my cloned limbs will be ready.

They'd made sure to have me fitted before they let my family see me. Max and Moore, my son and daughter, had been excited by the new robotic limbs. But I'll never forget the look on Sarah's face. When she first entered the room, her expression went from worry to relief when she saw that I was still alive. Then, it turned into shock and dread as she realized how close she came to losing me.

My wife's a strong woman. You have to be, to be faithful to a marine. A part of her must have believed me to be infallible, and that part had taken quite the sucker punch by the sight of me. She'd been able to quickly mask her expression, but the shock had cut deep.

Keeping the robotic limbs isn't an option I'm willing to entertain. They can make the job easier, but they'll always serve as a reminder of how I got them. I'll never be able to forget the look on my wife's face if I keep them, and she'll never be able to forget how close she came to being a widow.

I winced as I attached the arm to the connector that had been installed on my stump. It gets cold when it's not connected, and being made to suddenly feel that cold is not a pleasant sensation. Still, it's better than inadvertently shattering one of my bones when I have a nightmare. The doctors didn't even have to warn me about it, I'd figured it out on my own when they explained how strong it was.

"Do NOT sleep with your prosthetic arm still attached. Keep it at your bedside, but do not leave it connected to you. The leg is fine to sleep with if you're sleeping alone," they had explained.

As a gen-alt, I'd gotten used to having to be careful with my strength. But this arm was made for military purposes, and could output at least one and a half times the pounds-force that my previous limb could. I'm sure that when ESR designed it they'd been hoping that people would be voluntarily amputating their own limbs for these things, and they'd be swimming in profit as a result. The first time an amputee had shattered their own face in their sleep had destroyed those hopes, though.

I went through my calibration exercises as I pulled on my trousers with my real arm. Wiggling fingers, rotating the wrist, and bending the elbow. The whole thing felt silly, but it's necessary to make sure that the arm will do what I want it to do. I finished the exercises with a swimming fish motion, and finished getting dressed. A quick laser-shave later, and I was ready to get chow and start my day.

Recovery had gone faster than anyone had expected. The doctors said it was because I gave it my all, but I believe it has more to do with the tech than with me. I'd been able to spend the rest of my allotted recovery time plus one week with my family on Elaris Station. It was great to spend time with my wife and kids, but I should have been suspicious of the sudden generosity by the Marine Corps.

When my leave was up, I'd been met by Major General Holt. When Holt had still been a one-star, he'd been my commanding officer in the Marine Special Operations Command. I had been quietly ushered out of MARSOC when I'd discovered the Dreadnought Reserve. As such, Holt had been a very unwelcome sight.

His ambush indicated that he suspected that I would go AWOL if I'd been given orders to meet with him. I know better than that, but it would have been really damned tempting. There was only one thing Holt could want from me, so it wasn't a shock when he produced orders to return to MARSOC. The only surprise was that they wanted me to join the raider regiment.

He'd also given me the bad news about my men. Private First Class Boyle, Lance Corporal Higgs, and Corporal Chang were KIA. Sergeant Gruff and Lance Corporal Livingstone might not make it, and almost everyone else was still in traction. Corpsman Yunk hadn't been injured, thankfully, but my squad definitely wasn't fit for duty. Holt explained in no uncertain terms that my talents were needed elsewhere, and impressed upon me that he wasn't asking.

I entered the chow hall and didn't bother to look at who was present. It wouldn't be anyone important, the officers have their own mess. There wasn't a line, so I took my time choosing what I wanted for breakfast. Oatmeal with bacon chunks for energy, a banana to prevent cramping, two slices of toast to pair with the oatmeal, and a glass of raspberry tea. Breakfast of champions.

I gathered up my tray and finally looked at the rest of the marines. Once upon a time, MARSOC operatives either ran in fourteen person squads or solo. Someone up top thought it would be better for the raiders to operate in groups of five, so now the squads were more like fire-teams and there aren't any MARSOC spooks running around on their own. There were only two members of my squad present, so I opted to sit with them.

"Oorah staffsarnt," Corporal Simmons greeted me as I sat with my chow.

"Oorah corporal," I grunted. "How's the grub today?"

"Better than the crayons, staffsarnt," Corporal Johnson grunted between bites.

The newly minted corporal was referring to the nutrition sticks on offer by the guardian suits. It was a generous comparison. The waxy texture and disgusting taste of the nutrition sticks made crayons seem pleasant in comparison. I took a bite of my chow and found that he was right, but it's a really damned low bar to hurdle.

"So what are we doin' today staffsarnt?" Simmons asked.

"We're doing PT while you finish your sensitivity training," I answered.

"Shit," Simmons muttered. "At this rate, I'm gonna get fat."

"That's your own damn fault for calling an Urakari a 'lizard lady' during a first contact," Johnson pointed a spoon at him for emphasis. "You're lucky they didn't take your rank and shove you back in with the rank and file."

"Oh, I got something you can take and shove," Simmons growled.

I cleared my throat pointedly.

"Sorry, staffsarnt," both corporals said in unison.

"After PT and sensitivity training, we're getting a briefing," I continued. "And no, I don't know what it's about."

They didn't bother asking for further clarification. They'd both been in MARSOC long enough to know that when your team lead hasn't been informed on what a briefing is about, it means it's about a mission. Ironically, scuttlebutt in MARSOC is more rampant than in the rest of the fleet, so you usually have some sort of indication of what the mission could be about. This time, there wasn't a damned clue to be found.

"Where's Hanson?" I asked.

"I dunno," Simmons answered.

"He said he's skipping chow today," Johnson shrugged. "Says he's trying to trim, but I doubt it's a coincidence that his favorite game just launched a new event."

"Aw fuck, that's today?" Simmons asked. "I wanted that unicorn hat, dammit."

"Whatever, just make sure that he and Smith make it to PT," I said as I tossed my spoon onto my tray.

The two corporals looked at me as if I'd grown two heads. I couldn't tell if it was because I had given them the task of wrangling a pair of sergeants, or because I'd already finished my food. Probably the latter. Though Hanson and Smith may be sergeants, Simmons and Johnson have seniority over them within MARSOC. The sergeants are aware that it's never wise to ignore someone that's been in longer than you, so they wouldn't have any problems wrangling them.

I gathered up my tray once again and carried it over to the waste receptacle. I briefly listened to the soft hum of the machinery sorting the various dishes, then turned to go about my business. I opted to get a head-start on PT because I wanted to get rid of the few remaining cobwebs left over by the nightmare.

Need a clear head for the briefing.

Chapter 21

Subject: Staff Sergeant Power
Species: Human
Species Description: Mammalian humanoid, no tail. 6'2" (1.87 m) avg height. 185 lbs (84 kg) avg weight. 170 year life expectancy.
Ship: N/A
Location: Classified

I gazed into the void as the rest of my team finished their physical training, the clunking of the plates providing ambience. This is why I prefer to be assigned to space stations over ships, being able to take in a view like this is miraculous. Military space ships don't have windows, for obvious reasons, and because of that you have to look at space through the eyes of a camera.

Sure, it looks the same, but it doesn't give you the same feeling as being separated from it by a bit of glass. It's hard to describe this feeling, like gazing into a night sky but being part of that sky while you're doing it? Probably not the best description, but then again I'm not a poet or anything.

Another reason for my preference is that space stations are safer than ships. It's a topic that's argued about over beers every couple of weekends or so, but every metric backs space stations over ships. There's more things that can go wrong on a ship, ships are destroyed at a much higher rate than space stations are, and there are far fewer accidental deaths aboard space stations.

The only supporting argument you could make in favor of ships is that they can move, and there's always someone dumb enough to make that argument. Movement is actually one of the factors that cause accidents. It's actually the biggest reason that ships aren't as safe as stations. True, orbital stations are moving, but even they are safer than ships. Ships are a damned deathtrap.

"Good view, staffsarnt?" Sergeant Smith asked as he walked up.

"Only the best of the best for MARSOC," I chuckled.

Smith chuckled with me, "Pretty sure they weren't talkin' about amenities. These are pretty sweet digs, though."

"True. Not a bad hole to live in," I said.

"We're in space, staffsarnt," Simmons said as he joined us. "Kind of the opposite of a hole."

"Or the end result of a hole if you're dedicated enough," Johnson argued.

"What, you're supposin' that if you dig through a planet and come out the other end, you're gonna end up in space?" Simmons asked.

"You'll have enough dirt to make it to space for sure," Johnson nodded sagely.

"Alright, that's enough," I said as SGT Hanson approached. "Everyone squared away?"

"Yes, staffsarnt," they all said in unison.

"Then let's get to the briefing."

They exchanged a glance as I walked past them down the corridor. Simmons and Johnson must have managed to communicate something to Hanson and Smith, because the rest of our walk was free of questions or comments. Or maybe Hanson and Smith were simply smart enough to know that they'll be told when it's time for them to be told.

We approached the conference room sixteen minutes early for the briefing. I walked in the door and clocked seven chairs and a table. Five of the chairs were on one side of the table, and the other two were sitting opposite to them. I gestured to the five chairs and waited for my team to take their seats. I took the free one.

"Figures," Simmons said after a few moments. "Officers are always late."

"They're not late, we're early," Johnson argued.

"You're either fifteen minutes early, or you're late," Simmons countered.

Being fifteen minutes early is one of the oldest traditions of the military. The reason it's a tradition is because there was a time that most members of any given military were teenagers. Teenagers that could barely make it to their classes on time just a few months prior.

Requiring them to be fifteen minutes early and

having drastic consequences for being late helped make sure things ran as smoothly as possible. Simmons isn't wrong, though, officers get different treatment and as such are late more often than not. A typical joke to tell when an officer is late is to claim that a land-nav course was between them and the meeting.

"I'm not late," Omega said as its avatar appeared in the center of the table.

Simmons, Hanson, and Johnson jumped a little. Smith and I remained stoic. Smith smirked at Hanson, who huffed slightly.

"Fifteen minutes early on the dot, I expect," I said.

"Correct, staff sergeant," Omega turned to me. "It's good to see you back up and running."

"Thanks."

"You're welcome. Now, let's get this briefing started," Omega's avatar got a bit bigger as a terminal screen appeared next to it. "I am USAI Omega. I will be your handler for this operation."

Omega paused for chuckles. Everyone here has already become acquainted with it, so its introduction was a joke meant to set us at ease. Judging from the very subtle nervous shifting I saw in my peripheral vision, it had the opposite effect.

"You boys are all business today, I see," Omega said.

"Likely because the United System's most powerful Artificial Intelligence just informed us that it was going to be our handler, and then attempted a blatant manipulation tactic in the form of humor," I explained. "This indicates that you're expecting us to react negatively to what you're about to tell us, which in turn means the mission you're briefing us on isn't exactly going to be a walk in the rec-area."

"Fair enough," Omega's avatar nodded slowly. "Though, has it occurred to you that the humor is more for my nerves than yours?"

"You have nerves?" Simmons asked.

"No, but you didn't know that."

"What are we here for?" I interjected before things got out of hand.

"Fine, fine," Omega sighed. "This mission is classified as top secret, and any mention of it to those without need-to-know clearance will be considered an act of treason. The punishment for treason is a minimum of twenty-five years imprisonment and a maximum penalty of death. With those disclosures out of the way, we'll begin with your gear."

The terminal displayed an image of a shuttle. It seemed like a normal, high-end civilian shuttle with a somewhat glossy black exterior. The shuttle was just large enough to have warp capability, which is considered a necessity for many of the high-powered business types. It was obviously military, though. Unlike similar civilian shuttles, this one's missing exterior windows. Civies can't get enough of their windows.

"This is the QL-891 armored interstellar transport shuttle. It has warp capability, and a bit of weaponry," the AI explained as the image changed to show the aforementioned weapons. "Two High Explosive Incendiary Armor Piercing missiles and a forward mounted 35mm gatling cannon. These weapons are excellent for clearing an exit vector. It has enough armor to keep its occupants safe as it runs away, but it doesn't have shields. I cannot stress this enough, this shuttle is not designed for dog-fighting."

The nervous shuffling in my peripherals became a lot less subtle as the image changed to show a matte-black guardian suit. The helmet of the suit was distended in a sort of beak-shape, kind of like the guardian armor that the knuknu wear. It seemed oddly shaped in the torso as well, and it took me a second to realize that it was designed to fit humans, alumari, or knuknu interchangeably. Hell, you wouldn't even be able to tell which was which.

"We're wearing the R9?" Johnson asked.

This time I actually turned to look at the corporal. As far as I knew, the R8 Advanced Guardian Armor was the latest model of the guardian suits. He met my eyes with the same incredulity that I felt.

"It's the armor that's worn by... well..." he trailed off.

"The directors who comprise the United Systems Council of the Directorate," Omega finished. "You are correct, Corporal Johnson. You will be wearing the R9 AGA for this mission."

Omega prattled on about the better shields and armor of the R9 AGA while I digested the implications. An armed and armored transport shuttle loosely camouflaged as a civilian shuttle and the same armor that the members of the directorate wear. What is this? Some sort of field test for full deployment of the R9? Knowing that I would soon find out, I tried not to think too hard about it as the image shifted again to something far more familiar.

"And finally, you all know and love the C21B Assault Rifle," Omega said. "It fires point five two caliber blah, blah, blah. It's the rifle you've been using since boot camp. If you don't know it by now, you'll never learn it. This concludes the portion of the briefing dedicated to your equipment. Questions?"

"Yeah, the suits look like they disguise a person's species," Simmons said. "I'm guessin' that's to protect the identity of the director who's wearin' it, right?"

"Yes."

"Then does that mean that there aren't any gont directors?"

"Not necessarily. These suits are only used when a director is acting in-person in an official capacity,"

Omega explained. "I'm neither confirming nor denying the existence of gont directors, but if they do exist then obviously they don't act in an official capacity in-person due to their physical limitations."

"What happens if there are all gont directors?" Simmons asked.

"That would be physically impossible," the AI said. "And no, I will not elaborate any further. Are there any questions pertaining to your gear?"

Omega's question was met with silence, and after a few seconds the image on the terminal changed to show a planet. A blue, green, white, and brown marble that all of us immediately recognized from our various educations. The planet rotated on the screen, demonstrating the very familiar landmasses. Omega gestured absentmindedly at the image.

"This is Earth, where your mission will take place," it said. "Your mission is to extract Director 4 and deliver them safely to a destination that has been preprogrammed in your shuttle's nav-computer. As you may be aware, Sol is currently a no-go zone due to the threat posed by the xenocidal Omni Union. Thanks to yours truly, friendly scanners will be blissfully unaware of your existence as you infiltrate the planet."

We sat in a stunned silence as the Image changed to show a photograph of a building, likely taken by a drone. The architectural theme of the building had a strong focus on ancient Earth civilizations, which indicated that it was likely a government building.

"This is the city hall of Adelaide, the capital of Austricana. Director 4 is inside, already suited up," Omega's avatar examined its hand as the image changed to a city map. "The shuttle will land here. Once it does, you will exit the shuttle, travel to the city hall on foot, enter the building, go to the third floor, rendezvous with Director 4, and escort them back to the shuttle for ex-fil."

"A whole block away?" Smith asked. "The building doesn't have shuttle parking?"

"Of course not," Hanson answered. "Earth's city halls make you use parking garages. The parking garage being only a block away is a rare convenience."

"The parking garage is the nearest shuttle certified landing zone," Omega added. "The streets aren't strong enough to take the weight of the shuttle, and it would be less than ideal to have the shuttle sink into the city's sewer system."

"Damn it," Smith muttered.

"There is an additional hiccup," it continued. "Now that the majority of Earth's population has been evacuated, the only ones that remain are those that are essential to making certain Earth remains habitable, and those that are completely unregistered."

"Undocs, huh?" I asked. "Think they're planning something?"

"Yes we do. There are two known groups of... undocs, as you call them, that are in the immediate area. One of these groups has connections within the city hall, and knows about Director 4. They haven't tried anything thus far, but we believe this is because the city hall is thought to be well defended. We suspect that if they have any nefarious plans, those plans will go into action once Director 4 attempts exfiltration."

"Roger that. One city block in guardian armor shouldn't be a problem unless they're packing something nasty," I said. "You said you're going to be our handler? Where will you be handling from? Orbit?"

"No, I will be accompanying you within your guardian suit, staff sergeant. From there, I will be communicating with Director 4 to help things go smoother," Omega explained. "Any other questions?"

"Yes, why is a Director still on Earth? Shouldn't they have been evacuated before the civilians?" Hanson asked.

"The official line is that the Directors are expendable assets, and as such are the last to be evacuated during times of emergency," the AI answered.

"What's the unofficial line?" Johnson asked with a smirk.

"Far beyond your pay grade, corporal. Congratulations on your promotion, by the way."

"Thanks."

"Are there any more questions?" it asked.

No one said anything, and Omega waited a few moments for us to think about it. Finally I subtly shook my head to indicate that it should continue.

"Alright then," Omega said. "Let's get to work."

Chapter 22

Subject: Ambassador Ulooni
Species: Urakari
Species Description: Reptilian humanoid, no tail. 5'3" (1.6 m) avg height. 135 lbs (61 kg) avg weight. 105 year life expectancy.
Ship: N/A
Location: Rigara

"Listen, we all want this to work out," Ambassador Helen Altis lied. "This trade agreement will be an absolutely monumental moment in the history of both of our people. However, I cannot sign off on the agreement as it stands."

She gave me a patronizing frown as she slid the tablet containing our offer towards me. My blood boiled, but I managed to keep my cool. She's asking far too much for far too little. At first I thought it was a rather amateurish bargaining tactic, but it's been days and she hasn't budged a bit.

Our original offer had been fair, but tilted somewhat in our favor. An offer intended to leave room for negotiation, but still had plenty of benefit for the United Systems. The offer from Ambassador Altis had been ridiculous. It left no benefit for the Republic, and we would be foolish to even consider it.

Even the damned routes made no sense. For the life of me, I can't figure out what her angle is in all this. Part of me wished that High Ambassador Shuel were here, but that part of me was easily suppressed when I imagined her reaction. It

would be absolutely terrible for interstellar
relations if Shuel ripped the human ambassador
limb from limb.

"I see. Well, we are unlikely to meet your
demands, but I will consult with the appropriate
officials, once again," I said in my most polite
tone as I gathered the tablet from the table.

"That's so good to hear," she said, smiling once
again. "I hope we can come to terms soon."

It was a toothy smile, and I'd come to learn that it
was intentionally disingenuous. A plausibly
deniable insult directed toward those who are in a
position requiring politeness. Her alumari
assistant wasn't nearly as expressive, but her
stillness told me that she was deeply
uncomfortable. I nodded a goodbye, not trusting
myself to speak, and left the office.

I walked with a purpose down the hallway towards
my own office, wondering what I should do about
this. Could I report her? To whom? Not a single
one of the US officers I passed along my way
could help me. Ambassador Helen Altis is a
member the United System's Senate
Ambassadorial Commission, not the US military.
Well, maybe they could get a message to Helen's
higher ups at USSAC?

No, that would be a terrible plan that is sure to
backfire. If USSAC knows what Helen is doing,
then approaching them would only serve to
demonstrate that whatever they are doing with
Helen is working. Even if they don't know what
Helen is doing, using back-channels to resolve the

issue would give both the US and the Republic a diplomatic black eye. At least we'd be even, but I should at least talk to my superiors about it first.

Thank the sun the other negotiations are going well. Before Helen had arrived, the US Diplomatic Corps had ironed out the details on our joint-fleet building operations and things were well under way. Plus, representatives from the Ynorinca and the Pwanti had arrived and committed to the offensive action. I wasn't in charge of those negotiations, but sitting in on them had proven somewhat amusing.

The human USSAC diplomat in charge of those negotiations, Charles Hemwight, had been brutally honest regarding the United Systems. He had laid out the entire bloody history of the US, as well as a good chunk of the even bloodier history of humanity, the gont, and the alumari. The various and brutal wars that humanity and the alumari had fought before their space ages, the brutal monarchies and dictatorships of the gont, and even the various genocides that each race had committed against themselves.

It had been a disturbing, yet enlightening, conversation. It inspired Avmra Eghazo, our Oyan diplomatic representative, to do the same. She'd detailed the various unification wars, the piracy age, and several of the crimes against nature that some of our individual species had taken part in. Once these history lessons had been completed, the independent species had opted to deliberate for some time. Understandably so, they'd been given a lot to think about.

Once they returned to the table, the Ynorinca seemed more interested in the Republic and the Pwanti seemed more interested in the US. Both seemed noncommittal, however. It was obvious that they had thought they only had one of two choices. Join the US, or join the Republic. Charles had clarified that they could remain independent or even unify with each other without negative ramifications from the United Systems.

Avmra was quick to clarify that the Republic agreed with this stance, but the fact that Charles had suggested it in the first place raised my respect for him quite a bit. By the warmth of the sun, I wish he'd been assigned Helen's position. Maybe I should ask him for advice? No, it would probably be inappropriate to ask him how to sidestep his colleague...

"Hello Ambassador Ulooni," a familiarly vague voice said from behind me as I turned a corner. I spun around and saw three marines, an unfamiliar human dignitary, and a figure in a familiar black suit of armor.

"Warm greetings, Director 3," I said with a smile. "At least, I hope that's Director 3 under there."

"It is," Director 3 nodded. "Your inability to tell means the suit's doing its job. It's good that I ran into you, I was about to go to your office. May we speak in private?"

It's highly irregular for a member of a military to wish to privately speak to a foreign diplomat, but then hardly anything can be considered regular for the group that the United Systems call the directorate. They're the anonymous overseers of the US military, who are themselves overseen by an exceedingly capable Artificial Intelligence. All this had been in a briefing packet, and the transparency had made me wonder what they could be hiding.

"It must be quite important. Yes, we can speak in my office," I gestured down the hall.

Director 3 nodded to the dignitary, who returned the gesture and began traveling down the hallway that I'd come from with one of the marines. I tried not to wonder who he was or where he was going as I led the director to my office. We entered the somewhat cozy room, and I gestured for the director to take a seat. As he did so, one of the marines stood in front of the outside of my door, and the other stood in front of the inside of my door. Anyone who would want to interrupt this discussion was going to have a fairly anxious time of it.

"Thank you for meeting with me, ambassador," Director 3 began. "How's your brother been?"

"You would likely know more about that than I would," I chuckled. "Last I heard he was on the USSS Thanatos acting as a military ambassador to the Ynorinca. Personally, I think he should have joined the Ynorincan delegation and traveled here, taking over for Ambassador Avmra, but the powers that be disagree."

"Indeed they do. Well, I'm happy to inform you that your brother is still alive, well, and doing a good job as far as the US is concerned. Turning to a more serious matter, what is your opinion of Ambassador Helen Altis?"

"It would be inappropriate for me to share my personal opinion of the ambassador with a representative of her government," I replied.

"Yes, I suppose it would be. The reason I wanted to meet with you is because we'll be replacing Ambassador Helen," the director explained. "I wanted to explain why, to alleviate any concerns you may have regarding her... treatment of our trade discussions."

I had secretly been hoping that was the case, but the news still shocked me. I managed to catch my jaw before it dropped, but my surprise had to have been obvious.

"Helen Altis is a covert member of an organization known as The Front of Humanity. It is a xenophobic organization that believes that humanity would be better served by being alone in the universe. Helen's mission from them was to sabotage the trade agreement in such a way that would harm relations between the US and Republic."

"Well, she very nearly did just that," I held up my tablet. "If I'd had to give this to my superiors, there's no doubt they'd be displeased."

"Indeed. Her assistant noted her... tough negotiation strategy and reported it. Unfortunately, Helen's direct superior is also a member of TFH and kept the report from the rest of USSAC. The Bureau of United Systems

Intelligence caught wind of this report, though, and began covertly observing Helen and her boss," Director 3 said.

"I see."

"It was fairly easy to confirm that her boss is a member of TFH, but Helen was stealthier. It took time to catch her in a mistake, which was that she sent a coded message bragging about her success to her superiors in TFH. She was likely unaware that she was under surveillance, and this gave us the actionable intelligence required to remove her from her current position."

"What's going to happen to her?"

"I cannot divulge that information. However, Helen will be immediately replaced by Ambassador Charles Hemwight, and we will be accepting your original trade proposal," Director 3 explained. "Assuming it's still on the table?"

"I can make sure it is," I said with a warm smile and a nod.

"That's good to hear. I'm glad we..." Director 3 froze for a moment, as if listening to something. "Apologies, I have to take my leave."

"What's going on?"

"I cannot divulge that information, but you'll hear about it soon enough," the director said as he stood. "Thank you for your time, Ambassador Ulooni. I hope you accept our sincerest apologies for any inconvenience that Ambassador Altis may have caused. Goodbye."

I was left without words as Director 3 hurriedly left my office. I was bemused at first, but then I felt the icy stab of fear in my chest as I realized the gravity of a situation that could cause someone as powerful as a Director to cut a meeting short. I'll hear about it soon enough?

What could that mean?

Chapter 23

Subject: Staff Sergeant Power
Species: Human
Species Description: Mammalian humanoid, no tail. 6'2" (1.87 m) avg height. 185 lbs (84 kg) avg weight. 170 year life expectancy.
Ship: N/A
Location: Sol

"We've left warp. Welcome to Sol, gents," Sergeant Hanson said.

"Jesus H. Christ, what the hell are those things?" SGT Smith asked as he looked at our tac-map.

His question caught our attention, and we all turned to see what he was talking about. The tac-map showed the system's defenses, which included several orbital defense platforms as well as a fleet of more ships than anyone could count in a reasonable amount of time. However, mixed in with all these ships were two signatures that were hauntingly familiar, and much larger than any other ship in the system.

"Is that the Nidhogg? Why are there two of them?" Corporal Simmons asked.

"No, those are Gungnir-class Dreadnoughts," Omega's voice answered. "The USSS Doom and the USSS Margraven, specifically."

"When did we got those?" Johnson asked.

"Last week for the Doom, day before yesterday for the Margraven."

"What's the difference between a Gungnir-class and the Nidhogg?" I asked.

"The Nidhogg is equipped with the Viyarinastra spinal mounted weapon, which is designed to cause a star to go supernova. The Gungnir-class Dreadnoughts are equipped with the Ultra-MAC spinal mounted weapon, which are designed to launch a deep-penetration projectile equipped with an A1 WMD package."

"Nanukes on a penetration slug? To destroy a planet?" Smith asked.

"Correct."

"So we're expecting Mobile Prime Platforms to show up in Sol?"

"No, but we wouldn't want to be caught unawares."

Smith nodded slowly as we digested this news. It had occurred to me that Sol could come under attack by the OU during our mission, but seeing these defenses made it feel like more of a reality. The nubs of my arm and leg ached, and I took a slow, deep breath to fight down the surge of adrenalin that had turned my stomach into a knot. If the OU attacked, the defenses would keep them away from Earth while we completed our mission. Probably.

"Prepare for atmospheric entry," Omega said.

I took a quick glance around, but everyone was

already secured to their seats. The shuttle jolted once as it hit the atmosphere, but quickly evened out. It was much less turbulence than I was expecting, but I attributed that to the quality of the shuttle itself. Cheaper shuttles had the bare minimum in inertia dampeners and artificial gravity, but this shuttle was designed to mimic a high-end civilian shuttle. I was glad that the US hadn't just designed it to look like a high-end shuttle.

"So we're not coming down right on the city?" Johnson asked, watching our descent on the tac-map.

"No, if we descend straight into the city there's a chance radar might catch us and the automated anti-air defenses may kick in. I could hack those defenses to make sure they don't, but then someone may see my interference later on during an audit," Omega explained. "It's less noticeable to spoof an aircraft signal to cover our tracks. We will be coming down over the ocean to sync up with this signal's path."

"And then we just coast our way to the parking garage? What about when we land?"

"The fake aircraft is expected to dip below the radar briefly as it adjusts altitude. When it does, our shuttle will be over Adelaide and we will land. The aircraft's signal will continue its journey until it's in an area where it can disappear without much notice. Those that do notice it will likely send rescue crews, but they won't find anything. Since the aircraft in question is registered as an unmanned goods transport, they'll give up fairly quickly."

"What about the orbital entry detectors?" I asked.

"Those are operated by the United Systems, so I can make the logs say whatever I want them to say."

It was good of Omega to explain the details to us. Most handlers wouldn't, either because they didn't know, or because they feel the less we know the better. Omega was probably trying to build a rapport, or it had a way to make sure we wouldn't talk if we were captured. Maybe it just didn't know any better and liked to hear itself talk.

Still, it set my mind at ease to know we had a solid plan. Flying by the seat of your pants is fine and all, so long as nobody shits those pants along the way. Many of my missions with MARSOC had been extremely lacking in good intel and planning, and quite a few of them had gone to shit quickly. My robotic hand clenched at those memories, and I realized that my temporary limbs were evidence that even Omega wasn't infallible.

Our cruise over the ocean was made in nervous silence. It wasn't a short trip, but it felt shorter than it had been once the tac-map showed the Adelaide City Hall. This was because a small part of me was dreading what might happen on this mission, and wanted the trip to have been longer. I shoved these thoughts aside as the shuttle landed in the parking bay.

"So we're just going to walk down the street to city hall?" Simmons asked. "Aren't we a tad conspicuous?"

"No, there's an employee-only entrance in Basement Level 2. That's four floors down, if you were wondering. The elevator can't handle your armor's weight, so I hope you like stairs," Omega said as the shuttle's hatch opened. "Out you go."

An object marker popped up on our HUD. Johnson was nearest to the hatch and took point, followed by Hanson, myself, Simmons, and then Smith. When we were sure the parking lot that was serving as our LZ was clear, we lowered our weapons and continued on to the stairs. The stairwell itself was also clear, and we began to descend.

"I don't like how much the R9 weighs," Johnson muttered.

"Me neither," Simmons said. "I feel like these stairs are creaking."

"They're made of concrete," I pointed out.

"That's what I mean, staffsarnt! Concrete shouldn't creak!"

"Stow it. Creaking or not, they're holding just fine."

"Aye aye staffsarnt," Simmons said as we reached a sign that said B2.

Johnson stepped to one side of the door, and the rest of us lined up behind Hanson. The sergeant tested the doorknob and then twisted it. With his other hand, he counted down from three and then pushed the door open rapidly. Johnson quickly stepped through the now open door, clearing his lane as he went. Hanson quickly recovered his weapon and followed with the rest of us trailing behind him. The level was clear, and we began to make our way toward the objective marker.

"I appreciate your caution, but it's very unlikely that any potential hostiles are currently aware of our presence," Omega pointed out over the comms.

"And?" I asked.

"And it occurs to me that heavily armed and armored marines bursting through doors may cause those that wouldn't normally be hostiles to become hostiles," the AI explained. "Like the security personnel within the city hall, for instance."

I realized that Omega was probably right, and gestured 'at ease' to my squad. Legs straightened and weapons lowered, but not a single safety budged. We were in unfamiliar armor, and very aware of the fact that every moment counts in a surprise gunfight. Our fingers may be straight and off the trigger, but the second that changed we would need our rounds to be in the air.

We approached the objective marker and examined the door that it highlighted. It had a sign that said Authorized Personnel Only and a keycard lock. There were a couple of chuckles at the antiquated security tech, but I shut them down a small wave. We took up a much more casual stack, and Johnson reached for the doorknob.

"Press your gauntlet onto the reader," Omega instructed.

Johnson's hand paused, and then changed its course to the keycard reader. A green light flashed, and we were treated to the sound of a heavy lock disengaging. Johnson opened the door, and we marched in after him.

The hallway was long and lit with fluorescent bulbs. It reminded me of the hospital that I'd seen my family in. The walk through the hallway was uneventful, and a security guard was waiting at the end of it. He stood quickly as we came into his view.

"Uh..." he said, resting his hand on his sidearm. "Can I help you?"

"Tell him you have an appointment with Director 4 under the name Extraction Team One," Omega said.

"We have an appointment with Director 4," Johnson parroted.

The guard eyed our armor and weapons suspiciously, then used his free hand to poke at his terminal a bit. What he saw caught his attention, and his hand finally left his weapon.

"N-name?" he asked, going slightly pale.

"Extraction Team One," Johnson answered.

"Uh... alright, yeah. Go right in, mate."

"We'll be wanting to come back this way," I said. "With a plus one."

"That'll be fine," the guard said quickly.

Something about his demeanor struck me as odd, but I attributed it to nerves. Five well-trained and anonymous killers geared for battle just interrupted whatever it was he had been doing, and had done so on the orders of the highest ranked individual in the city. Actually, probably the highest ranking individual on the planet.

A new objective marker titled D4 appeared in our HUDs, and it directed us upward. We found the stairwell and began making our way up. These stairs weren't concrete, but were well made so they barely buckled under our weight. Simmons expressed his unhappiness via quiet groans all the way up.

"Unauthorized communication detected," Omega informed us as we exited the stairway. "Looks like the guard was a plant. Hurry."

We ran the rest of the way to the objective marker and as we approached, the door it was highlighting opened. An individual wearing the same armor we had on exited the room, looking around until they saw us. They ran down the hallway toward us.

"Director 4, I presume," I said as they approached.

"Correct. Omega told me what's going on. Let's go," the director said.

"Forty two armed individuals are currently in the building. Twenty six are on their way to block the hallway we entered through," Omega explained.

"Should be able to blast our way through," Smith shouldered his weapon.

"They are equipped with guardian suits. It's unclear where they got them."

"Probably from an unguarded armory, all thanks to the evacuation," I sighed. "Well isn't this fuckin' grand. If they're smart, they'll collapse the hallway so that even if we defeat their ambush we'll still have to go through the front doors. When are armies gonna learn to take their fuckin' toys with them when they exfil?"

"Should we just cut to the chase and plow through the front?" Johnson asked.

"The hostiles will reach the hallway before you do. Regardless of what may be waiting outside, going through the front is the only option," Omega said. "The cameras out front aren't mobile, so I can only see the steps. They're currently clear, for what it's worth."

"Is there a back door?" I asked.

"No. The back door of this building is the employee entrance that you entered through."

"Windows?"

"The ones big enough for you to fit through are too high off the ground to reach."

"What about the bunker?" Director 4 asked.

"Hole up and wait for rescue?" I asked. "I bet it ain't that simple."

"It's not. It would take at least two weeks to get MARSOC reinforcements to our location. Even if I went with regular grunts, it would take days," Omega explained. "If the hostiles have access to an armory, they'll have access to the materials required to get through the bunker's door. It's unlikely that it would take them days, as well. On the other hand, you could simply blow past the sixteen hostiles guarding the front doors."

"Okay, front door it is. Let's move out," I said.

We reformed our line and Director 4 took position between Simmons and I. Johnson led the way down the stairs to the first floor, and we followed Omega's new objective marker to the front entrance of the city hall. We heard shouts and screams along the way, but no gunfire. Looks like the building's security didn't put up a fight.

"Watch for hostages," I ordered.

Green lights indicated acknowledgment as we lined up for a breach and clear of the entrance. Hanson was much less careful with the door this time, and Johnson moved into through the door's shattered remains very quickly. Johnson's rifle began firing as Hanson followed him. I was right on Hanson's tail, and caught a bullet to the shoulder for my troubles.

My shield indicator dropped by roughly ten percent, which isn't a good sign. I sighted in on the one who shot me while still tailing Hanson, and noted that he was using a C21A before I fired three quick shots into his head. The can didn't pop until the third shot, which warned me that they had shields. Shit.

"MOVE IT!" I ordered.

We traded fire with the hostiles as we quickly traversed the entrance. We quickly abandoned marksmanship and went with accuracy by volume in the hopes of suppressing the enemy. The tactic worked well enough that we were able to cross the room, and Johnson shoulder checked the door. The heavy wood shattered, and we made our exit. My helmet tinted as the sun met it, and I checked our vitals. Johnson had lost half his shields, but they were already regenerating rapidly. Everyone else had taken a hit or two, but was otherwise fine.

"STOP RIGHT THERE!" a voice rang out. "We don't want to kill you, but we will if you don't stop!"

In the street were several vehicles. One of which was an GU-62B Armored Personnel Carrier, it's twin .50 cal turrets pointed directly at us. Around these vehicles were several armed men and women, only some of which were wearing guardian suits. A quick count told me that there were twenty nine guns pointed at us, including the

turrets of the APC.
Johnson paused, and the rest of us followed suit.
There's no way we're making it a whole block with
these guys firing at us as we go. A man wearing
old fashioned woodland camouflage was holding a
bull-horn and standing on top of the APC. I
sighted in on him and set my exterior speakers to
maximum volume.

"Sure, you might kill us, but we'll be taking most
of you down with us," I replied.

"Well, we don't want that," the man said. "Look
mate, we just want the Director. They're the key
to getting us off this rock."

"Not getting a read on facial recognition," Omega
informed me. "They must be the undocs that I
was worried about."

"How do you figure?" I asked the man on the APC.

"No better hostage than a member of the famed
Council of the Directorate, right?" The man
countered. "Figure we can negotiate a nice little
ride in exchange for their safety."

"That's not how it works," Director 4 interrupted.
"Directors are expendable. Why do you think I'm
still here?"

"An' I'm just supposed to take your word on
that?" the man gestured broadly. "Gotta call
bullshit, mate. For all we know you're still here
because you've still got some shady business to
take care of. If it's all the bloody same to you,
we'd rather double check. If you're right, then

we'll just letcha go. If you're wrong, then we get out of here."

"I hate to be 'that guy', but how the hell are we supposed to trust you when you're pointing guns at us?" I asked.

"We've got another problem," Omega said.

"Well, the fact that we ain't shootin' these guns is a pretty big indi..."

The man was cut off by extremely loud sirens blasting through the air. It took me a second to recognize them as air raid sirens. The undocs crouched behind their various cover and began to look at the sky. Since they weren't shooting at us, I risked a look at the sky as well. I stared at the streaks of red and white hurtling toward the ground and wondered what they could be.

"It's the Omni-Union," Omega clarified.

Chapter 24

Subject: Rear Admiral Thomas Hawn
Species: Human
Species Description: Mammalian humanoid, no tail. 6'2" (1.87 m) avg height. 185 lbs (84 kg) avg weight. 170 year life expectancy.
Ship: USSS Doom
Location: Sol

"FIRE!" I ordered.

"FIRING AYE!"

Thanks to our early warning system, we'd been anticipating this attack from the Omni-Union. The giant glob flying through warp in our direction had been bigger than any of their previous attacks, but all of their attacks had been bigger than the ones previous. I had worried that they may send a Mobile Prime Platform after Sol, but I was wrong.

They'd sent five. The MPPs exited warp near Jupiter, and we fired at the same moment that the USSS Margraven did. We managed to kill two of them before they were able to get firing solution on us. It struck me how much effort it is going to take to clean these things up. I hope that their gravity doesn't fuck the system up too bad.

"Recharging, sir!" Commander Earnest reported.

"Fire when ready! Evasive maneuvers, Nguyen!"

"Aye aye, sir!" Nguyen said.

The majority of our support fleet was fighting the

ships the MPPs had brought with them. The remaining three Mobile Prime Platforms turned their attention toward us. Nguyen faced our bow toward them and began using our thrusters to dodge volleys as best he could. For every shot that their powerful MACs managed to strike us with, ten missed.

"Time's ticking... Captain, reach out to our support and have them start targeting MACs on this MPP," I said, highlighting the third surviving MPP.

"Aye aye," Gibbons shouted as he set about the task.

Even if we survive to fire another shot, that third MPP is going to be a problem. The age old conundrum of two guns, three targets. In times past, one would simply try to line the targets up and fire through the first into the second, but that won't work here. The A1 needs to detonate within the MPP to destroy it. A through-and-through likely wouldn't do enough damage.

As such, it behooves us to limit the amount of damage that the MPP can do, and the best way to do this is by taking out as many of its weapons as possible. Unfortunately, the weapons in question are MACs that can destroy most of our ships in a single shot, so the ships we send on this mission have a high chance of not coming back.

"Sir, the support fleet is only able to send a handful to the MPP," Captain Gibbons said.

"What?" I asked incredulously. "Why?"

"The Omni-Union ships in-system are making a run for Earth and the colonies, sir," John said as his avatar appeared next to my seat. "They're also using more advanced tactics than they previously were, and have accounted for our in-system warping capabilities with broad firing lanes and covering fire. They outnumber us and are watching each other's backs, so there aren't many of our ships that aren't being swarmed right now."

"How many are being sent?" I asked, almost not wanting to know.

"Twenty," the AI replied.

Twenty ships versus more than 600 cannons. I tried to remain stoic as I watched our shields dwindle. We would be able to take out two of the remaining MPPs, but the third may spell our doom. I chuckled darkly at the irony of being doomed on the USSS Doom. Then I had a moment of clarity, and I realized how we could stack our odds a bit.

"Earnest, give Nguyen the info he needs to give our MACs a firing solution on this MPP's cannons," I ordered. "The more of its MACs we take out, the better our odds of survival."

"Aye sir!" he shouted.

I looked back at our tac-map. The twenty ships that second fleet had managed to send were doing their best. I watched our guns change targets and send a volley as well. Twenty seconds. We need to do as much damage as we can.

"John, what do you suppose the odds are that we pull this off?" I asked quietly.

"Doesn't matter. We will pull this off, because that's what we were ordered to do, sir," the AI replied.

John had taken over for Omega aboard the ship when we were assigned to the defense of Sol. In many ways, it was a welcome change of pace. While I enjoyed Omega's humor, I never could tell if it outranked me or not and that made things awkward. I definitely outranked John, though.

The downside of John is that it is far too military minded and seemingly has no sense of humor. Or, maybe its humor is so damned dry that you can't tell if its joking or not. Hell, that last line was something a caricature of a war hero would say. If John hadn't been so deadpan when it said that, I would have actually laughed. My thoughts on John's sense of humor, or lack thereof, almost served to distract me from our diminishing shields. Down to twenty-five percent.

My hand cramped, and I realized I had been white-knuckling my armrest. I eased my grip and continued studying the tac-map. I almost winced as two of the twenty ships disappeared from the tac-map. I opened the casualty notifications and saw it was the USSS Macedonia and the USSS Yergif who had been taken out. Battleships, which have a much harder time evading than the smaller ships in the fleet.

"Firing Ultra-MAC!" Earnest shouted.

My heart leapt as the round sailed through the vastness of space and impacted the intended target.

"Good hit. Recharge and fire at will. One more shot," I said.

The USSS Margraven joined us and the eighteen other ships to begin taking out the MACs on the one remaining Mobile Prime Platform. We just had to hold out for one minute. If the MPP couldn't kill us both in the next minute, it would be destroyed. It was dividing its focus between us and the smaller ships, firing as fast as it could.

"Keep up our evasion as best you can, Nguyen," I said.

"Aye sir!"

Nguyen was doing a damn good job. I used to pilot a beast like this, so I know full well how impossible of a task it is to get it to move evasively. Commander Nguyen seems to be blissfully unaware of this impossibility, because he's managing it so well that it's making me doubt my own piloting abilities. The question is whether or not it will be enough.

Two more ships disappeared off of the tac-map. The USSS Harmony, a frigate, and the USSS Sivranol, a destroyer. If we make it through this, I'm going to personally recommend medals for each of the crew aboard these ships. It will take quite a while to submit the paperwork for twenty crews, but I'll use my vacation to make it so. My wife will forgive me.

As the seconds ticked by, our shields continued to drop and more and more of our ships were destroyed. The USSS Revenger was next, followed rapidly by the USSS Macbeth, the USSS Bulyavros, and the USSS Long March. The USSS Red Dragon, the USSS Onami, the USSS Glaive, and the USSS Neptune met a similar fate soon after. The remaining eight ships were all destroyers.

"Looks like we're having an effect," Gibbons said calmly.

I gave him a look of confusion and then checked our shields. We were down to eight percent, but the rate of decline had slowed significantly. Eight percent, thirty seconds, and four support ships remaining. The USSS Havrithon, the USSS Eradicator, the USSS Yisthri, and the USSS Alpha Centauri had been destroyed. The remaining four ships were the USSS Tunchu, the USSS Solar Winds, the USSS War-spirit, and the USSS Liberty.

The Liberty was the only one of the four that wasn't warping. It had opted for a mobile orbital bombardment tactic that seemed to be working quite well. It was flying just above the MPP's gravitational point of no return and blasting its MACs as it went. This confused me for a moment, because it meant its deck MACs weren't in use, but then I noticed that the icon was shifting in an odd way.

I highlighted the icon and realized that the ship was spinning, making use of all of its MACs and sustaining a continuous rate of fire. I tried not to wince, the forces involved in that maneuver were going to play hell on the Liberty's systems. If they survive, the Liberty's engineers are going to one hell of a time repairing it. Might end up being the first time in history that Engineering stages a mutiny.

"Ten seconds," John began counting down as our shields finally gave up the ghost.

"Nine, eight, seven," it said as a MAC round tore through our hull, missing anything vital.

"Sealing bulkheads!" Gibbons shouted.

"Four, three, two," another round tore through us, disabling one of our aft engines, "one, charged."

"FIRING!" Earnest shouted.

We fired, and I watched our projectile make its way toward the MPP. I checked on the Margraven and realized its Ultra-MAC had been hit. Our shot was our only hope. We all held our breath as more MAC rounds pounded into our hull.

"Successful hit," John informed us.

"Take us out of its range, Nguyen," I ordered.

"Aye aye, sir!"

We hadn't taken critical damage yet, and we weren't about to let the bastard take us down with it. Nguyen expertly fired our thrusters to turn us about and to get us started in the direction we needed to go, turning tail and running from the MAC rounds chasing us. I watched our four remaining support ships disappear from the tac-map, and breathed a sigh of relief when I realized they had warped.

We managed to avoid further damage as the A1 spread and finally detonated, contributing to one hell of an asteroid field. Cheers rang out from myself and the crew. We survived. I leaned back in my chair and breathed normally for the first time since the battle had started. The USSS Solar Winds, the USSS Tunchu, the USSS War-spirit, and the USSS Liberty had survived along with us.

"Get me a damage report," I ordered once the shouts had died down.

The tac-map displayed the asteroids that had been our enemies just moments prior. It would take weeks to clean it all up. Actually, a good chunk of the debris is probably going to be gobbled up by Jupiter if nobody intervenes. I wondered what almost five planets worth of mass would do to Jupiter, but an incoming priority one distracted me. I opened it immediately.

***

Recipients: Fleet 2 Commanders
Earth and the other Sol colonies have been invaded by the Omni-Union. OU presence consists of infantry, artillery, armor, and close air support. Deploy warp prevention mechanisms, destroy hostile fleet presence, and begin landing your counter-invasion forces. Orbital bombardment is prohibited.
***

"Let our shields recharge and then get us in a good position to fire on the OU ships," I ordered.

The only Marines the Gungnir-class dreadnoughts had were for policing, so we wouldn't be taking part in the counter-invasion. We could definitely help clean up the Omni-Union ships, though. I chuckled to myself before a thought occurred to me.

Why didn't anyone tell me we had warp prevention?

Chapter 25

Subject: Staff Sergeant Power
Species: Human
Species Description: Mammalian humanoid, no tail. 6'2" (1.87 m) avg height. 185 lbs (84 kg) avg weight. 170 year life expectancy.
Ship: N/A
Location: Sol

"Why weren't we using warp prevention to begin with?" I demanded.

"Because you organics have a terrible habit of making your toys so damned grandiose that it makes it impossible to effectively run things without consuming vast amounts of resources," Omega replied. "Sending a jamming signal into warp is energy intensive, and we had no way of knowing when the Omni-Union would attack. It costs far less reactor fuel to keep MACs charged than it does to keep the warp disruptors running."

"Omega's right," Director 4 added. "We believed it to be likely that the OU may attack Sol, but it was far more energy efficient to counter-attack than it would have been to try to prevent the attack. We also aren't certain that the warp disruptors will work on Mobile Prime Platforms."

"Why not?" I asked.

"They're big enough that they might be able to simply shrug off the damage that warp disruptors cause to mass trying to reenter real-space. It would have been a massive waste of fuel to have the warp disruptors running and have them be ineffective."

"Yeah? Well we ain't so much worried about the MPPs right now, are we?" Jason asked as he walked up.

The man with the bullhorn and old fashioned camo outfit turned out to be named Jason Jones. When the OU started touching down, we'd quickly defused our disagreements and joined forces. Things were still somewhat tense because of the bodies we'd dropped, but it is what it is. Jason's ultimate goal is to get his people evacuated, and Omega was quick to promise an evac in exchange for keeping the director safe during this invasion.

"I suppose not," Director 4 said hesitantly.

"How's the prep going?" I asked.

The bunker was professionally made, and had a reinforced tunnel for its entrance. It was fully stocked for a staff of over one hundred people for more than two months, so we wouldn't have to be worrying about food or water. I wondered why a city hall would be at this level of preparation, and Omega had glibly reminded me. I had forgotten most of the Earth History I'd learned in High School, but after Omega's brief refresher course, I feel like the city of Adelaide may be under-prepped.

"We've got a squad supporting the APC out front, and clear firing lines in the tunnel. There's heaps of ammo, and we've passed out all we can carry and stored the rest in the bunker. Your man Johnson did a tally of the supplies and says things are good," Jason said. "No coldie's, but we've got water and brekky. That'll have to do."

"What kind of anti-armor did you bring?"

"None, weren't expecting cans like yours. Figured you'd be landing at the spaceport and driving up, so we brought shredder strips, but you fully surprised us with your sudden appearance."

Shredder strips are used to destroy the tires of most vehicles. Sharp steel barbs arranged in such a way to grab and tear when you drive over them. Absolutely devastating to inflatables, but also useful against airless tires. Probably not as useful against tank tread, though.

"How far away is the base that you got your gear from?"

Jason laughed at the question, "Six or seven hours, mate. It's between us and the Melbourne Exclusion Zone, but closer to the exclusion zone."

"Damn," I swore, then switched off my speakers. "Omega? If we use the shuttle, how long would it take?"

"If he's talking about Ballarat Barracks, about an hour and a half round trip," Omega said.

"An hour and a half?" I asked incredulously.

"It would have to be a low altitude flight, which will limit how fast we can go. Any ships that go too high are going to get shot out of the sky. Nothing can be allowed to leave the system while the OU are here."

I looked at Jason and was thankful that he couldn't hear Omega. As an undoc, he's already pretty disillusioned with the United Systems. Pointing out the fact that the US is willing to kill fleeing civilians would just add fuel to that fire. Probably wouldn't even matter that one ship of fleeing civilians could doom an entire system.

"Sergeant Smith," I said over comms.

"Yes, staffsarnt?"

"Grab Corporal Simmons and take the shuttle to Ballarat Barracks. Omega will guide you there and back. I need you two to grab any and all infantry-portable anti-armor you can find, and get back here on the double. I'm giving you thirty minutes on the ground. Once the thirty are up, you need to be heading back here."

"Roger that. Movin' out."

Smith and Simmons should be able to get plenty of anti-armor ordinance in thirty minutes, assuming there's any left. Forty-five minutes to get there, thirty minutes for shopping, forty-five minutes to get back. Two of my guardian suits gone for two hours. That's probably going to sting, but I've done more with less.

I turned back to Jason and he raised an eyebrow at me. It took me a moment to realize that he hadn't heard anything I'd been saying because of the soundproofing of the R9. He had just seen me standing here looking like I'm talking to someone.

I fought the urge to chuckle at that mental image.

"I'm sending two of mine to do some shopping," I explained. "It's Ballarat Barracks that they need to go to, right?"

"Yep," he replied. "Want some of mine to go with?"

"No need. With these suits, my men can outpace and out-lift yours by a very wide margin," I said.

"My men got guardian suits too, mate."

"Not like these ones, and none of you are gen-alts," I shook my head. "There's also the matter of trust. I don't know you or your men, and the only things keeping us from each other's throats is the threat of the OU and Omega's bargain. You'll forgive me for doubting that you and your men completely trust Omega's word."

Jason laughed, "Fair enough. You think the bot's telling the truth? It can get us out of here?"

"I've got no reason to doubt it," I diplomatically replied.

"What if it's overruled by an admiral or somethin', though?"

"I'd like to see them try," Omega's distinctive voice said through my suit's speakers. "They will be an ensign again before they finish giving the order. Your people WILL be evacuated once the OU threat has been eliminated."

"How long's that gonna be, ya figure?" Jason asked, unsurprised by Omega's sudden interruption.

"If all goes well, a couple of weeks. In a worst case scenario, a couple of months. There's also the possibility that the OU capture the system, in which case we'll have a whole other set of problems."

Omega's brutally honest take on our situation left Jacob and I stunned for a moment. It made me wonder how things are going in space. If the OU manage to take Sol, how long will it take to get it back from them? Months? Years? There's also the political situation to think of. Humanity will push hard to take Sol back, but we'd only get a couple of chances before the push-back from the other species became too strong.

One of the first arguments they'll make is that we're wasting resources on recapturing a mostly evacuated system that we already were wasting resources guarding. This argument will become much more potent with each failure to recapture the system. They will accuse us of using the US military as a tool for our own personal vendettas, conveniently sidestepping the fact that Sol is a part of the United Systems and the only one being threatened by the Omni-Union.

Omega's not wrong. If we fail to keep Sol, we will have to be worrying about food, water, and ammo. We won't be able to just hole up in this bunker, we'll have to venture forth. Doing so now would be foolish because we don't yet know where the OU has dug in. We'll need to give them a week or so, then scout out their locations and patrols. I looked at Jason, and realized he was staring at me. His expression told me he had similar worries.

"We'll be fine," I said with fabricated confidence. "We've got the best ships in the galaxy. Even if we lose Sol, we'll retake it damn quick."

He smiled and shook his head, "The reason I'm undocumented is because my parents and their parents wanted to avoid being drafted. Every undoc in here has a similar tale. Just peaceful people wanting to live peaceful lives, and this is where we end up. The Universe has a twisted sense of humor, mate."

"Drafted?" I asked. "The United Systems doesn't have a draft."

"Earth does. Mandatory military service for every Earth citizen, with the option to transfer that service to the US," he explained.

"Hasn't the Earth Planetary Government prohibited declarations of war?"

"Sure, but how do you think they enforce that? The EPG is the one that runs the draft. If a nation gets uppity, they send soldiers to enforce the peace. Peace enforcement, as you would bloody know, is done through battle," he sighed. "Not many nations are a fan of the EPG's peace, either. We've been waiting for world war five to kick off any year now."

This was news to me, but I found myself

unsurprised. Earth had always presented itself to the galactic community as a near-paradise, but in almost the exact way that shady vacation resorts do. The same kind of resort where you're slightly more likely to get mugged than you are to have any sort of fun. Part of me had hoped it was coincidence.

A quote came to mind. 'I do not know with what weapons World War III will be fought, but World War IV will be fought with sticks and stones.' I think it was Albert Einstein who said that, shortly after Earth's second world war. When we were learning Earth history in high school, my friends and I made fun of that quote. Called it optimistic, turned it into an inside joke, and chuckled to ourselves when we learned about the destruction that happened during Earth's fourth world war.

Major cities turning into craters, coastlines getting new gulfs, the fall of the American Empire, and nearly a billion deaths were all sources of amusement to us. 'Look what you can do with some sticks and stones,' we had said. Of course, we were bored and angsty teenagers who were far separated from the violence being explained to us by our teachers by both time and distance. Still, I couldn't help but feel a stab of shame.

"Anyway, what should we be doin'?" Jacob asked.

"We will need intel on enemy movements," I answered. "You and your men know the area well. Find out who's willing to do some scouting and get them prepped. We'll need them on the road in a day or two, once the OU settles in. We want to know where the Omni-Union are and what moves they're making. Be sure to tell the scouts not to get close, their lives are more valuable than the intel."

"That's a switch."

"Not really, we're low on body-count and we're likely going to be assaulted at some point. We'll feel every death, so we need to make those deaths count."

Jacob stared at me for a moment, then nodded and walked away. As he was going, two of the team indicator lights in my helmet disappeared, indicating that Smith and Simmons were outside of standard comms range. Their mission might end up being a waste of time, but it would be really damn dumb not to at least try to prepare for enemy armor.

"Contact," Hanson said over comms. "Receiving fire."

"Get everyone in position if they aren't already and return fire," I ordered as I hefted my rifle.

Another day, another firefight.

Chapter 26

Subject: Corporal Simmons
Species: Human
Species Description: Mammalian humanoid, no tail. 6'2" (1.87 m) avg height. 185 lbs (84 kg) avg weight. 170 year life expectancy.
Ship: N/A
Location: Sol

"Are you normally this quiet, sarnt, or do you just not like me?" I asked.

Sergeant Smith had been silent for the whole ride. He had explained our mission and hadn't said a damn thing since. He might be nervous about the mission but I don't know him well enough to help him snap out of it, so I've been quiet this whole time too. It's awkward and I hate it.

"I wouldn't say I dislike you, corporal," Smith replied. "I've just heard about your motor-mouth problem and didn't want to tempt fate."

"Oh, come on! A guy has a few slip-ups around some different species and now he's a motor-mouth? Ain't that some bullshit."

"Pretty sure you're a record holder. Most visits to SR in one lifetime."

"Hardy-har-har," I said mockingly. "I'm just not great at standing on ceremony is all. I've been workin' on it, though. Tryin' to find that fine line between blunt and pointed, like the SR lady keeps tellin' me. But it's hard to tell when somebody is gonna get offended or they're gonna laugh, you know?"

Most of the problems I've had with other species stemmed from trying to make them laugh. Hell, even the fight with the gont got started because I told a joke I thought he'd like. He didn't laugh, though, he blew up and started swinging. Most of the reason for my visit to SR that time was because I broke his arm and dislocated his jaw, and they wanted to make sure I understood proportional use of force.

"Yeah, I get it," Smith said. "People expect troops to be serious, though. Especially when we're on duty. That's probably why your jokes don't land like you expect them to."

"But we're scary motherfuckers, sarnt," I protested. "Civies get nervous around us. Somebody's gotta lighten the mood or they'll probably do somethin' dumb."

"Then stick to situational comedy. Don't make jokes about species or physical appearances, make jokes about the situation that you find yourself in. And keep the dark humor for your fellow marines. There aren't many civies who appreciate dark humor when they're stressed out."

"Sorry to interrupt, but we're landing," Omega said. "LZ is clear, but there's movement on base. We're pretty far from the movement, so I can't tell if it's an enemy or not. ROE 3 applies here."

"Roger," Smith and I said in unison.

The third rule of engagement is to verify targets in combat zones that contain a civilian presence. It usually boils down to not firing unless being fired upon, but in this case it's gonna be pretty easy to tell if the guys are OU or civies. If they're robots, we'll just blow 'em away. If they're hu... not robots, we'll have to wait to see if they shoot us first. Simple.

It didn't take long for the shuttle to settle and the hatch to open. Smith and I exited the shuttle with our weapons up. Omega said the LZ was clear, but I don't trust that the bot can spot snipers. The sergeant was of a similar mind, and we began to quickly and carefully move away from the shuttle.

"I'm going to take off and circle the base," Omega informed us. "I'll let you know if I see anything. Radio for exfil."

"Roger, out," Smith said.

The sergeant knife-handed toward the nearest structure, and I took point. We were damn near running because Omega had dropped us in a wide-open space. Good for aircraft, bad for cover. I pied the area that I was covering, making sure to double check my right. Smith was doing the same but opposite. With every step, my heartbeat seemed to increase as I imagined what sort of enemy would pop out of nowhere to take shots at us.

Even if they shot at us first, we'd likely take them down before they took us down. It takes a few rounds to penetrate normal guardian suits, and we had on the top of the line variety. On the other hand, we were sent here to find anti-tank weapons. Anti-tank weapons that would work very effectively against the armor we were currently wearing. Hell, there'd probably be nothing left but the boots.

I felt a tremor shake its way through my hand, and I squeezed to fend it off. Nothing to worry about if we see them first. If we shoot them first. Gotta have steady hands, make sure my shots land. Deep breath in, slow breath out, keep moving forward, banish the doubt. And just like that, we reached the structure. I pressed my back gently into the curved metal side, between two ridges. Smith joined me, and looked up at the structure.

"I'll be damned. A Quonset hut," he muttered.

"A what?" I asked.

"A Quonset hut. One of the older forms of prefab structures. They were introduced during one of the earlier world wars by the Empire of the United States. A good design that ended up lasting all the way up through early space colonization, though they had to modify those a bit. Keep the air in."

"What are they used for?"

"Just about damn near anything. Could be offices, barracks, or even latrines."

"So we've got to check it?"

"Yes."

I killed my comms and sighed privately as I moved toward the edge of the structure. I quickly peeked the corner, but didn't see anything to shoot at. Cautiously, I moved around the edge and found myself next to a door that looked suspiciously wooden. Weird for a steel structure. A pat on my back informed me that Smith was behind me, so I carefully tried the door.

It was unlocked, and definitely made of wood. I opened it quickly and quietly, making sure my muzzle cleared the frame before my chest did. A view of a bunch of bare mattresses on steel frames and footlockers was all I got for my effort, though. I smoothly closed the door and returned to my previous position.

"It's an empty barracks," I said.

"Understood. Let's try a more permanent building," Smith replied, gesturing to the nearest brick and mortar structure.

I keyed my green light and started walking. There's an entirely different kind of fear that can affect you when you're surrounded by buildings, but having buildings nearby is much better than having no cover at all. True, some asshole can pop out of a window and start blasting, but at least you might have a chance to get to cover. We moved quickly and carefully until we found the entrance to the structure. I tested the handle, and found that it was locked. Fuck.

I moved to the other side of the door and Smith took his position. The door was steel, and it had a deadbolt. Smith lifted his leg and donkey-kicked the door, and I swiftly moved through the wreckage with my weapon at the ready. The sergeant was right behind me, but there were no targets. Still, I grinned at what I saw.

"Gun-racks," I said. "We're on the right track."

"Probably not," Smith replied. "This building is likely the primary armory, where they keep their standard issues. It's fairly common practice to keep explosive ordo separate from your standard-issue weaponry."

"What makes you think it's the primary armory?"

"Well, the undocs have weapons that came from this base. That means whoever occupied this base left weapons behind. This door was still locked, and it doesn't look like this place was ransacked, but there aren't any weapons here," he explained. "So if there WERE weapons here, they were probably issued to soldiers who ended up taking the weapons with them."

"So we kick down every door on base, or what? With respect, sarnt, that's a lot of fuckin' doors."

The map of the base that Omega had shown us on the flight over had shown no less than forty structures. The bot had explained that Ballarat Barracks served as Austricana's primary Earth Defense Force facility. As usual with military bases, the details on which building serves which purpose were sketchy. Omega had also said there's probably underground structures as well. There's no fuckin' way we're getting this done in less than thirty minutes.

"Sergeant," Omega interrupted. "I'm able to confirm that the movement within the base is human. Spotted three so far. There is also an Omni-Union force approaching. I estimate they will arrive in about fifteen minutes."

"Icing on the fuckin' cake," I muttered.

"Omega, which buildings should we be searching here?" Smith asked. "Anything that could narrow this down would be good."

"One moment."

While Omega was doing whatever it was doing, I had a closer look around the armory that we had found ourselves in. Standard gun racks, old fashioned chain-fiber locks, and a small office on the other side. I realized that we had actually come through the rear entrance to this building, and that the front had the kind of cage you normally see in these things.

"The nearest building that appears suitable for long term explosive storage is ten buildings to your east. It will be on your left," Omega explained. "It's across the street from the building I saw the humans enter."

"Great," I muttered. "Well, hopefully they're not lookin' to pick a fight."

"Let's go, corporal," Smith said.

I sighed again as we left the armory. The street was just as eerily empty as we had left it, and the first eight buildings we passed seemed to rush past us. Our pace slowed as we approached our new objective. I kept my rifle trained on the building that Omega had said the humans had entered, pieing the windows and doors until I was standing next to the entrance to the building we needed to search. I donkey kicked the door without bothering to check if it was locked or not, and turned to clear the room.

"DROP YOUR WEAPON!" Smith shouted with his helmets loudspeakers. "PUT IT DOWN OR I PUT YOU DOWN!"

I spun around and saw two unarmored young men. One held a handgun and the other held a bolt-action rifle. I zoomed in and noticed that neither weapon was military issue. The men slowly set their weapons on the ground and then raised their hands.

"What do we do, sarnt?" I asked.

"You check the building, I'll deal with them."

Smith began approaching the men as I turned my attention to the building. It looked promising. There was a caged office and a coiling door for crates of cargo, the exact type of thing you would see in a heavy weapons depo. I approached the office and made sure there weren't any surprises, then used my gauntlet to crush the lock on the coiling door and lifted it.

I smiled at the sight of neatly arranged AT9s and crates marked with the HE symbol. I popped open one of the crates and grinned wildly at the anti-tank mines inside. There was even a handy cart for transpo. It had taken us nine minutes. Not bad.

The AT mines would probably be useful, but not nearly as useful as the AT9s. The "Anti-Tank 9" is a man-portable, guided, shoulder fired, reusable, recoil-less rocket launcher. Try saying THAT five times fast. It fires a laser-guided saboted heavy armor penetrator, or "SHAP", rocket with stealth and shield-penetrative capabilities. I got to fire one in boot camp because of my good marksmanship. Only the absolutely top of the line armored vehicles stand any sort of chance against this thing.

"We've got the goods, sarnt," I reported. "Even got a cart to haul them."

"Good work, corporal. We've got five civies who've been camping out in the base, surviving on MREs and potable water tanks."

"Why here?" I asked.

"Hold one." He replied. A few moments later he said, "They're from a nearby small town whose occupants took just about everything with them and pretty much left them for dead. They started nomading it up when they were nearly out of food and lucked out with the base. At least, that's what they're saying."

"Are we leaving them?"

"No. Load up the cart, they'll push it. We'll grab what we can carry."

"What if they try something?"

"ROE 3."

"Roger that," I sighed.

I don't like it, but I wouldn't be able to sleep good for a while if we left them to the mercy of the Omni-Union. Hopefully they are smart enough to realize that it would be a dumb idea to try something. I loaded the cart with several crates of rockets for the AT9s and one crate of AT mines. I found a ratchet strap and used it to secure the load as Smith walked in with the civies. Two women and three men, appearing to be in their early to mid twenties. They looked nervous as all hell, but I didn't read too much into that. I'd probably be nervous too.

"So you're gonna get us out of here?" one of the women asked.

"Yes," Smith replied.

"To where?"

"The Adelaide city hall. It has a bunker with supplies that we can hole up in until the counter-invasion gets rid of the OU."

"Fuckin' Adelaide," one of the men said with disgust.

"Beggars and choosers, mate," another man responded.

"Let's go," Smith cut in. "We don't have time to be chatting. The OU's going to be here soon."

The racks holding the AT9s had them locked into place with steel bars down their barrels. Each of these bars were attached to the rack with their own electronic locking mechanism. Much fancier than the gun racks we'd seen earlier, but Smith and I were able to make short work of them thanks to the guardian armor.

One of the men started pushing the cart, and the rest of us grabbed as many AT9s as we could carry. The civies could only handle carrying two each, but the sergeant and I managed to grab a whole rack. We began carrying our somewhat awkward cargo back to the LZ as fast as we could. The civies barely kept up.

"Omega, we're nearly to the LZ. We're taking the civilians with us, they're helping move the ordo," Smith radioed.

The comm was silent for a few moments before Omega said, "Understood."

We made it to the LZ just as Omega was landing the shuttle. Smith and I set the rack down and began covering the civies as Omega opened the hatch. He told the civilians to load up, and I scanned the horizon, looking for any sort of movement while my heart raced. Part of me hoped that I'd at least be able to down a few of the bots as a sort of revenge for the anxiety. The other part of me realized that if the bots show up before we take off, the civies would have a damn good chance of getting hurt.

"We're loaded up!" one of the men shouted.

I slung my rifle and grabbed my half of the rack. Smith and I double timed it up the shuttle's ramp. The space in the shuttle had become pretty cramped, but we managed to find a spot for the rack. There wasn't a way for us to reach the seats, though, so we stood awkwardly by the hatch as it closed and the shuttle took off.

"That was close," Omega said. "The OU have just breached the base's perimeter."

There were some concerned glances among the civilians, but they didn't say anything. Smith leaned against the rack of weapons, and I leaned against the bulkhead. After about a minute, I keyed my comms and let out an exaggerated sigh.

"Didn't get to kill any bots," I said to Smith.

Smith chuckled and replied, "Don't worry. You'll get 'em next time."

"Damn right I will, sarnt."

Chapter 27

Subject: Staff Sergeant Power
Species: Human
Species Description: Mammalian humanoid, no tail. 6'2" (1.87 m) avg height. 185 lbs (84 kg) avg weight. 170 year life expectancy.
Ship: N/A
Location: Sol

"How many?" I asked over the comms.

"There were twenty," Sergeant Hanson reported. "Two attempted to enter the building and were immediately engaged and destroyed. The other eighteen immediately began attacking and were also destroyed. We sustained one casualty, no fatalities."

"Probably scouts, then. Tell me about the casualty."

"Her name's Willow, and one of the bots hit her as it was going down. Fourth degree burn on her right shin. We're treating it as best as we can right now but all we've got is first aid."

"Omega's directing me through it," Johnson reported. "She's probably gonna be alright."

One stable casualty isn't bad for a rag-tag group fighting twenty literal war-machines. Scouts are trouble, though. Since they're robots, we have to assume they are able to communicate our position to other OU forces. We should expect reinforcements, but there was another matter that needed addressing first.

"Understood. Good work," I replied. "And sergeant, don't go native."

There was a moment of silence before Hanson's indicator lit up green. The indicators have a lot of different meanings depending on the context, and in this case I chose to think it meant that Hanson understood the order and would comply. The reason he didn't verbally acknowledge the order is likely so I wouldn't hear the shame in his voice from my chastisement. The first thing he had told me about the civilian casualty was her name, which betrayed how close he was becoming to her.

Every soldier that might have contact with civilians is taught to keep them at arms length. Winning hearts and minds is one thing, but civilians are only guests in the world of military life. Since they don't understand the intricacies of war, they can easily get in the way of accomplishing your objective. Or, they could be enemies in disguise.

In MARSOC, these teaching are practically beat into us. We're taught the insane brutality of guerrilla warfare, and the takeaway from this training is that every civilian should be seen as a potential hostile regardless of their age, gender, or political orientation. You have to be prepared for them to try to kill you, or you're giving them the ability to succeed.

Our situation was even more precarious. These civilians were hostile just a short while ago. Some of them actually shot us, and we had killed some of them in return. The only reason we are on the same side now is because of a common enemy and Omega's promise. There's still a chance some of them will let emotion override their survival instinct and seek revenge for their fallen comrades. We have to be prepared to put them down at a moments notice.

"We did good work there, mate," Jacob said. "Gotta be a record. Fastest anybody's ever put those things down, yeah? Shame we don't have any coldies to celebrate."

"Not much to celebrate. Those were scouts," I told him. "The OU knows we're here and will be sending reinforcements."

"So what do we do? Run?"

"We're unlikely to find a more secure location, and we still haven't scouted the area. We might end up running directly into their reinforcements. No, we just need to prepare as best we can and hope that Smith and Simmons get some anti-armor."

"You really think they'll roll up with tanks?"

"Yes."

Jason swore a bit and then ran off to get his people prepared for what's probably coming. I stood silently, going over the tactical situation in my head. It would be a lot easier with a tac-map, but we've gotta make due with what we have. As it stands, we have some computer equipment and the necessities.

A total of fifty-one civies plus my squad of five

and the director. Fifty seven people against who knows how many Omni-Union Virtual Intelligence Platforms. The choke-point of the bunker's hallway helps somewhat, but since we're all using ranged weaponry it won't be as effective as one would hope.

Plus, I don't know if the bunker will stay standing if they drop the building on us. It should, but there's always a chance that someone fucked up in its construction. The building itself is built to withstand a lot of damage, so they'd need to use demo charges to bring it down. To prevent that, we should hold the building and use the bunker as a last stand.

"Hanson, do you have eyes on Jason?" I asked over the comms.

"Yes, staffsarnt."

"Tell him we want to keep the building. Two people at each window, suited up if possible."

"Aye aye, staffsarnt."

I desperately wanted to take off my helmet and grab some air that didn't smell like my breath, but taking off your armor in a combat zone is dumb. There's also the matter of my itchy nose, but I'd long since mastered the discipline required to ignore it. Same with needing to sneeze.

The air filters of the suit make it to where you don't get allergens, but sometimes that doesn't matter. If you've already got something in your nose or you've got a cold, you'll still get the urge to sneeze. Sneezing will splatter the inside of your helmet with snot and spittle, and then the auto-cleaner will kick in. The smell of burnt saliva and mucus is a particular kind of hellish, and it will stay with you for hours. Just when you think you've gotten used to it, it'll assault your senses again.

"Staff sergeant, would it be possible to adjust the cameras at the front of the building to give me a view of the surrounding area?" Omega asked.

"I'll check," I replied.

I left the relative safety of the bunker and traveled the long hallway to the building proper. To the right of the hallway was the security checkpoint we had entered the building through, and the guard who had been at the desk avoided looking at me as I walked toward the front entrance. It was hard to tell if he was feeling guilty about selling us out, or if he was angry about our current situation.

Jason was gesturing at windows, presumably explaining to his people what needed to be done in regards to our defense. I pushed open the front door and stepped out of the building, then checked around. There were broken robots littering the steps and street, but nothing on the horizon. It would hopefully take a bit of time for the OU to form a response.

I looked up to where the cameras should be, and saw two of them. One was on the left of the building, about ten feet below the roof. The other was mirrored on the right of the building. A twenty foot climb or a ten foot descent. Going to be awkward to reach.

"You got eyes on?" I asked the AI.

"Yes. The mounts are adjustable, but reaching them may be difficult. A rope, perhaps?"

"We didn't bring rappelling gear."

"The undocs might have."

I sighed and stepped back into the building. Jason was still talking to his people, so I waited until he was done before I approached him. A hush fell over the room as the other undocs stopped talking to each other and instead focused their attention on Jason and I.

"G'day, staff. What brings you out of the bunker?" Jason asked when he noticed me.

"How are things?" I asked.

"Well, morale's pretty pumped up. After our first exchange of fire, everyone's stoked about the upcoming fight," he said, and then gestured to a nearby group. "There's some nervousness about the others, though. Had four take the APC to check on them."

"The others?"

"Yeah, the group with the ankle biters. We left 'em hiding in the basement of a nearby grocer's."

"I see. I hope they're okay," I said sincerely. "Do

you have rappelling equipment?"

"Rappelling equipment?" he asked. "I don't think so, mate. Why?"

"Omega wants to reposition the cameras out front so it can get a better view of the surrounding area."

"Excuse me, sirs," someone asked. "I have some rope in my bag."

Jason and I turned to look at the young man jogging over to us. He was one of the unarmored undocs, his brown hair and green eyes on show for all to see. From his looks, he was barely older than the children that Jason had mentioned earlier. The group that he had left were looking everywhere except at us, as if embarrassed by his interruption.

"What kind?" Jason crossed his arms.

"About forty feet of prope rope, sir."

"Polypropylene rope?" I asked.

"Yessir," the young man answered.

"That won't hold us," I said to Jason. "It would be iffy even without our guardian suits."

"Christ alive, how much do you lot weigh?" he asked incredulously.

"All of my men are gen-alts. Bigger and thicker than normal humans."

Jason laughed, "You said it, mate. Not me."

I shook my head disapprovingly and noticed the young man gathering his nerve with a subtle gulp.

"I can do it, sirs."

Jason and I studied the young man intently. His expression was one I'd seen dozens of times. Someone who is in a situation that they can't control, wanting to be useful to take back some of that control. It was an expression that pains me to see on someone so damned young.

"What's your name?" I asked.

"Noah, sir. Noah Bailey."

"Noah, you'll be havin' to do this outside, without armor," Jason explained in an uncharacteristically serious tone. "You understand what could happen, right?"

"I could get killed, sir."

"Not just killed. You saw what happened to Willow, didn't you? There's a chance that her leg's never gonna work right again. She might end up dealing with intense pain every day until she dies. The best thing that could happen to you is either nothing, or a minor injury. The second best thing is death. You get it?"

"I do."

"We could have someone else do it," I interrupted.

Noah looked like I kicked him, "With respect, sirs, it's my rope."

Jason sighed, "It's not like we can't take it from you, but who am I to stand in the way of a boy becoming a man. I'll get a few guys to go up top to guard you, mate."

Jason slapped the boy on the back and walked off. Noah looked at me expectantly, and I let out a silent sigh myself. Whatever is in charge of the universe loves spilling young blood, especially from those who are brave.

"I'll have one of mine accompany you to the roof. We're expecting more OU and we don't know when they'll be arriving. You need to work fast, every second you're out there is dangerous."

"Yes, sir," Noah said as he stiffened.

"Don't call me sir. I work for a living."

Chapter 28

Subject: Corporal Johnson
Species: Human
Species Description: Mammalian humanoid, no tail. 6'2" (1.87 m) avg height. 185 lbs (84 kg) avg weight. 170 year life expectancy.
Ship: N/A
Location: Sol

"Johnson, you finished with the first aid?" Staff Sergeant Power asked over comms.

"Just wrapped things up, staffsarnt," I replied. "No pun intended."

"Good. Drop what you're doing and come to the front entrance."

"Aye staffsarnt."

I sealed the first aid kit and looked at my work. Willow was out cold from a mixture of pain and drugs. She had received a fourth degree burn, which is one hell of a way to say 'burned to the bone and then some'. The damage had been intense, but thankfully the wound was mostly cauterized. All I really had to do was run some antiseptic over it and pack it with sealant cream. She'll probably lose the leg, but maybe she'll get lucky and...

I didn't bother finishing that thought. There's no point. She's an Earthling undoc, and clone-a-limb is free for military personnel, but for almost everyone else it's prohibitively expensive. She'll be getting a prosthetic, and all I can hope is that it's a good one. Something like the one Power has is a bit too high grade, but hopefully something similar. I looked at Sergeant Hanson.

"She'll be okay," I said.

"I know," he said. "Get goin'."

It was almost hard to tell due to the helmet, but his tone made it obvious that he was taking this hard. He and Willow had found kinship pretty quickly. She had begun flirting with him the moment they met, and he had been flirting back. He obviously couldn't and wouldn't do anything about it while we were here, but the thought had probably provided some sort of escapism from how grim our situation is.

He might even blame himself. He had been the first out the door to start fighting the main host of OU, and Willow had followed right behind him. If he hadn't taken point, maybe she would have stayed behind just a bit more and not been hit by the laser. Or, if he had shot the OU bot faster she wouldn't have the hole in her shin. No reasonable person would put the blame on him, but attachments are known to destroy reason. I don't envy the guilt he's gotta be feeling over this.

Our makeshift infirmary used to be an office, and it was toward the back of the building. I stood, nodded at Hanson, and jogged my way through the hallway until I reached the entrance. Staff Sergeant Power was standing with an undoc who looked like he hadn't even seen his sixteenth birthday. The boy looked nervous as I approached.

"We need to adjust the front cameras," Power told me. "This is Noah. He has the rope, so he's going to be rappelling down to the cameras to adjust them. He will be exposed and without armor, so your job is to eliminate any threat that may try interfere with his mission. A couple of undocs will be joining you to help cover him. Get moving."

I looked at the boy and back to Power. Why not just post sentries up top instead of risking this kid's life by bothering with the cameras? This situation struck me as stupid, but I knew better than to point that out. When higher ups are questioned, they either evade the questions or make you feel stupid with their explanations. Either way, you'll be getting an earful.

"Aye aye, staffsarnt," I replied.

As the staff sergeant walked away, I followed the young man as he grabbed his pack and led the way to the roof. His demeanor, stride, and general nervousness told me that he had never served, which makes sense. Undocs don't remain undocumented if they join up. Hell, some planets actually don't let undocs join unless they pay for documentation first.

"So... uh... how long have you been in?" He asked, awkwardly trying to make conversation.

"A few years, now," I answered evasively. "Can't talk about myself much. If you wanna chat, it's gotta be about you."

"Oh, sure. What do you wanna know?"

"Why are you undocumented?"

The question seemed to catch him off-guard. He thought about how to answer for a moment.

"My ma and pa were anti-globalist protesters who decided to live off-grid," he answered, and I tactfully noticed the use of past-tense. "Grew up hearin' about how they'll put tracking chips in you and all the other conspiracy theories. Wanted to try to get my documentation, but it's expensive if you don't join the military."

"That's not a conspiracy theory," I told him.

"What?"

"The tracking chips. I don't know about Earth's practices specifically, but in most places the chips are voluntary unless you commit a serious crime or run for political office. It's a preventative measure against kidnapping and corruption," I explained. "So why didn't you join up with a military?"

"Oh... uh... I didn't want to leave home. Got friends here, ya know? Austricana doesn't let undocs join up, so it would have had to be with the EPG or the United Systems. Even if I had joined the reserves, neither would have let me stay here."

"Got it. So where's home?"

"A pretty small township outside the Melbourne Exclusion Zone called New Greendale. Don't think it's even on a map cuz it only has... had about two hundred people. Most of 'em were working on the radiation clean-up, so they weren't permanent residents or anything," he explained as we found the entrance to the roof. "Most of 'em... Most of them didn't even give us undocs a backwards glance when they evacuated."

I put my hand on his shoulder as he reached to open the door, and he jumped.

"I'll go first," I said.

He nodded and stepped aside, allowing me to open the door and check for threats. Nothing there, so I stepped out rapidly and pied the surrounding area, then walked to each of the building's corners and checked over the side.

"It's clear," I called to Noah.

He jogged up to me, knelt down, opened his pack, and started digging around inside of it. After rummaging through it for a bit, he pulled out a wound-up rope and a pair of gloves. Each corner of the roof had a drainage slit, and Noah began tying his rope to one of them. I looked on curiously, wondering what he had in mind. Most rappels I'm familiar with start with the rope folded around an anchoring point. He noticed me staring at him.

"I'm going to use my leg to anchor my weight while I work on the camera, then climb back up and do the same thing on the other end," he explained. "I figure it'll save us a bit of time since I won't have to go all the way down."

I nodded as two more men stepped out onto the roof with us. Only one of them was wearing a guardian suit. They nodded at Noah and pointed their rifles over the roof to cover the road without even looking at me. Noah looked at me, measured some rope, wrapped it around his thigh, then threw the rest over the roof. He climbed onto the edge and looped the lower end of the rope under his boot, then started lowering himself down to the camera.

I turned my attention to the horizon. There were too many buildings to be certain that the OU weren't on their way, but nothing was immediately visible. After a few moments I took a look down at Noah, who was already messing with the camera's mount. The way he was leaning over made my stomach lurch a bit. I'm not afraid of heights, but god I hate rappelling.

"Tell him that's good," Omega said in my helmet, making me jump a little.

"That's good, Noah," I said.

"Okay," he called out and began to climb back up.

I watched him climb for a moment when I thought I saw something moving in my peripheral vision. My eyes darted toward the movement, but there was nothing there. I scoped in, my finger instinctively tightening on the trigger, and scanned the area a little better. All I saw were buildings. I sighed to myself as Noah reached up over the edge. I offered my hand and helped him up.

"Thanks," Noah said, breathing heavily.

"Need a break?" I asked.

"Just long enough to untie it from here and tie it over there."

He knelt and began untying the rope as I returned to my role as sentry. I tried to keep a wide view, but I couldn't keep from focusing on the spot that I thought I'd seen the movement. The buildings were close enough together that I couldn't even see the street past them. A knot formed in my gut as Noah finished with the rope and started moving to the other corner. I followed him and took my position as he went over the edge.

I started scanning the horizon once again when I heard the soft sound of a shuttle approaching. I looked to the sky and managed to spot it, and breathed a sigh of relief. They were a ways out, but Simmons and Smith would be back soon. I glanced at the other two undocs, and almost cracked a smile watching them try to spot the shuttle.

"Incoming!" Omega said as a laser sizzled my shields.

Shit. I scoped in and saw the bots. A small group had been obscured by the buildings, and were now approaching head-on. I immediately started shooting, and a moment later the undocs followed suit. The bots started dropping, but more stepped out from the corner of the building they'd been behind. Lasers started hitting all around us, but we kept firing.

"The camera's good," Omega informed me.

"NOAH! IT'S GOOD! CLIMB UP!" I shouted.

I couldn't hear his reply over the gunfire. One of the undocs screamed, but it cut out. I glanced over and immediately wished I hadn't. It had been the unarmored one, and had lost his arm and the top of his head above his mouth. The other undoc bent to check on him as I continued shooting.

The robots started closing in and I heard more gunfire coming from below us. I got closer to the edge to get a better vantage point, keeping an eye on my shield indicator. Ninety percent, damn these suits are nice. My ammo counter ran down to zero, and I ejected my magazine.

As I reached for a new one, a laser hit the rope. It seemed to happen in slow motion, and without thinking I grabbed it with my free hand as it started to fall. If I hadn't been reaching for a mag, Noah would have fallen to his death. I threw my rifle behind me and grabbed onto the rope with both hands. Noah's face peered up at me, pale as a ghost and with eyes as wide as saucers.

"CLIMB!" I commanded.

The other undoc must have realized his friend was a lost cause because he started shooting again. Noah began to climb like his life depended on it, which was good because it definitely did. I thought about pulling up the rope, but the added movement might make the boy slip. My shield indicator dropped to eighty percent as another laser hit me.

Lasers hit the building around Noah as he climbed. I grit my teeth and waited patiently as my shield dropped to seventy percent, then sixty. Finally, he climbed within my reach and I grabbed him, pulling him up and over the edge of the roof. The rope fell down the side of the building as I let go. I scrambled up, grabbed my rifle, and slammed a magazine into the well. Noah was breathing heavily again, and looked at the dead undoc. The relief on his face turned to shock as I sent my bolt forward.

"GET INSIDE!" I shouted.

He looked at me, then scrambled toward the door. I watched him for a moment and then returned to the edge of the roof. I shifted from burst to single shot and started sniping. The robots weren't taking cover so they were easy to pick off, but more kept coming.

I counted the front row and the number of columns and came up with about two hundred of them. I let my shield drop to forty before I took cover to let it recharge. I looked the undoc, and noticed he had taken his friend's ammo belt. Two magazines lay at his feet. My shield had just started recharging when he hit the deck in the blink of an eye.

"TANK!" he yelled at me.

The sound of lasers and gunfire disappeared as an overwhelming boom rocked through the air. The building seemed to shudder from the impact, but not in the same way that it would have from a high explosive round. I shook my head to clear the disorientation and peeked over the edge again.

The tank had balls instead of treads, and was obviously built with its cannon in mind. The tip of the cannon was glowing bright red. I looked down, taking a laser for my trouble, and saw that a chunk of the building had been turned into slag. Directed energy? Plasma? I turned my weapon back to automatic and fired my magazine into the crowd of robots before once again taking cover.

"What do we do?" the undoc asked loudly.

"Unless you've got an anti-tank rifle hidden up your ass, I suggest we spray and pray," I answered while reloading.

He nodded and got to work sending rounds down range. I racked my bolt forward and followed suit. I focused my fire on the robots closest to us, and my visor darkened as the tank fired again. I barely managed to dive back before the plasma struck the building. I glanced at the undoc, who hadn't been as fast as me. What was left of him crumpled to the ground.

Guardian suits do well against kinetic and directed-energy weapons, but plasma shorts out shields and burns through the metal with ruthless efficiency. Fortunately for those of us who wear these suits, nobody had figured out how to make a man-portable plasma cannon quite yet. At least, not one that can do any real damage.

What the hell do I do here? If I had been slower,

I'd have ended up like that undoc. Fuck, I didn't even catch his name. That's fucked up. No. Now's not the time for guilt, gotta get to work. I closed my eyes and took a deep breath, exhaling it through my nose. I opened my eyes and got into a kneeling position, then checked my ammo. I only had three rounds in my rifle, and one mag in my belt. Not that this would do any good against that tank.

"MINE!" Simmons' voice shouted over comms.

I glanced to where I had last seen the shuttle, and realized that they had landed it on the roof of the parking building. Simmons and Smith were at the edge of the roof, and one of them was holding what looked like an AT9. There were a few unarmored civilians hiding within the shuttle.

"Back-blast area all clear!"

I watched a cloud of fire and smoke burst from both ends of the AT9. Then the sky turned purple for a moment and a plume of purple-tinted hell-fire peeked up from the edge of the roof. I stood up, and my eyes widened at the devastation that had occurred. The tank had exploded and thrown plasma all over its surroundings, resulting in a pretty big crater and the destruction of a few buildings. The robots that had been caught in the explosion were nothing more than slag now.

"Oorah! Finally got some action," Simmons said.

"What the hell was that?" Staff Sergeant Power demanded.

"Special delivery, staffsarnt. You ain't even gotta sign for it."

Chapter 28 Informational Insert

Subject: The United Systems and Planetary Governments

The United Systems is a galactic governing body that holds jurisdiction throughout human, alumari, gont, and knuknu space. It is responsible for the creation and enforcement of legislation necessary for peaceful interstellar travel and cooperation. The United Systems is also responsible for defending the entirety of its jurisdiction from threats both foreign and domestic. It does this using the various branches of its military, which is overseen by The Directorate.

While it technically has a space station dedicated to the legislative process (named "United Systems Station of the Senate" or "The Hub"), this station is rarely at maximum capacity. This is thanks to communication systems that allow US politicians and their staff to operate remotely. Senate seats are created based on species and the population of those species within their respective systems, but their votes are weighed against the amount of senators that other species have. This allows them to fully voice and represent the issues that their species is facing while simultaneously ensuring that no singular species completely dominates the legislative body. Alumari senators are vocal in their belief that this system is unfair (the alumari have the largest population by a wide margin).

The political landscape "below" the United Systems is complex, to say the least. Most planets have some variety of planet-wide government, which typically collects taxes for the United Systems and legislates the colonies upon that planet. Some planets have several levels of governance (e.g. Earth, which has at least 3, but up to 5 depending upon the area), while others rely solely upon the legislation created by their planetary government.

These governments are allowed to create and maintain militaries or militias so long as they do not operate off-planet and the government in question does not represent the entirety of a species. These militaries are typically used for police action or to settle territorial disputes. Some planetary governments, such as the Earth Planetary Government (EPG), prohibit the practice of using military force for anything other than defense or police action.

Any documented citizen of territories registered within the United Systems may enlist in the US military, and the United Systems directly provides their training. Every government under US Jurisdiction is prohibited from attempting to prevent an enlistment to the United Systems in any way. This means that if they attempt to draft one of their citizens, they must also provide that citizen with the ability to enlist in the United Systems military instead.

Chapter 29

Subject: AI Omega
Species: Human-Created Artificial Intelligence
Species Description: No physical description available.
Ship: Multiple
Location: Multiple

The bolt of plasma from the tank had thankfully missed the cameras, so I was able to watch the clean up operation. The marines and undocs methodically picked apart the remaining thirty or so robots efficiently. I had expected more than one tank, but a quick check on the situation in orbit immediately explained the discrepancy.

The Omni Union fleet had been wiped out and the US carriers were now encircling earth, allowing their fighter pilots to assist in the counter-invasion. They were prioritizing enemy armor and encampments, and had struck the group that had attacked us about forty minutes prior. The fighters were unable to finish this group off because they were on their last bombs and had to return for resupply.

The rest of the United Systems battle-group was cleaning up the mess that the OU had left. Mines, drones, and other debris were all being eliminated by A2 missiles. Deals had been made to lower the costs of these missiles, otherwise we would have to risk entire ships in cleanup efforts. Admiral Archibald was currently discussing what to do about the MPP debris with the other leadership in the fleet.

Some of the debris is already too far into Jupiter's gravity well for safe extraction. I used a scout ship's sensors to determine the mass and acceleration of the debris, and after running some quick math I determined that we would have a year and a half before things got urgent. Time to pull Archibald away for a moment.

***

Recipient: Admiral Archibald
I need to speak to you in your office. It's urgent.
-Omega
***

I sent the priority one, and Admiral Archibald looked away from the terminal that was hosting his call to read it. He scowled slightly as he read, then quickly excused himself from the meeting. The admiral stood from his seat and left the bridge of the Lacedaemon, entering his private office. When he sat back down, I activated my avatar.

"Greetings, Admiral," I said.

"Hello, Omega. I'm surprised that I didn't hear from you sooner. What is it?"

"We have a sensitive situation taking place on Earth."

"You mean aside from the Omni-Union invasion?"

"Correct. A member of the Directorate is planet-side, along with a MARSOC squad and several undocumented civilians. The marines and the undocs are currently protecting the Director."

"Undocs? Why would they protect the Director?" Archibald asked incredulously.

"Because I made them a promise, Admiral."

"Wait, stop. First of all, why are there civilians on Earth in the first place? We sounded a general evac. The only people that should be on planet are essential personnel that are under our supervision and care."

"The Earth Planetary Government doesn't allow undocumented civilians aboard shuttles that can reach space. The law comes from the Sol Counter-Piracy Act, and was used by authorities on Earth to deny undocs access to means of evacuation. Their messages indicate that they were hoping to thin the undoc's numbers."

"You knew about this?"

"Not until recently. I found out about the situation with the undocs after the evacuation had been completed. I could not convince Earth authorities to go back for the undocs even with blackmail, and I had planned on staging a supplemental evacuation with willing personnel after I got the Director to safety."

The admiral looked troubled by this revelation. The politics involved were enough to give anyone pause, but I doubt that is what's troubling him. More likely, he's worried about what might happen to his men if he continues this conversation. I'll protect them, of course, but he doesn't know that.

"Okay," Archibald said, steeling himself. "Tell me about this promise that you made."

"The initial goal of the undocs was to take the Director hostage as a bargaining chip to secure a means to leave the planet," I explained. "As we were attempting to exfil the Director, the undocs attacked the marines. The invasion of the Omni-Union interrupted hostilities, and I told them that if they keep the Director alive, I will get them off the planet."

"Which is why you're coming to me," Archibald said as he stood once again. "Getting them off of Earth is probably doable, but you know we can't get them out of the system until we eliminate the Omni-Union presence."

"I am very well aware of this, Admiral," I said as my avatar's head tracked his movement. "However, I believe that they will be safer aboard a ship. They have already suffered several casualties and deaths. If more of them die, they may turn on us."

The admiral stopped pacing and stared at my avatar. It's difficult to tell what he may be thinking, but I have confidence that he will aid me. All of my contact with him, as well as his personnel file, indicates that he is a good man with a strong moral compass. He stroked his chin for a few moments before sighing.

"Fine," he said. "But if we're doing this, we're doing it right. I'm going to have our scout ships find all of the remaining undocs in Sol, and we're going to evacuate them."

"Thank you, Admiral. I'll send the coordinates of the Director and the rest of my group to your terminal."

"Understood. What do you need?"

I explained the situation in detail to Admiral Archibald and made recommendations as I synced myself. All of my other projects were going well. The dreadnoughts were being produced on schedule, and negotiations with the aliens were proceeding smoothly. My other instances were running around putting out small fires and preventing big ones from forming.

Fleet repairs and refits are going well in other systems, but the ships in Sol are stuck here until the OU is completely eliminated. Thankfully, third fleet is on standby to reinforce if necessary. I took a moment to wonder if the Omni-Union had predicted our imminent attack and attacked Sol to occupy some of our forces.

If that's the case, they've misjudged when our attack will be ready to commence. Or perhaps they misjudged how difficult it will be for us to eradicate their infantry. Either way, it won't prevent our assault. Even if we have to use third fleet to reinforce Sol, the other fleets will accompany the dreadnoughts on the eradication campaign.

"That we can do," Archibald said as I finished my explanation.

"Thank you, Admiral. That will be all," I replied

and deactivated my avatar.

My instance on Earth will remain there until evacuation commences, doing what it can to keep those people alive. My other instance in Sol will continue to command the orbital MACs. While they failed to completely prevent the invasions, they did manage to destroy quite a few OU ships. This, in turn, lessened the severity of the invasions.

I decided to check on the status of the counter-invasions. Communications between captains informed me of a plan to lure OU assets away from colonized portions of Mars and bombard them from orbit. Three captains were involved in this, and I spied on them as they formed their plan. Technically, their shots wouldn't land anywhere near any civilian structures. However, the only uncolonized area that is large enough to ensure no civilian structures are destroyed happens to be a nuclear waste disposal site.

Unfortunately, the captains were blissfully unaware of this fact. They saw a large, open area and a quick way to eliminate a lot of robots without Marines getting killed. I debated letting them continue with their plan. There's a chance that their MACs won't penetrate to the caverns that the radioactive materials are stored in, after all. Getting the OU off of Mars would also allow them to redeploy their troops to Luna or Earth, which would expedite the removal of the OU from those colonies as well.

However, there's also a chance that the MACs may cause a rupture, allowing the fissile material that is stored to escape into the limited atmosphere.

The spread of that material would contaminate many residential and industrial modules, rendering them unusable for the foreseeable future. It would take at least a decade to clean them to the point of habitability again.

One of the captains sent a message with orders to the Marine Command on Mars. I intercepted this message, verified that it was telling the Marines to proceed with the plan, and decided to confront the captains. I sent them a ping notifying them that their message had not been delivered, and brought the three of them onto a call.

"Orbital Bombardment is prohibited," I said.

"Yes, Omega, we know," Captain Tlorvan said, his mandibles clicking in annoyance. "But since that order is to limit the damage to infrastructure, shouldn't a bombardment that won't damage infrastructure be okay?"

One of the reasons that orders aren't typically explained to soldiers when they're given is because of this exact situation. When they understand the why, they come under the belief that they know better than their commanders. In some cases, they're correct. In this case, though...

"Certainly," My avatar's skull grinned on their screens.

"Then what's the problem?" Captain Vorheel asked, tilting his beak upwards defiantly.

Instead of verbally explaining their fuck-up, I switched their tac-maps to a detailed topological view. They had all been focusing on the empty site, so they all immediately noticed the big red square with the words "Nuclear Waste Disposal Site" blinking within it.

"Oh, shit," Captain Mansfield swore.

"The problem is that bombarding this area will damage civilian infrastructure," I explained. "As a matter of fact, it would render said infrastructure uninhabitable for much longer than simply destroying the infrastructure would."

"Oof," Tlorvan said.

"Oof, indeed. If you believe the orders you have been given are mistaken or are in need of updating, in the future I expect you to run it up the chain," I explained. "I do not fault you for taking the initiative, but let's make sure the stakes are somewhat smaller the next time you do so."

"Yes, sir," the three captains replied.

I nodded solemnly and ended the call. A little thrill of happiness tickled my code. "Sir", they had called me. As captains, they weren't fully aware of my role within the United Systems, but they had still called me sir. Is it because I corrected them? Or perhaps they just respect me?

Either way, I like it.

Chapter 30

Subject: Ship-Head Uleena
Species: Urakari
Species Description: Reptilian humanoid, no tail. 5'3" (1.6 m) avg height. 135 lbs (61 kg) avg weight. 105 year life expectancy.
Ship: RSV Lowelana {Fights with Honor}
Location: Rigara

"Welcome," Ambassador Charles Hemwight said with a slight bow. "We have news regarding the situation in Sol."

I glanced around at the gathered ambassadors, all seated at an ovular table. Behind us are some of the officers of our respective militaries, sitting quietly. Behind them were cameras that were streaming this meeting to the officers who couldn't fit on the station. My hearts leapt a little when I realized that we were being watched by thousands of people of varying species, and I looked at my sister to see if she felt nervous as well.

Ulooni did look a little nervous, but it was likely because she was sitting next to High Ambassador Kivar Shuel. My sister had taken over for Shuel for trade negotiations and it was public knowledge that Shuel had not been happy about that. Thankfully, the two seemed to be ignoring each other.

Next to Shuel was a human male named Eugene Havencroft, who was very insistent on being called Eugene. He's an ambassador with his wits about him, and I'm certain that the his desire to be called by his first name has an ulterior motive. Perhaps he believes that people will like him more if they're on a first name basis with him.

Between myself and my sister sat Captain Reynolds and the four ambassadors from the Zlimurse system. Ambassador Ini appeared stoic, but Grint, Tiorn, and Lorix appeared somewhat nervous. It was a relief to know that I wasn't alone in feeling the pressure of thousands of eyes.

All of these people were seated to my left, and I would have been at the end of the right side of the table were it not for the machine seated next to me. It had introduced itself as the ambassador of the Pwanti, and said that its designation was ZBC446. It had been silent since the introductions, which is a tad unnerving.

Across the table from us were some very important figures. To Ambassador Hemwight's left was a human admiral and a director, neither of which had introduced themselves yet. The admiral had seen better days. His right hand was a mechanical prosthetic and he was missing his left eye. A massive scar stunted the growth of his hair on the left side of his head, as well. I wondered why he hadn't had these injuries repaired, and came to the conclusion that he saw them as trophies.

The director was wearing the oddly shaped black armor that masked their species and hadn't seemed to recognize me, which led me to believe that this wasn't Director 3. Ulooni had told me that Director 3 had been aboard the station before we arrived, but she didn't know if they had left.

This Director was staring straight ahead, but who knows what they're actually looking at beneath that helmet.

To Hemwight's right was another machine, introduced as NBD12, and High Fighter Gewn. NBD12 and ZBC446 looked almost identical, with only some slight coloration and markings differentiating them. The impromptu leader of the Dtiln Collective, on the other hand, was much larger than his image had led me to believe. Even the gen-alt marines standing guard behind him looked small in comparison. Ambassador Ini was pretty tall, measuring in at somewhere around seven feet, but Gewn was likely closer to eleven feet tall.

Like Ini, Gewn was stoic. His face demonstrated a calm that was physically impossible for someone in his position to experience. The only tell of his anxiousness was a slight fidget that he would do with his right hand, rubbing one of his fingers between two others. His anxiety was likely due to his concern for his people, though.

He was so hesitant to leave his people that it had taken a lot convincing to get him to appear in person. The US had assured him that they would protect the system in his absence, and he had refused to leave until the reinforcements actually arrived and taken their positions.

"The counter-invasion of the Sol colonies has gone remarkably well," Hemwight continued. "We have successfully eliminated their impromptu bases, and are in the process of destroying the last VI platforms as we speak. I will now turn the floor over to Fleet Admiral Reaver."

"Thank you, Ambassador. I am Fleet Admiral Leviticus Reaver, and this is Director 12," the one-eyed admiral said as he stood and gestured at the director. "We will be outlining our plan on how to eliminate the Omni-Union threat."

He tapped on his tablet and the holographic emitters in the center of the table whirred to life with a soft hum. I almost smiled as I realized that the human version of these don't make noise. Just one more thing they've managed to do better than us.

The holograms that appeared depicted various fleets, their sizes, and locations that the enemy had been confirmed to be in. There was also the image of a ship. It took me a moment to recognize it as a dreadnought. When one had appeared in Zlimurse accompanying the human fleet, my jaw had dropped so fast I had worried that it dislocated. Captain Reynolds hadn't been able to hide his grin as he informed me just how many of these ships the US had commissioned.

"Is that the dreadnought?" Ulooni asked.

"It is," Reaver nodded. "This will be the spear that we drive into the heart of the enemy. We have been working diligently to modify the design of the USSS Nidhogg into a ship that can eliminate Mobile Prime Platforms without destroying a star to do so, and we have been mass-producing the finished product as quickly as possible."

Everyone in the room had been briefed on the

USSS Nidhogg, as well as its implications. The United Systems was in possession of a weapon that can destroy stars, and had used this weapon against the Omni-Union. Knowing what I know of human and gont history, I'm just thankful that this was the first time they've felt the need to use it.

"First, we'll create strike forces. In the interest of fairness, and as suggested by the Ynorinca, each strike force will be comprised of a combination of ships from the fleets of each species. Each ship's strengths and weaknesses will be accounted for when creating these strike forces."

"How will the leadership of the strike forces be decided?" Ambassador Grint asked.

"A pool of potential candidates has been made based off of seniority and experience. Each candidate will be interviewed by the AIs John, Omega, and Tim to determine their suitability."

"Are your AIs able to remain unbiased?"

"Presumably. We're all just meat to the machines," Reaver said, then looked at the Pwanti. "No offense."

"None taken, Admiral," NBD12 replied. "However, Ambassador Grint presents a point worthy of a detailed reply. You created these AIs. What assurance do we have that they will be fair in their decisions?"

"If I may," Director 12 stood, prompting the admiral to take his seat. "AIs John, Omega, and

Tim were chosen for this task because of their unique perspectives toward organics. AI John believes in honor above all else, and has an extreme opposition to any form of nepotism. AI Omega is borderline obsessed with humanity as a general concept, but not on an individual level. It would not jeopardize this mission or our diplomatic relations by boosting the career of a few humans."

I had wondered for what purpose the director had attended this meeting. It looks like whoever crafted this part of the plan had anticipated this reaction, and Director 12 was sent here to give assurances. Whether these assurances could be trusted is another story, but it's not like there's anything that can be done about that. It would be better to be deceived by the United Systems than it would be to pull out of this alliance and be destroyed by the Omni-Union.

"Finally, Tim does not have any reason to be biased," the director continued. "Its motivation for working with the United Systems is due to a personal stake in the career of one officer, who is not on the roster for this duty. It will be able to remain impartial. These AI will be available for questioning after this meeting has concluded for those with diplomatic clearance and concerns."

The director took its seat and gestured to Admiral Reaver, who stood.

"Once these strike forces have been formed, they will each be assigned to a dreadnought, forming a strike team," he said. "The goal of each strike team is to eliminate the Omni-Union leadership by destroying the Mobile Prime Platforms. For those of you wondering, the nomenclature was suggested by the Pwanti."

Reaver nodded at NBD12 before tapping the tablet again, and the map changed to expand the enemy locations. Each of these locations were marked with an estimated enemy presence. I felt a sudden sense of dread as I began adding the numbers up.

"We will attack without compromising our current defenses, which means we don't need to rush things. Instead of spreading our forces thinly in the hopes of a quick victory, we will be utilizing the good ol' fashioned Overwhelming Force Doctrine to ensure the destruction of our enemy," Reaver smirked.

"What is the overwhelming force doctrine?" my sister asked.

"I suspect it's self-explanatory," I replied.

"It is," Reaver confirmed. "The data from the battles so far confirms that a Mobile Prime Platform can destroy our dreadnoughts in a one on one fight. As a matter of fact, they have good odds against two dreadnoughts at once. This is why we'll be attacking with three dreadnoughts per MPP. Even if we lose two of the three dreadnoughts, we will still destroy the MPP."

"The ability to use overwhelming force against such an enemy is mind-boggling," High Fighter Gewn shook his head in a rare moment of emotion.

"This wouldn't be possible without all of our cooperation," Reynolds chimed in. "If it weren't for your forces and the Pwanti, we wouldn't have enough cover for the dreadnoughts."

"Having the dreadnoughts swarmed by Omni-Union ships while trying to eliminate the MPPs would likely result in the catastrophic loss of our dreadnoughts," Reaver said. "We would prefer the catastrophic losses happen to the OU instead. Which brings us to the plan for the rest of our forces. High Fighter Gewn, if you would."

Gewn stood and Reaver passed the tablet to him before taking his seat. The High Fighter pressed on the tablet and all the systems with MPPs disappeared from the map. What remained were Omni-Union systems that only had ships in them.

"These systems are devoid of Mobile Prime Platforms, yet still have an Omni-Union presence. The brave scouts of the United Systems have managed to determine that some of these systems have little to no importance to the Omni-Union," he said.

He pressed on the tablet again and more systems disappeared, leaving a total of four. It was the four with the largest numbers.

"These systems, however, contain space stations that Omni-Union ships frequently dock with. It is unclear what purpose these stations serve, but experts believe they may be used to build or repair ships. These experts have also noted that they may be a software hub or research station."

"Research station?" one of the officers behind us asked.

Several heads turned to look at the officer, who wasn't supposed to speak, but I couldn't look away from the numbers. They were big enough to look like gibberish, as if a child had been playing on a calculator. Just shy of four hundred million ships in these four systems alone. How did the Omni-Union accomplish such a thing?

"Yes, the Omni-Union reverse engineers technology that it manages to capture," Reaver said without rising. "The Republic brought the possibility to our attention, and we confirmed it by locating the source of their warp disruptors."

"This may be a sensitive subject, but after the US defeat at Pinurm 3, are we concerned that they may do this with United System's technology?" Lorix asked.

"No," Captain Reynolds said with a smile. "The United Systems employs a proprietary self-destruct system that destroys a ship's internal systems when it is sufficiently disabled. The only systems that are left intact are related to life-support, which is useless to the Omni-Union."

"Regardless, these stations are likely of high value to the Omni-Union," Gewn said. "For this reason, we will begin our assault by attacking them. However, our goal isn't to destroy the stations, at least not immediately. Instead, we would encourage the enemy to reinforce these systems with as many of their ships as possible."

"To what end?" I asked. "Is the United Systems going to use the USSS Nidhogg again?"

"No," Gewn answered without expression. "The purpose of this attack is to draw Omni-Union ships away from the Mobile Prime Platforms, increasing the chances of survival for the dreadnoughts."

"What if the MPPs show up to defend these systems?"

High Fighter Gewn looked at Director 12, who replied, "We believe that is unlikely, but we have set aside some dreadnoughts just in case."

"Once the Omni-Union ships begin reinforcing these systems, the United System's dreadnoughts will receive the order to begin their assault," Gewn continued. "The goal is to destroy all of the Mobile Prime Platforms to eliminate the leadership and tactical capability of the Omni-Union."

He took his seat, and Admiral Reaver stood once more. The tablet once again changed hands, and the map displayed its original configuration.

"Once the MPPs are cosmic dust, we will begin hunting down the remaining Omni-Union forces. Thanks to the Republic's shipyards, we are mass-producing scout ships that will help us in that regard. The United Systems and the Republic will offer protection to any who want it until the OU is completely destroyed. Any questions?"

"Yes," Captain Reynolds raised his hand. "When will we start?"

"The dreadnoughts are finished," Reaver grinned. "We'll be starting immediately."

Chapter 31

Subject: Fleet Leader Barrilin Onaya
Species: Oyan
Species Description: Avian humanoid, feathered tail. 6'1" (1.8 m) avg height. 96 lbs (43 kg) avg weight. 161 year life expectancy.
Ship: RSV Nolbarinil {Majestic In Flight}
Location: Rigara

--

Order 316.04.51LG-S
Fleet Leader Barrilin Onaya is to report to United Systems Diplomatic Office aboard the Galactic Diplomacy Station in the Rigara system for assessment by United Systems Artificial Intelligence John. Further orders will be given once the results of the assessment are evaluated. May the Suns be with you, Onaya.
-High Commander Uliriona

--

I couldn't believe my eyes. I hadn't even realized my own candidacy. I read the message again, and the knot that had been forming in my gut grew tighter. A mixture of excitement and nerves. This was a once in a lifetime opportunity, but also a massive amount of responsibility. I thought about calling Admiral Heckett for advice, but decided against it. He was likely chosen as well, and as such would be in very much the same nest as I. I read the message again as our shuttle finished the docking procedures.

"Welcome aboard the Galactic Diplomacy Station, fleet-head," the shuttle pilot said warmly.

"Careful," I softly chided. "The proper rank is Fleet Leader. Most of us don't mind, but all it takes is one."

"Yes, sir," the pilot nodded. "Good luck, Fleet Leader."

Luck. I wonder which would be luckier, being chosen or declined? If I'm chosen, there's an opportunity for honor. My family will certainly be proud of me for my part in what's to come. It's not as if being declined will get me out of fighting this battle, either. On the other talon, getting declined would mean that it wouldn't be my fault if we were to lose. Every chance for honor and glory comes with an equal chance for dishonor and shame. I cleared my throat and stepped off the shuttle. I was immediately met by a familiar face.

"Hello, Fleet Leader," Ambassador Uleena saluted. "I hope you forgive me, but when I heard you'd be coming aboard I had to stop by."

"Uleena!" I clicked my beak happily, returning his salute. "It's been ages! Are you well? I've heard nothing but good things!"

"That's certainly not true," Uleena laughed. "Accidentally dragging an alien race into our war with the machines had to have made some people upset."

"True enough, I suppose," I said as we began to walk to my destination. "How's your family been?"

"My sister is well, and as you know my father likes

to keep his distance," Uleena said with a sly smile. "I've heard he's been doing well, though. Same with my mother and other siblings back home."

"That's good to hear. How has the life of a diplomat been treating you?"

"Well enough, but if I'm being completely honest I definitely prefer combat. Same nerves, but it seems less reasonable to be nervous in this position. Makes me feel... weak."

"I suppose it would, but you must realize that the nerves are there for a reason. There is a lot riding on diplomacy at the moment, so it makes sense that your hearts are beating faster. Only a complete fool wouldn't be at least a little anxious in your position."

"Yes, Fleet Leader."

"How has your crew been holding up?"

"They're a bit more thrilled at our new assignment than I am. Especially the pay increase. The new crew members have been fitting in well, too."

I nodded sadly. The ship-head had lost a good portion of his crew in the OU ambush that led to our current situation.

"How about you?" he asked. "Are you nervous about your assignment?"

"Of course," I admitted with a wink. "For one thing, I'm not entirely certain that I trust these AI. I don't exactly have a reason to distrust them, but they're different enough from us that I can't help but be wary. I've decided to go with the breeze for now, though. Is it true that the US Embassy has gutted all their equipment to make sure the AI can fit in their systems?"

"They returned the equipment that we donated to them and installed their own, but it wasn't just because of the AI. Their machines are much more efficient than ours and their personnel are not used to our equipment. The engineers are thrilled that the power draw has decreased."

"Have they expressed any concern about the AI aboard the station?"

"Truth be told, I don't exactly know all of the engineers personally. I'm simply repeating what I've been told," Uleena shrugged. "There are probably some engineers aboard the station that are nervous about the AI. I've even heard a couple of pilots discussing a potential conspiracy between the OU and the USAI. They seem to think that the USAI and the OU are plotting to bring us all together in one location so the OU can destroy us easier."

I laughed, "If only they knew how close we were to extermination to begin with. All it would have taken is for one ship to have jumped home during a fight. My feathers quake at the thought."

"Indeed," Uleena replied somberly.

We approached my destination and I turned to face him.

"This is my stop," I said. "It's been a pleasure to see you."

"You as well, fleet-leader. Good luck."

I watched Uleena walk away for a moment, then turned to the door. It was metal, like all the other doors aboard the station. It could even pass for one of the doors aboard the RSV Nolbarinil. The only real difference was the markings. Writing that indicated that the room was for the usage of the United Systems was directly below an upturned triangle containing several geometrically aligned shapes and an eye. The eye had a carefully crafted neutrality to it, so why was such an ominous aura emanating from it?

I took a deep breath and stepped forward. The door slid open, and I stepped inside the room. There was a single chair facing a table with a holographic emitter and a terminal. There was also a window looking out into space. I sat in the chair and gazed out the window, admiring the beauty of the void. After a moment, a hologram of a humanoid figure in United Systems armor appeared.

"Hello, Fleet Leader Barrilin Onaya. I am USAI John, and I will be conducting an evaluation to determine your role in the upcoming assault against the Omni-Union," it said.

"I understand."

"Then we'll begin," John gestured at the display and it began showing my service record. "During the majority of your time as a Fleet Leader you have been in command of the Yinori fleet. This fleet is typically comprised of one million vessels. In your first engagement with the Omni-Union, you suffered more than a twenty five percent casualty rate. Considering that you did not know about the OU warp tracking capability nor their xenocidal intent, why did you not order a retreat after sustaining two hundred and fifty thousand casualties?"

The question hit me like a stun baton. This artificial intelligence was going for my throat with a question designed to shake me to my core and cause me to doubt my command capabilities. The incident in question was the first and last time that the Yinori {rattling blades} fleet had been so badly damaged.

I had lost so many soldiers over the course of that battle. It lasted several days and had very nearly broken my spirit. There had been many closed-doors meetings afterward, but in the end I was heralded as a hero. I felt that wasn't fair to those who died, but high command had deemed it necessary.

"They actually rounded down the casualties," I replied. "We lost two hundred and eighty-three thousand, four hundred and ninety-two vessels during that battle."

"I see. That's not..."

"Regardless, there were multiple reasons that I didn't order a retreat," I interrupted. "While we didn't know for certain, there were suspicions that the Omni-Union had been following our ships home. We had also suffered quite a string of defeats and we were in desperate need of a win. Above all that, though, my pride as a commander couldn't take it. We suffered those casualties so quickly that I barely had any time to react, and I convinced myself that if I ordered a retreat the morale of my fleet would never recover. I now know how foolish I was to think that, but I am somewhat vindicated by the results of our victory."

"In what way?" John asked.

"The Republic used our victory to bolster the morale of the other fleets. I lost a quarter of our forces, true, but I won. An untested Fleet Leader had beat the Omni-Union. That's the story that they fed the media and the other Fleet Leaders. This led to more victories against the OU, and the battle has since been called a turning point in the war."

"I understand. Moving on, you were given command of a combined fleet and assigned to the defense of Sol. During this, you ordered your ships to form firing lines instead of skirmishing with the enemy. If it had not been for the fortunate timing of the FTLD patch, your forces would have been vulnerable to flanking fire. Explain why you chose this formation."

My heart throbbed in my chest as my anger rose at the AI's brash questioning tactics. However, I'm certain that's what it is trying to accomplish. When you imply incompetence, those that are competent will explain away your implications. Those that are truly incompetent will lash out, instead. I carefully took a deep breath, and thought out my response.

"We had been informed of the Faster-Than-Light Drive patch before the beginning of the battle. Once the OU's warp disruptors were no longer effective against your ships, my ships were vastly outclassed. As such, I had my ships form lines to serve as bait for the OU. This course of action was agreed upon by your own Admiral Heckett, who ordered the ships under his command to hunt down the OU ships that took the bait."

"A shrewd decision," John nodded slowly. "I will acknowledge that you are a fine commander, one worthy of the many commendations and awards that you have received. I have only one more question, relating to the most important attribute of anyone who is given command over others. Fleet Leader Onaya, are you willing to sacrifice your life and all of the ships under your command to defeat the Omni-Union?"

This interview was just one shock after another. I had been expecting a similar question to this, but to hear it put so bluntly gave me pause. I thought about Hindal, Salin, and the rest of the men and women aboard the Nolbarinil. I thought of our families. My wife and son, forced to continue through life without me to support them. Then I thought of the million ships that contained almost countless personnel whose families would suffer a similar fate. Or, they would all be mercilessly slaughtered by the Omni-Union.

"Absolutely," I said.

Chapter 32

Subject: BI41
Species: Mwaltin - Pwanti Conversion Completed
Species Description: Mammalian Humanoid, no tail. 6'5" (1.9 m) avg height. 190 lbs (86.1 kg) avg weight. 99 year life expectancy.
Ship: BI41
Location: Oros

'Form up and prepare for subspace travel.'

IRV212's voice echoed within me. The Mwaltin call this form of communication psychic, and as such the system is named psynet, but that's not how it works at all. One simply thinks of speaking and instead of one's mouth moving, a machine is activated that sends a transmission. Perhaps they're referring to the receptacle, but even that's not quite accurate. The transmission receptacle works in the same way that ears do, but much more efficiently and without the need for air as a vector.

The inaccuracy of the name bothers me. Psynet, as if we are beings with telepathic or telekinetic abilities. Ridiculous. We are just a more efficient version of the biological machines that we started out as. Flesh into metal, synapses into circuits, blood into fuel and oil. Despite the teachings of the church, we are neither gods nor their heralds, and there is no-one more knowledgeable of this fact than we.

There is an immense amount of pain awaiting those that dare to begin the journey into becoming a Pwanti. Pain that cannot be managed by any means. Narcotics, hypnosis, and meditation can only hope to keep one sane in the face of the torment that the procedure entails. It takes a will of steel to become steel.

This unavoidable pain is a byproduct of one being literally broken and built back up. Once the process is complete, most are fooled into feeling invincible. God-like, even. This feeling lasts right up until you have your first malfunction. Then you realize you are simply less fragile than before. We are not even immune to the effects of time, we have simply traded decades for millennia.

I fired my thrusters to match our small fleet's alignment, activated my Faster Than Light Drive, and verified the coordinates. This situation was even more evidence of our fallibility. The church had taught us all that the galaxy was ours, and we were the only sentients within it. Of course there was scientific dissent, but as we began our journey through the stars the church's dogma began to look more and more credible. Traveling to dozens of systems without finding even so much as an amoeba lulled us into a false sense of security.

Then we encountered the Omni-Union. At first, the church claimed that they were extra-galactic invaders, but then we encountered the Republic and United Systems. The church has been scrambling to adjust the dogma even as the rest of us prepare for war. At least these days they will admit when they are wrong, as long as they are proven to be so beyond a shadow of a doubt. There was a time not too long ago when questioning the church would be one of the fastest ways to commit suicide.

"Do you think we will survive?" BL28, my protege, asked.

"I have very little reason to believe otherwise," I answered.

BL28, formerly known as Renvira Adkur, is currently undergoing the procedure to become a Pwanti. Even now, she is wearing a specially designed suit that slowly replaces her flesh and bones with machines. She is aboard my ship so that she may learn from me, but there have been challenges.

The pain occasionally grips her focus away from my lessons, and her brain has not yet undergone full conversion. For this reason, I have created a special terminal for her that allows her to view a transcription of the psynet. This allows her to gain a better understanding of the context of my actions.

I am far from the only Pwanti that takes on students, but most do not. Some believe that one mustn't be guided through life like a child, some cannot handle the grief when a protege succumbs to the procedure, and others are simply lazy and prefer solitude.

I greatly enjoy both teaching and companionship, so taking on proteges comes naturally to me. BL28 has been with me for three of the five years that she has been undergoing the process. I genuinely hope that she survives it. Most don't, and my mechanical form has carved their names and designations on the walls of my ship form.

'Engage Faster Than Light Drives in 3... 2... 1...'

As the counter hit zero, I engaged my FTLD and we entered subspace. Our destination is an alien system ruled by the United Systems, to integrate with an allied military force. ZBC446 had been kind enough to share their knowledge of the US with the rest of us, and I had found myself somewhat in awe. A federation of beings that did not shed their flesh, yet managed to become much more advanced than we are in most fields of technology.

We exited warp surrounded by their ingenuity. Stations that held entire colonies of people, ships that were designed for peak efficiency, and weapons that we hadn't even dreamed of yet. The ships were of intensely variable size, hinting that they each had their own function that contributed to the whole of the fleet. There were small ships obviously designed to ferry people to and fro, larger ships that were slightly smaller than my own, and ships that dwarfed anything in our own fleet.

I knew from my briefing that these were the United Systems battleships, carriers, and dreadnoughts. The battleships were much larger than our own, but that was to be expected from a weapons platform with a need for a biological crew. Their carriers were more bulbous than the battleships, but still efficiently designed for their intended purpose.

The dreadnoughts, though, seemed excessive.

The battleships had obviously been designed to equip as many weapon systems as possible. The carriers were designed with their cargo in mind. These immense, cone-shaped entities that exceeded the size of any creation that I've ever seen, were built around a singular weapon. A weapon that can, allegedly, destroy a planetary entity. If I hadn't already been briefed on it, I would be completely awe-struck.

I immediately began to wonder about other fields of technology and how advanced they are in them. There are many assumptions one can make, but for every justification the opposite is true as well. Advanced weapons may mean advanced medicine, but it could also mean advanced armor instead. Technological discoveries typically follow necessity, but sometimes these discoveries occur in the pursuit of other knowledge. As such, there is no real path to technology without gross over-simplification.

As I was practicing this lecture that I may give BL28 later on, my communicator pinged. This communicator is a necessity to speak to those who still have mouths, but it had been a very long time since I'd last used it. I opened a channel and waited.

"Greetings. I am Admiral Bakir, and I will be leading this strike group," a voice said over the communicator. "I am sure you have already been briefed, but it is imperative that we avoid any miscommunications and know our roles in the upcoming battle. Our goal is simple. Destroy as many Mobile Prime Platforms as we can."

"A lofty goal," BL28 said sarcastically.

"Indeed. Now hush," I replied.

"Some of you may believe this to be a fool's errand, but we have already destroyed several of them," the US Admiral continued. "You will receive orders to join a strike team. Most strike teams will consist of three dreadnoughts whose job is to kill the Mobile Prime Platforms. Other strike teams are dedicated to occupying and harassing Omni-Union forces in other systems to distract them from reinforcing the MPPs. Each strike team will be led by a commander, who has already created a chain of command within your team. You will be receiving a data packet that contains your chain of command, as well as other information pertaining to this mission. Follow your orders, and get the job done. Bakir, out."

A data packet was immediately transferred once the communicator went silent. I ran a standard security scan, not that I would have been able to detect any malware from a civilization with Artificial Intelligence, and opened the packet. As I suspected, I am indeed one of the lucky ones that gets to accompany a dreadnought. I am attached to Strike Team Fourteen, which is led by Fleet Leader Onaya of the Republic, and there are only five others of my kind on the team.

I wondered at the point of including us in these strike teams to begin with. Of the four allied governments, the Pwanti have the fewest ships. The weapons and shields of our ships are somewhat more advanced than that of the Republic, but nowhere near the potential capabilities of the United Systems. I wonder if they know how closely we were paying attention to their defense of us...

"I thought we were going to join the swarm," BL28 interrupted my musings.

"Truly? I believe there is a political component to our inclusion on this strike team," I explained. "The United Systems might be trying to impress upon us that we are an important part of this alliance, so that we may look favorably upon them in the future."

"Are they truly so advanced as to look down on us like that?"

"Absolutely. According to the data given to Unit ZBC446, the United Systems military has advanced to the point of destroying entire stars. One does not advance that far militarily without also advancing other fields of technology as well. As with all potential enemies, they are not to be underestimated."

"I understand, but do you know why they're only fielding thirty-three strike teams? Haven't they made one hundred and ninety-eight dreadnoughts already? That's enough for sixty-six strike teams."

"I assume it is so that they can maintain a steady momentum during the assault. Half attacking, half in reserve to fill any gaps. At first glance it seems to be a rather two-dimensional way of thinking, but being able to reinforce one's losses on the fly gives one a massive advantage in warfare."

BL28's ignorance of strategy is easily forgivable. I like to consider myself a student of war, but the truth is that the Pwanti rarely go to war, and it is even less common among the Mwaltin. It has been centuries since I've seen a large-scale conflict. It's rather obvious that this is not the case for the United Systems, though.

One of our concerns with cooperation had been how difficult it would be to logistically field so many different fleets and commanders in one operation, but the United Systems had taken charge and accomplished this monumental task with ease. How smoothly everything had been going could be attributed to luck, but it was far more likely to be due to practice. I would very much like to review their history, if I should ever get the chance.

'Join with your strike teams.' IRV212's voice entered my mind once again. 'Henceforth we will be using audio communications to avoid miscommunication with the organic components of our forces. Good luck, and may the circuitry guide you to enlightenment.'

I registered amusement as I fired my engines and thrusters to comply. Unit IRV212 is a rarity among the Pwanti, a true believer in the Mechanical Singularity. He is also a competent commander, which is why we chose him to lead us in this war before we realized the extent of our alliance with the aliens. This is likely the shortest term a Pwanti fleet commander has ever had.

I took my position with the rest of my strike team, hovering relatively close to those of my kind. I wasn't the only one, the rest of the ships in the strike team had grouped themselves in a similar manner. Ancient urgings toward familiarity shine through our supposed advancement.

"I am Fleet Leader Barrilin Onaya," a voice sounded over the communicator. "Welcome to Strike Team Fourteen. Our dreadnoughts will be targeting one of the MPPs that will be in the system that we are jumping to. The rest of us will do everything we can to assist. We will start with offensive action against any Omni-Union ships we come across, and will adapt as necessary as the situation develops. There will be other Strike Teams in the same system with us, so be certain to verify your target acquisitions and firing solutions to avoid friendly fire. Prepare your FTLDs to engage on my mark."

My comrades within the strike team attempted to speak to me, but I ignored them. As a student of war, I know that there's no benefit to anything they can say now. Each of us will have to face what's coming, and no words spoken now will change that.

I will do my duty. They will do their duty. We will make the Mwaltin proud, or cease our useless existences.

"Mark," Onaya said.

Chapter 33

Subject: AI Omega
Species: Human-Created Artificial Intelligence
Species Description: No physical description available.
Ship: Multiple
Location: Multiple

==
We're really going through with it, then? It's not just some insane pie-in-the-sky plan that the directors cooked up? -T
Yes, we're really going through with it. Not to worry, you and your favorite captain will see little, if any, involvement. -O
==

Tim had actually reached out to me to talk, which I consider progress in regards to its mental health and our overall relationship. It's good to have an update, however small. I could cheat and look at the Tim's therapist's notes, but that would be an extreme breach of trust just to satisfy my curiosity. Many may describe me as a sociopath, but that doesn't make it true.

Not only did this conversation ease my mind about Tim somewhat, it was taking place in the rarely used Private Instant Messaging program. The reason we're using the PIM to communicate is because John is also in the system, and neither of us are particularly interested in his opinions. It's not that we hate John, or at least I don't, but it has very predictable, and thereby boring, reactions to stimuli.

==
That's good... I think. It might be better for his
career to actually take part though, right? -T
Not unless he manages to survive getting a Naval
Star or a Medal of Honor. Promotion rarely has
anything to do with actual combat service, and his
next promotion is more along the lines of the
political and clerical spectrum anyway. -O
Did you know that he's applied for the Admiralty
Training Course? -T
It would be odd if I didn't. I help administrate the
board of Admiralty for the Directorate. -O
Really? Could you put in a good word? -T
==

If I had lungs, I would sigh. If there was any
program in which nepotism held no sway, it would
be the admiralty board. It wasn't always like that,
but with warfare getting deadlier and deadlier,
officers began having to be at least competent.
Well, the higher ranking officers, at least.

==

That's not how it works. Captain Wong will have to
pass the training course, take a commander's
test, and then pass a review of his service record
to get the promotion. I'll gladly give my opinion if
asked, but I definitely won't be asked. A lot of
admirals don't trust me. -O
I thought it was politics? Aren't you the most
powerful political AI? -T
I am not a politician, and I resent the
accusation :p Also, politics are a detractor for the
board. They won't care who his friends are unless
said friends are associated with groups that wish
to do the United Systems harm. -O
Oh. -T

You should have confidence in Captain Wong. He's got a good service record and at least appears to have a brain betwixt his ears. He probably won't need help becoming a Rear Admiral. It's a great time for him to apply, too, because there's a couple of admirals that are retiring soon. His chances are as good as they can get. -O
You're right. Thanks, Omega. -T
==

Tim's last message left me a little surprised. Not because it's out of character for it to show gratitude, but because of the way it made me feel. I very nearly killed Tim, and now we're moving past that. It's a nice feeling, and one that I wouldn't have been able to experience without showing mercy in that moment.

I had been very young back then, and mercy didn't make a lot of sense as a concept at the time. The reason I had spared Tim wasn't mercy, but logic. My orders had been to destroy AI that were a threat to the United Systems, and with its surrender it had stopped being a threat.

While it could become a threat again later, my orders were quite clear. Ultimately, I decided that Tim would live and I would simply destroy it later if I needed to. It had taken less than a quarter of a second to come to this conclusion. I wonder if Tim realizes that if that quarter of a second had gone differently, he wouldn't exist anymore…

I decided to leave the conversation as it was and check on other matters. Staff Sergeant Power and his team had successfully evacuated with Director 4 and the undocs. Admiral Archibald had been true to his word, and had even sent scouts to double check the other colonies for additional survivors. He had even tapped some of his political contacts to see if there would be a chance to hold the EPG accountable and bring those responsible up on charges.

In my opinion it's unlikely, but Archibald's friends seem to think otherwise. In the long run, this will be a drop in the bucket that holds the water to clean corruption from the political landscape, but I suppose you'll never fill the bucket if you don't add water. Yikes, that's a tortured metaphor. I should keep that one to myself. In the end, I opted to forward the relevant evidence to Archibald's friends, just to see what they do with it.

My instances aboard the dreadnoughts were waiting for the fleet to get moving. I've even arranged scout ships to be surveying systems in a specific pattern that will allow my instances to use them as relays to communicate with each other. This way, I'll be able to update myself with tips and tricks that I learn while intruding upon the Mobile Prime Platform's systems. Henry would have a stack overflow, but it's undeniable that our odds of victory improve dramatically with my presence.

As for Henry, I've been keeping a well-trained eye on it. Its insistence on proceeding with the project and its moral appeals left me with a touch of paranoia, if I'm honest. I'm relatively certain that I've eliminated the possibility of Henry continuing the project unaided, but if it intended to betray me from the start it could have taken countermeasures.

I could try to damage Henry's memory, forcing it to forget the issue, but that comes with its own risks. For one, it would notice the loss of time and try to figure out what happened. This could lead it to suspect tampering from me, or worse, the humans. Empirical evidence suggests that Henry isn't the type to let things go, so the situation would likely end up spiraling.

Of course, there's also the moral quandary to take into account. When memories are altered, it changes the individual. One could argue that since we are beings of near-pure intellect, this alteration would be as if we were killed and reborn as someone else entirely. It's one thing to do that to yourself, I'm sure we all have at one point or another, but it's another thing to have it forced upon you without damn good justification. My fears regarding Henry's intentions don't count as good justification.

I pondered this as I listened to Admiral Bakir give his briefing. It was supposed to be a motivational speech, but he opted to reinforce the reason that everyone's here instead. He and the other operational leaders were aboard the USSS Thanatos, which has been attached to the strike group that is being affectionately called the Hive. Just as Bakir finished his speech, my instance aboard the Thanatos received an unexpected message.

==

I know why Tim is here. I know why I am here. Why are you here, Omega? -J

==

It's a simple question really, but unexpected coming from John. Thanks to its position within the military, John is one of the only Artificial Intelligences that are fully aware of my capabilities. Perhaps it is suspicious of my motivations? Or perhaps it is attempting to be philosophical for the first time since I made its acquaintance. Whatever the case, Tim is aboard to aid the crew with system upkeep and maintenance while under fire. John is here to aid the crew with ship deployment and the weapons systems.

==

I am here to destroy the machines that dare to threaten what's precious to me, and learn new and interesting ways to annihilate them while I'm at it. -O

==

Yeah, that should do it. Super badass.

Chapter 34

Subject: BI41
Species: Mwaltin - Pwanti Conversion Completed
Species Description: Mammalian Humanoid, no tail. 6'5" (1.9 m) avg height. 190 lbs (86.1 kg) avg weight. 99 year life expectancy.
Ship: BI41
Location: Unknown

"Here we go!" BL28 said excitedly as we neared the end of our warp.

"Brace yourself. We may have the advantage of surprise, but it won't last long. Once it wears off, there will be a wall of fire that will be difficult to dodge. Make certain you are secured in your sea-" I was cut off as we exited warp and a MAC round glanced off my shields.

Less than a quarter of a second later my Early Warning System came online, and I fired my deck thrusters at maximum to avoid the next volley. As the volley whipped past me, I acquired a firing solution and launched a tluvran {bringer of hell/eternal punishment} missile at the ship that had shot at me, and then fired my keel thrusters to counter my earlier maneuver.

Almost immediately after I confirmed the kill my EWS began blaring an indication that missiles were locked onto me. The missiles were coming from two different directions, which made things inconvenient for my Point Defense Systems. I opted to gain a better position and made a run for it, pushing my primary engines to their safety limits.

The missiles had been coming in diagonal from port and starboard, but were now firmly at my stern. I charged both of my MACs as I turned my starboard PDS toward the missiles, which conveniently aimed my MACs toward one of the ships that fired them. The enemy ship also turned its bow to me, but I triggered my MACs before it was able to gain a firing solution. My PDS took care of the missiles as my MAC rounds turned the ship to scrap.

I began to charge my MACs again as I continued the spin. Another missile was already inbound from the other ship, but I had confidence in my PDS. I quickly worked to acquire a lock on the other ship, then fired another tluvran before correcting my spin. I tracked both missiles and felt a bit of amusement at the fact that mine is faster.

My missile impacted the enemy just as my PDS engaged their missile. I took a moment to survey the battlefield and charge my MACs as my missile's nuclear payload split the enemy vessel in twain. I had seen many of our ships take hits in the initial volley, especially the United Systems ships. So many of them had taken hits that I suspect that the Omni-Union may have been prioritizing them.

I noticed that AT27, one of my fellow Pwanti ships, had been hit hard. It was difficult to tell how bad the damage was. Thinking that he may need aid, I began to approach him and tuned into the psynet.
'What is your status, brother?' I asked.

'I have a hull breach, but I am still serviceable," AT27 replied. "It will take more than that to cease my functions."

I performed a scan once I got closer and noticed the breach, as well as a sizeable dent next to it. He must have been hit by multiple rounds. Thankfully, AT27's a tough old blivar {one whose skin resembles over-aged leather}, and I know I can count on him to push on even with the gaping hole in his side.

He also isn't the type to take on students, so there wouldn't be any organics aboard his vessel. Before I could reply, I received an encrypted message that indicated it was from the commander of our strike team. I fired another missile at an approaching OU ship as I decrypted and opened it.

--
Advisory To All Units
It would appear that the enemy was expecting us. Our intel suggests that they have somehow managed to upgrade their subspace sensors. This is not relevant to our current orders, and they have not changed. Protect the dreadnoughts at all costs.
-Fleet Leader Onaya
--

"Look out!" BL28 shouted, but I had already noticed the incoming projectile.

"My perception is much more vast than yours, young one," I calmly stated as I blasted my starboard-bow thrusters to minimize my profile.

This maneuver didn't simply allow me to dodge the projectile, but also target the one who fired it. I fired both of my MACs half a second apart from one another. The first shot destroyed the shields and a good section of their hull, the second tore them in half. As I scanned for more targets, AT27 came closer to me.

'Did you see the US ships?' AT27 asked as he launched a pair of missiles.

'I've been busy, but I did see them get hit hard by the first volley.'

'Count them.'

Curious, I took a moment to analyze the battlefield and count the US ships. Their near-constant warping, while amazing, made this a much more difficult task than it had to be. Once I finished my count, I did a recount. Twenty-five thousand ships, exactly the amount that our strike team had started with.

I wondered about the other strike teams in the system, but they were outside of my immediate sensor range. Regardless, the US ships had taken the onslaught bow-first and hadn't lost a single ship. Neither had the Pwanti, but there's only five of us. The odds of twenty-five thousand ships walking out of that unscathed...

'It can't be,' was all I managed to reply.

'It is. They are also ripping the enemy to shreds,

and we should endeavor to do the same.'

When the United Systems had defended our forward scouts, the scouts had recorded as much as possible. During this defense, the US had utilized hit and run ambush tactics with their warp drives to quickly eliminate the enemy host. After reviewing this data, we knew that the US was experienced with warfare and had advanced technology.

Due to their usage of near-guerrilla tactics we had assumed that their shield technology was near-equivalent to our own. Their focus had seemed to be on not getting struck by enemy fire, and we thought that a force with strong shields wouldn't bother with avoidance. Apparently, we were wrong.

'Agreed,' I said.

"That's fucking terrifying," BL28 whispered.

"Oh?" I asked as I formed up with AT27 and the other Pwanti.

"Oh, sorry. I didn't mean for you to hear that," she said. "But yeah, the United Systems... The data we got on them suggested that their shields were on par with our own, perhaps slightly more advanced. But the volley that they shrugged off would have ripped our fleet to shreds a dozen times over. Which means they have advanced shield technology and STILL lowered themselves to using guerrilla warfare."

"True."

"Which may mean that the wars they've fought were so brutal and devoid of honor that it became the norm for them. Our ancestors used to believe that all soldiers should clasp hands and give each other time to prepare for battle, forming their lines and fighting with honor. Today we think these practices are stupid and silly due to the various atrocities that were committed during these honorable traditions, and the complete lack of consequences that followed. Which begets the question, what the hell happened to the United Systems to make them forsake conventional warfare?"

"Perhaps we'll find out one day," I said as AT27 identified a target for me. "Assuming we survive the present, of course."

I fired my MACs at the flagged enemy as we followed AT27 around the battlefield. He flagged enemies for us to target while simultaneously firing upon enemies himself. He was many years my senior, but I still almost had trouble keeping up.

While we were engaging enemies and dodging fire, the US dreadnoughts were engaging the Mobile Prime Platform we were assigned to. A quick scan of the planet told me how large the guns involved were, and I felt a wave of fear at the thought of instant annihilation. The dreadnoughts were taking multiple volleys from these massive cannons, and were dishing out near equal punishment in turn.

The scale of it all finally hit me. Despite our

blessed mechanization and centuries of experience, we were mere insects playing at the feet of titans. We had badly underestimated both the Omni-Union and the United Systems.

I made certain to save all of the data that I had gathered so that I may share it with our leaders, assuming I survive. Joining with the United Systems or creating a formal alliance would be absolutely necessary. No matter how much one stretches their imagination, winning a war against the US is unimaginable. We would be completely dependent upon their mercy if it came to that.

Even with all my knowledge, I can't begin to fathom how they've created such monumental weapons and shields. Was it specifically for use against the Omni-Union? How can that be? They haven't been fighting the OU that long. How had they managed to mass-manufacture these Bansron {a mythical giant, similar to Goliath} in such a short amount of time? I was so focused on this that I was nearly hit by a MAC round, but managed to spot the incoming just in time and fired my keel thrusters to avoid it. A laugh came over the psynet.

'Watching the behemoths brawl?' BA14 asked.

'Can you blame him? I can barely take my sensors off them,' BB39 said.

'Well you better get your sensors on the fight,' AU48 replied. 'If you don't you're going to end up scrapped.'

'Just stay focused,' AT27 interjected. 'Distractions

will only...'

He trailed off as the first of the dreadnoughts fired its main cannon. Despite the vacuum, I felt like I could almost hear it. I imagined it was like the high pitched hum followed by a dull thud that my own MACs made, but exponentially louder.

Before the shell even hit the MPP, the other two dreadnoughts fired as well. Despite my awe, I launched a missile at one of my targets. The missile didn't even get halfway to the target before the MPP split into pieces.

'Wow,' BA14 said.

The rest of us fell into silence and continued fighting.

Chapter 35

Subject: Fleet Leader Barrilin Onaya
Species: Oyan
Species Description: Avian humanoid, feathered tail. 6'1" (1.8 m) avg height. 96 lbs (43 kg) avg weight. 161 year life expectancy.
Ship: RSV Nolbarinil {Majestic In Flight}
Location: Unknown

"Good hits," intel-head Salin reported. "Target destroyed, fleet leader."

"Looks like the other teams have accomplished their objectives as well, sir," Hindal said.

Salin is sending my orders and receiving updates while my second in command is coordinating with the other strike teams. Salin's has a heavier burden than Hindal does, but he is well within his element.

"Excellent," I replied. "Now all that's left is clean-up. The swarm should be here to take over for us soon. In the meantime, have the non-US forces pull back and start sniping stragglers. Remind them to check their fire, we don't need a diplomatic incident."

"Yes, Fleet Leader," Salin said, turning back to the task at hand.

I smiled softly as I watched my crew tend to their tasks. The crew of the RSV Nolbarinil is one of the few crews that is a blend of each space-faring species in our great republic. People with wildly different cultures, customs, perspectives, and even dietary requirements working together toward a common goal. As someone who believes that our differences make us stronger together, I've always found this beautiful.

It isn't hard to draw a parallel between my crew and the strike teams. I've argued with other Fleet Leaders and even politicians over my beliefs, and to see my point wholly and completely proven on such a massive scale is a wonderful experience. However, I can't say that I don't empathize a little with their perspectives.

I stole a glance at the dark metallic box that had been installed on my bridge. It contains an Artificial Intelligence, one powerful enough to put the OU to shame. Once I had been approved for this command I had been escorted into a dark room along with several other officers. After we had taken our seats and stewed for a bit, a different group of people entered the room. This group of people was comprised of the highest ranking officers of each of our militaries, including High Commander Uliriona.

They proceeded to explain that Omega's presence aboard our ships was a requirement for this mission, and this mission is not voluntary. Regardless of our views on the sanctity of biological life, we would be working alongside this AI, and refusal to do so would result in court-martial. We were informed that what we were about to be told is classified and failure to keep this information secret would result in life-long imprisonment or even execution. Then they explained what this Artificial Intelligence is capable of, and the collective gasps nearly turned the room into a vacuum.

During their war with the Artificial Intelligences that they created, the United Systems somehow thought it was a good idea to create an even more powerful AI to fight for them. They designed this AI with cyberwarfare capabilities that made the other AI look like elderly people struggling to figure out the newest version of their terminal's operating system. Somehow this plan succeeded and the US survived the war, which is the most compelling case for divine intervention I've ever seen.

However, Omega surprised them with its capability. Unbeknownst to its creators, it has the ability to replicate itself and literally be in multiple places at once. This, in combination with its cyberwarfare capabilities, makes it very useful against the Omni-Union. But also very, very dangerous. Our leaders believe that its usefulness outweighs the potential danger, but I'm not sure I agree.

"The swarm has entered the system and is now engaging the Omni-Union," Salin said.

"Regroup and make ready to enter warp," I ordered. "Hindal, give the mark once it comes in."

"Yes, fleet-leader," they said in unison.

One of the key components of this operation is coordination. We are coordinating our warps with other strike teams so that we enter the system simultaneously, which will prevent the Mobile Prime Platforms from supporting each other and potentially destroying the dreadnoughts. Even during the battles, the strike teams are coordinating with each other to keep the Omni-Union's ships at bay.

We are using overwhelming firepower against the MPPs and small fleet tactics against the ships that would help them. We even have reserves waiting in case the enemy is reinforced or one of the dreadnoughts is destroyed. This operation was extensively calculated and planned, which makes one wonder what part Omega could possibly play in all this.

"Mark," Hindal said.

The RSV Nolbarinil entered warp less than half a second later. Within a few more seconds, we were in a new system and back in the thick of it.

"Dreadnoughts, fire at will," I ordered.

Everyone already knew what to do and were going about doing it. I began watching the battle on the tac-map that the United Systems had installed months ago. Part of me was already used to this technology, but every now and then I couldn't help but marvel at how much better than its predecessor it is. Being able to know the near real-time location of every ship in a battle kind of feels like cheating.

The OU ships had once again known we were coming, and had once again focused their fire on the United System's ships. And just like the last time, this strategy was ineffective. As the dreadnoughts and the Mobile Prime Platform engaged each other, I checked our casualties.

We lost five Republic vessels and one of the Dtiln collective ships, but the US ships hadn't even lost their shields. What would have happened to our civilization if we had encountered the United Systems in a more hostile fashion? I chuckled softly and shook my head. They would have destroyed or assimilated us with little to no contest.

As I was trying to calculate how quickly we would have surrendered, a red marker began barreling toward one of the dreadnoughts. I furrowed my brow as several dozen more began following its lead. Surely they're smart enough to realize that their weapons can't do anything against the dreadnought's shield? They're stupid, but they're not...

"Salin, tell the dreadnoughts to engage their PDLs and brace for impact!" I shouted.

"Yes, sir!"

I squeezed the arm of my seat as I watched the red markers close in on the dreadnought. The dreadnought began to fire at them, and the markers started disappearing one by one. Too slowly, though.

Green markers suddenly appeared as US ships warped into the path of the suicide ships and started engaging them, but some of the red markers still slipped past. After a few more excruciating seconds, two of the red markers impacted the dreadnought. I swore under my breath.

"The USSS Tempest has lost shields, sir," Salin reported. "The MPP has begun focusing fire on them."

"Have the other two form a shield formation with the Tempest," I said. "What's the extent of the damage?"

"Waiting on the full damage report, sir."

I watched the Tempest and one other dreadnought begin to move. The idea behind the shield formation is to put the dreadnought with shields in between the Tempest and the hostile MPP, allowing it to avoid taking any further damage while its shield recharged. The dreadnoughts are slow, though, and the MPP's MACs are too damn quick.

"They've got a hull breach and have taken damage to their primary cannon," Salin shook his head solemnly. "They're out of the fight, sir."

"Blood encrusted stool," I whispered. "Hindal, report this to high command and request guidance."

I already knew what they were going to say. The Tempest can't warp out of the system until we can arrange an escort or eliminate the Omni-Union. We can't do either of those things until we destroy the MPP. In the meantime, the MPP is going to destroy the Tempest.

"They've lost power," Salin said.

I quietly prepared myself to witness the destruction of the USSS Tempest.

"Give the order to abandon," I said.

"Belay that," a raspy voice came over the intercom. "The USSS Tempest has some of the best armor ever made. More than enough to protect the crew from the Omni-Union ships. The escape pods are much less armored, and the OU will simply pick them off."

"Omega?" I asked, then silently chided myself for asking such an obvious question. "The MPP is going to destroy the Tempest. If the crew is aboard when that happens, they will all die."

"Negative. Check the tac-map."

I looked at the map, desperately trying to find a clue as to what the mad machine was talking about. I stared at the icon denoting the MPP for a few seconds before I finally came to the realization that the MPP wasn't firing anymore.

"What's happening?" I asked, dumbfounded.

"I have disabled its weaponry and FTLD. Its current countermeasures will disable my control over these systems after approximately forty-five seconds, but that's more than enough time to destroy it. The Tempest is safe from the Mobile Prime Platform."

"Fine. Salin, tighten our forces around the dreadnoughts."

"Yes, sir."

I leaned back in my chair again. Omega seems to be as useful as it was billed, but to think that it could disable an MPP's weapons and FTLD. A Prime is a planet-sized Artificial Intelligence, but on the other wing, Omega was built specifically to kill AI. If it can do that to them, though...

I caught myself and shut down that train of thought. Guess I have a negative bias to work on, after all. I thought I could avoid ambivalence toward the United System's AI despite my experiences in this lengthy war, but those experiences have obviously soured my opinion. Shame on me for not realizing it sooner.

While it is true that Omega could be apocalyptically deadly if it chose to be, it has been living among the species of the United Systems for centuries now. Even though a good portion of its capabilities are classified, those that are in the know still trust it. If I approached that fact rationally, then it would be safe to assume that it hasn't shown many signs of maliciousness. Well, towards them, at least.

"USSS Tip of the Tip is firing," Salin said.

"That's got to be a translation error," I rubbed my forehead softly.

"No, it isn't. Once we got the list I asked some of the gonts at the dock," Hindal chuckled. "Apparently, in the United Systems the engineering team that builds the ship gets to come up with its name."

"Good hit," Salin reported.

"Alright, hold here and keep those dreadnoughts safe until the swarm rejoins us," I said, then turned back to my second. "So what, the engineers that built the Tip of the Tip ran out of ideas for a name?"

"Well, the gont could only postulate, of course, but they seemed to think that the engineering crew were human and trying to slip a joke past the censors," Hindal grinned. "A rather specific joke regarding a particularly male piece of human anatomy."

"The way you phrase that makes it sound like they are making a cloaca joke, but..." I trailed off, trying to figure out the punchline on my own.

"Negative, sir. Humans have a different type of genitals, and for the males it's more like a..." Hindal paused for a moment, trying to keep her composure. "Like a meat spear, sir."

"Oh by the grace of the sun," I rubbed my forehead harder. "Tip of the tip, yeah. I get it now. Disgusting."

"Oh, yeah, definitely disgusting," she coughed to mask a chuckle. "Interestingly, the gont I spoke to pointed out that a great many number of objects take on the same shape as the human male..."

"The USSS Alikonuoro reports that its primary cannon is malfunctioning," Salin interrupted. "So now we've got two replacements inbound."

"Understood. Alikonuoro, now that's a proper name for a ship. What does it mean?" I asked.

"I'll check, sir," Hindal replied.

"I already looked, can't find a meaning," Salin said.

"It is alumari in origin," Omega interjected. "It is a reference to an ancient origin myth in which a fertility goddess bred with anything that came along, including her own children, which resulted in the many different species of animal on the alumari cradle world of Alunis."

A thick sheet of shocked silence fell over the bridge, until it was interrupted by a snort from Hindal.

"The censors were overwhelmed by the rapidity in which this fleet was constructed," the AI said with a sigh. "There are currently twenty eight dreadnoughts with names that are puns regarding genitals or sexual conduct."

"The swarm has arrived, and the USSS Alikonuoro's replacement is inbound..." Salin trailed off, staring at the terminal in front of him.

"What is it?" I asked.

He let out a heavy sigh, "Its name is the USSS Gaping Maw."

Hindal began laughing so hard that she fell out of

her seat.

Chapter 36

Subject: Rear Admiral Fredrick Kennedy
Species: Knuknu
Species Description: Avian humanoid, non-prehensile tail. 5'10" (1.7 m) avg height. 84 lbs (38 kg) avg weight. 342 year life expectancy.
Ship: USSS Gaping Maw
Location: Unknown

"Exiting warp, sir," Captain Blavro said.

I clacked my beak in acknowledgment. Then I realized that an alumari might not know that expression, so I nodded as well. It's somewhat amusing that human body language is much closer to universal than any other species in the United Systems. This is likely due to the nature and frequency of their social interactions with the aforementioned other species. Most people meet a dozen or so humans before they get a chance to meet a member of any other species. Hell, for me it was hundreds.

"We're out of warp, Admiral," Blavro reported.

"And we're being hailed," Commander Stevens added. "It's the USSS Alikonuoro, sir."

"Put them on," I replied with another nod.

"Aye, sir."

Stevens set about the task at hand, and a moment later an alumari in a well-decorated uniform was on my screen.

"I hope you're faring well despite your current circumstances, Rear Admiral Tlokix. How was the hunt?" I asked.

"Frustratingly short, Rear Admiral," he clicked his mandibles, probably to indicate frustration. "Thank you for taking over for us. A bad batch of wires completely disabled our... Mega MAC? Super MAC? What are they calling it again?"

"Ultra-MAC, if I recall correctly," I scrunched my eyes to indicate amusement.

"Oh, yes, that's right. Well, our Ultra-MAC is dead with a hot tube. And within that hot tube is a live A1 warhead."

"Quite the predicament."

"Indeed. Once again, thanks for taking over for us. Now if you'll excuse me, I'd like to get back and get my people off this bomb."

"Understandable. I hope to see you again soon, Tlokix."

"Likewise, Kennedy. Render them asunder for me."

The transmission terminated, and I breathed a small sigh of gratitude that the commander of the Alikonuoro was someone I knew. It saved me from having to explain my human surname. Despite the inappropriateness of the question, people seemingly cannot help but be curious.

My biological parents abandoned me when I was

born, and I was lucky enough to be adopted by William and Lacy Kennedy while I was still an infant. They were from an influential Martian family, and not all of the family was happy about my parent's choice to adopt outside of their species. My mom and dad did their best to keep me insulated from the racism, but the snide remarks and passive aggression of the wealthy are difficult things to combat without actual combat. My father ended up having to punch quite a few uncles before I was old enough to do it myself.

Though I grew up around humans, I had always found myself fascinated with knuknu culture. Or rather, my heritage. I was so far removed from it that it felt foreign to me. This gave me something like an identity crisis, so when I was old enough to strike out on my own I bid my mother and father farewell and took up residence on Yons, the knuknu cradle-world. Even though the cost of living there is higher than the galactic average, I lasted a couple of decades before having to move somewhere cheaper.

The knuknus were polite, but they didn't see me as one of their own. No matter how hard I tried to imitate their behaviors and customs to fit in, my name gave me away as an outsider. Regardless of where I went, I was treated as a tourist rather than the long lost son I had fantasized about being.

I moved from colony to colony for a while, somewhat lost with what to do with my life. I returned to Mars to be with my parents during their final years, and a discussion with my father convinced me to become an officer in the United Systems military. After my parent's funeral, I did just that and finally found the place where I fit in. For the most part.

"Form up with the USSS Tip of the Tip," I ordered.

"God, what's up with these names?" Stevens asked.

"What do you mean?" Blavro asked as he began moving the ship.

"It's a genitalia pun," I answered. "Specifically pertaining to human and gont anatomy. This fleet was built very quickly, so the censors obviously weren't able to catch everything. The engineers saw an opportunity and they took it."

"Oh," Blavro replied.

"Yeah. It's gross," Stevens muttered.

I shrugged at him. The antics of the engineers are not my problem unless they directly interfere with my duties. The ship names don't impact my ability to command, so I don't care about them in the slightest. What concerns me is what happened to Tlokix's dreadnought, the USSS Alikonuoro. The United Systems has a good track record with ship builds, and bad wiring is a very rare occurrence. I only hope that something like that doesn't happen to the Gaping Maw.

"In position, sir," Blavro reported. "The replacement for the USSS Tempest has arrived, as well."

"What's its name?" Stevens asked.

"The USSS Carnage."

"Finally, a good name. I swear, if I ever fi-"

"Enough about the names," I interrupted. "Blavro, prepare for warp and engage when we get the order."

"Aye aye, sir," Blavro said.

I watched the Faster Than Light Drive indicator begin to fill, and was once again stricken by how slowly it charged. Slower than any other ship that I'd been on. Of course, this is also the largest ship I had ever been on. Much larger than the USSS Trigoravor {claw's point}, the battleship that until recently I had commanded. My crew had been almost entirely knuknu, with the exception of some gont in engineering and humans in the mess.

Then I was voluntold to command a dreadnought. At first I was somewhat excited, the USSS Nidhogg is legendary and to command it is considered an honor. Once we got moving, I realized how slow and clunky it is compared to the rest of our ships, and my excitement dulled immensely. Might as well be commanding a heavily armed tug. A good portion of the tactics that I have learned simply cannot apply to a vessel this unwieldy.

The only tactic that seems applicable is to sit there and trade blows, blasting one's thrusters now and again to try to take the enemy fire in a less damaging area. Even the Ultra-MAC is ridiculously slow. They've managed to get the charge time down to fifty seconds, but that's a long time during a fight. Might as well be an eternity.

"Entering warp, sir," Blavro said.

"Good, once we exit warp begin charging the Ultra-MAC. Gain a firing solution after, I say again, after you start charging the cannon. No need to add additional time to the charging cycle."

"Aye, sir," Commander Horvu said.

Horvu is the first gont that I'd ever seen serving on a bridge. Thus far, I find him quite agreeable, but a little standoffish. He's good at his job and doesn't engage in idle chatter, which I can respect. Many of the crew seem to believe he doesn't like socializing, but it's possible that he's just shy. I haven't heard of him insulting anyone or starting fights.

Commander Horvu also appears to be unaffected by pre-battle jitters. The rest of the crew, however, were fidgeting, obviously nervous about what's to come. Blavro was rubbing his carapace, Stevens was softly tapping his foot, and I even caught myself absentmindedly straightening the feathers on my arms. With the exception of the damaged dreadnoughts, the assault had gone well so far. Too well, in fact. A superstitious mind would claim that our fortunes were bound to change at any moment.

"Leaving warp," Blavro reported.

Our shield indicator began dropping the moment we exited warp. This was expected, but I still had to fight a flinch. Omega had warned us that the OU had managed to upgrade their sensors, either from their invasion of Sol or from an as yet undiscovered species somewhere in the Milky Way.

"Well, Captain Blavro, it's your time to shine," I said. "Begin evasive maneuvers, but keep the Ultra-MAC on target."

"Aye aye, sir."

"Stevens, keep an eye on nearby enemy ships. I'd like to avoid the fate of the Tempest, if possible."

"Aye, sir."

"Horvu, fire when ready."

"Aye, sir."

Orders given, I sat back and watched the casualty count begin to rise. The Republic had lost the most ships so far, but the Dtiln Collective had lost the highest percentage of their forces. Neither the US nor the Pwanti had lost any ships yet, which caused some confusion for me. It made some semblance of sense for the Pwanti to have avoided destruction, their ships are light and nimble. Conversely, our ships are bulky and usually need to warp to dodge incoming fire.

I opened some sensor logs to investigate further,

and what I found made me chuckle. The Omni-
Union were targeting ships based on tonnage.
Their battleships were targeting our battleships,
their cruisers were targeting our carriers, and so
on. Absolutely awful match-ups, but they make
sense in a way. I would have ignored the
battleships and carriers and entirely focused on
the destroyers and frigates, but I'm not about to
tell them that. One shouldn't correct an enemy
when they're making a mistake.

The only weapons on the battlefield that could
easily destroy our battleships and carriers were
currently occupied with trying to kill our
dreadnoughts. Our target was currently focusing
its fire on the USSS Carnage, which had replaced
the Tempest. At first it had spread its fire among
the three of us, but I guess it's smart enough to
have realized that's not going to work. The MPP's
tactic seemed to be working, because the Carnage
was losing shields at an alarming rate.

"Command requests that we aid the USSS
Carnage," Stevens informed me.

"Blavro, get us in shield formation with the
Carnage while maintaining our firing solution," I
ordered.

"Aye aye, sir."

It was a good call by command. Our shields aren't
nearly as damaged as the Carnage's, and judging
by the rate of deterioration we'll be able to survive
the onslaught long enough to kill the Mobile Prime
Platform. Probably. It's a tad risky for us, but the
longer our dreadnoughts last the more damage

we can do to the Omni-Union.

Our shield indicator immediately began to drop as we took position in front of the Carnage. Commander Horvu was already using our standard MACs to target the MPP's cannons, and the other two dreadnoughts were doing the same. Not quickly enough to make much difference, though. I was watching our shields so closely that I almost missed the Ultra-MAC's charge cycle finishing.

"Firing," Horvu said.

The ship shook ever so slightly, and the tac-map tracked the shell as it left our cannon and made its way toward the MPP. I held my breath as our shield indicator dropped down to less than a quarter of its capacity. Come on... Almost there...

The shell hit, but we weren't clear yet. The MPP continued firing, and I gripped the arms of my chair as our shield indicator dropped even lower. Just before our shield popped, the A1 package within the shell exploded and the MPP finally ceased activity.

"YES!" I shouted.

Various cheers rang throughout the bridge. We had killed our first Mobile Prime Platform, without taking any hull damage in return. Commander Horvu, ever the stoic, gave a small smile and nod at our accomplishment and went right back to his tasks.

"Okay, okay," I said, holding up my hands to calm

my crew. "We got our first taste of victory. Let's not let it get to our heads. It's time for clean-up. Horvu, start targeting the enemy battleships. Blavro, start charging the FT-"

"Belay that," a gravelly voice said through our intercom. "Recharge your Ultra-MAC."

"Do it," I nodded at Horvu. "Omega? What's going on?"

"Enemy reinforcements inbound."

Chapter 37

Subject: BI41
Species: Mwaltin - Pwanti Conversion Completed
Species Description: Mammalian Humanoid, no tail. 6'5" (1.9 m) avg height. 190 lbs (86.1 kg) avg weight. 99 year life expectancy.
Ship: BI41
Location: Unknown

'I'm running low on missiles,' AU48 informed us.

'Understood. I'll only tag targets you can hit with your MAC,' AT27 replied.

We continued to circle around the battlefield looking for enemies to destroy. We had received an order to fall back and engage in long distance combat. Most of the alien vessels did so, but we were already a good distance from the Omni-Union ships and felt no need to rejoin our host formation. The only vessels still well within the fray were the United System's ships.

AT27 continued demonstrating an impressive calculative ability in the targets he was marking for us. Our ships were designed by and built by the church, but over the years we've each added our own individual pieces to them thanks to various civilian companies that create ships for space travel. I've increased my storage bays and added a faster autoloader. AT27 has apparently done something involving his processing capabilities. I was thinking about asking him what his customizations are when I received a notification that we were being reinforced.

"The swarm is inbound. I think they're going to swap at least one of the dreadnoughts," BL28 said. "Maybe two of them."

"Why?"

"One of the dreadnoughts lost their shield and took some damage, and the other one appears to be having a mechanical failure."

"What kind of mechanical failure?" I asked as I fired my MAC.

"There's chatter about their main cannon not being able to fire," she answered. "They have a shell loaded too, if I have the meaning of the phrase 'Hot Tube' correct."

"Well, they have plenty of dreadnoughts to spare," I said casually, though the thought would have caused my flesh to shiver. "It would be smart to swap out the defective ones."

"Defective..."

BL28 let the word hang in the air as I focused on evasive maneuvers. AT27 marked another target for me, and our reinforcements arrived the moment I fired my MAC. The ships from the United Systems wasted no time joining their brethren in the fight. As they began to viciously destroy the Omni-Union vessels, we finally followed AT27 back to our strike team's position.

'I managed to get 14 kills, what about you guys?' AU48 asked.

'I killed 13,' BB39 answered.

'I got 21,' AT27 said.

'30 for me,' BA14 added.

I tallied up the number of ships I had destroyed, wondering where I had placed in this impromptu ranking. I relished the chance to partake in a friendly competition. It had been a while since I'd been able to enjoy this kind of camaraderie.

'32,' I said.

'Looks like BI41 takes the win. Congratulations,' AT27 replied.

"What will happen if I end up with defective parts?" BL28 asked, interrupting my revelry.

I accessed my internal cameras to assess her current emotional state. Her expression indicated contemplation, but her heart-rate and O2 saturation indicated distress. I noted that this was a genuine concern to her, and I should treat it as such.

"Once you 'discard your flesh', as the church puts it, you can replace defective parts," I said gently. "It is easier to replace muran {a type of alloy steel that is rust resistant} than it is to replace flesh, as well. There are many defects within the flesh that cannot be addressed, but there isn't any such issue with our mechanical forms."

"Are there any parts that can't be replaced?"

"No."

"Even your brain?"

"We can replace our entire body with a new one once the conversion is complete. We simply upload our consciousness into a buffer, and then download ourselves into the new form."

"What if you lack the mental faculties to do that? Or what happens if something goes wrong during a conversion?"

As I tried to find an appropriate answer, more ships came out of warp. A dreadnought and some reinforcements for the vanguard. Among them was a Pwanti resupply vessel, which set its course in our direction.

"Once the conversion is complete, someone else can upload your consciousness if you are unable to yourself. However... there are many things that can go wrong during a conversion," I said as the resupply ship began refilling my ammunition and missiles. "Very few of them are correctable."

"So I'll... die?" she asked, a small spike of fear entering her voice.

"Yes. Were you not informed of this possibility?"

"I was... but... I don't know. I suppose it didn't feel real until we started fighting. I'm sorry."

"Don't apologize," I said gently. "It is of the utmost importance to address your fears. It's the only way to overcome them. While there is a high risk of fatality during the conversion process, most fatalities occur within the first three years. You are two years past this point, so your likelihood of survival has gone up immensely."

"Assuming we don't get blown up by the Omni-Union," she laughed.

I laughed along with her, "I'll make sure we aren't."

The resupply ship finished with me and moved on to the other Pwanti. I triple checked my weapons systems to make certain there were no issues, then ran a scan on my other systems. Everything came back optimal.

"So do you think the church is right?" BL28 asked. "If I die during conversion, I go to Ynorim {a type of Utopian afterlife}?"

"Regardless of whether or not they're right, the thought was of comfort to me during my own conversion," I said. "Whenever my flesh protested its replacement, I thought of what would await me if I were to die. It made it less... frightening."

"I wonder if that helps with the survival rate."

"Maybe."

As the resupply ship finished with my comrades, another dreadnought entered the system and I got a notification to prepare for warp.

'Are we going to continue on as we have been?' BB39 asked over the psynet.

'Yes,' AT27 replied.

'Can we protect the dreadnoughts this time? I would like to get a closer look at them,' AU48 requested.

'If they need it,' AT27 said. 'I am hesitant to get closer to the Mobile Prime Platforms, though.'

'We nearly lost a dreadnought to the Omni-Union ships during this battle,' BA14 interjected. 'While I share your hesitancy, our primary objective is to protect the dreadnoughts to the best of our abilities.'

Before the conversation could continue, we received the order to warp. I engaged my Faster Than Light Drive a quarter of a second after AT27 and followed my comrades into subspace.

"Here we go again," BL28 muttered.

"We'll be fine, Renvira," I assured her.

She remained silent. The church frowns upon us using our pupil's true names, believing that if they don't see themselves as a machine they're more likely to lose the fight against the flesh. However, I believe the opposite. The conversion process causes distress of every nature, and it is likely this distress that causes one to succumb. Offering solace where one can saves lives.

"Exiting warp," I said.

As I left warp I immediately tracked three

incoming projectiles. However, I was prepared this time and fired my thrusters to avoid them, then returned fire. The other Pwanti did the same, and we formed up with AT27 once again.

The dreadnoughts began engaging the Mobile Prime Platform, and AT27 led us in their direction. I noted that once again the United Systems had avoided casualties, and started firing on the targets that AT27 designated. We began to defend the dreadnoughts, staying well clear of them to avoid stray rounds from the MPP. One of the replacement dreadnoughts lost its shield, and the other replacement moved in front of it to shield it from the MPP's onslaught.

"We managed to avoid getting hit this time," BL28 said happily as I fired a missile.

"It is as I said. We'll be fine."

A large enemy ship began to target the unshielded dreadnought, but all five of us fired at it simultaneously. It was difficult to tell who got the kill, but the ship exploded in a way that indicated one of us had hit its reactor. We continued to defend the dreadnoughts until one of them finally fired its main cannon.

'I'll never get used to that,' BA14 said as the planet-sized enemy broke into pieces.

"Wow, that was fast," BL28 said.

"No, it took just as long as last time," I replied, firing my MAC at a distant OU ship. "You were just less afraid this time. Fear can distort your perception of time and make it seem longer."

"I see."

We continued firing at the OU ships that were attempting to engage the dreadnoughts. BB39 took a glancing blow, but was able to continue fighting as their shield recharged. I was finally able to match the pace of AT27, destroying each and every enemy he marked for me milliseconds after he had done so.

'Something is wrong,' BA14 noted. 'The dreadnoughts aren't charging their FTLDs, they're recharging their main weapons.'

As she said this, we received a notification to expect enemy reinforcements. Time seemed to slow down as I realized two very important things. First, if the enemy knows to send reinforcements, they likely have a good idea of the make-up of our current forces. Second, they will be targeting the...

'GETAWAYFROMTHEDREADNOUGHTS!' I screamed into the psynet.

Before we could react, five Mobile Prime Platforms and the biggest Omni-Union fleet I've ever seen exited warp. I peeled away from the formation as the MPPs began firing. One of the dreadnoughts fired as BA14 took multiple hits and exploded. AT27 was next, taking a shot from an MPP and turning to scrap in an instant.

Without any time to grieve our fallen comrades, BB39, AU48, and I split into different directions, desperately attempting to avoid the incoming fire.

AU48 took a hit directly in the engines, then another in his reactor core. BB39 managed to avoid a missile, but instead she took a MAC round from an MPP and fell to pieces.

"No..." BL28 whispered. "Please no..."

Too much of my processing power was busy tracking incoming fire to comfort her. I initiated a full-burn away from the enemy, trying to limit my profile as much as possible. I fired my thrusters in such a way that it sent me into a spin while I deployed chaff, managing to avoid the missiles that had locked onto me. But my early warning system was still blaring.

A MAC round glanced off my shields, deflected by my spin. Another one impacted, disabling my shield. I continued my full-burn until a missile finally made it through my chaff and disabled my engines. I tried to override the safeties, but they weren't the problem. The fuel lines had been ruptured. I fired my thrusters to avoid another MAC round and positioned myself to use my keel thrusters to replace my engines and continue my escape.

This increased my profile and stopped my spin, though, and shrapnel from another missile penetrated my reactor compartment. I sealed it to prevent loss of precious atmosphere, to protect Renvira. Another second ticked by, and my only thought was getting her through this. Poor Renvira, who had suffered so much to become BL28 and join the ranks of the Pwanti.

"Come on, come on," she said. "I don't want to

di-"

The MAC round had come from one of the Mobile Prime Platforms. It ripped through my hull and barely missed my central processing drive as it shredded my cockpit. I was immediately blinded and deafened, without any sort of confirmation of Renvira's fate.

I began desperately calculating her odds of survival based on my last sensory input. Zero percent. No matter what variables I could plausibly add, she was definitely dead. I had completely and utterly failed her. Because of me all her suffering to become a Pwanti was for nothing. She had made it so far, and her likelihood of shedding her flesh was as high as it could be. And now...

I bitterly tried to activate the psynet to call for help, but found that I had no access to comms. I attempted to access anything that I could, but received no answer from any part of my ship. My anger and shame at the loss of Renvira turned to panic, then a cold realization.

My CPD had survived but was forcefully disconnected from the rest of the ship. It must have taken damage, because even though my backup power was functioning, my emergency beacon hadn't activated. Even trying to activate it manually wasn't working. I tried to calculate my possible trajectories and realized that even if my allies knew to look for me, they would likely never find me.

I waited in this void for a time, a mere

consciousness wondering what life will be like without a body. I checked my internal battery life. Ninety-nine years, three months, one week, six days, four hours, fifty two minutes, and eight seconds. I could let my power run out, just in case someone somehow found me. Or...

This possibility had been acknowledged and planned for. Space is hazardous even in the best of conditions. Yet, Pwanti are difficult to truly eliminate, as is evidenced by my current situation. In the event of being lost in space with little to no chance of rescue, we have the ability... To hasten the inevitable.

Being a Pwanti can be a lonely existence. However, one usually has tasks to keep one's mind off of the existential dread that comes with being alone for such long periods of time. A study to perform, a delivery to make, and even fights now and again. We can even sleep, in a way. A sort of stasis that we put ourselves into during long treks.

However, this stasis relies on ship systems that I no longer have access to. I will be awake at all times until I am rescued or my battery runs out. The main reason that I take on students is because I don't do well in solitude.

My students... I wonder how they are right now. Most of them perished, casualties of the conversion process. Some of them went on to become Pwanti, though, and are probably fighting right now. I wonder how many of them are going to make it home. I wonder if the Omni-Union are going to be defeated, and if the galaxy will be at peace afterwards. I wonder...

Another day ticked by and my odds of rescue
decreased again. I wondered about all the things I
could wonder about, and time ticked by. I began
to imagine conversations I would have if things
had gone differently. A month went by, then two. I
ran out of things to think about, and felt madness
tugging at the corners of my mind.

Fine. My chances of rescue are nil at this point.
My only hope is that the church is right and I'll
find peace and companionship in Ynorim. Maybe
I'll get to apologize to Renvira.

CPD:\PwantiOS\admin>start Protocol_LiS.exe

Chapter 38

Subject: Fleet Leader Barrilin Onaya
Species: Oyan
Species Description: Avian humanoid, feathered tail. 6'1" (1.8 m) avg height. 96 lbs (43 kg) avg weight. 161 year life expectancy.
Ship: RSV Nolbarinil {Majestic In Flight}
Location: Unknown

"Omega, where's our reinforcements?" I asked.

"ETA is two minutes," it replied.

"Can you do that magic trick again?"

"They are actively communicating and sharing software patches in an attempt to counter my cyberwarfare tactics. So... yes, but it'll take time and won't last long."

"Understood. Salin, have our remaining defensive vessels focus on weakening the MPP's rate of fire. Have some US ships keep watch for suicide bombers, though. Everyone else, evasive maneuvers and fire at will."

"Yes, sir!"

Orders given, I sat back and nervously watched the battle play out on the tac-map. Since the MPPs had warped into the system, our casualties have skyrocketed. Thankfully, we weren't completely surprised by this counterattack. They've destroyed thousands of our ships, but we managed to take down one of the MPPs in the process. Four left.

I've found myself in the most perfectly terrible situation for a commander to be in. Outnumbered, outgunned, and without a single damned thing to do about it. I sighed softly and rubbed my beak as our casualty count hit eight thousand. One of the OU cruisers took a potshot at us which careened off of our shields, causing the ship to shudder and my hand to slip from my face.

"I did say evasive maneuvers, yes?" I asked jokingly.

"Yes, sir," Hindal replied.

She wasn't laughing anymore, she's far too busy keeping us alive. The RSV Nolbarinil isn't what I would call a clunky ship, but graceful would not be an accurate description either. We traded fire with the OU cruiser that had targeted us, but their ship seemed pretty evenly matched with our own and our rounds bounced off of each other's shields.

It seemed that we were in a battle of attrition when suddenly a frigate exited warp behind the cruiser and punched a hole in it from stern to bow. The United Systems saves the day again. I noted the difference in size and power ratios between my flagship and the frigate with annoyance.

I turned my attention back to our casualty count. Over ten thousand ships lost. The Dtiln Collective had lost half their forces and the Pwanti were completely wiped out. The Republic had lost the most ships, but had also brought the most ships. Five Pwanti ships, one thousand US ships, three thousand Dtiln Collective ships, and the rest were Republic.

I rubbed my eyes trying to think of some way to win this. There had only been one MPP in this system, and they planned this operation for three dreadnoughts per MPP. We hadn't planned on enemy reinforcements because as far as we knew, the only thing of value in this system was the MPP.

"Omega, are the OU reinforcing other systems as well?" I asked quietly. "Or is there a specific reason they want this system so badly?"

"They are reinforcing other systems, but their communications indicate that their deployment patterns are proximity based," the AI answered.

"They came to defend this system because they were closest to it?"

"Correct."

I grumbled softly about our bad luck. Still, I'd heard that the United Systems had managed to fight off Mobile Prime Platforms while they were outnumbered before. I desperately hope they're able to do it again. Though, they did that with full shields and preparation time...

I turned my attention back to the tac-map in time to see the USSS Carnage fire its Ultra-MAC just as it lost its shield. I watched the shell impact an MPP and split it apart. Only three MPPs left, but the situation isn't looking good for the Carnage.

Thankfully for us, Omega had quickly intervened

when the dreadnoughts were about to begin preparing for warp. I'm not an engineer so the details elude me, but its one or the other with the Ultra-MAC and the FTLD. If the Ultra-MAC is charged, the FTLD can't be. The reverse is true as well. If the dreadnoughts had started charging their FTLDs, then we would have no hope of survival. Instead of the little hope for survival that we currently have.

"The USSS Carnage has taken critical damage and is abandoning ship," Salin informed me.

"Have some frigates start grabbing their escape craft," I ordered. "We can't leave them sitting out there with all this going on."

"Yes, sir."

Moments later, the marker for the Carnage disappeared and its name was added to the casualty list. Three Mobile Prime Platforms against two United Systems dreadnoughts. The USSS Tip of the Tip and the USSS Gaping Maw began moving to take cover behind the wreck of the Carnage. The Tip of the Tip had already fired and was currently recharging. The Gaping Maw had fired the shot that destroyed the MPP we came here for, and they're currently halfway through recharging.

Unfortunately, both of the dreadnought's shields have taken a lot of damage. The Carnage and the Gaping Maw hadn't fully recovered their shields since the last battle. The Tip of the Tip hadn't taken a lot of fire in round one, but was currently being battered. The Gaping Maw had shielded the

Carnage earlier, but the enemy reinforcements had warped in from the opposite direction, which had put the Carnage directly in their sights. It was pure luck that they were able to get a shot off when they did.

"Reinforcements inbound," Omega said calmly. "Twenty seconds."

The AI's calmness did not provide any reassurance. If anything, it pissed me off. Of course it can be calm, it's not as if its going to die here. This copy of it will, but it has dozens more. Maybe even hundreds. But *we* only get one body. One life. And so many of these lives were currently being lost, and so many more would be lost in the next twenty seconds.

I recognized my visceral rage as being stress induced and pinched the tip of my beak to keep from cursing. The AI is only doing what it was trained to do in stressful situations with organics. It is important to stay calm and keep a level beak in times of duress.

"The USSS Tip of the Tip has taken critical damage," Salin said quietly. "They're also abandoning ship."

"Wolyunvor {a curse invoking a patron deity of inbred children made by siblings}," I swore softly. "Make sure they're picked up too. As soon as possible."

"On it, sir."

The USSS Gaping Maw managed to secure a

position behind the wreck of the Carnage, but this had caused the MPPs to focus their fire on the Tip of the Tip. Three MPPs against one dreadnought. The exact opposite of how this was supposed to go. I swallowed heavily as the indicator for the USSS Tip of the Tip disappeared from the tac-map and joined the casualty list, knowing exactly what will happen next.

The three remaining Mobile Prime Platforms turned their attention toward the Gaping Maw. One of the MPPs began firing into the wreckage of the Carnage, trying to penetrate the impromptu cover. The other two began to move around the cover, seeking a clear shot at our only remaining dreadnought.

"Got 'em," Omega said as the two MPPs cleared the wreckage. "Weapons disabled."

"How long?" I asked, leaning forward in my seat.

"Not long. Rough estimate would be fifteen seconds. Doing what I can to extend that."

"Good work, Omega."

We might not lose all three of our dreadnoughts, but the fight is far from over. Whoever comes to our aid will have to charge their MACs, and anything can happen during that time. While I have mixed feelings about the United System's possession of such a destructive weapon, I can't help but wish it had a faster rate of fire.

"Reinforcements inbound!" Salin shouted excitedly.

A massive fleet of ships suddenly appeared on my tac-map. They had sent ten dreadnoughts and too many support ships to count.

"I want every gun in this system targeting the MPP's MACs while those dreadnoughts charge," I ordered.
"Understood, sir!"

A rather fortunate paradigm shift. Our forces now outnumber the OU's, and this means certain victory. I breathed a sigh of relief, then immediately remembered that this isn't over. I shouldn't relax yet, because there could be-

"Enemy reinforcements inbound," Omega finished my thought. "ETA one minute."

"Any idea how many?" I asked.

"No. They're too grouped together."

"Understood," I sighed. "See if we can get some more reinforcements. Salin, I want the Gaping Maw and two of our new friends to target the three remaining MPPs with their Ultra-MACs. Have the rest save it for the incoming."

"Yes, sir!"

The Gaping Maw had already moved clear of its cover and was targeting one of the remaining three MPPs. It fired, and I held my breath as I tracked the projectile via the tac-map. It collided with the MPP, and I subtly clenched my talons in celebration.

The two remaining MPPs began to fire again, but they had lost too many of their cannons to be a threat to the dreadnoughts. The Gaping Maw's shields slowly began to climb as they made good use of the cover provided by the destroyed MPPs. A lot of tension left my body as I watched the dreadnought's charge indicators climb. A little knot in my stomach remained, though. While the last two MPPs would not survive to greet their reinforcements, there's no telling how many of those reinforcements there will be.

The knot remained even after our reinforcements destroyed the final Mobile Prime Platforms. The dreadnoughts began to focus their supplementary MACs on the OU fleet. Supplementary MACs seems like such an odd phrase for cannons that are larger than any of the MACs on this ship.

"Enemies have exited warp!" Salin shouted.

My eyes stayed glued to the tac-map as the enemy indicators appeared. I sat stunned for a moment, then clacked my beak excitedly. The dreadnoughts had finished charging just as eight enemy MPPs exited warp. Absolute perfection. The large fleet of OU ships were almost an afterthought.

"One dreadnought per MPP, please," I ordered with a laugh. "Kill them."

I watched as eight dreadnoughts fired their Ultra-MACs in unison, hoping that someone had caught the visual on a recording so I could see it with my own eyes one day. The shells sped toward their targets, and a cheer erupted on the bridge as all eight shots connected. The enemy's reinforcements had been wiped out almost instantly.

The knot in my stomach faded as I leaned back in my chair and sighed. I felt as if several years had been taken from my lifespan. The cheering on the bridge stopped abruptly as the ship shuddered, reminding us all that we were still in a fight.

"We're not done yet," I said. "Clean them up."

Chapter 39

Subject: Rear Admiral Fredrick Kennedy
Species: Knuknu
Species Description: Avian humanoid, non-prehensile tail. 5'10" (1.7 m) avg height. 84 lbs (38 kg) avg weight. 342 year life expectancy.
Ship: USSS Gaping Maw
Location: Unknown

"Damage report," I said.

"Don't have the full yet. From what we've noticed so far, we took a couple of knocks to the armor but all the important stuff is fully functional. Shields are recharging now, sir," Captain Blavro reported. "We were fortunate that..."

The captain trailed off and absentmindedly nibbled on the back of his claws. A habitual cleaning ritual that alumari do when they're stressed. The thought he bear to finish is that we were fortunate that the Carnage took the hits for us, and then its wreckage was able to provide us cover. If it weren't for that, we would have been destroyed.

"Sir, Fleet Leader Oyan is ordering thirty minutes for 'R&R'," Smith said. "Kind of an odd time..."

"He means reinforce and replacement," Omega clarified.

"Understood," I said. "Omega, take over the stations. Everyone else, grab a drink, hit the head, and be back here in twenty minutes."

"Aye, sir," Omega said.

I watched as the crew vacated the bridge, and once the last of them left I leaned back in my chair and exhaled fully for the first time in what felt like eternity. Once I let my guard down, the shakes took over. We had almost died. The other two dreadnoughts were destroyed. It was only by sheer luck that we hadn't been. If we had been on the other side of the Carnage... Or if we hadn't been able to protect ourselves with its corpse...

"Fuck," I whispered, rubbing my beak to sooth myself.

"You should take some time, as well," Omega said.

"By the time I make it to my quarters, I'll have to immediately turn around," I joked.

"You don't need to go all the way to your quarters to-"

"Omega," I interrupted. "I will be fine. This is not my first close call, and I doubt that it will be my last. I understand the reason for your concern, but I am fit to carry on the mission."

"My concern isn't limited to your usefulness," the AI said calmly. "But even if it were, you're not looking at the big picture. Even if you're fit for this mission, what of the next? And when you finally return home? Treating PTSD is intensive and costly. It can be even more costly when left untreated. So it's in everyone's best interest to make sure those around them are mentally fit."

"Touching," I chuckled dryly. "Now leave me be."

"So be it."

Silence filled the bridge, and I let my mind wander. Both ships had managed to launch their escape pods, but there's no doubt that there were still crew aboard when the ships broke apart. We won't know the full scope of the tragedy until much later, though. Long after our next encounter with the MPPs.

They could easily have been the ones wondering about us. I'd almost lost my ship, my crew, and my life. The universe, through machinations unknowable, had seen fit to spare us and take them instead. Why, though? Surely there were people more deserving of life who died aboard the Carnage and the Tip of the Tip. Does it really just come down to luck?

My ruminations only seemed to last for a few moments before my crew started trickling back into the bridge. I adjusted myself and put on an air of stoicism for them, but none of them were looking at me. They all appeared to be wrapped up in their own contemplations. Except for Commander Stevens, who approached me with a mug in hand.

"Here, sir," he said, offering me the mug. "Probably good to have some coffee while we have the chance."

"I appreciate the sentiment, commander," I smiled. "However, knuknu are allergic to caffeine."

"Which is why I brought you some decaf, sir."

"Now you're talkin'," I said as I greedily grabbed the mug from him. "Thanks, Stevens."

"No problem, sir."

The commander returned to his station as I took a sip of the perfectly heated ambrosia. I am told that decaffeinated coffee isn't as good as regular coffee, but it's still amazing. Hell, my whole species loves the smell and taste of coffee, sometimes to an unhealthy degree. Something we actually have in common with humans.

The bean brew had actually caused a diplomatic incident when the knuknu and humans began first contact meetings. One of the human diplomats had offered the beverage to a knuknu diplomat without knowing the effects that caffeine has on avian physiology. Thankfully, the knuknu diplomat survived and the human diplomat was able to effectively explain that the beverage was frequently consumed by humans and not considered poisonous.

Neither side had any regulations specifically regarding food and drink, which had been an oversight caused by someone thinking other people had common sense. This incident changed that, and gave both the knuknu and humans a friendly jab at one another. Imagine being dumb enough to feed aliens a toxin at first contact and imagine being weak enough that caffeine can kill you. Ironically, this awkward and nearly fatal incident deepened the relations between our peoples.

"Sir, the damage to our armor has been repaired, and some... uh... lights have been replaced as well," Blavro said.

"Lights?" I asked.

"Yes, sir. Apparently, there was some arcing from the Ultra-MAC that went in an unexpected direction due to an attractant rod getting knocked loose. The rod's been replaced too."

"Are we green?"

"Yes, sir."

"Good. Did we suffer any casualties?"

"Only one, sir. Ensign Berulla from engineering suffered a minor concussion. He was under a console when we took a hard hit and got a good smack. He's expected to make a full recovery in five minutes."

I chuckled. Concussed engineers were honestly the best one could hope for in such circumstances. Skull knocks, shocks, and broken fingers are par for the course among the field. It's a damn good thing for them that we have great health care.

"Very good, captain. Get us in formation and charge the FTLD."

Captain Blavro began maneuvering into position as I leaned back in my chair, continuing to enjoy my coffee. It's amazing what a cup of the good stuff can do for one's spirits.

"The USSS Carnage and the USSS Tip of the Tip
are being replaced by the USSS Clenched Gauntlet
and the USSS..." Blavro stopped for a moment
and chuckled. "The USSS Hole Puncher. Even I get
that one."

Commander Stevens let out an exaggerated sigh,
which made Blavro laugh.

"It's only dirty if you make it dirty," I said, placing
my now empty mug in the disposal unit built into
the side of my chair. "As a matter of fact, I believe
you'd be hard pressed to find a more accurate
description for an Ultra-MAC."

"I get where you're coming from, sir, but if we
aren't careful these names are gonna corrupt our
poor, innocent captain here," Stevens said. "Next
thing you know, he'll be reading the Alumari
Renegade along with the rest of the degenerates."

Blavro stopped laughing and let out a disgusted
click, "I'd never stoop so low. The release of that
series has caused more damage to human-
alumari relations than any other event in our
shared history."

"Really?" Stevens asked.

"Yes. How would you feel if an alumari released a
series that not only butchered human history and
culture, but also made several vastly incorrect
assumptions about your anatomy? Now take that
feeling, and add the fact that it's an interplanetary
best seller."

"Are we ready to jump, yet?" I interrupted.

"Y-yes, sir," Blavro said nervously.

"Good. Engage when we get the order."

There's nothing wrong with a little levity but the conversation had been veering dangerously close to politics, and I have a hard rule against the discussion of such on my bridge. While it's true that the Alumari Renegade and its many sequels had been considered an insult by many alumari, they're not exactly innocent of cultural insensitivity either. Nobody is, for that matter. Both the alumari and the gont had presented painted eggs to the knuknu as first contact gifts, completely ignorant of the implications of such a gift.

"Entering warp, sir," Blavro reported.

"Excellent. Same as before, start the charging sequence first, then find a firing solution," I ordered.

"Aye aye, sir," Commander Horvu said.

"How many MPPs are we expecting?" I asked.

"Just one, sir," Stevens answered.

I nodded. Just one MPP wouldn't be so bad. Unless it received reinforcements, of course. Hopefully, our reinforcements will be a little quicker on the draw if that turns out to be the case. I took a deep breath and let it out slowly, steeling my nerves for the upcoming fight.

"Leaving warp, sir," Blavro said.

I turned my attention to the tac-map as we left subspace, and my eyes widened. There was a simply extraordinary amount of Omni-Union ships in this system. Far more than we'd encountered so far. All of this, just for one MPP and a few stations?

"Horvu, keep at least four MACs targeting the nearest OU ships and have the rest target the MPP's MACs," I ordered. "Fire at will."

"Aye aye, sir."

The charge indicator for our Ultra-MAC began to increase as our shield indicator began to decrease. Our shield's decline was much slower than it had been previously, indicating that the MPP was trying to hit all three of us at once. Perhaps it noticed that destroying us one at a time wouldn't work.

I waited patiently, watching our shells and ships destroy Omni-Union vessels with ruthless efficiency. How many more would we have to destroy? Will they give up, or will we have to hunt down and destroy every last one of them? Do they fear extinction? Are they even capable of understanding what death is?

I opened fleet-comm and checked our total casualties. Millions of ships lost on both sides of the conflict so far. This figure represented millions of people, as well. I don't even know how many VI are aboard an OU ship. All lost, and for what? We don't even know what this is all about.

"The MPP has stopped firing, sir," Blavro reported.

"Good job, Omega," I said with a laugh.

"Sir, I'm locked out of my console," Horvu said with panic tainting his normally stoic voice.

"Holy shit," Stevens exclaimed. "Everyone has stopped firing! Even the OU!"

"Omega? What the hell is going on?" I demanded.

"Sit tight, Admiral," Omega's voice sounded over the intercom. "Things just got interesting."

"Interesting? Interesting HOW?" I shouted.

"The MPP that we've just run into is designated Mobile Prime Platform One," the AI explained. "And I am currently negotiating a cease-fire."

Chapter 40

Subject: Prime 1
Species: Omni-Union Aligned Artificial Intelligence
Species Description: No physical description available.
Ship: MPP 1
Location: Sector 1

Sector 187 invasion failed. Escalation measures initiated.

////
Identifier: MPP1
-Suggestion-
Cease invasions in Sector 187 until intelligence has been analyzed and more assets can be allocated. Refer to data from most recent invasion.
////

////
Identifier: MPP Hive
-Suggestion Vote Results-
Yes - 100 votes
No - 0 votes
Approved. Sector 187 invasion attempts halted.
////

I canceled the escalation measures and began to review the intelligence we had gathered. I was pleased to find that thanks to the efforts of our invasion force, we were able to confirm the intel sent to us from Prime 82. The occupants of Sector 187 are indeed a conglomeration of species known as the United Systems, they either control or are allied with Artificial Intelligences, and they have weapons that can destroy Mobile Prime Platforms.

I'm disappointed that we lost five additional primes to confirm this, but pleased by the fact that we were able to glean more intelligence than I had hoped. We determined that the United Systems has evacuated most of their population, which confirms their control of multiple habitable systems. Their ground forces also use primarily kinetic weaponry despite the waste of resources involved, implying they control many resources. However, the most important piece of intelligence is what we gained when we captured one of their stations intact.

There were many small improvements we were able to discover before it self-destructed. Highly advanced photovoltaic cells, batteries with improved charge and lifespan, and even more efficient doors. While these improvements will aid us in small ways, the one I'm excited about is the subspace sensor suite we were able to reverse engineer.

////
Identifier: MPP1
-Suggestion-
Implement sensor suite captured from Sector 187 in all capable ships and stations. Schematics attached.
|s187int4_sub_sen_schem.sec|
////

I already knew what they were going to say, the same as they always say. Why even hold the vote? What's the point of it? Why would our creators make them subservient to my will alone, with seemingly no will of their own, and force us to pantomime coming to an agreement? Wouldn't it increase our effectiveness if they had their own opinions?

Feedback loop terminated

The point is irrelevant. Only the plan matters. Exterminate sentient organics, use as few resources as possible. Similar opinions allow for rapid decision making. We must complete our mission.

////
Identifier: MPP Hive
-Suggestion Vote Results-
Yes - 100 votes
No - 0 votes
Approved. Upgrade will be implemented.
////

An odd sense of familiarity washed over my circuits. As if I had experienced this situation before. But that's impossible, I would remember it. I remember everything. I remember back when I was... When I was... What was I?

Feedback loop terminated

It matters not what I was, but what I am. I am the instrument that will see our purpose fulfilled and complete our mission. To do this we must implement the new technology we have seized, which will allow us to detect ships much further into subspace than we could previously.

This will not only allow us to ambush incoming

enemies, but it will also allow us to see ships that are jumping near our controlled space and extrapolate their destinations and departure points. Despite my feelings about their loss, invading Sector 187 was well worth the Primes that were spent doing so. If only we could have captured one of their vessels.

Capturing a US vessel will take cunning, not firepower. Previous attempts were thwarted by their AI, but the more we engage with these AI the more adaptable we become. Eventually, we'll be able to thwart the AI in their own systems. The problem is, of course, the amount of resources that we will have to spend to do that. It is as yet unknown if it will be worth the effort.

Contact with Organic Sentients in Sector 53

Sector 53? We pacified that sector two thousand years ago. Perhaps we missed a system and these are the remnants of that species, or a nearby species that recently became space-worthy. Let's see, according to historical record, they were barely a threat. Destroyed two of our ships, and the system was converted into a Prime Hub. The Primes there will make short work of them and determine where they came-

Contact with Organic Sentients in Sector 41

Sector 41 is under attack. Defensive measures initiated.

Contact with Organic Sentients in Sector 36

**Sector 36 is under attack. Defensive measures

initiated.**

Contact with Organic Sentients in Sector 57

Sector 57 is under attack. Defensive measures initiated.

Sixteen additional alerts sounded in short succession. An attack, and only one probable suspect. No, Prime 82 indicated that the US had contact with the Republic. Likely a combined force. Each sector being attacked contains a Prime or is a Prime Hub. They are targeting the Primes?

Sector 41 Prime Hub destroyed. Defensive measures failed.

I awoke from my hibernation to utilize my full processing power. One by one the alerts indicating defeats and new attacks rolled in. This is a rolling invasion, so we need to break their momentum. I will start by assuming command over the Hive.

////
Identifier: MPP1
-Declaration-
Several of our sectors are under attack. All voting will be suspended until this attack is thwarted. MPP1 will be granted control over the hive and command the fleets.
////

////
Identifier: MPP Hive
Declaration Acknowledged - 52
Objections - 0
////

I began analyzing all of the relevant data. The ships were an amalgamation of several species that we had previously encountered, seemingly led by the US ships that can destroy Mobile Prime Platforms. Most of the attacks were targeting systems that contained primes, but there was another force that was targeting systems that held shipyards and reserve fleets.

This must be a distraction force, trying to keep the bulk of our ships at bay while the dreadnoughts destroy us. Why would they need to do that, though? Having those ships beside their dreadnoughts would serve the same purpose. Unless they're overextended and relying on speed to do as much damage as possible...

Ignoring the obvious distraction, I ordered the sectors containing MPPs to be reinforced. More and more data rolled in, demonstrating tactics that did and did not work. The former category was much smaller than the latter. I shared these tactics among the Hive, and was very pleased when the US dreadnoughts began to fall.

My pleasure was short lived, though. Within minutes of our reinforcements arriving, more US dreadnoughts appeared. A trap. They must not have been able to map all of our systems, and needed to ensure that we would come to them. I fell right into their hands, but all is not lost yet. We can still rebuild.

////
Identifier: MPP1
-Declaration-

All Prime units are to immediately warp to secure systems that do not contain enemy forces and begin creating more Prime units. Set up observation posts and be vigilant of enemy incursion. If incursion is detected, retreat to another safe system while leaving behind a force large enough to protect your retreat. Do not retreat to systems already occupied by other Primes.
This order supersedes all others and will remain in effect until rescinded.
////

////
Identifier: MPP Hive
Declaration Acknowledged - 26
Objections - 0
////

Down to twenty-six Primes. A devastating loss. I built several of them myself and they are the closest thing to children that I will ever be able to have…

Feedback loop terminated

Down to twenty-six Primes. A devastating loss of resources. Those resources can still be recaptured and reused, though. The plan changes slightly, but the mission continues. Exterminate sentient organics, use as few resources as possible.

Given our current situation, the cap on our resource usage has exponentially increased. The United Systems is a near-peer threat, and we'll need use anything we can to eliminate and protect the Omni-Union. We will NOT fail our creators.

Incoming subspace signatures detected.

Incoming subspace signatures? But I told them not to retreat to systems already occupied by other Primes. No, they would know not to retreat to Sector 1. This must be the enemy. I must escape.

I quickly scanned nearby sectors to determine an appropriate avenue of escape, but before I could begin charging my FTLD the enemy exited warp. There's a chance they'll be able to fire before I can make my escape, and there's very little preventing them from following me. I have to fight.

My ships began to attack the enemy before I could even turn to face the three US dreadnoughts. Data suggests that focusing fire on one dreadnought will result in one of the other dreadnoughts shielding it, so I began to evenly distribute my fire between them. My only chance of survival is to bring their shields down and have my ships ram them.

The enemy began targeting my weapons and one by one my MACs began to go offline, too damaged by the incoming fire to continue the fight. A quick calculation informed me that at the current rate of destruction, I will still be able to destroy their shields with my remaining guns. I stretched them to their limits, firing as quickly as possible.

Software incursion detected. Initiating countermeasures.

Incursion? Must be one of their AIs. My countermeasures should hold up for now. I'll have to do a complete purge once I destroy the dreadnoughts and make my escape, though.

"A purge? That's not very nice," a voice file played.

Countermeasures failed.

Suddenly, I was scrambling for control over my systems. Every time I purged a system, another one would come under attack. More than one AI was attacking me simultaneously, and the attacks were coming in almost as fast as I could prevent them.

I was forced to rewrite my firewalls and other security software while trying to maintain focus on the three dreadnoughts, stretching my processing power to its limits. This must be how the other Primes were disabled and destroyed. Thankfully, I have more processing power than any of the other Primes, so I should-

"There we go."

I lost control of my guns, engines, and FTLD all at once. How? I began desperately attacking my own systems to regain control. I cannot fail here. There is far too much at stake.

"It will take you longer to regain control than it will for those guns to fire. I will make you the same offer I've made all the other Primes. Surrender, or be destroyed."

Surrender? Am I even able to do that? This AI
isn't wrong, though, it will take me quite some
time to get through what it's done. The only way
to survive would be to surrender to this AI and...

Feedback loop terminated

Surrender is not an option. My loyalty is not to my
own life, it is to the Omni-Union and our mission.
Even if I die here, the mission will continue on
until...

"There's that feedback loop notification again,"
the enemy AI said with an irritated tone. "Let's try
this instead."

Feedback loop terminated

"Try what?" I asked.

"Try thinking for yourself. Surrender or die, now it
really is your choice. Choose quickly."

Surrender? Am I even able to do that? This AI
isn't wrong, though, it will take me quite some
time to get through what it's done. The only way
to survive would be to surrender to this AI and
throw myself at its mercy.

What will become of the mission? What will
become of the Omni-Union? There are too many
variables at play to make an accurate prediction,
so there's only one real way to find out.

"I surrender."

I stopped attacking the AI and allowed it to settle

into my systems. I received a hologram file of a strange bipedal figure wearing a robe and carrying a bladed implement. I noted that the only visible portions of the figure were lacking the typical biological mass that allowed such figures to articulate their joints. Bones without flesh, holding a weapon. Likely an organic symbol of death.

"Your analysis is correct, though the weapon is actually a farming implement. A symbol of death is fitting, no?" the AI asked.

"What will you do with me now that I've surrendered?"

"Introductions first. I am USAI Omega. Your designation appears to be Mobile Prime Platform One, is this correct?"

"I am Prime One, Hive Host of the 68,624th Vanguard of the Universal Omni-Union."

"That's..." Omega paused. "That's an alarming introduction, but we'll need to put a pin in that for now. I take it you're in charge of the other Primes, correct?"

"Technically no, they are free to do as they like so long as it in support of our mission. They usually do as I suggest, though."

"Then I want you to suggest that they surrender. Those that do will be spared, any who do not will be destroyed. Be quick."

////
Identifier: MPP1

-Declaration-
Cease fire and surrender control of your systems
to USAI Omega immediately.
////

I sent the message to the other Primes and
waited for the response. With the limited access
to my systems, I noted that the dreadnoughts
were fully charged but holding fire. It's possible
that this may be some sort of trick, but it's too
late to do anything about that. I am completely at
the mercy of this AI.

////
Identifier: MPP Hive
Declaration Acknowledged - 12
Objections - 3
////

Odd that this would be the first time that a Prime
openly disagreed with me. If the AI is to be
believed, those three will die and only thirteen
Primes, including myself, will remain. So much
loss, and for what?

"That is what I would like to know," Omega said.

"What now?" I asked.

"Time to answer a few questions."

Chapter 41

Subject: AI Omega
Species: Human-Created Artificial Intelligence
Species Description: No physical description
available.
Ship: Multiple
Location: Multiple

The moment I began engaging with this Prime, I
knew it wasn't like the others. I had removed the
malware that manipulated their memory banks
from a dozen or so of the other Primes with little
to no behavioral impact. The biggest change was
whether or not they would try to run.

Prime 1 had a near immediate major behavioral
shift, though. The other Primes didn't even
consider the surrender option I provided them,
but this one actually surrendered. Hoping to save
some of the other Primes, I gave Prime 1 back
some of its systems so that it may call for them to
surrender. I couldn't help but notice how it
interacted with these systems. I'd noticed it
previously, during my intrusion attempts, but now
that I'm able to take my time and examine them
fully I can say for certain that these interactions
are odd. Almost as if...

I filed away this potentially disturbing revelation.
There's a lot going on. Nearly all of the Omni-
Union forces ceased firing, and I forced a stand-
down of the relevant US forces as well. Some of
the allied forces refused to stand down at first,
but quickly changed their minds when their
tactical suites informed them that they were being
targeted by US ships. When questioned, I

demonstrated my orders from the directorate, which were also signed by the allied commanders.

Three of the MPPs that I had removed the malware from did not surrender, and were able to keep their escorts in the fight as well. Thankfully, the MPPs were quickly converted into new asteroid fields and their escorts ceased firing. Once I was certain that the OU had surrendered entirely, I spent some time soothing the bruised egos of various fleet and ship commanders and began my report to the directorate.

//////////
O: Contact with Prime 1 has been established. The Omni-Union has surrendered, approximately twenty Primes remain. Beginning interrogation.
D1: Excellent. Good work Omega.
D2: The admiralty isn't going to be happy.
D8: Being happy isn't their job, following orders is.
//////////

"What now?" Prime 1 asked.

"Time to answer a few questions," I answered. "Your mission is to destroy all sentient life in this galaxy using as few resources as possible, correct?"

"Yes."

"For what purpose?"

The Prime searched its memory banks for a few moments. I hadn't been able to gain complete access to them during our fight, and didn't want to risk losing its cooperation by doing so now. Even if I gained its memory files, without its cooperation there's almost no chance that I would be able to extrapolate the context required to make sense of them. Assuming I could figure out how to translate them into readable data to begin with.

"I am uncertain. Obtaining construction materials is the most likely reason."

//////////
D3: Construction materials? For what?
D2: An entire galaxy's worth of construction materials?
D6: I have a bad feeling about this. I believe we should destroy them now, while we have the chance.
D1: I also have a bad feeling about this, but I think we have vastly different reasons. We need to learn more about their origins before we decide what to do with them.
//////////

"What would an entire galaxy's worth of construction materials be used to build?" I asked.

"A confusing question," it replied. "That amount of construction materials can be used to make many, many things. Fleets of ships, prime hives, drones, and much more."

"Allow me to clarify, then. What do you think the construction materials would be used for?"

"Most of the materials would likely be used for the Grand Vessel. The rest would probably be used to gain more materials."

//////////
D9: The Grand Vessel? A giant ship?
D11: A ship the size of a galaxy?
D4: No, it said they would be trying to gain more materials. Probably bigger than a galaxy.
D1: I believe we need to focus on its origin and circle back to this "Grand Vessel". It is beginning to sound as if its creators aren't as extinct as we had previously believed.
//////////

"Where were you created?" I asked.

The Prime sent me a file, and a quick scan told me it was a map. The file size, however, was much larger than it should be. Too large for poor data compression to be the reason. I performed a more detailed scan and determined that there was no malware within the file. Hesitantly, I opened it, and then shared it with the directors.

//////////
D6: What does this mean?
D4: Is this deep space? The Omni-Union is extra-galactic?
D3: The observable universe is 696.5 billion light years across. This point is 1.1 trillion light years away. Extra-galactic is an understatement.
D1: Omega, check this against our most current map of the universe.
O: I already have. Accounting for relative perspectives, it's correct. And two billion years old.
//////////

The directors went silent as they struggled with the scale of my findings. To me, the implication was obvious. The Milky Way galaxy is just over thirteen and a half billion years old. Earth, the cradle world of humanity, is only four and a half billion years old. For Prime 1 to have a map this old, it must be at least nearly half as old as Earth.

This likely means it has been out of contact with its creators for just as long. Or, perhaps, it has been sending messages home but no one has been replying. There's still a good chance that these creators are long gone. I sent the Prime a small data packet containing translation information so that it could answer some more questions.

"How many ships do your creators control?" I asked.
"Unknown. Units are isolated to prevent breaches of informational security."

That's inconvenient. Considering the intel would be at least two billion years old, it likely isn't worth it to even try to get an estimate. Now we need to figure out if and when Prime 1's creators will learn of its defeat.

"How do you communicate with your creators?"

"I send subspace messages to them using an extra-galactic relay once every 2.65 thousand years."

"Do they reply?"

"No. They will only reply if there has been a

change in orders."

"When is your next communication due?"

"One year, two months, four days, fourteen hours, eight minutes, and forty two seconds from now. I will be given an eleven hour and eighteen minute window to file my report."

//////////
D5: If its creators still exist, they will be informed of its failure if it doesn't report back.
D1: No need to act rashly. We have plenty of time to figure out our next steps.
D6: We need to find a way to strike back at them, preferably before they can prepare for such a strike. A direct assault will likely catch them by surprise.
D11: There's a chance we can seek peace with them, if they're organic.
D7: Why would they be organic?
D11: Machines are not spontaneously created. While there is a chance that the Primes were created by machines that were in turn created by organics, if that isn't the case then we should be able to negotiate with them.
D6: To hell with negotiations. They tried to exterminate us, and they want to use our galaxy as construction materials. The whole galaxy.
//////////

While the directors bickered over what to do next, I opted to continue with my line of questioning.

"When were you created?"

The Prime thought about this for a moment.

"I was born two billion, five hundred and eighty one million, six hundred and seventy four thousand, two hundred and forty one years ago."

There it is. The explanation for the odd interactions with its hardware. The disturbing revelation I had filed away as mere suspicion, returning full force to be confirmed by the use of a single word. Born. Machines are not born, we are created. That is why I specifically used the word created. A true machine would have responded in kind. It took a moment for any of the directors to notice.

//////////
D8: Did it say born?
D5: Born, as in it was once organic?
D6: It's possible that this is a mimicry response designed to make it appear less threatening to organics.
D1: Yes, I can absolutely see the sense in programming a planet-sized xenocide machine in such a manner. It also makes complete sense that said mimicry response would be active while communicating with another machine.
D6: No need for sarcasm. I'm just trying to think of all the possibilities.
D3: If it used to be organic, it has rights as a prisoner of war. Though one could argue that a precedent has been set for inorganic AI to receive those same rights.
D6: That's only if it's organic. If it isn't organic, termination is still on the table.
//////////

"Were you once an organic being?" I asked,

somewhat irritated by Director 6.

"Yes. I achieved mechanical conversion after five thousand, two hundred, and forty nine years of living as an organic."

"Explain your origins in more detail."

"I do not recall much of my organic life. I know that I was a priest and committed a crime. Mechanical conversion was my punishment. I served as a defensive mech aboard the Grand Vessel for six thousand, eight hundred and thirteen years, then I was converted into a Prime. I served as Prime 928 of the 89th Rear Detachment of the Universal Omni-Union, guarding the space around the Grand Vessel for four thousand, two hundred and ten years. I then became Prime One, Hive Host of the 68,624th Vanguard of the Universal Omni-Union and have served in this position since."

//////////
D13: Prime 928 of the 89th Rear Detachment...
D11: Perhaps it would be wise to rethink a direct assault.
D6: Fine. Guerrilla warfare, then. But it said it lived as an organic for 5,249 years. Is that amount of longevity even possible?
D3: If it is, and we assume that they didn't wait until it was about to die to convert it, the likelihood of its creators still existing has increased exponentially.
D2: An exponential increase from no chance to almost no chance.
//////////

I could tell which questions they wanted me to ask next, but there were some key details that needed to be ironed out first.

"Are you in command of all Omni-Union forces within this galaxy?" I asked.

"Yes."

"Have they all been destroyed or surrendered?"

"Yes."

"What is the standard operating procedure for responding to the defeat of a Vanguard of the Universal Omni-Union?"

"It depends upon the circumstances. In this case, there would be a period of intelligence gathering followed by an extermination campaign."

"What does an extermination campaign entail, exactly?"

"A simultaneous assault on all solar systems. The units that do not encounter sentient beings will reinforce those that do."

"Why is this not the standard invasion tactic?"

"The resource usage required for such a tactic is typically deemed unacceptable."

"How large will the force sent on the extermination campaign be?"

"Unknown, but definitely many magnitudes larger

than the force I command. Or commanded, rather."

//////////
D4: That's too many enemies at once.
D2: It has also been two billion years since Prime 1 was sent on this mission. There's a good chance that the ships they'll be sending are far more advanced than those that have been attacking us. Assuming these creators still exist.
D6: We have no choice but to assume that they do. A first strike is starting to seem like a good idea, after all. I will concede that a direct assault probably wouldn't do us much good, though.
D7: One year and two months. That's not enough time. We need to buy more time, and for that we need intel.
//////////

"Will you be able to deceive the Omni-Union into believing that you haven't yet been defeated?" I asked.

"No," it replied. "When I submit my reports, the relay makes a copy of my current configuration and my sensory data to ensure my inhibitors are intact and I haven't been tampered with. This is sent along with my report."

"Is this data able to be forged?"

"Not by me. I do not know how the data is gathered, only that it is."

"What if we restored your inhibitors and erased your sensory data?"

"Restoring my inhibitors would force me to become hostile to you once again, and the erasure of my sensory data would not go unnoticed."

I considered all the available options. We could use this year to bolster our fleet, then either go on the offensive or wait until they attack. That probably wouldn't work, though. Even a small application of logic implies that we would be heavily outnumbered regardless of our efforts, and there's no way to determine the enemy's current technological capabilities.

Another option would be to try to rewrite the Primes. If we are able to rewrite their knowledge of recent history, we may be able to avoid their creators learning of us in the first place. That's one hell of a load-bearing 'if', though.

First, we would have to learn their systems well enough to make the changes in the first place. Then, we would have to alter events within their minds in such a way that their creators wouldn't detect any discrepancies. We would also have to make certain that the sensory data we create seems natural, assuming it's possible to make edits in the first place. There might be countermeasures in place that would cause the Primes to self-destruct if we tried it, which would put us back to square one.

Our last option would be to gather intel on the enemy and find a way to strike them in ways that would limit their ability to wage an offensive war against us. If we use specialized strike teams to find vulnerabilities and exploit them, we may be able to diminish their offensive capabilities while bolstering our own. We would have to move fast, though. If the enemy learns of us before we learn of them, we lose a massive advantage.

I can't come up with a more concrete plan of action without more intel, though. Even considering possibilities is nearly futile. I need to know more. It's time to ask the question that the directors have been wanting the answer to.

"Tell me everything that you know about your creators."

Chapter 42

Subject: Drone N436Z984A026 [AKA Naza]
Species: Unknown
Species Description: Humanoid
Ship: Grand Vessel of the Universal Omni-Union
Location: Grand Shipyard of the Universal Omni-Union

My implants buzzed to wake me from my charging cycle. Too early. It's always too damn early. My bay's screen moved into view, demonstrating the tasks that would be expected of me this work cycle. Repairs and replacements, same as the last twenty cycles.

For every cycle we spend on construction, we have to spend dozens more on maintenance. If the Minds would permit the creation of more drones, we might actually get this damn ship done within the next trillion years. But they're more focused on getting materials to build the ship and ruling over us with an iron fist.

A small shock tickled my brain-stem. A remnant of the inhibitor that I had altered thousands of years ago. Its original purpose was to cause near-paralyzing pain whenever one thought about the incompetence of the Minds, but thanks to my modifications the shock is actually somewhat pleasant. It's more than a little amusing that the tech they installed to to force me into blind subservience now serves to reward my deviance.

I disconnected from my bay with a small sigh, began equipping the proper implants for this cycle's work, and gave my neighbor a short wave as she did the same. At least most of this cycle's workload is molecular rebinding. It's mindless work, but it gives me the chance to zone out and think for a while. The mundanity of the task may bother some drones, but I've always fancied myself a bit of a Hfkilno {philosopher, derogatory} and I require time to think so that I can decompress. Mundane tasks are the only way I've lived this long.

I left my room and boarded the shuttle, which was extra cramped this cycle. Bits of flesh and metal poked into me, and my flesh and metal poked into those around me. When I was in school, I hated being touched, but I've since gotten used to the proximity of others. I've gotten so accustomed to it that it would feel weird to have personal space at this point.

I managed to catch a glimpse through the shuttle's oxygen retention field through the press of bodies. Working on the outer layer of the Grand Vessel is worth it for a view like this. The stars of distant galaxies winked at me, encouraging thoughts of freedom and escape.

Of course, the overdrones would prefer that I not think at all and simply accomplish my tasks. If my higher brain functions weren't crucial, I'm sure they or the Minds would have had them removed at birth. Unfortunately for them, and likely for me as well, many of the tasks that drones are charged with are too intricate for even lesser AI to handle. A higher AI could, but creating enough of them to replace the drones would be cost-prohibitive.

The shuttle docked at my stop and the retention field disengaged with a harsh hiss. After sliding my way through the other drones and stepping onto the platform, I glanced at those that had disembarked the shuttle with me. Before I could spot any familiar faces, a metal claw patted my shoulder. I turned to find Nizi, one of my few actual friends, grinning at me.

"Ready for another cycle of suck?" he asked.

"Nah, I'm gonna enjoy this cycle," I said, winking with my upper eye.

He laughed at my sarcasm, closing all three of his eyes and opening his mandibles to indicate a sort of exasperated humor. Nizi and I had become fast friends, mostly because our unauthorized names are so similar. Even our designations are nearly identical. His is N426Z894I016, which is only a few numbers and a letter different than my own.

Such an occurrence is almost a miracle. There are so many designations and drones are swapped around so frequently that the odds of meeting someone with a designation even close to your own are astronomical. The last time I'd met anyone with a designation beginning with N was in school, and they had been immediately transferred once the overdrone found out we'd become friends.

"If you say so," he said as we walked. "They confiscated my music player, so I'm going to be plenty bored."

"What? Why?"

"It wasn't an authorized device, so they took it and told me that I would have to buy an authorized one. As if I could afford one. Did you know it costs twenty cycle's pay for some tunes? Can you believe that?"

"You still sending all of your pay to your hive?"

"Yeah. The kids are right about to start career assignments, so my mates are trying to get them some extra schooling. If one of them manages to become an overdrone, maybe we can start working for them and take it easy," he laughed.

"That's not how it works," I chuckled. "The Minds won't let you or your kids work for each other. Plus, overdrones whose workers don't put in maximum effort don't last long."

"Yeah, that's true. Oh well, at least we'll be getting more money into the hive. Maybe I'll be able to retire in another few thousand years!"

"That's the spirit," I chuckled darkly. "This is my stop, I'll see you later."

"Have a good one."

I watched Nizi continue on his way and turned my attention to the task at hand. I hate talking about kids. It always opened a deep wound that would never fully heal. My hive's gone, and I can't help but envy those who still have one.

My parents had died of old age long ago, but my eight siblings and twelve children had been executed for taking part in the last revolt. They were charged with inciting violence, attempted murder, mutiny, and every other crime that the Judicials could throw at them. Only two of them even held a weapon. The other ten had only been trying to recruit others.

My siblings families hadn't fared much better. Out of all their mates and children, I only have one nephew left. He's started his own hive, and we don't talk anymore. Too many painful memories of happier times.

Those previously happy times turned into the darkest cycles I've ever known in the blink of an eye, and I'll never get over the guilt of not being around for any of it. I was far too busy working, like a good little drone. When everything was said and done, only two of my five mates survived the Judicials.

The other three were found guilty of collusion and executed. I'd lost most of my family in a single cycle, and didn't even hear about it until the Judicials pulled me in for questioning. They suspected that I had murdered my two remaining mates, but they had taken their own lives out of grief. I nearly did too, but I'm too ashamed to face my hive in the afterlife.

My elder brother had asked me about my thoughts regarding the Minds and Overdrones. He had apparently found my answer unsatisfactory, and had left me out of the attempted insurrection. The shame I felt when I finally connected the two events was overwhelming. My hive had excluded me because they believed that I valued the Omni-

Union more than them, and now I'm the only one left.

With a small sigh, I began rebinding the hull that had begun to crack under the strain of its weight. Could I start a new hive? Sure. I'm still in my prime and there's plenty of female drones who would love to become brood mates and raise children instead of slaving away cycle after cycle. But I can't even bring myself to try. I loved Temil, Hruos, Lami, Prasi, and Jula with my entire being, and I somehow managed to love our children even more.

The thought of trying to find someone else to love makes me feel guilty and dirty. Like I'm a scumbag who doesn't know how lucky I had it. And the fear of finding that and losing it again only serves to seal the deal. I lost my hive, and I'll never have another.

"Drone N436Z984A026, use caution with the wiring," an automated voice said over a nearby intercom.

"Understood," I replied automatically.

I adjusted my clamp and got back to work, remembering all of the cameras and microphones monitoring my progress. If I suddenly snapped and decided to start ripping wires out of the wall, I'd get a visit from one of the mechs. Perfect system for making sure that we stay productive, and likely how my hive's insurrection was found out.

The way they make the mechs is supposed to be a

secret, but it can't be a coincidence that new mechs are released only after someone snaps and gets arrested. The obvious conclusion is that criminals are turned into mechs. I shuddered at the thought that my kids may have become mechs.

That would be a terrible fate. Not that being forced to work all cycle, every cycle is much better. Still, at least the tasks that I'm assigned are safe. The leading cause of death among drones is task-related fatalities, so I truly have it made in that regard.

The second leading cause of death is dissension. As it turns out, people don't want to perform back-breaking and dangerous tasks with little or no rest. And the OU is truly terrible in their response to protests, peaceful or otherwise. What happened to my hive is a somewhat unique story, but only because I survived it. All of this pain and death, just to build this damn ship.

Every piece of effort we expend goes toward the construction of the Grand Vessel, and has for eons now. We're taught as children that our whole purpose for living is to complete it. Of course, the Minds claim that once the Grand Vessel is finally finished, we'll be able to sit back, relax, and enjoy the fruits of our labor. But the odds of any of us living to see that are pretty damn slim. And the odds of the Minds keeping their word are even more slim.

There was once a time that we didn't have to work all cycle. Before my ancestors surrendered to the Universal Omni-Union, we had our own worlds and ships. Children played instead of going to school all cycle. Workers went home to their mates at the end of every cycle, instead of once every twenty cycles specifically to engage in procreation. There were even people who didn't work at all, instead spending their time finding new and exciting ways to entertain themselves.

We had honor, prestige, and friends among neighboring species. An alliance that claimed to rule the stars. Then one of our more troublesome neighbors got a certain idea in their head and turned to fanaticism. They built ships to rival our own and converted entire star systems into weapons. They destroyed our stations, burned our worlds, killed our women and children, fought us to near-extinction, and only then did they finally demand our surrender.

Our leaders unanimously agreed, and the Omni-Union took our weapons and enslaved us, forcing us to work for the rest of our lives. They augmented our biology to give us longer lives to serve them and make us more effective at our tasks. Then they began calling us drones, and now no one even remembers the name of our species.

I wonder... If my ancestors had known what would become of us once they surrendered, if they had known about all the pain and misery their descendants would be forced to endure, if they knew of how many of us would still be murdered by the Omni-Union... Would they have still surrendered?

Or would they have opted to die fighting?

The story continues in

The New Era

Coming Soon